The
Truth About
Love

Also by Jane Elizabeth Varley

Wives and Lovers
Husbands and Other Lovers

The
Truth About
Love

JANE ELIZABETH
VARLEY

First published in Great Britain in 2007 by Orion Books,
an imprint of The Orion Publishing Group Ltd
Orion House, 5 Upper Saint Martin's Lane
London WC2H 9EA

1 3 5 7 9 10 8 6 4 2

A CIP catalogue record for this book is
available from the British Library.

ISBN-13: 978 0 7528 7389 3 (hardback)
978 0 7528 7390 9 (export trade paperback)

Typeset by Deltatype Ltd, Birkenhead, Merseyside

Printed in Great Britain by Clays Ltd, St Ives plc

The Orion Publishing Group's policy is to use papers that
are natural, renewable and recyclable products and made
from wood grown in sustainable forests. The logging and
manufacturing processes are expected to conform to the
environmental regulations of the country of origin.

www.orionbooks.co.uk

For Adam

Acknowledgements

I am indebted to Jane Wood, Susan Lamb, Lisa Milton, Alison Tulett and the team at Orion. Also to Clare Alexander and her assistant Justin Gowers.

Many people helped me with the research for this novel. Thank you to Alison Baguley, Stephen Boniface, Linda Empringham, Sarah Graham, Sue Hart, Robert Scott, Vivien Sultoon, Peter Ward, Elizabeth Winter and Professor Richard Wright.

Special thanks, as always, to my husband.

Chapter 1

Sally reminded herself that she was very lucky to be spending part of her afternoon in the quiet occupation of writing birthday party invitations. The invitations, in their duck-egg-blue box, tied with a ribbon and edged with a balloon pattern, were a luxury they couldn't afford, and yet had been irresistible in Village Voices, a little artsy stationers that had just opened in Church Road. She had stacked them on the kitchen table next to a lined A4 pad, on which she had written a list of invitees who were asked to come and celebrate Louis's second birthday.

She ticked off her parents, saw the next name and put down her pen. She looked up. The weak February sun fell through the leaded French windows, slicing over the blue-green slate floor and across the edge of the kitchen table. The garden beyond was showing promise beyond the developer's carelessly laid turf and ragged beds. Edward had spent most of the previous Sunday clearing leaves and digging the beds, pointing out places for planting rhododendron, azaleas and hostas, and other plants that she was not sure she could identify. The rear boundary was marked by a rickety larchlap fence, beyond which rose up their neighbour's majestic plane tree.

Louis would be awake soon, his afternoon nap seldom lasted longer than an hour. So determinedly she returned to the task at hand, reached for her pen and wrote her stepdaughter's name on the top right-hand corner of the card – *Hope*. As she did so she felt a surge of irritation that she was powerless to resist. Nothing could shift Sally's enduring resentment that her son's March birthday fell on the same day as that of her stepdaughter – or that this year was Hope's twenty-first. She knew it was ridiculous. It was not as if it could be changed. Moreover, her husband Edward did not feel the same way. On the day of Louis's birth he had said blithely that it was something the two of them could share, Louis and Hope, united by one birthday. She had not been able to think of anything to reply to this and two years later she was still struggling to find a good word to say about what was at best a bloody big inconvenience and at worst a perpetual reminder of his ex-wife Pia.

Edward was infuriatingly vague about Hope's plans for her twenty-first birthday. Sally had tackled him about it again last Sunday in the garden as he dug the back border.

'Are you positive Hope hasn't said anything? Surely she's having a party?'

He had continued to dig. 'No.' He had stopped, leaned on the fork then looked up into the branches of the neighbour's tree, which loomed over them. 'Plane trees soak up the water. The lawn needs a wet summer.'

'Edward! What about Pia? Have you spoken to her?'

He shook his head. 'Nope.' He resumed digging. 'Why don't you call her?' he added helpfully.

Sally had turned on her heel at that point. She had never believed in so-called friendships between past and present wives. In the beginning she had thought that some civilised, very grown-up, pulling-together-for-the-sake-of-the-children effort with Pia might happen – and for a time there had been polite exchanges and stiff telephone calls. But all that had ended with the events of last Christmas: how was it possible for two intelligent women to get so worked up over a pile of dirty laundry?

She pushed Hope's invitation into an envelope and wrote out the address at the university. More often than not Louis refused to take a nap these days but when he did she would select one or two of the tasks that required silence or concentration to be performed in his absence. She still hadn't totally unpacked the top floor. After the initial flush of enthusiasm she had lost interest in unpacking another box and she now understood how it was possible to be boxed years after moving in.

But Sally loved her new house. The light and spacious kitchen-dining room was set at the back of the house. At the centre was a kitchen table, a flyweight expanse of light oak set on slender tapered legs, the chairs fashioned in a single, smooth curve of matching wood. Edward, spotting the table in the Conran shop, had pointed to it. 'That's the one.' He could still surprise her like that: his easygoing demeanour snapping into decisive mode; his tastes and preferences unpredictable.

It was a white wood kitchen. Allegedly hand-painted, with a beech countertop that looked fantastic and was laughably impractical, the walls were panelled in three-inch timbers to waist height and painted white, the plaster above finished in magnolia. Edward now suspected that the panelling had been installed to conceal some residual damp, since the wood in the corner on the outer wall was lifting.

But there were nice touches – a wall rack on which hung her blue Le Creuset saucepans, the convenient bookshelf above it for her cookery books, a white butler's sink and beautiful antique-style brass taps – and best of all the view onto the garden. The French windows opened onto a brick terrace and lawn. Edward said that in the summer the terrace would be scorching at midday and they would need an umbrella for shade.

She hadn't realised that Edward knew so much about gardening. There had been no opportunity in the rented Putney flat and before that the Barbican. It had been out of the question to remain at the Barbican. Pia had stayed there more than once.

They had been house-hunting for months, growing ever more demoralised, each property dingier and more expensive than the last. Sally had protested that there was no point in going to see 12 North Walk, 'It's way out of our price range.'

But Edward, drinking coffee one Saturday morning, had been adamant. 'We need a house. And we want to be in it for Christmas. So, we're going to find one this weekend.' He had picked up the telephone, set up six viewings for that afternoon and suggested that she leave Louis with her mother.

North Walk had been last on the list, the light failing as they pulled up outside the red-brick Victorian terrace on a narrow street close by Cannizaro Park.

The youthful agent greeted them by looking at his watch. 'It's newly converted into one house and a basement flat.' He took out the keys. 'The builder's open to offers,' he added, wrestling with the Yale lock.

Finally, he opened the door and switched on the hall light. Then she saw the colours in the delicate design of the Victorian stained-glass front door and the broad staircase framed by elaborately turned oak balusters and carved newel posts.

'A lot of the original features have survived,' said the agent, leading them into the front room. 'It was rented out for years.' The spacious room, the bay window accented by a window seat, had the high ceiling of the era, a centrepiece ornate carved medallion of leaves and roses and a broad plaster fireplace.

Edward led the way out into the hall, gesturing at the new carpet. 'There might be some of the original floor tiles under that.' Then he turned to the agent. 'We'll take a look around on our own.'

'No problem.'

They admired the kitchen, stopped by the red-painted cloakroom on the ground floor and by the time they had reached the master bedroom on the first floor Sally wished they had never come to see the house at all. First she set eyes on the small exquisite Belgian rouge marble fireplace, then on the sash windows giving out onto a view of the Wimbledon Common golf course. Nothing else they had seen in months of searching came close to this.

But Edward was looking around with far more than a casual eye. Next he took a hard look at the second small bedroom on the first floor. 'Spare room or office?' Then he bounded up the stairs, pausing at the white-tiled bathroom on the half-landing to point out the power shower, and onto the attic bedrooms. 'So, that's two attic bedrooms up here and two downstairs.'

'Edward! It's way beyond our budget.'

He looked unconcerned. 'Everyone ends up borrowing more than they think they will.'

'But—'

He interrupted her. 'Sal, we need a house. This is the best one we've seen. We'll make it work.' He went over and pulled up one of the sash windows, peering out at the brickwork. She thumbed through the particulars. At the end there was a 'historical note'.

'Hey, listen to this,' she said, as Edward closed the sash. She read out loud, 'The property has a famous heritage. In Victorian times 12 North Walk was owned by Mr and Mrs Robert Latham. Love letters between the couple were dramatised in the award-winning BBC television series *Letters of a Victorian Lady*.'

She looked up. 'My mother raved about that programme.'

Edward turned round from where he was looking at the ceiling plaster. 'There you are. You could write a history of the house.'

She liked the idea, caught up now in his enthusiasm. He came over to her, taking hold of her waist. 'Sal, I want the best for us.' He pulled her towards him. 'It's a stretch, but if he takes a low offer we can make it. Of course, there won't be much over for extras. You might as well tear up your passport.'

They were in for Christmas. Edward had cashed in some life assurance policies and she had blocked out of her mind the reality of twenty-five years' worth of payments on a 90 per cent mortgage. Somehow, in the divorce, Pia had escaped with all the assets, notably the house in Gerrards Cross and half of Edward's pension, but none of the liabilities. There were times when it made Sally furious. And at other times she felt guilty that Edward was starting all over again when some of his contemporaries were paying off their mortgages altogether.

She had met Edward when she was appointed as his temporary PA at Porter Stone. Porter Stone was a bank that guarded its reputation for exclusivity and discretion, dealing only with 'high net worth clients' and having just three London branches located in Fleet Street, Sloane Street and Grosvenor Square. At each branch a liveried footman opened the door for clients, dressed in a tailcoat in the bank's burgundy colours, a short top hat and tan pigskin gloves.

To open an account at Porter Stone, Edward had briefed her on her first day, it was necessary to show assets of one million pounds.

'That's clear assets of a million,' he said casually. 'Not mortgaged.'

The staff were by and large privately educated, the clients increasingly not. Edward's job was to recruit new customers.

'We don't necessarily make any money out of the banking,' Edward had explained, 'at least, not if the customer maintains a minimum balance of ten thousand pounds in their account.'

She had tried not to look surprised at that. She aimed simply to be in credit, if only by forty-five pounds, which was her current balance. 'But we do make money on all the other things that follow once they become clients,' Edward continued. 'Tax planning schemes, life assurance, legal services ...'

They were in his second office in the bank's headquarters in Fleet Street with a view of the turrets of the Royal Courts of Justice.

'I don't suppose your clients go overdrawn,' she had ventured.

He had raised an eyebrow. 'More often than you might suppose. Fortunately, you and I don't have to deal with that. We reel them in, pop them in a basket and send them along to be filleted by the private client department.'

She noticed that he was already including her. And he was always doing that, implying that they were a team, never seeking the credit or pulling his weight at her expense.

He put her at her ease. Arriving at the bank she had still not been sure she even wanted the job. But something of the atmosphere of Porter Stone had touched her, even as she had been escorted through the building: the thick carpet, the smell of beeswax, the absence of banter and laughter, all set Porter Stone apart from the offices she had hitherto worked in. It was an institution with its own rituals, language and codes: daunting at first and then compelling.

She had liked Edward immediately. He was a big man, not fat but with a rugby player's physique, unruly hair, a ready smile and a genuine laugh. But his eyes were tired, she had noticed, and she had understood at once that there was something out of kilter with him, that he was weary and heavy-hearted beneath his affable exterior. She had guessed that he was about forty and married with children from the photograph on his desk. In fact, he was separated and living in a flat in the Barbican. He had not said so at the time. But he had gestured to the photograph. 'My daughter, Hope – she's hoping to go to university to read History. I see you read History, too. And my son, Dan. He's hoping to go to Welton.'

It was nice of him to recall her degree subject. He had taken the trouble carefully to read her CV. She learned in time that Edward always paid attention to detail. He was intelligent enough to conceal his ambition, however. Outwardly it was his natural charm and high energy that caught the attention of clients and colleagues.

She had heard of Welton, a Buckinghamshire public school. She had not herself gone to private school. When the agency had first suggested Porter Stone she had hesitated, not least because she could not envisage herself there. But Eileen at the agency had been enthusiastic.

'It's a maternity-leave vacancy.' Eileen had consulted her notes. 'He travels frequently and entertains, and there needs to be precise follow-up. And discretion.'

'I'm really looking for something in the media,' she had ventured.

But Eileen had brushed that aside. 'So is everyone else, dear. Porter Stone is very good for your CV. Banking always is. I'll send you along.'

In the event, Edward's permanent PA had decided that she did not, after all, want to return to Porter Stone. And so it was that a five-month placement as the PA to Edward Kirwan-Hughes had stretched into three and a half years until she left, now Mrs Kirwan-Hughes, and seven months pregnant. They had discussed her leaving sooner but they needed the money even more then. Between Edward's divorce and her credit card bills, it felt as though they would never get their heads above water. Then there was the wedding, small but costly, and the honeymoon, a long weekend in New York and a trip back on the *Queen Mary II*.

So far they had had the house to themselves but two weeks ago a *Sold Subject to Contract* sign had been affixed over the agent's *For Sale* board and last weekend she had come down to the kitchen on Sunday morning to see a couple standing in the middle of the back garden. The woman was holding a tape measure and an A4 notepad. Sally had stood back quickly, conscious that she was wearing her pink fleece maternity dressing gown, making a mental note to replace it as soon as possible. The woman was casually but fashionably dressed: distressed jeans, a navy blue pea coat with a striped scarf that looked like it came from Paul Smith and a pair of sheepskin boots, with a low heel and an overlap at the top. She had an outdoor look about her: she appeared unmade up, with mid-length rather scruffy brown hair, but she was good-looking in a sporty way. The man looked like a professional type. Observing them, the woman doing most of the talking, Sally guessed they weren't married and they didn't have children. They had stayed for ages. Later, looking out of Louis's bedroom, she had seen them get into a red BMW convertible, the woman driving, pulling out confidently in the direction of Wimbledon Village.

She wrote out an invitation to Vickie and the other girls from playgroup and then one to Brickie. Brickie, who was the PA to the Chairman of Porter Stone, had been her closest ally there and remained a friend. She considered whether to invite Mad Auntie Mary, her mother's sister, who was not mad but was very loud, and then put her on her mental list of possible invitees if numbers were down. But all the while, as she wrote names and addresses on the pale blue envelopes, thoughts of Hope's birthday intruded and with it the prospect of seeing Pia for the first time since that call. Edward's silence on the matter, the date was only three weeks away, was not encouraging.

She came to Edward's parents. Did Edward's mother know what was going on? Sally knew that Pia still saw her. What was being planned? They must have organised something by now. Why hadn't they told Edward? Maybe they *had* told Edward? It was hopeless. She got up. She already knew there was nothing in the fridge to snack on. The fruit bowl was uninspiring, a couple of apples and some overripe bananas. She opened a cupboard and ate a handful of mini rice crackers. She really needed something sweet, though. She ate a box of Louis's raisins. But she was doomed. *Why* couldn't she stop herself? She felt a surge of irritation towards Edward. She had asked him, *please, please, please* no chocolates. But still they had come, for Valentine's Day, the huge pink heart-shaped box filled with a plain chocolate assortment.

She had gained too much weight during pregnancy, a combination of her desk job and lunches in the Porter Stone dining room. Now Porter Stone seemed like another life altogether. For work she had worn dark tailored suits, inventively combined with fitted shirts and silk scarves in pinks and reds and creams, her shoulder-length auburn hair tied back or pinned up in the house style. Her mother, noticing her wearing more make-up, objected. 'You have perfect skin! Foundation clogs the pores, you know.'

Her father had looked up from his newspaper. 'You're an English rose!'

It was true. She did have good skin, the pale type that goes with blue eyes and only tans with enormous effort. Nowadays she was lucky if she found time to smear on tinted moisturiser and a dash of lipstick. Her hair would be much easier to manage if it was shorter but Edward always vetoed having it cut.

'I like it long. It suits you. You're beautiful.'

He still said that, though not as often as he used to.

As for the suits, with their close-fitting, knee-skimming skirts, there was little point in unpacking them. On a good day, if she weighed herself as soon as she got up, it was possible to say that two years after Louis's birth she had lost nearly half of the weight she had gained.

The last stone was notoriously difficult. But spring was not so far off and on New Year's Day she had vowed that this would be the year she lost the weight, in time for summer and sunbathing in the back garden.

Not today, though. She went into the living room, got down on her hands and knees, and pulled out the box from under the claret-red calico-covered sofa. Out of sight, out of mind did work occasionally. She lifted the lid, then the white corrugated paper, then the piece of thin russet tissue paper that covered the five remaining pieces. She was depressed to realise that she did not need to consult the guide. She already knew there was an orange cream, a coconut, a raspberry, a lemon and a coffee. The plainest had gone first, little bars of un-adulterated chocolate luxurious in their own gold foils, then the nut clusters, then the truffles, then the toffees, until all that had remained was the nougat and the bloody creams. She ate the orange, then the raspberry and then, even though she did not want it, the coffee. With its sticky sweetness coating her teeth she pushed the box back under the sofa and thanked God that Edward didn't have a sweet tooth or a taste for thin women. Then she pulled the box out again, took off the lid and the card and the tissue paper and ended the temptation once and for all by eating the lemon and the coconut. The coconut was surprisingly good.

Brickie had said she was crazy even to think about coming back to Porter Stone. She had come to see the house last weekend while Edward was at a Welton hockey match and they had sat in the kitchen eating shortbread fingers and drinking tea while Louis played with a farm set that Brickie had bought. Brickie, a brunette, was in her weekend uniform of chocolate moleskins and fisherman's polo-neck.

'Even if they take you back, they'll give you some awful job in settlements or complaints.'

She knew Brickie was right. The women who returned from maternity leave were given terrible posts involving huge amounts of travel and rotten clients until, worn-down, they left.

Brickie shook her head as Sally pushed the packet of biscuits towards her. Her eye was on the wall next to the boxed-in chimney breast. She stood up, peering closely at the wall. 'Look! You can see that there was a bracket here once.'

'A bracket?'

'For lighting,' Brickie explained. 'Candles and then gas lights until they converted to electricity. If you looked in the basement you might see where the servants' bells used to hang.'

After that, she had shown Brickie round, up to their bedroom, sparsely furnished with a *Bedknobs and Broomsticks* brass bed and two small teak chests, which served as bedside tables, and a trouser press.

'We need more furniture,' Sally had commented, almost apologetically.

'Oh, all in good time. That's the fun, isn't it, doing it bit by bit.'

It was so typical, Brickie, whose parents could buy up all of Wimbledon Village, had none of the airs and graces that so often went with old money.

Brickie had wowed at Louis's attic room, at his curtains with their tin-soldier motif in red and blue, his aeroplane mobile, framed Babar posters – Babar on one, Celeste on the other. Sally wondered if Brickie felt regrets that she did not have children. It had been astounding to her when Brickie had revealed that she was forty-four. She had thought her somewhere in her mid-thirties.

'Probably a result of not having a husband,' Brickie had said wryly. Brickie had looked round at Louis's room with a searching eye. 'Really, the builders didn't change the layout at all. This room must have been freezing.'

'How can you tell?'

'It's the attic. There was no roof insulation. Only a tiny fireplace.'

Brickie put her hand on Louis's radiator. 'Louis doesn't realise how lucky he is. Think what it must have been like up here in the winter ...'

For Sally, the birth of Louis had brought a belated realisation of how lucky she was, of how much her parents had done for her. Once, when she was five or six, playing in the garden, she had overheard through the open kitchen window Mad Auntie Mary talking in an urgent whisper.

'You're spoiling her! It's too much.'

She never did find out what was too much. There were no Caribbean holidays, no private school, no ponies. But there was ballet and drama and new dresses, never second-hand or hand-me-down. Much of it was the inevitable dominion of the only child, seated between her parents, enjoying the attention of two adults. And now the spoiling had begun all over again with Louis, his birth healing the disappointment her parents were unable to conceal at her marriage to a divorced man.

'So, Edward has two children, Sally?' Her mother had made it sound like an incurable illness.

But Louis had changed all that, from the first time, minutes after the birth, that her parents had seen him, her mother crying over his little red face and his swaddled body, and her father briefly embracing Edward.

It had all seemed so promising back then. Louis's birth had inspired Sally with a new consciousness of the importance of family. She had been full of good intentions and positive resolutions. Hope, slight with her mother's dark brown eyes, had come to the hospital and pressed a wrapped present into her hands. It was a Wedgwood Peter Rabbit child's set, a bowl, plate and cup. Sally had felt a novel surge of warmth towards her stepdaughter. Stiffly, they had embraced.

'Hope, thank you. We want you to come and visit.'

'Of course,' Hope had said, a little too quickly.

But though she had come to Louis's christening, Hope had been only once to the flat and never to North Walk. Dan came. At Christmas Edward had collected him from Welton. Dan arrived smelling of cigarette smoke, laden with dirty laundry and fresh from an argument in the car about his housemaster's insistence on a haircut.

The back and forth between Edward and Dan continued in the hallway as Dan dropped several duffel bags on the floor. 'Everyone has it this length,' Dan argued, rolling his eyes.

Edward sounded weary. 'If he says you have to get it cut, you don't have much choice.'

'He's a prat. No one listens to him.'

It had been a chaotic holiday: most of the house still unpacked, Louis growing each day more over-tired and over-excited, Dan and Edward locking horns over Dan's hair and smoking – *Dad, I'm really, really not smoking* – and non-stop television viewing.

Sally had brokered a truce for Christmas Day. 'Let's just drop it for today,' she had appealed to Edward.

Edward had held up his hands in mock surrender and Dan had cast her a grateful glance.

Nonetheless, Christmas Day had seen the chaos intensify, her parents staggering in with presents for Louis, and soon the living-room carpet was covered with plastic, boxes and wrapping paper – mixed in with a forest floor of dead pine needles from the tree that had started dropping as soon as they brought it in. Her mother had pulled out a garish red velvet mini Father Christmas suit, its hood trimmed with white fur, the middle accessorised with a black felt belt.

'I know it's only for one day,' her mother said cheerfully, teasing Louis's arm into the sleeve, 'but I couldn't resist it.'

'I'll film him in it,' her father added, taking out the camcorder.

Sally had exchanged glances with Edward.

'Drink?' he said, by way of a response.

The day had passed in a blur of cooking, eating and clearing up. At eight o'clock she had fallen asleep on the sofa.

So, in the circumstances, on Boxing Day, Sally had thought it a very generous gesture on her part to do Dan's dirty washing for him. He would arrive at Pia's in ship shape condition, apart from his hair. Loading the washing machine she had not noticed the red Father Christmas outfit inside, changed after Louis dropped a gloop of cranberry sauce down it, then helpfully left in the machine by her mother.

Dan, seeing her pull out five, pink tie-dyed school shirts had said just one anxious word: 'Mum.'

She found the offending Father Christmas suit and read out the label resignedly. 'Hand wash cold separately.' Then she saw the anxious expression on Dan's face. 'Hey, don't worry. Tell her it's my fault.' Should she offer to replace them? No, they paid out a fortune in school fees already. 'Your mum can get some Dylon and run them through. They'll be good as new,' she added optimistically.

Later, waiting for Edward to return from dropping Dan at Pia's house, she wondered if she ought to pay for new ones after all.

Then the telephone had rung. Without any prelude Pia had started yelling. She sounded drunk. 'They're ruined! Utterly ruined. I've just unpacked his bag and found them.' She said this in the tone of a customs officer discovering a drugs haul.

So Dan had blamed Sally.

She kept her voice even. 'It was an accident. I didn't realise that Louis's Christmas outfit was in there.'

'A red one?' Pia made this sound scandalous. 'Surely you knew it would run?'

'I didn't see it in the machine.' Too late she realised how defensive she sounded.

Pia's tone made clear her opinion of Sally as an imbecile. 'You need to check the machine before you place a load in it.' Pia's voice gathered momentum. 'And separate your whites from your colours.'

Any residual impulse to pay for the shirts disappeared. 'You can use Dylon.'

'Dye them!' Pia sounded horrified. 'These are Welton school shirts.'

Sally was losing patience. 'I'm sure other shops sell them. How about Marks and Spencer?'

'Out of stock!' Pia shouted. 'All the school stock is cleared out by now. And it's the sales. Do you expect me to traipse into Slough in the middle of the sales? None of this would have happened if you had been more careful.'

With anyone else she would have apologised. Instead, she said, 'I'm sure you can find some.'

Pia snapped back. 'Why should I? You've no idea of the trouble you've caused.'

'It was an accident.'

'I shall be sending you a bill!'

At the mention of money, Sally's voice took on a harder edge. 'It's not my responsibility.' She searched for words to end the call.

But Pia was not finished. She spoke more slowly now. 'No. It's never your responsibility, is it? It's always mine. I have to pick up the pieces for the devastation you leave in your wake. Well, I've had enough. In future, stay out of my way – and my children's lives,' Pia gathered her breath, 'before you do any more harm.'

And then Pia had slammed down the phone. Sally had sat down, shaking. The truth revealed was nonetheless shocking: the polite façade had been ripped down. Later, when Edward arrived home and she relayed the call to him, he had been sympathetic but detached.

'Just ignore her.'

A bill never did arrive. She had spent several weeks scouring the post, anticipating its arrival by composing letters in her mind that she would send in reply.

Please note that I am not liable, legally or morally, for this amount.

There had been no contact since then. But surely there would be, at whatever party was being planned, a party she grew more convinced was being kept secret from her by Pia. A party at which the pretences of the past would no longer be possible. A party about which she was getting increasingly obsessed.

She could hear Louis now through the baby monitor. She put down her pen and cleared the table, putting the invitations on a high shelf out of his reach. He sounded happy. Sometimes he could be foul when he woke up from a nap, whining and scratching her and kicking. It was too cold to walk so she would wrap him up and take him in the car down to Cottenham Park. By the time she had stopped off at Sainsbury's it would be dark. It took an age to get round any supermarket because so many people stopped her to coo at Louis. He was adorable, with his chubby face and stocky legs, and she dressed him cosily in corduroys and woollens and little shirts. She would give him his tea and they would watch *Pingu*, his current favourite, and before she knew it, it would be time for Edward to come home and she would wonder, yet again, where on earth the day had gone.

Chapter 2

Anna Miller had decided that she hated lawyers and that her next programme might well be an exposé of the legal profession, focusing on conveyancing solicitors. She held the telephone under her chin as she addressed envelopes stacked on her desk. It was quicker to do it herself than try to find her assistant, Ethne, who seemed to spend as much time as possible hiding in the kitchen. The same do-it-yourself principle could be applied to her flat purchase.

Simon Archer's voice droned on. 'The searches are back, the mortgage offer is through, but I would urge you to consider the issue of the plane tree. There is the option of a structural survey. I'll put that in writing to you.'

'But I've already had a survey!'

'No. That was a mortgage valuation. It affords no warranty as to the condition of the property. You need a full structural survey for that. It's a common misconception amongst the public.'

She recalled that Simon Archer was a lawyer recommended by a colleague for his thoroughness.

Anna could hardly believe that yet another obstacle had emerged. 'Why didn't you tell me about this before? Then we could have dealt with it weeks ago!'

Simon sounded wounded. 'I wasn't aware of it. It is a major purchase and I would be failing in my duty to you if we didn't at least consider the issue of the tree.'

'The neighbour's tree?'

'Yes.'

'Look, Simon, I've sold my flat. I'm buying this one. If I don't exchange soon they're going to sell it to someone else. If the tree falls on the house who cares? I'm in the basement. And if it sneaks up through the ground, I'll sue the neighbours.'

Simon sounded alarmed. 'That assumes that your prospective neighbours have funds to pay and further assumes that the court thinks fit to grant such an order.'

Where and when had he learned to speak like this?

Simon continued. 'I'm not sure that I can condone—'

She cut him off. 'I'm not asking you to condone it. Just do it. Let's exchange contracts.'

'But—'

'Today, Simon. Then send me a letter telling me that you told me to have a structural survey and I wilfully and recklessly ignored you.'

There was a silence. Then, at last, 'Very well.'

'Thank you.'

She put the phone down before Simon could change his mind. She crossed off his name from her to-do list, which consisted of two columns of an A4 pad. She wanted 12 North Walk and she was going to have it. Fifteen minutes' walk downhill to the station, a garden for entertaining, and more light than in any basement flat she had seen.

More than that, she felt she was destined to live there. When the particulars had first arrived in the post, she had searched her mind to recall from where she knew the name North Walk. Later that day it had come to her: the BBC sound archive. The memory took her back to her very first BBC job, cataloguing tapes in the archive basement. There were hundreds of them, lined up on dusty shelves, each marked with a yellowing and peeling label bearing the name of a London street. North Walk was one of them. The tapes were interviews carried out with people who lived in those streets in the 1960s, recording their recollections of life at the turn of the century. The idea was to select the best and make an anthology for sale to the public.

At the time she had been given the assignment she had been mutinous, arguing with Des, her personnel officer, to be moved. 'This is ridiculous,' she said, waving the assignment notice at him. 'It's completely irrelevant to what I want to do. I joined the BBC to make programmes! I've already won a student film award.'

Des, Yorkshire-born with thirty years of BBC service, had been unmoved. 'You need to get experience. You can't run before you learn to walk, pet.'

Now she was running faster than ever, but no longer with the BBC. She had swapped the corridors of Television Centre for the narrow staircase and cramped Charlotte Street offices of 7–24, the country's most successful independent television production company. 7–24 was started and still wholly owned by Rick Roth, though it was widely rumoured that 7–24 was soon to go public with a share issue. She was, since two months ago, the company's senior programme producer. Her first assignment was 7–24's first venture into the making of a serious series documentary. *Marriage Menders,* as described by the in-house proposal document, was a programme that followed over six episodes the stories of three couples 'in crisis and on the brink of divorce' as they 'made tough choices'. Personally, Anna thought *Marriage Menders* was long on cliché and short on innovation. But most of the format work had been done before her arrival.

Marriage Menders was intended to demonstrate that 7–24 could do in-depth documentary work. Rick hadn't said so but it was clearly a strategy designed to appeal to the City institutions Rick needed on board if he was going to go public. And he'd needed someone with her experience to do it.

She finished addressing the envelopes and made a note to call Simon Archer in an hour to check that he hadn't found another reason not to exchange contracts. Then she needed to get to the basement edit suite and look over the first set of films, of a young couple from Slough whose three young children could have caused sound problems. Rick might want to see them when he signed off on the final choices. She made a note to start outlining the voiceover script. Why did the list never get shorter? Axing the BBC committees, the corporation form filling and the indispensable networking was supposed to give her more time for a private life – as Tim had pointed out last night when she had phoned him from Slough where filming had overrun to say she couldn't make dinner. But he was used to it by now – and it would change, just as soon as *Marriage Menders* was out of the way.

She had met Tim at a summer party thrown by Natasha Webster, a television presenter, in the back garden of Natasha's Putney house. It was a farewell party held on a very hot and humid July evening. Natasha, recovering from a divorce that had lasted longer than her marriage, was leaving to go and spend three months living and filming in an Ethiopian village school set up by Save the Children. It was a career move Anna could only describe as 'gutsy'. Natasha had introduced them and, Anna realised in retrospect, set them up.

'This is Tim Meah, the leader writer on *The Times*. And this is Anna Miller. Anna's the BBC's star producer ...'

He was sexy: linen trousers, white shirt, dark eyes.

She was slightly unnerved. She jumped in. 'So you're the leader writer?'

'Actually, there's a team of us.'

He looked like a very cool professor, the kind all his students had a crush on. But decent, not the type to take advantage.

She was struggling to be natural. She wished she looked like Natasha, in a floaty dress, instead of white capris and a strappy navy and white T-shirt. At least she had a tan. And her hair, usually defiantly unmanageable, had responded well to treatment with an extortionately expensive anti-frizz shampoo recommended by the manageress at Space NK. 'Do you choose what you write about?'

'Sometimes. Usually it's an obvious topic. Like today – we're going with the pre-Budget leaks. But if I get the chance I like to write about the very strong case for the abolition of the BBC licence fee.'

She laughed. He had got her. He didn't ask any of the usual questions. *Have I seen anything you've worked on?* The Holiday Programme? *Do you get sent anywhere exotic?* Later, after just the right amount of red wine and while a joint was being passed round, he'd asked her why she went into television. She inhaled, he didn't. She liked that about him.

'To make a mark. To get across what I wanted to say.'

Fortunately, he didn't ask what she had wanted to say. It was such a long time ago. Instead, he'd smiled. 'Our generation has been lost to the media. Forget politics. Or making things. Or teaching. All the ambitious kids want to be on TV.'

Normally she would have argued that that was because television was the route to power and influence. Instead, she had leaned against him and he had driven her home and kissed her in his car outside her Shepherd's Bush flat. The next week he had invited her to see *Eugene Onegin* at Holland Park Opera. As he parked she asked him the plot.

'Man meets love of his life, doesn't realise it, lives to regret it.'

Tim knew things. He read novels. He hadn't stopped reading serious books when he left university. He knew the first lines of poems; he knew the names of stars and trees and birds. He knew about massage. He knew how to give and receive in bed in equal measure. He knew how to kiss her deeply and run his hands over her body in one slow, possessive motion that still made her heady. He didn't control her, crowd her or flirt with other women. Natasha, on her return from Africa, told her she looked like she was in love and that Tim was the best thing that had ever happened to her.

Last weekend she had taken Tim to see the flat. By then she had already put in an offer. But at least she was making an effort to involve him. The agent, a young girl shivering in a thin black suit, and holding a list of Sunday-morning viewing appointments, looked harassed as she had let them in.

Anna had seized the opportunity. 'We may be a while. We have to measure up.'

The girl's face had fallen.

'Why don't we lock up and bring the keys back to the office?' Anna continued.

The girl looked doubtful.

'We don't want to make you late,' Anna concluded.

The girl's mobile had begun to ring. Flustered, she reached for it in her handbag, saying to Anna as she did so, 'Well, I'm not supposed to …' But she handed Anna the keys with her free hand.

'Thanks.'

The girl hurried off, answering her call, 'Hello! I'm on my way …' and slamming the front door behind her.

'Very smooth,' observed Tim drily.

Anna couldn't see why he felt the need to make a comment. 'It helps both of us. I hate being followed around.' There was a fractional tension – as there so often was. 'Let's start at the front.'

'Fine by me.'

The moment passed. 'Very big,' he said approvingly as she showed him the front room. They moved on to view the galley kitchen, fitted out in beech with black fake-marble countertops, located at the rear of the flat. Above the sink was a newly installed side window looking out onto the well of the patio.

At the opposite end, the kitchen opened out into a dining area. The flat was set out so that all the living rooms had natural light.

The floors were laid throughout with very pale wood laminate, which added to the impression of space and light. The bathroom, situated in the middle of the flat, had no window and relied on recessed halogens and an extractor fan for light and ventilation. Last she showed him the bedroom at the back with a door opening onto a small, square patio.

'I saved the best for last,' Anna exclaimed. She found the key to the lock lying on the floor. 'Here, let's have a look.'

She had stepped out into the chill January morning and bounded up a short flight of stone steps leading up onto the neighbour's lawn.

Tim, standing on the patio, looked doubtful. 'Anna, it is their garden.'

'They won't mind.' She waved him onto the main lawn. 'You see, there's no one about.' Inside her new neighbour's house the kitchen was unlit. A tricycle was parked next to the glass door and the sticky fingerprints of a small child were smudged onto the glass. Hopefully he or she was a quiet child.

As they looked up at the brickwork of the house she told him about her plans for the flat. 'I want to put in a totally integrated entertainment system and wire the flat for sound.'

'Fantastic. It's a great flat.' His voice told her he was holding something back.

'But?' she asked.

'It's just very different from Shepherd's Bush. Wimbledon's for families, isn't it?'

'Yes. Families and couples. Both.' As she said this she wondered if that was what she was looking for. A place that kept her options open? There was a momentary awkward silence.

Tim walked back down the steps to the basement patio. 'You could have some raised beds built there,' he pointed out.

'Yeah.' She hadn't a clue about gardening. But there must be hundreds of gardeners in Wimbledon who could do it for her. They had walked back into the flat and discussed the size of the kitchen table she would need and afterwards they had dropped the keys back as promised and gone for breakfast in Café Rouge. But nothing had been said about Tim moving in and she wondered if in this – as in everything that related to her personal life for as long as she could remember – she wanted her options open, too. It was not that the idea of marriage and a family was so bad. It was the thought of actually doing it: running behind that tricycle and wiping fingerprints off glass and all the other unseen, unrewarded and unglamorous tasks that constituted motherhood.

Work, in contrast, rewarded her in every sense. Anna reviewed her list. She needed to forget about Simon Archer and concentrate on her meeting with Rick. *Marriage Menders* came first – for her and for 7–24. That had been another reason for leaving the BBC. If all went well, and 7–24 did go public, the stock options she had negotiated in her contract would set her up for life. A successful share issue would leave her rich enough to work freelance – when and if she felt like it. She would be set up financially so that she could ease off … get married, start a family, live a little. Or she could start her own company – where she would be the occupant of the top-floor office.

The sight of the invitations for Louis's party seemed to have prompted Edward to recall that he had indeed been told something about Hope's birthday. He stood, loosening his shirt, the other hand holding a glass of red wine.

He sipped it and pulled a face.

'It was on offer,' Sally explained, chopping an onion.

'Drink!' commanded Louis from his booster seat, banging his beaker, a little king surveying them as they brought him food and drinks.

The wine budget had been slashed at their last 'financial summit', so called by Edward – monthly meetings, following the arrival of the bank statement and the credit card bills, where they would make solemn resolutions to economise.

She filled the beaker with water and handed Louis a bowl of chopped banana.

'Juice!'

'There's a party in the evening,' Edward volunteered. 'Pia sent me an email.'

'When?'

He didn't answer. He was rooting through the cupboard, presumably looking for something to snack on. He pulled open a packet of Wotsits.

She ignored the issue of exactly when the email had arrived. She suspected Edward delayed opening anything from Pia. For now, she was impatient to know more. 'Where?'

'At Pia's. She's getting a marquee.'

The horrible thought that Sally genuinely had nothing to wear occurred to her. She could hardly lose a stone in less than a month.

'Wots,' mewed Louis, abandoning his drink and his banana. 'Wots.'

'And there's a lunch beforehand,' he added.

So. It was just as she had suspected. 'Well, how are we going to have Louis's party on the same day?'

'Wots, Wots.'

'Oh, let him have one,' she said resignedly. Before she had had children she had always thought that consistency was essential.

'In the morning? It really isn't a problem,' he said reasonably, passing a Wotsit to Louis. 'What's for dinner?'

'Not a problem!' she exclaimed. 'I've written all the invitations! For 3.00 p.m.'

'Have you posted them?'

She hesitated. She could exaggerate, she had no difficulty in omitting certain facts, but she had never been able to tell an outright lie to Edward, not even a small one. 'No.'

His gaze lightened. 'Well then, can't you just alter the time?'

Yes, she could, but that was not the point.

'I don't see why you couldn't have told me earlier,' she said, irritated. 'And no one has a children's party in the morning; they're always in the afternoon. How can we possibly have a birthday party in the morning and get to Gerrards Cross for lunchtime? And what about Louis? He's going to be exhausted – a party in the morning and then this lunch.'

He turned to face her. 'Darling, it's not that kind of lunch.'

'What?'

'It's a formal lunch.'

'What do you mean a formal lunch? Do you mean there are caterers?'

He took a large sip of wine. 'It's at the Compleat Angler.'

'The Compleat Angler! The one at Marlow?'

Edward nodded. She had never been but she had seen the receipts for client lunches there. It was no place for a two-year-old, not unless he was an exceptionally sophisticated and well-behaved toddler. Louis was disqualified on both counts.

'Well, who's paying for that?'

'Pia,' he said defensively.

She was slightly mollified by that. But only slightly. 'Who's going?'

He sighed. 'Hope. Dan. Pia. Me. My parents. Pia's mother. And Gabriel, I guess.'

'Gabriel!' she said derisively. Edward was loath to discuss his marriage to Pia but made no secret that Gabriel, Pia's brother, had been a thorn in his side for its duration.

She repeated the names while counting them off on her fingers. 'And me. So that's nine.'

He said nothing.

He took a deep drink from his glass, put it down again and looked out of the window into the darkness.

Then he said, 'Sal …' He took hold of her shoulder. 'Sal …'

And she knew then before he told her, so that at that moment his touch was nothing to her and their eyes met.

She looked away, out of the kitchen window into the black, refusing to hold his gaze. 'Sal, I'm sorry. Really.'

But she had broken away from him now and gone over to stand by the window. Her face was flushed, her stomach sick and the hot tears that had come into her eyes were ones of anger and betrayal and confusion. But she could say nothing because she could not trust herself to speak.

She heard his voice.

'It's just a couple of hours and then we'll be together in the evening. It's just one day, Sal. We have all our lives together.'

And it was true. She had him all the time and yet it was not enough. Because the only thing that would satisfy her on this occasion was that which she could not ask for – *don't go, stay with me, stay with us.*

Even though she knew it would give her no comfort, still she was compelled to ask him, '*Why* can't I come?' It was hard not to pout and she was aware that her mouth had formed a hard-set line.

She heard his sigh. 'Darling, I didn't make the arrangements.'

'I know you didn't!' She swung round. God, why were men always more anxious to escape blame than to explain themselves? 'I'm not

23

saying you did!' No, Pia and Hope had made the arrangements, that much was obvious. 'I'm asking *why?*'

He gave a half-shrug of his shoulders. 'Sal, you'd hate it.'

'I'd like to decide that for myself.'

He paused. 'It would be awkward, that's all.'

The truth was that he was right. It would be awkward and she would hate every moment of it. She could visualise it now, trapped at a lunch table with Pia, besieged by her family as they shot off well-worn anecdotes and family jokes.

She turned her back and went back to preparing dinner. Louis began whining to be let down. And then Edward dealt with awkwardness as he always did.

'I'm going to get changed.'

He left the room to go upstairs.

Chapter 3

Hope sat waiting for her father just before noon in the Pret a Manger located on the corner of Fleet Street and Arundel Street. It was convenient for both of them, a short walk from Porter Stone and the King's College library. They were meeting early so as to be able to sit down. She held a stack of 3 × 5 lined record cards, a hundred or so, on which she had written essential facts relating to the English Civil War in different colours. Blue for the Royalists, red for the Parliamentarians.

Short Parliament April–May 1640
Cromwell forms New Model Army April 1645
Cromwell dies August 1658

Did she need to learn all the months? And once she had done the Civil War there was all the nineteenth-century European stuff to do. The notes filled two thick lever-arch files. She began to panic, as she always did, when she let herself think about all there was to do before the mock exams at the end of the spring term. It was barely a month away. And there was the dissertation to write too.

No one else panicked like she did. Oh, they all proclaimed that they were going to fail and bought caffeine pills to keep themselves awake. But no one else had even thought about starting their revision. They were all too busy doing as little work as possible and enjoying themselves. And in the middle of it all was her party. Mummy was doing everything, but there was still something to find to wear for the lunch. For the evening Hope was wearing a black cocktail dress, with a tight, boned bodice and a floaty skirt, that they had found in Selfridges last week. So she had lost most of her study day, the one day per week without lectures or tutorials, and had to stay up until 2.00 a.m. to finish her assignment. Meanwhile, Mummy was texting her all the time asking her this and that.

'I don't want you to think I'm taking over,' Mummy had said last week when she had come to Kennington to collect her to go to Oxford Street. She had looked up to the minute, in a new boxy fuchsia-pink jacket, but tired. Privately, Hope thought that her mother's short, layered and heavily highlighted hairstyle – she had cut her hair short after Daddy left – made her angular features appear sharper. But she would never say so.

'Are you sure you want to go shopping?' Hope had asked anxiously. 'We don't have to go today.'

'Why ever not? We've made a plan to go!'

Her mother had come from an interview at the BBC for a pre-Budget news reports in which she had been asked for her predictions on how the Budget would affect women. Hope had said that Mummy ought to sit down. She made them green tea in the Bridgewater mugs Mummy had given her as a moving-in present, four of them, each with a different set of birds.

Something for uni, Darling!

She really wished her mother wouldn't say *uni*. Hope took the robins and handed her mother the barn owls. When Hope moved in, Mummy said the flat was a fine example of 1960s brutalism – a sixth-floor university flat with low ceilings and worn-out grey commercial-grade carpet. It needed painting, the ceilings were stained yellow and the Formica kitchen had several of the cupboard doors missing. A machine answered calls to university maintenance. No one ever got back to them. They sat surrounded by the washing airer in the corner and a pile of mugs waiting to be washed up when someone bought washing-up liquid.

Her mother had lit a cigarette. 'Just one. And it's menthol.'

Her mother was careful not to smoke in public. Pia Kirwan-Hughes advised women on how to manage their lives, not shorten them.

She had taken out a file from her slim tan briefcase and opened it. 'Now. We have seventy-six acceptances for the evening, fourteen declined, and forty-two still to reply. So I'm going to say provisionally one hundred to the caterers.'

Pia reeled off the latest names to reply, most of them Hope's school friends, the newer university friends Hope had chased up herself.

Hope was wondering where her mother planned to put Jo and the other two flatmates. It would be good if they could all be together.

'And I've confirmed the menu: smoked salmon followed by chicken pie and then either chocolate cheesecake or apple strudel.'

On the other hand she wanted to sit next to Jo and that would be on the family table.

Pia looked up. 'Hope!'

'Oh. Yes. Good.'

Her mother returned to her notes. 'Now. Fireworks. We could have some fireworks at the end of the evening. But then again, if you're all going to be merry ...'

'*Merry!*'

'Or whatever term you want to apply to describe being blind drunk, perhaps it would be safer not.'

'I think fireworks would be fun!' Hope exclaimed.

'Well, we'll see,' concluded her mother briskly. 'And really, apart from that, everything's done. I've sent an email to your father with all the details so he's in the loop. I'm still waiting for a reply.'

Her mother was really good at saying things that weren't an obvious criticism. She took a sip of tea and pulled a face.

'It's the water,' Hope explained.

'I've told Dan he can bring one friend – no more. But not to the lunch. That's just family.'

Good. Hope knew that the phrase 'just family' was code between them. 'So what are we doing about Frumpy?'

Pia raised her eyes heavenwards. 'We'll just have to make the most of it, darling. I have to invite her for the evening.'

Hope knew why – because Daddy might not come without her. It was a bitter thought and she pushed it away. At least she wasn't going to be at the lunch. Mummy had been firm on that from the outset. 'I'm damned if I'm going to pay for her. It's bad enough that I have to pay for her incompetence.'

Hope had accompanied her mother to buy Dan new school shirts after Christmas. Really, she had wanted to stay at home and study. But her mother had plans. 'Slough will be ghastly. Let's go to Windsor. We'll hit the sales and have lunch at the Castle Hotel, darling.'

Her mother, thumbing through the pile of wrapped two-pack

school shirts in the Windsor branch of Marks & Spencer, had been vocal on the subject of Sally's miserable housekeeping skills. 'We're very lucky that they happen to have shirts in stock. Ordinarily they don't. Of course, I brought you up to take special care of other people's things. But not everyone has standards, sad to say.' They had stood for ages in the queue of bargain-hunters waiting to pay. 'I could send her the receipt. But sometimes one has to be the bigger person. Of course, if she had any class at all, she would send me a cheque voluntarily.'

To be fair, on the few occasions they had all been together Frumpy didn't say anything nasty or behave badly. It was just so much more relaxed when she wasn't there. Hope found herself thinking before she said anything because every topic of conversation seemed full of potential pitfalls.

She had just reached the dates of the Long Parliament when Daddy arrived, late – but only five minutes. He kissed her and said, 'I'm famished. BLT?'

'Yep.' She thought about leaving her record cards on the table to try to save their place. But it would be catastrophic if she lost them so she grabbed them and her bag. There was a queue of office workers ahead of them and some sort of delay caused by a problem with the coffee machine.

She told him about her dress and then about the menu for the evening. 'Smoked salmon with a salad garnish thing. Then chicken pies. Mummy thought because it was March we should have some-thing hot.' She stopped herself. Perhaps he knew all about it? 'She said she sent you an email telling you everything.'

He nodded but did not comment. Hope wondered if he read emails from her mother. She generally skipped bits, they were always so long.

Instead he said, 'I hope she's heating that marquee.'

'We've hired every hot-air blower in Buckinghamshire. There isn't going to be a formal top table. Mummy thought that would be really old-fashioned. We're going to sit on a round table like all the others. And Mummy's going to get one of the chefs to stay on and cook a kind of survivors' breakfast.'

'You should get him to make you pancakes. Get some proper maple syrup.'

'Mummy thought omelettes and fruit salad.'

He snorted. 'For the girls. The boys will want more than that.'

It would be brilliant if he could be there. He would make it a hundred times better. He would get the boys up and do something stupid and fun with them, take them in the garden despite the morning chill and play football or three-legged rugby. Mummy was a fabulous organiser but sometimes it was a relief to be spontaneous. And it was so tempting to ask him but if she did that it would spoil everything. Not because he would get cross. Just because he would say something like '*We'll see*' and they would both know that he meant no.

'We're calling it "The Morning After The Night Before Pyjama Party",' she explained.

The queue had begun to move. Edward pulled out his wallet to pay for lunch. Turning to her, he gave her a wry smile. 'Well, you must have something nice to wear.'

He handed her a fold of notes. 'Get yourself some decent PJs. And I mean *decent*,' he said mock sternly.

She could see they were twenty-pound notes. 'Thanks!'

And then they had reclaimed their space looking out over Aldwych and St Clement Danes Church. They talked about Porter Stone and his clients and the new house, which she had yet to visit.

'Why don't you come down this weekend? Sally would love to see you.'

'I have to work,' she said firmly.

He said nothing more. So she jumped in and they talked about lectures and her dissertation, *Victorian Women – their rights and responsibilities*. Jo had thought of the title.

It was her favourite historical period. 'Did you know that married women couldn't even own property until 1870? Their husbands got it automatically.'

'What's wrong with that?' he asked innocently.

She knew how to ignore him now. 'And I want to look at how the universities discriminated against women and I want to research the lives of working-class women, too.'

'It's a big subject,' he said cautiously. That was one of the things that was best about her father. He really listened. He didn't just say '*Super, darling*' like her mother. 'Just make sure you do an outline. Keep it structured.'

'I know,' she said gloomily. 'They take marks off if you go over the word limit.'

'That's life,' he said. 'You have to work within the rules. Not that you need to think about that right now,' he added hastily. 'No interviews.'

It was her father who had put a stop to all that, before Christmas, when she had burst into tears in the Fleet Street Starbucks, worn down with essays and ten-page application forms for marketing jobs she wasn't sure she even wanted. Daddy was brilliant. He told her firmly to go back and tear up all the forms, then concentrate on getting her degree and apply again next year. Why hadn't she thought of that?

He had hit his stride now. 'And no working right through the Easter holidays. You need a break. Is Mummy taking you anywhere?'

She rolled her eyes. 'Mummy's working.' They used to ski at Easter but when he left, Mummy refused to go on her own with them.

'The book?'

'What else? She's got interviews and book signings and all sorts of stuff.'

Sometimes he asked her other personal questions about her mother, not in an intrusive way, in a nice way that made her feel that he was still keeping an eye on them. Like the time Granny went into hospital. And after Mummy split up with Roger and Daddy asked if Mummy was OK about it. Roger ran an art gallery in Beaconsfield and liked going to the races. He was fun.

He sounded concerned. 'But you're going home?'

'Everyone's going home. We have to. We get thrown out of the flat because the university uses them for conferences.'

Thoughts of her well-being were clearly on his mind because he said next, 'What about Jake?'

She hated it when he asked her those sorts of questions. It made her want to curl up with embarrassment.

She shrugged her shoulders. 'He's still in Costa Rica,' she said noncommittally, and in truth she knew little more than that. Jake's Politics with Spanish degree required him to spend a year overseas. Jake had pre-planned his career in the Diplomatic Service while at Welton. Jake emailed her, but usually only as part of a round robin. She doubted whether he would remember her birthday and she didn't care. But this was not the time or place to go into all of that.

'Well, don't forget—'

'I'm too good for him. I know, Daddy!'

He had disliked Jake, whom she met when she joined the sixth form at Welton, dated on and off for the two years of sixth form and attempted to date when he went to Southampton and she went to London. Daddy didn't say why exactly, but once he said that Jake was 'clever' in a way that clearly wasn't a compliment. She and Jake had decided to have a break during their first year of university. She had known long before that that something was very wrong but had not known what it was.

Already Daddy was looking at his watch. 'I have to run.'

Her disappointment must have shown because he added, 'Same time next week?'

'OK.'

'I'll check my diary and call you.' Sometimes they emailed but he used his Porter Stone account, which didn't feel very private. He got up and looked at his watch again and she knew that his mind was now on work. He kissed her at the exit to Pret a Manger and she watched him cross the road until he was lost in the crowd thronging Fleet Street. There never seemed to be enough time. It was always a snatched lunch or early dinner here and there. She was invariably left with the feeling that he was stopping off to see her on the way to his ultimate destination. Her father had become a visitor in her life. And when they were together the old familiarity could not be relied upon. It came and went, so that at times it was as if he had never left home and at others their words were uncomfortably loaded with meaning. They had lost some of the old easy understanding. Sally had it now. Hope tried very, very hard not to think about it but, as she lost sight of him in the Fleet Street crowds, she could not suppress the image of Sally hearing his key in the lock, going up the hall to meet him and welcoming him home.

Chapter 4

Sally's father had a number of favourite sayings. His belief that the road to hell is paved with good intentions came to mind as Sally stood in the reference section of Wimbledon library looking at the book pages of the *Daily Mail*. The trip to the library had been well intended, a high-minded combination of intellectual stimulation plus a calorie-burning walk. But Louis had wriggled through toddler story-time while a crying baby held ineptly by a thin teenage girl with another child in tow had all but drowned out the librarian's voice anyway. Later, as she bribed Louis with a packet of mini cookies so she could snatch a look at the library newspapers she had seen in the *Daily Mail* book review pages a column headed 'Ones to Watch'. There was a thumbnail photo of Pia and a short review of her new book: '*Smart Women, Smart Choices* (6th edition) – Pia Kirwan-Hughes makes finance accessible and offers sensible tips for making your money go further. A must-have for the money-wise woman.'

She left to check out Louis's books and the boxed DVD set of the series *Letters of a Victorian Lady*. She pondered if Edward knew about the review. She knew they talked, of course they did, they had two children together. Maybe at the last Welton hockey match? She pulled herself up. She had made a solemn resolution that she was not going to think about Pia or the bloody lunch.

Because what was the alternative? Edward simply refused to discuss it. She had broached the subject on several occasions. Each time, his tone growing testier, he simply asked her what she thought he was supposed to do. Not go? And at that point she had backed off. Because the only answer was yes, don't go! Don't go to your only daughter's twenty-first birthday. Or, if you must go, please insist that I come too, even though I don't want to go because I will look fat and I will feel like an alien who has just landed on Planet First Family. So she had changed Louis's invitations to read Sunday instead of Saturday and tried to forget all about it.

But not being invited to something she didn't want to go to continued to make her mad.

They reached the library counter. Ahead of them an elderly man was standing stooped, slowly taking books out of his wheeled shopper trolley. Watching the books scan, she thought about all the money Pia must make from her books. It was so fucking unfair that Pia paid nothing at all towards Dan's school fees or Hope's university costs. Louis, who hated being stationary in the pushchair, was kicking so hard that it was rocking violently.

Sometimes, usually at these moments, she thought how her life might have been different if she had never gone to India with Chris. Probably they would have stuck it out as boyfriend and girlfriend for the final year. And she would have left with a decent degree, a degree good enough to secure her an interview and a high-paid career, instead of a third, which triggered an automatic rejection letter. In retrospect, she was a fool not to have moved out of their shared student house when they came back from Christmas in India. Some stupid sense of pride, combined with the false hope that they would get back together, stopped her. She would sit in her room, her books spread out in front of her, supposedly revising, before realising that she had failed to register a word of what she had read. Or she would flee to the offices of the university student newspaper and spend night after night sub-editing until the point came when most people thought she was the editor. At the time, she had thought Chris, a fellow history student, was the love of her life. A week before her finals, a girl, a first-year anthropology student, emerged from Chris's bedroom wearing one of his shirts.

It was a wonder she had got a degree at all.

They had their final row in the sacred location of the Holy Lake at Pushkar in Rajasthan, on the steps that led down to the water's edge. Chris had spent the trip making jibes about her middle-class background and criticising her relentlessly. 'You give too much to the beggars. It upsets the balance ...'

At the lake, Chris was half-stoned and enthusing about 'the people'. 'They're so open and spiritual. It's so real.'

'Real?' she repeated askance. 'Seeing everything through a drug-induced haze. How is that helping the ordinary people? Chris, I'm going.'

He had looked surprised at that, he knew she was afraid to travel on her own, but he had let her go. At the station, amid the fumes and dust, she had met up with two New Zealand girls and they had travelled together for the twenty-hour journey.

If only she had known at the time that one day she would meet a man who loved her for all the things that Chris despised.

Not that she had imagined when she first started working at Porter Stone that she would end up married to Edward. At the beginning Pia had been very much in evidence, calling frequently. It had been some weeks before Edward told her about the separation. But one Monday morning after she had been there for a couple of weeks she came into the office and checked his voicemail. It was rare for there to be any messages. Top clients had Edward's mobile and another line was manned twenty-four hours a day for banking business. But today there was a message. It was from Pia. Her voice was angry and she sounded drunk.

'Edward, it's Sunday night and I can't get hold of you. I've called the flat and the mobile, which is switched off. What is the fucking point of a mobile if it's switched off? Will you please call me as soon as you get this? I need to speak to you, the boiler's broken down and we've got no hot water. None whatsoever! And I can't find the plumber's number. God knows how much it will cost if I use the Yellow Pages. Where are you? It's just fucking irresponsible.'

There was a second message.

'Edward! Call me as soon as you get this!'

Sally deleted the messages. Edward was away in Geneva. He had left on Sunday afternoon. She typed out a fax: *Please call Mrs Kirwan-Hughes regarding a broken-down boiler at the Gerrards Cross house.* When he was away he had asked her to send him a fax updated in the morning and before she left in the evening so that he had a written record of any changes to his diary. Edward could use email but much preferred not to.

It was a revelation how much she liked Porter Stone and the Porter Stone way of conducting business – sure, sedate, almost serene. And, of course, she liked Edward.

He broached the subject of his marriage as they sat in his office at the end of a long day running over background information for a lunch with Joe Saltzman. Joe, a property millionaire, would be a major catch for the bank. Edward had reached across his desk and picked up a photograph of his children, of Dan when he was a toddler and Hope aged nine or ten, taken on a beach, as they posed side by side in swimsuits, the sea in the background.

His tone was awkward. 'My wife and I separated in the summer.'

She had heard that on the office grapevine but feigned ignorance. 'I'm sorry.'

He seemed uncertain of what to say but reluctant to leave the subject. 'We waited until the end of the school term. We wanted Hope to finish her GCSEs.'

'Of course.'

'Not that one can protect them entirely.'

'No.'

'You may well come across certain … appointments. They're … meetings I have with Pia. I put them in the diary as Cavendish Square.'

She had noticed those and known that they must be personal. She had not known what to say, made nervous herself by this unaccustomed hesitation she observed in Edward. She nodded.

'Naturally, I would like this kept between ourselves.'

She spoke a little too quickly. 'Of course!'

She was slightly offended that he might think otherwise. Discretion came naturally to her. Already in the short time that she had worked for Edward she had developed a loyalty to him.

He hesitated again and looked at the clock. It was nearly seven. And she knew then that he was thinking about returning to his flat in the Barbican, to the alien feeling of a key in the lock of an empty home, to reheating some ready-made meal and eating alone in front of the television. And she felt a pang for him.

He must have said something to Pia after the boiler calls because there were no more voicemails. She observed as Pia moved out of his life. Her calls to the office tailed off and then stopped, although sometimes she could hear him through his closed office door sounding fraught on his mobile. The Cavendish Square appointments ceased abruptly. There was a lull for a while. But then other calls started. For a couple of weeks or so from a girl called Beth. One from a girl called Jemima. And then from Louise. Even now the recollection of those messages from Louise Winter had the power to unnerve Sally.

Ed! Just reminding you – La Pot au Poule at eight.
Ed! Do you need me to arrange the car for Thursday? I usually allow two hours for the journey.

That last had been a black-tie dinner party in Wiltshire. Louise Winter, a forty-something divorcee with time to fill and alimony to spend, had been a regular caller, keen to engage in long chats and to 'liaise about Edward's diary', anxious to book him for dinners, concerts, gallery openings, first nights and more than one charity ball. That had not been the worst of it. After a few weeks of Louise's calls, Edward had asked Sally to book two tickets on the Eurostar to Paris. Louise had come to the office on the Friday afternoon prior to their departure. She was radiant – her figure svelte, her complexion tanned in the depths of winter. She carried a long sheepskin coat and a Louis Vuitton holdall..

Edward had returned on Monday with a box of Fauchon Marrons Glaces, which he left on her desk with a note in Louise's handwriting on George V Hotel headed paper.

Sally,
Thank you so much for organising such a fabulous trip. Merci beaucoup!
Louise

Ordinarily she would have at least kept the box but the knowledge that Louise had picked it out made her sour. She threw it away, contents and all, in a wastepaper bin on Fleet Street. She had been very conscious of her weight in those days. Later, she was to find out that Edward had broken up with Louise on their return from Paris. If she had known that she would have spent a much happier weekend, kept the Marrons Glaces and avoided recurrent conversations with her mother about how little she was eating.

They fell into a comfortable working routine. But one day, when Edward was away on a day trip to Frankfurt, there was a sharp knock on her open door. She looked up to see the six-foot, expensively suited figure of William Overton.

'Hello.' He apparently did not feel the need to offer his name, even though they had never been introduced. But she knew who he was: he had been pointed out to her by Brickie as one of the bank's rising stars, a former Guards officer recently graduated from the Harvard Business School.

'I need the Joe Saltzman file,' he said casually.

She felt an instant pang of anxiety. Joe was proving tricky to reel in. But Edward had confided to her that he was close to persuading Joe to move all his personal and business banking to Porter Stone. It would be a major success for Edward.

'Oh?'

'Yep. Nothing to worry about,' William Overton said patronisingly. 'Saltzman mentioned he wanted some advice on OMDs. I need to look over the file.'

OMDs? Orchestral Manoeuvres in the Dark? No. Offshore Money Deposits.

It would be much the easiest, simplest thing to give the file to William Overton. He had walked over and was leaning presumptuously against her desk. She observed his eyes flick over her papers. Something didn't feel right.

'I'll need to check—'

'No need to trouble Ed,' William interrupted smoothly. 'The Chairman wants me to hurry it along.' He shot her an insincere smile. 'Top priority. So, if you would ... I'll take it now.'

His voice sounded light but she could see the tension in his face. Now she was sure. She knew his game. He wanted to swipe Joe from under Edward's nose, take advantage of all the painstaking groundwork that Edward had laid, and bag him as his own catch for the bank.

Her heart was beating so hard she wondered he couldn't hear it.

'No, I can't. I'm sorry.' She stopped herself. She needed to sound more serious. 'I have to check with Mr Kirwan-Hughes.'

He could not conceal his surprise. It was the same shocked, reappraising look that Chris had given her when she picked up her bag at the Pushkar Lake and told him she was leaving. It was the glance several smart-mouthed student journalists had shot her when they finally understood that she was going to cut down their piece whether they liked it or not.

There was an impatient edge to his voice. 'Look …' She realised then that he didn't know her name.

'Sally.'

He lost a little of his composure. 'Look, Sally, I can see that you like to follow procedure.' He made this sound like a character weakness. 'But this is a business matter. The bank could stand to make – or lose – a substantial amount of money over this. I'm sure you don't want to be the one responsible for that.'

He really was unbearable. Her resolve not to let Edward lose Joe Saltzman hardened further. She paused. 'No. You can't have it.'

She watched him closely. It was as if he was considering walking round and rifling through her office drawers.

She pre-empted him by picking up the telephone. 'Excuse me. I have a call to make. To Brickie. She's the Chairman's secretary. I need to confirm our lunch arrangements.'

He stood up straight. There was an agonising pause of four or five seconds.

'Very well.' He walked over to the door and turned back to her. He could not completely conceal the agitation in his voice. 'I only hope this doesn't rebound on you.'

She put down the phone. There was no lunch arrangement with Brickie. She felt shaky but victorious. Edward, when she told him about it the next day, had been aghast.

'Sally, I'm really sorry.' He had looked angry. 'Hell. You shouldn't have been put in that position. It's disgraceful.' Later, Brickie told her that there was a rumour going round the bank that Edward had gone up to William Overton's office and raised voices had been heard through the closed office door.

William Overton had never come down to her office again, Joe Saltzman finally signed with the bank and there were no other women after Louise. A couple of weeks after the Saltzman file incident, Edward had casually suggested that as it had been a hard week they ought to treat themselves to a drink after work. They had slipped into a taxi and headed off to the seclusion of the Dorchester Bar. It was there, over a glass of champagne, in the mirrored bar with the piano playing 'Strangers in the Night' in the background that he had turned to her and said too casually, 'When I was in Paris I kept thinking how much you would enjoy it. It's such a beautiful city.'

And she had taken his meaning, heady from the champagne and the admission that he had been thinking about her. She had known that he was testing the waters, understood that his position was difficult, but revelled in the moment. She held his gaze a fraction too long. 'I'm sure I would have loved it!'

Rick's office had recently had a makeover. Spanning the top of the building, the style was ultra modern: white walls, limed oak floors and at one end sliding doors opening out onto a roof terrace. At the other end there was a kidney-shaped desk with a smoked-glass top and huge black revolving chair. To one side hung a vast flat-screen television, on the other side big blown-up photos of his wife and children. Rick's second wife used to be a presenter on MTV.

Rick's office was in contrast to the cramped accommodation in the rest of the building. The entire accounts department of six people worked in two windowless basement rooms; the post room, run by Oliver the Post, a Welsh psychology graduate, was little more than a cupboard. There was a tiny kitchen off the second-floor landing equipped with a kettle and a microwave but most people went out or bought sandwiches from Allegra, a horsy type who turned up every day on a sit-up-and-beg bicycle. But these days every graduate wanted to work in television: some eight hundred people had replied to their last *Guardian* advertisement for a researcher. So everyone put up with it.

Rick and Anna sat on facing black sofas arranged next to the glass doors. Anna opened her *Marriage Menders* file. 'We've selected three couples and done short films with each of them. They're all good on camera.'

Rick nodded.

She read from her notes. 'First are the Michaels. They live in a council house in Slough but they're originally from Carlisle. He moved down here for work. He's a tyre fitter.' The Michaels' Carlisle origins had worked in their favour. 'Three young kids. Big debts. She's a full-time mother.'

'What does she look like?'

'Very pretty.'

'Good.'

She looked up at Rick. He was forty but looked in his thirties, with the ageless media look of close-cropped hair, Diesel jeans and expensive black shirt. And a Breitling watch.

'They're a nice couple, under strain, they could really use the help and the money. The most likely to make it – and the public will love them.'

He nodded his approval. 'Who else?'

Anna turned to the next page of her notes. 'Second are the Zarkoskys. They're our older couple. Both in their fifties. They live in a huge house in Beaconsfield. The two daughters have left home – now they have nothing to talk about, blah blah. Mrs Zarkosky is a big wheel in the local Catholic mothers' group.' She looked up, interested to see his reaction to her next snippet. 'Peter Zarkosky was involved with another woman.' He hadn't called it an affair. She checked her notes. It was a 'dalliance'.

Rick looked impressed. 'Will she talk?'

That could be problematic. 'The other woman? I don't know.'

But before she had a chance to explain Rick interrupted. 'So what's the line?'

'Bad things happen to rich people.' There was more to say. Peter Zarkosky had been very clear that their participation was conditional on the exclusion of his 'friend', as he put it.

But before she could raise this with Rick he cut across her. 'Who else?'

She reminded herself that Rick didn't expect to hold her hand. Her salary was twice that at the BBC, with a BMW convertible thrown in, and a golden hello that had provided the deposit for 12 North Walk. So she made a mental note to fill in some research on the Zarkoskys and moved on. 'Last we have the Ramseys. Nina and Rob. Probably the least appealing – they've got it all but they're still bloody miserable. Modern couple, no kids. They live in a new four-bedroom house on a snooty estate in Bracknell. She owns her own recruitment company. Rob is five years younger than Nina. He's trying to start a landscape gardening business.'

'He was her gardener?'

'Yep.'

'What's the diagnosis?'

She turned over a couple of pages. 'The psychologist thinks they're locked in a mother–son dynamic, replaying childhood patterns. Nina was forced into a caregiver role as a child.'

'Fuck! I meant what's the story, Anna?'

She thought for a couple of seconds. 'She's a control freak and he's a wimp.'

He sat back frowning. 'Where's the viewer identification?'

'Identification? Loads. Women are out-earning men, snapping up skilled jobs, men are redundant. It's a big issue in relationships.'

He mimed a yawn. 'OK. I think it's a good mix. Be careful with the Ramsey husband – wimps are boring. And get a bloke to do the voiceover. This is prime time, nine or ten p.m., not daytime.'

She was about to object to that but he looked at his watch and got up. Walking away from her to his desk he said, 'Good. Sounds like you've got it all under control. Move it along.'

She had barely been there ten minutes but it was clear that her time was up. Anna was on her own. As she left his office and descended the stairs to her own, she felt it.

Dan rested against the backboard of the goal. The nylon padding of the hockey goalkeeper's suit, in which he resembled the Michelin Man, rendered him lumbering but warm. A sleety rain drifted across the Astroturf onto the players and the small huddle of midweek spectators, his parents not numbered amongst them. The game was close to halfway and he had seen little action. He swung his hockey stick listlessly. Who the hell played hockey now anyway? They didn't even cover it on TV. He liked football. He had played at his last school, scored the occasional goal and got to run instead of waddling around in a fat suit.

After the game there would be tea in the pavilion, if orange squash and a stale iced bun could be described as tea. It was not even a proper bun, more of dry bread roll topped with sickly white icing. No currants or butter. He would have liked a cup of tea and a toasted teacake with melted butter like his grandmother used to make before she got ill. But tea and coffee was only available to the fifth-form prefects: there was a kettle in the prefects' room. The sixth-formers had shared study-bedrooms and a kitchenette on each corridor with a microwave. His year slept in four-bed dormitories. It was all very well for Hope. She'd only gone to Welton in the sixth form, as his mother conveniently forgot.

'You'll have fun!' she had enthused. 'It's such a sociable way to live.'

The rain was falling more heavily now. But they would not call off the match. The players' shirts were stuck to their backs and their hair was matted white from the sleet. His bloated gloves made it difficult to rub his eyes clear of the rain. It was forty-one days to the end of term. Two years to the end of the fifth form. He would not stay on to the sixth form – his mother absolutely could not make him do that. And two and a half hours before study hour, when the teachers were drinking coffee in the staff room and the prefects were supervising lower-school homework; two and a half hours until it was safe to meet Pascoe in the amphitheatre and roll a joint and feel that sweet relief, that heady high. Two and a half hours until life became bearable again.

Sally had forgotten that weeks ago she had ordered Iain Braden's *History of Wimbledon Village*. The librarian had handed it to her as she went to check out the DVDs and Louis's books. Now, reading it in the kitchen while Louis played at her feet, she was frustrated. Iain Braden mentioned the Lathams' connection with North Walk but nothing about their life there.

12–18 North Walk was constructed in 1876 as part of the development of the north side of Wimbledon Common. The four terraced houses were typical of the family homes built for the prosperous middle-class merchants and City men whose influx into Wimbledon since the coming of the railway in 1852 transformed a once-rural hamlet into a thriving town (see Chapter Two for the development of Wimbledon 1850–1914). The Lathams resided at number 12. Mrs Latham was the younger daughter of the Duke of Wakemont whose ancestral home, Selton Park, holds a place in the popular imagination as one of England's most grandiose stately homes. History records the Duke of Wakemont as a trusted advisor of Queen Victoria.

E.D. Irvine's study, A History of the Wakemont Family, *records that the Latham marriage was seen at the time as a love match.*

Mr Latham, whose occupation was recorded as a journalist, pre-
sumably lacked independent means, accounting no doubt for the
couple's move to Wimbledon.

One can only surmise as to the new Mrs Latham's reaction to
her reduced circumstances, the gay ballrooms and gilded salons of
London high society forsaken for modest suburban brick.

There it ended. The Lathams appeared in Chapter 8, subtitled 'Famous Faces of Wimbledon', the extract illustrated by a studio photograph of Bella Latham taken with her sister Camilla. They faced each other, hands crossed, wearing identical high-necked dresses, their hair pulled back. Bella, aged eighteen according to the caption, was the prettier of the two, with large dark eyes, a confident gaze and delicate features.

Sally found herself staring at the photograph. She felt a compulsion to know more, provoked by Iain Braden's speculation. If she were ever to write a book she could never be satisfied with leaving a question unanswered. Had Bella's risky love affair survived? She put down the book. It would be time-consuming and there were so many other more pressing things that she needed to get on with. But, unbidden, the image of the cover of Pia's last book came to mind, glossy white with a gold embossed pound sign, Pia's name in heavy black print at the top. How difficult could it be? Pia had written books and brought up two children at the same time. She wrote a note on a Post-it and stuck it to the fridge.

Lathams
Order 'Letters' book from library

In the meantime she would try to persuade Louis to have a nap, long enough for her to watch episode one of *Letters of a Victorian Lady.*

Chapter 5

Hearing sounds of the crew drinking tea with the Ramseys in their kitchen, Anna felt uneasy about her choice of couple. They had the type of problems that many people shared – but they also had heaps of money to compensate. She was not sure that Rob and Nina would generate sympathy from the viewer.

Nina Ramsey had been only too keen to vent her frustrations on camera, waving her French-manicured hand around the expensively furnished living room of their modern Bracknell house. 'This all has to be paid for, you know.' She had turned back to her boyish husband Rob, saying accusingly, 'Not to mention the credit cards and your van payment, too. That's why I'm too exhausted to cook and clean.' Nina had rolled her eyes at Anna. 'His mother waited on him hand and foot. So now he leaves all his clothes on the floor for me to pick up! And she never liked me! She's never even given me a chance!'

Anna was under pressure from Rick to produce rushes. Juggling three couples with only the help of Ethne, her virtually absent assistant, was giving her a headache. And that evening she was due back in London by seven o'clock to go to the theatre and dinner with Tim and a Conservative MP whose name she had forgotten.

There was a time when all she had ever wanted to do was make television programmes. It had been her dream to see her ideas come to life on the screen. It was odd then how lately she had begun to think back with nostalgia to the early days of her career. At the time she had disliked being a researcher – or so she thought. Now, she recalled the days at Glastonbury, the all-night parties in London, and the pleasure of doing one thing well. Even the sound archive had ended up being fun. Unable to persuade Des the Personnel Officer to transfer her, she had settled down resentfully to the job of reviewing the hundreds of hours of audiotapes held in the BBC archive. The tapes, recorded in the 1960s, were the result of a joint project by the BBC and the University of London Social History Department. A team of young university researchers had gone out to the homes of working-class men and women, by then in their seventies and eighties, and interviewed them about their recollections of working-class life in Victorian and Edwardian times.

But the twelve weeks she had spent locked away in the basement had been a revelation. Often she had stayed, listening through her headphones at a corner desk in the deserted archive, until ten o'clock at night when Bernard the security man would come and startle her with a touch on the shoulder. 'Time to pack up, dear.'

The tapes gripped her in a way she would never have expected. The voices of working people telling their stories would play in her head long after she had left to travel home on the tube: she heard tales of hardship and sadness recounted in varying tones of indignation, self-pity and occasionally anger. There would be laughter and the softening of the voice as the speaker recalled the early blossoming of a love affair or a carefree moment in time. There was surprisingly little nostalgia for the good old days but frequently relief for having made it through years of poverty and war. It had not been possible to listen to all the tapes: instead she reviewed the first couple of minutes and decided whether to continue. She had listened to as much as possible and made a list of the best excerpts to be made into a two-tape edition provisionally entitled *Hard Labour: Voices of Working People.* In the event, the project was shelved, deemed months later at a BBC funding committee meeting to be insufficiently commercial. That had been her first taste of BBC politics. And her first lesson in her lack of power. It was not one she had needed to be taught again. So why was it that now, holding more power and influence than she had ever done before, she felt only nostalgia for the dimly lit and dusty archive she had long ago left behind?

'It's been a while since anyone's asked for this.'

The librarian scanned the paperback copy of *Letters of a Victorian Lady.* He handed it to Sally. 'Have you watched the series?'

'Oh, yes. I loved it.' She put the book in her bag. 'Now I want to read the letters themselves. The Lathams lived in my house,' she added by way of explanation.

The library assistant, an elderly man in a beige cardigan who looked as if he should have retired years ago, said enthusiastically, 'Goodness. How fascinating.'

She felt encouraged by his reaction to say more. 'Actually, I'm thinking of writing a history of the house – the story of the Lathams after they moved in.'

Why did she say 'I' not 'we'? Perhaps because when she had asked Edward if he wanted to watch episode two of *Letters* he had mimed a yawn and said couldn't they watch the European Championship football instead? When Edward had suggested that she should write a history of the house, he had apparently meant exactly that.

There was a time before Louis was born when all day spent together with Edward at work was not enough. They would slip away from the office for dinner at the small Italian in Floral Street that had become their regular: a no-nonsense checked tablecloth and spaghetti bolognese restaurant where the wine was poured from a wickerwork bottle-holder and the window sill was lined with candles stuck in empty Chianti bottles. Franco showed them to a table at the back and remembered that Edward didn't take ice in his whisky. When they got engaged Franco brought out champagne '*Complimentary!*' and admired her solitaire diamond at length.

In time, the routine changed. At Sally's insistence, Edward gave up the Barbican flat. Once she found out that Pia had a key and had on one occasion slept in the bed, she had never felt right there. She wanted a change. They chose Putney, renting while the divorce dragged on and Edward's legal bills rose accordingly. Pia was determined to argue every point. They stood close on the tube and walked side by side to the flat where they would eat in the kitchen. If you stood up you could just see the river from the kitchen window. Edward would sit at the table with the broken fold-down leaf that the landlord never did make good his promise to repair and watch her as she cooked.

Only later, when they moved into North Walk, as she observed Edward energetically set about the house and garden, did she realise how much he had missed owning a house.

Back then, they would talk about the day: the foibles of the clients, the chronic hold-ups in compliance, the ambitious plans of the new

Chairman. Of course, in those days she knew the clients. In the two years since she had left it had all changed so quickly.

Sally still listened attentively when Edward told her about work. Lately he had begun to talk about the bank's plans to open an office in Shanghai.

'It would be an extension of the Hong Kong office, serving high net worth clients. They've set up a steering committee – The Far East Planning Team. We're meeting twice a month …'

But the old days of bantered suggestions and observations were gone, and it was impossible to feel that her stories and anecdotes were as interesting as his. Vickie from the playgroup had a sweatshirt that said *Motherhood – The Hardest Job You'll Ever Love*, but Sally was not sure that she agreed. She loved Louis, but she would be more than happy to leave behind the rest of the repetitive, cleaning-up stuff that went with him.

Now, standing in the library, the librarian was giving her his concentrated attention. It was a while since anyone had done that.

'You should go direct to the original sources. Maybe it would be worth searching the local records?' he suggested. 'The electoral register's a good place to start. Or the family papers?'

She felt like a dilettante. What he was saying was so obvious.

And then a stern woman called closing time and began switching off the lights and he gave her a wave goodbye.

'Good luck!'

Sally had watched the six hour-long episodes of *Letters of a Victorian Lady* on DVD over the course of two days, albeit in snatches and over the top of Louis's head as he played with his favourite toy, a parking garage with a lift that carried the cars up to the top deck from whence he would send them hurtling down before loading them up again.

The series was addictive, with a starry cast and some terrific set pieces: the shooting party; the debutante ball; the Duchess of Wakemont's funeral cortège leaving Selton Park in the early-morning mist, as servants lined the steps and gravel driveway.

The programmes had been filmed at Selton Park itself, the house an expanse of Victorian Gothic brickwork adorned with an array of decorative turrets and towers in a romantic style of architecture suggestive of a medieval castle.

The house was the perfect setting for the melodrama that followed. Bella Latham was the beautiful, wilful, idealistic youngest daughter of the Duke of Wakemont, who was in turn a man torn between the duty he owed to Queen and country and his dedication to all the pleasures of the flesh. The Duchess indulged him, distracted from his philandering by her determination to see her daughters marry well. Camilla, her elder daughter, had done just that and was locked in a loveless union, unburdening her unhappiness to Bella in the morning room. Camilla stood in front of a wall painted with scenes of the British Empire, misted mountains and fortified towns dotted with British officers.

You must understand, Bella, that this is the condition of women. To be dutiful, unthinking, unfeeling items of property. I am as much an object in my husband's house as this vase or this table.

Later, the Duchess of Wakemont was dismissive of her daughter's unhappiness.

Why do you protest? What would you be? Mistress and master? You must make the best of it as I have done and many better women than you.

Into this loveless family came Robert Latham, a university friend of the Duke of Wakemont's eldest son. Robert Latham was the scholarship-educated son of a shopkeeper, a journalist by occupation, a believer in votes for all men and a supporter of trade unionism. Robert Latham's radical views, quick wit and dark good looks captivated Bella. The Duchess's response to Bella's pleas to marry Robert Latham was to take her to Italy for the summer.

The lovers persisted, however, exchanging letters and meeting secretly on Bella's return. But marriage appeared an impossibility.

In the end, it was the Duke who unexpectedly intervened. The Duchess died and in his grief the Duke lamented his unhappy marriage. The Duke of Wakemont, a serial adulterer, pheasant slaughterer and all-round villain of the piece, relented to Robert Latham's impassioned speech.

Since God first ordained marriage, no man would be truer than I to your daughter. No husband more conscious of his wife's wellbeing. No son-in-law more dutiful...

It was compulsive viewing. But at the end of it Sally was no closer to uncovering anything about the Lathams' subsequent life. The hope she had harboured that they would be filmed arriving in a horse-drawn carriage outside 12 North Walk was dashed.

It was frustrating: why didn't anyone seem to care about what happened after the lovers got married? The published *Letters* themselves offered no clue. There were just twenty letters contained in a thin paperback. Reading them, Sally was shocked that anyone could have based a six-part television series on these. The letters were a blend of light romantic talk, domestic trivia and political discourse, often jarringly intertwined.

Robert Latham wrote: *There is no woman alive more able to appreciate all that is fine and beautiful. Spent the day at the British Library ...*

But the two did not write as though they were distraught at being parted. Bella was enthusiastic about the trip to Italy: *It is well that I should see something of the continent. It is my sincere hope that the climate of the Alps will restore my mother to good health.*

Presumably their relationship had intensified after Bella returned from the continent not before? Sally had turned to the internet to try to find out more, only to find herself swamped by thousands of reviews of the television series. She had been about to log-off when a heading caught her eye: *Letters and Licence*. It was an article by Hart Rutherford for the *Guardian*, published six months after the series had aired and timed to coincide with the Baftas.

The success of Letters of a Victorian Lady *has provided the BBC drama department with a much-needed fillip. Viewers beguiled by the historical authenticity of the drama should be warned that though each bow and bustle is passed by the wardrobe department, no such care for historical accuracy applies to the storyline.*

So, someone else agreed with her. She read on keenly.

By and large the letters consist of faltering declarations of mutual attraction interspersed with domestic detail. There is no evidence in the letters that the dramatic meeting between the Duke of Wakemont and Robert Latham ever took place. Or even that a romantic attraction existed between the couple at the time they were written.

That was exactly her impression. Sally felt a revival of faith in her own abilities. But Hart Rutherford knew more.

There was no happy ending for the star-crossed lovers. The Latham marriage was short-lived. The lovers married in 1900. Robert Latham left for America in 1905, never to return.

That piece of information had come as a complete shock. Hart ended his article by arguing that the television series ignored the real story.

Moreover, for a man portrayed as prostrate with grief, the real-life Duke got to his feet remarkably quickly. Fourteen months after his wife's death he was remarried to a woman with three daughters of her own. Bella Latham's marriage occurred a year later. Robert Latham was in real life a shadowy figure. No examples of his journalism can be uncovered. His fate in America remains a mystery.

She felt inspired. There was a story to tell here, several, in fact. Why had Robert Latham left? Where had he gone? And what had happened to Bella? It was time that someone followed this story to its end. She would take the librarian's advice and go direct to the original sources – and she knew exactly where to begin. She picked up the telephone and dialled Directory Enquiries.

'Selton Park, Berkshire, please.'

It was proving near impossible for Pia to get Edward's attention. His gaze was fixed on the far goal, where Dan shifted apprehensively from foot to foot, anticipating a shot from the opposing team's striker. Pia couldn't remember the name of the team Welton were playing. All the schools in the league were private, though. When the shot came, Dan deflected the fast-paced ball with ease.

'Good save,' Edward shouted, and there was a polite round of applause from the fifty or so weekend spectators at the Welton home match. The day was dry but very cold. She was wearing her white full-length puffed ski-coat and a black faux-fur hat.

She couldn't resist making a point to Edward. 'It's so civilised – the way parents clap good play from either team. That's what one is paying for.'

Edward glanced at her but said nothing.

But it was a point well made. Welton was about so much more than academic excellence. Edward had been lukewarm about sending Dan. 'Are you sure he's the communal type?'

He ought to admit that she had been right. Here was Dan, on a Saturday morning, joining in happily with a purposeful team activity. At home he'd be in bed or watching television or getting ready to go and hang out with a crowd of undesirables in McDonald's.

Pia seized the moment when the applause died down. 'Edward, about the party ...'

But then some long-legged Welton player started a run for the opposite goal, hurtling down the outside of the pitch. Edward was off again. 'Go, Michael! All the way.'

He knew the names of all the players on the Welton team and most of the parents' names as well, which was surprising given that he came less than she did, only at the weekends, whereas Pia came in the week when she could. It was vital to be seen to support.

'Edward.'

He was watching the game intently. 'Yep,' he said distractedly.

'We must talk about the party.' She pulled off her gloves and reached inside her handbag for her list.

'Hope said it was all done.'

Really! Was he being deliberately obtuse as to the considerable amount of work still remaining? 'No,' she said tartly. 'It's not. For a start, there's your speech.'

'Speech?'

'Well, of course,' she said irritated. 'It's Hope's twenty-first. You have to make a speech in the evening. I think you should make it during dessert and then at the end you can announce the dancing. I've sketched out some ideas for you.' She began reading from her list. 'Baby, childhood and teenage anecdotes. Then achievements – academic and sporting. Then helping others – old people, young people and animals.' She looked up. 'These are all areas that need to be covered.'

'Whatever.'

She suppressed a sigh. This had always been a problem: Edward's failure to get to grips with the detail of a project. Of course, that attitude wouldn't bother Sally who was clearly a slapdash sort of person.

She persisted. 'Why don't you sketch out a draft and email it to me? Then I could make editorial suggestions.'

Edward was still watching the game. 'Why don't you write it? You seem to have a good idea of what to say.'

She paused for effect. 'Because you're her father.'

Edward turned round. 'Are you sure Hope wants speeches?'

It was ridiculous. 'Of course she wants speeches. She wants a proper twenty-first.'

He looked as if he was about to argue the point but instead said, 'I'll thank everyone for coming. Then I'm going to sit down. It's a party for young people – they don't want to listen to me droning on.'

Standing with Edward it was as if they were still married. Edward had never supported her properly. The plans for the garden landscaping, the choice of ski resort, the inspections of possible schools: it had all been the same. She would suggest that they first carried out careful research and then conducted a thorough review of all the options. And in response Edward would say, 'Whatever you like.' She would wave a sheaf of quotes at him. But the answer was always the same: 'Go for the mid-priced.'

It drove her mad then and it was starting to drive her mad now. But before she could tell him exactly why a speech was essential – social rituals exist for many good reasons – he was engaged in conversation by the Bishops, a neat couple whose son Harry was top in maths. She had suggested to Dan several times that he should invite Harry over in the holidays, his father was a neurologist, but Dan never had.

She caught a snatch of the conversation. Mrs Bishop was gazing up at Edward. 'Dan has really helped the team rise in the league this term.'

Throughout their marriage women had always fawned over Edward. If only they knew the truth! Sally probably still hung on his every word. Admittedly, she did see how a less intelligent woman would find him entertaining enough.

Pia turned her attention to the game, resisting the impulse to look at her watch. It could only be a few minutes to half-time. She thought about the speech and concluded that the best thing would be for her to write the speech and hand it to Edward on the night. Then all he would have to do would be to read it out. As usual, the quickest and simplest way was to do it herself. But she continued to feel resentful. If she was going to do all the work on this party – and pay for it, Edward needless to say hadn't offered a penny – she was damned well going to have it her way. She couldn't stop Sally attending in the evening, much as she would like to. But that woman's place would be in the shadows – she had devised several ways of making sure of that. It was Hope's day in the spotlight and Pia was going to do everything in her power to make sure that no one stole a moment of it from her.

Chapter 6

A veil of sleety rain fell relentlessly outside. Inside, despite the fact that it was three o'clock, Sally had switched on all the kitchen lights and turned up the thermostat. Snow had been forecast for later that day. She paused to pour boiling water into two mugs of instant coffee, she only ever bought instant these days, and turned back to Vickie who was sitting at the kitchen table.

'First of all he took three days to call me back. I left two messages with the office at Selton Park. I get the impression the archivist only comes in occasionally. And then he said no! He didn't even ask me first if I was a researcher or a journalist. He said that the Selton archive was closed and that was that.'

Vickie was rummaging through her baby bag. Sally could hear the sounds of cars and the babble of Louis and Vickie's son Rory coming from the living room.

'Oh.' Vickie took out a brochure. Her voice was excited. 'Look what arrived today! It's the brochure for Stokeby. It's the new school on Parkside.'

Some recollection of talk of the opening of yet another private prep school came to mind. But Sally was still seething from the off-hand tone of the Selton Park archivist. 'I mean, don't you think it's outrageous?'

'Yes. Awful.' Vickie was leafing through the pages. 'Look. They even have a yoga class. Isn't that sweet! They can start yoga when they're five.'

'I pointed out that it's an archive of national historic interest. And they won't even let you visit Selton itself. He said that it was a private home. It's unbelievable! Some of the artwork in there is by Alfred Jackson. And the architecture is amazing. There's a Pineapple ...'

Vickie looked up. 'Pineapple?'

'It's a smoking room shaped like a pineapple. It's built on one of the corners of the house. The leaves hide a chimney. The men would go there after dinner to smoke cigars. It's one of the best country house examples of a smoking room.'

'Amazing,' said Vickie. She pulled out some loose papers tucked in to the back of the brochure. 'God, these registration fees are extortionate. And we've got to do it twice over.' She was expecting another baby.

Sally sat down. 'But he just said that they're private papers and went on about how the archive has been extensively catalogued and how the papers relating to state affairs have been lodged at Christ Church College Library in Oxford.'

Vickie nodded sympathetically.

'But the whole point, as I explained to him, is that I'm not interested in the state papers. I'm interested in Bella Latham.'

'So, what are you going to do now?' said Vickie politely, getting up. Before Sally could tell her about the good news – the copy of E.D. Irvine's *A History of the Wakemont Family* that she had, after much searching, located and ordered online – Vickie raised a hand. 'I'll be right back. I'll just go and check on the boys.' It was always like this. Efforts at conversation interrupted by surveillance checks, wails, falls, screaming and a stream of whined requests for juice. She never had got to reply to Vickie's question.

Later, as Sally waved goodbye to Vickie and Rory, she felt a stab of irritation at Vickie's lack of interest in her Selton Park research. Frankly, if they didn't have children the same age and live within easy walking distance, she was not sure she would choose to spend any time at all with Vickie. It was, she admitted to herself, a friendship of convenience, born of circumstance and lacking in intimacy. As she walked back towards the kitchen a moment of clarity occurred: right now, while Louis was still playing with his cars, she would do what she had been procrastinating about since her unsatisfactory conversation with the archivist: seize the moment, telephone the *Guardian* and speak to the only other person in the world who seemed interested in Bella Latham – Hart Rutherford.

When Tim was angry it made Anna want him more. Something perhaps to do with the thrill of skating on thin ice? Tim was no longer angry but for the last few days he had been distant, not calling her during the day, and unenthusiastic about their plans for the weekend. It made her determined to win him back.

She had missed the pre-theatre supper and arrived halfway through the first act of the play. The staff wouldn't let her in so she was forced to wait in the bar. It had been difficult at the time, observing Tim emerge with the MP David Stratford and his wife at the intermission, to judge how annoyed he was at her late arrival. Outwardly he had seemed unperturbed. Smoothly, he had handed out flutes of champagne and made introductions, describing her as his girlfriend to the Stratfords, the four of them pressed together in the small crowded bar of the Duke of York theatre. Anna, in her filming clothes of Urban Outfitter jeans and Fat Face olive fleece, was clearly underdressed. This was the first week of a new production. Excellent reviews had brought out the City men and their wives.

She had meant to read up on David Stratford. Tim had told her he had overcome a checkered marital past to eventually secure a safe Home Counties seat and was tipped as a future leader of the party. He certainly seemed to fit the bill: tall, well informed and charming. While his wife, elegant in a black silk trouser suit, made small talk with Tim, David Stratford quickly engaged Anna in conversation about her work at 7–24. He listened to her solicitously, paying her his full attention.

'I met Rick Roth at a City lunch,' he responded. '7–24's going public?'

'Yes, that's our plan.' It felt natural to say 'our'. After all, she was a senior player now.

As the bell sounded to signal the end of the intermission, David Stratford placed his hand on her arm and said warmly, 'We've just bought a place in the country. You and Tim must come down for the weekend.'

So she had relaxed, soothed by the champagne and the fact that any awkwardness caused by her late arrival had been quickly assuaged. Briefly she tried to figure out the plot of the play before losing interest and letting her mind wander to Rob, Nina and the script for the voiceover.

But when they got back to Shepherd's Bush Tim had exploded. It was the first time she had seen him really angry. He was even more cross than when she had missed his parents' wedding anniversary lunch. But, as she had told him at the time, that wasn't her fault either: her flight back from Brussels had been delayed.

'Where were you?'

'On the M4. I called you! We got caught in traffic.'

'Couldn't you have left earlier?' he snapped, his voice thick with frustration.

They were standing in the kitchen. She opened the fridge and pulled out a bottle of wine, pouring herself a glass. He shook his head as she proffered him the bottle. He had not taken off his coat.

He really was making no effort to understand. She took a good drink of the wine. 'No. It was our first session, Tim. I can't just go in and point a camera at these people. I have to get to know them on a personal level.'

It was part of the job: making the participants in *Marriage Menders* feel that they and the crew were all one big happy family.

'But you knew about this! I gave you weeks of notice!'

'I have a deadline.' It seemed self-evident to her. 'Rick needs to see some footage.'

'Fucking hell, Anna!' He was shouting now. 'I had to entertain them both with no idea when you were going to turn up. Sitting in J. Sheekey with an empty place setting is not the ideal pre-theatre supper.'

'You could have got the waiter to clear it,' she retorted defensively.

Too late she realised this was the wrong thing to say. Tim looked livid. 'I did! When it was clear you weren't going to show up.' He ran a hand through his hair. 'Hell, I need to be able to rely on you, Anna. You're not the only one whose work matters. I need to look credible in front of these people. I need to get to know them.' He gestured to a copy of *The Times* lying on the counter. 'I don't fucking make this stuff up, you know. I have to get out there, cultivate people, and win them over so that when a story breaks I'm the one they call. Stratford is tipped for the top, for God's sake.'

'I know! And you *can* rely on me!'

She had gone over to him at that point. Despite the fact that she really felt it wasn't her fault, some instinct told her to give some ground. 'You can!' She rubbed his shoulder. 'Tim, this is temporary. It's the first few weeks in a new job. I'm finding my feet ...'

He looked unconvinced. 'Maybe it will always be like this.'

'No! It's just until I get settled in. I promise.'

Tim had left soon afterwards and she had let him go, drained by the day's filming and sleepy from the wine drunk on an empty stomach.

Now, with the Saturday sun cutting through the gap in the curtains, she edged over to him as they lay in bed at his Pimlico flat on the first floor of a stucco-fronted Sutherland Drive house. Anger she could cope with. His coolness, evidenced last night over supper at the Ebury Street Wine Bar, she could not. They had made desultory conversation about the US Presidential contenders.

Anna ran her fingers lightly along his back then began to massage his neck, pushing her fingers up into his hair. He stirred involuntarily then turned his neck as if to loosen the muscles, working against the pressure of her fingers. She gently pushed him onto his stomach and, naked, sat astride him, working the muscles of his strong shoulder blades and slowly down to his lower back until her hands had reached his thighs.

He was awake now. She leaned over him and whispered in his ear, 'Good morning.'

His voice was sleepy but insistent. 'Don't stop …'

'You need to turn over,' she whispered to him.

She did not need to repeat the suggestion. She reached down, massaging his hard cock steadily and rhythmically just the way he liked. He groaned with pleasure. She continued until he was on the edge of coming then stopped and eased herself on top of him, bearing down hard so that he thrust into her, working her hips against him and bracing herself against his shoulders.

He murmured, 'Oh yes.' Tim was not a talker during sex. She liked that. She adored kissing him and touching him and fucking him. She loved the way he could take control and then give it back; the way he could take his time or force the issue. He was confident and unpredictable and very well endowed. He was perfect.

So it was a surprise but not a great one when he shifted, grasping her waist to pull her off him, pressing her down onto her back and then screwing her hard, his mouth against her neck so she felt his breath, going deeper as she drew her legs up around his back. He made her come again and then he finished, quickly and hard, afterwards holding her tight in the way that she so wanted. He never rushed away.

Eventually he got up and grinned at her, pushing a strand of hair out of her eyes. 'I'll make some coffee. And then I'm going to buy you breakfast at Oriel.'

Yes, Tim was perfect. And they were going to have a wonderful weekend. Except for Sunday, of course. She would need to go into the office to prepare for the week's filming. But she didn't have to tell Tim about that right now.

Sally's worst fears had been confirmed the day she got her degree results, the lists of names pinned up outside the History Department office. She had known before she read her name, waiting to get past the crowd of students huddled round the papers, that she had got a third because Julie Harrod was telling everyone so in a very loud voice.

Sally got a third! Can you believe it!

And then Julie Harrod had looked up and seen her and fallen quiet. Sally had looked at the list, a handful of firsts, the vast bulk of seconds and ten or so with thirds. Some of the names of her fellow thirds she didn't recognise, presumably because they had rarely attended lectures. Embarrassment had flooded her face. She had ignored the mumbled commiserations of her fellow students and rushed away, her head bowed. She had got in her car, driven home in a daze and walked into the kitchen where her mother and father were standing expectantly. Her father was holding a bottle of champagne. Her mother was grasping three helium balloons – silver, gold and red – each bearing the word *Congratulations!*

'Oh, Daddy!' She had burst into uncontrollable tears.

Later that day her father had called Dr Hobbs. He reported back, perched on the end of her bed where she lay immobilised. 'Apparently it was very close. It was a matter of a couple of marks. He said they have to draw the line somewhere. Apparently you got a "D" in the medieval paper.'

'I think we ought to appeal,' said her mother who was standing in the doorway. 'It's ridiculous. You worked so hard!'

Had she? The last year had been a blur in which she had reeled from the break-up with Chris, learned to live independently for the first time in her life and spent far too much time sub-editing that bloody student newspaper.

Dr Hobbs, when she had summoned up the courage to go and see him two days later, had been excruciatingly kind. In his book-lined study in the new Arts Faculty building overlooking Kingston Bridge, he had gestured to her to sit down. Dressed in his usual fawn corduroy suit, he regarded her kindly from across his desk, his face deeply lined, his hair a shock of white.

'I've seen some very good students get thirds. It doesn't reflect your abilities. The medieval paper was a bugger and some of Professor Stanley's marking on the Stuarts was very tough. Unfortunately you just slipped below the line.'

Gently he ruled out an appeal. Instead, he looked at her hard and said, 'The important thing is to carry on undaunted. It isn't what you wanted or deserved, granted. But try to think of it as a bump in the road. Don't let it put you off your stride.'

But it had put her off her stride: her dreams of pursuing a postgraduate course were dashed and one too many rejection letters made her abandon all thoughts of graduate training schemes.

We are not able to offer you an interview on this occasion. Thank you for your interest.

She enrolled at secretarial college. Thereafter, she couldn't settle. In every job she felt she had something to prove. She checked every detail, added up every figure twice, proof read important documents and letters until she was seeing double. It was a protocol that had served her well at Porter Stone. As the years had gone on, her degree diminished in importance. No one ever asked her 'First, second or third?' But it was still a part of her past that caused her a twinge when she thought about it. It lingered in her memory with a sense of injustice. At the age of thirty-five and married with a small son she was a teenager in this one respect, continuing to look for her niche in the world, still with something to prove, still carrying the feeling that she had a purpose in life yet to be fulfilled.

The woman had come back again to the house. Sally had seen her yesterday as she returned from a trip to Sainsbury's. She had parked behind a red BMW but did not immediately recognise it, her view obscured by falling rain and the darkness of the late afternoon. Turning off the ignition, she had opened the door of the car and saw that a light was on in the basement flat. When she got out, she could see the woman in the front room. This time she appeared to be alone with the agent, without the man. Louis would have to stay put until she unloaded the shopping from the boot. He had entered the run-away phase of child development, making unpredictable dashes for freedom when not under close confinement. If she let him into the house he might, once again, clamber down the front steps and start hotfooting it in the direction of the golf club pavilion. She opened the boot of their Volvo estate.

Louis, twisting to observe her, turned up the volume. 'Get out! Get out!'

'Mummy will get you out. Wait a minute ...' She gathered up bags of shopping, careful of her footing on the road and pavement, which were coated with thin, grey slush from the recent light snowfall.

She dashed up the steps. Behind her, the wind carried a mournful wail: 'Mummy!' As quickly as she could she located her keys in her handbag and opened the front door.

It was when she returned to the car and took out the final four car-rier bags, her hair now damp and Louis in the throes of what Edward dubbed a Code Red tantrum, that the woman and the agent ascended the basement stairs.

'Mummy! Get out!' Louis sounded enraged that his command-ment had not been obeyed.

Sally's gaze met that of the woman as she stepped onto the pavement to draw level with her. 'Hi!' Sally said brightly. 'We live at number 12.'

But the woman was looking at Louis, screaming himself senseless and pounding the window of the car.

It was difficult to tell, looking at her expression, what proportion of the woman's reaction constituted pity and what was sheer horror. 'Hello.'

'He's teething,' explained Sally. It was her universal excuse.

'Oh.'

'Terrible Twos!' said the agent with a smile. She turned back to the woman, appearing anxious to hurry her away from Louis, a human blight on the neighbourhood. 'If there's anything else you need do call.'

'*Mummy!*'

The woman had already taken her car keys out. She turned to Sally. 'I'm just measuring up.'

Presumably that meant she had bought the flat. 'Oh. Congratulations!'

As soon as she said this, Sally realised how inappropriate it sounded. *Yes, congratulations on buying a flat below a bawling child whose mother appears to have no clue how to stop him.*

'Thanks.' The woman peered into the car as if to check whether one child alone was responsible for all that noise. 'I'll leave you to it.'

'I'm Sally,' she was about to say. But the woman was already walking away. She clicked her car key fob and the car unlocked automatically. Despite the recent snow it was immaculately clean and polished. She must have it professionally valeted. Inside, Sally imagined, it would be an oasis of soft, smooth leather, accessorised by a pair of designer sunglasses on the centre consul, the interior suffering at worst the odd drop from a Starbucks latte.

She looked like a woman who knew where she was going, in every sense. The type of person who had known from an early age what she wanted to be and whose career had progressed in a swift and proficient manner. She looked, in many ways, like the woman that Sally would once have liked to have been. A sudden gust of miserable inadequacy blew over her. She saw herself through the woman's eyes: overweight, damp and ineffectual. She wanted to shout after her: *This isn't really me! I can do so much more!* But she had a feeling that the woman wouldn't believe her, that she would smile politely and say, *Of course you can.*

Besides, the person she really needed to convince of that fact was herself.

Chapter 7

The front room of Hart Rutherford's Victorian cottage doubled as his office. A state-of-the-art computer and screen sat on a desk built into one of the alcoves on either side of the fireplace. A fax machine and printer were located on an antique two-drawer oak desk in the bay window. Above it and on the other side were bookshelves, the titles Sally could make out from her chair mainly international affairs and British history. On a side table lay a reporter's notebook and an elegant Cross fountain pen.

Hart returned with two cups of coffee.

'Tell me if it's too strong. Jumping Java's got quite a kick.'

A small unkempt Jack Russell trailed Hart into the room and jumped up onto Hart's lap as soon as he sat down.

'Get off,' he said brusquely. But his hand had reached down to caress the dog's ears as it sank sulkily to his side. 'This is Mutley. Don't let him manipulate you.'

Hart had taken so long to answer the door that Sally had wondered if he was in at all or whether she had got the wrong address. But when the door finally opened she had immediately recognised the man in the photograph. Her internet research had disclosed a BBC photograph of Hart Rutherford receiving a journalism award for investigative reporting in Northern Ireland, some two years before the article on *Letters*. The accompanying article said that Hart Rutherford, engaged on an investigation into paramilitary protection rings, was found in a ditch in County Londonderry close to death. She had noticed as she followed him down the narrow hallway, that he walked stiffly.

Now, taking a sip of the coffee, which was very good, she guessed he was about forty, still with the longish hair and athletic figure of the man in the photograph.

She had expected to ask the questions. She had prepared a sheet of them. But once they sat down he was the one who started talking first.

'So, why do you want to know about all this?'

Of course. He would be curious.

'I live in their house – the Lathams' house. In Wimbledon.'

He was making her nervous. Something in his eyes was not what she had expected. Hart Rutherford possessed the intelligent, appraising look of the professional journalist. She felt like a rank amateur.

'North Walk?'

'Yes.' So he had remembered that. 'They moved there after they got married and I thought it would be fun …' No. That was not the right word. 'And *interesting* to carry on the story.'

'Are you trying to make money?'

'No.' Actually, she had begun to entertain wild thoughts that she could write a book that might get made into a screenplay that might be made into a Hollywood film. But she wasn't about to make a total fool of herself by sharing that fantasy with Hart Rutherford.

'It's just a hobby. I mean, I'm not a professional journalist.' At that point she was distracted by Mutley jumping up onto her lap.

'What do you do for a living?'

Nothing. 'I'm a mother. I used to work in banking.'

'Where did you work?'

'Porter Stone.'

He raised an eyebrow. Now he surely had her marked down as some nitwit posh girl.

But the questions appeared to be at an end. He reached down for a notebook, pulling back the cover.

'I looked out my notes,' he said, pulling on his glasses. 'It was all a fluke, really. I had drawn the short straw for temporary television reviewer while the regular guy got dried out in rehab. So I was holed up at home watching preview tapes. *Letters*, I must confess, would not have been my choice of viewing.' He cracked a smile. 'But the editor wanted it covered. And it was good. I presume you've seen it …'

'Oh yes!' Three times now. It was becoming something of a compulsion.

'Little did I know,' he added, 'what a lot of tosh *Letters* would turn out to be.'

'But *how* did you know?' Sally asked keenly.

'I went to the Selton Park family archive ... Let me guess. They won't let you near it, right?'

'Right. I called Selton Park and the archivist said no.'

'I can imagine. Don't beat yourself up. It wouldn't matter if you were the editor of *The Times* ...'

He really was incredibly nice. She felt herself relax back in her chair.

'As soon as the television series took off they closed up all access,' he continued. 'The new Duke had big ideas of taking *Letters* to Hollywood. Probably still does. So he wasn't going to let anyone else pinch the story. Not that it's been optioned. I made a couple of calls before you got here.' Hart took a sip of his coffee. She took the opportunity to glance at his left hand. There was no wedding ring. 'But remember, I went down there before *Letters* was broadcast,' he continued. 'When they were grateful for the publicity. I checked out the birth, death and marriage certificates for the family. And then I looked through the diaries.'

'Diaries? What diaries?'

'Bella Latham's.' He paused. 'Well, there would be no reason for you to know that. Actually, calling them diaries is something of an exaggeration. They were jottings really, a sentence here and there, in four hardcover notebooks.'

She was fascinated. 'What did she write?'

'Basically how happy she was and how perfect her marriage was. Life was sweet. And why wouldn't it be? She had a nice house in Wimbledon, servants to do all her work, a husband who must have worshipped the ground she walked on ...'

'Why so?'

'Because Bella was the catch of the season and Robert Latham's passport to London society. Latham was a penniless journalist. You don't get much lower than that.'

She laughed. 'So why do you think the Duke let the marriage go ahead?'

Hart settled back into his chair and she found herself imitating him. 'I'm speculating here, but my guess would be that he wasn't that concerned about the money. Wakemont had diversified out of farming – officially into steel and heavy industry – but in reality most of the new fortune came from armaments. That's the reason the Wake-monts still own their house when all their neighbours are showing coach loads of tourists round National Trust tea rooms. Bella Latham didn't need to make a good marriage. And by 1900 Wakemont himself had already remarried.'

Sally knew this from Hart's article. 'I think that's very important, actually. Did the diaries say anything about Bella's relationship with her stepmother?'

'Not that I recall. Bella Latham started keeping a diary when she married and continued until her death in 1953. But they're patchy.' She was impressed by his easy command of the facts. He seemed as familiar with the story as if he had written it yesterday. 'The early years were virtually daily, except for when her son was born up until his death when she writes only occasionally. After a few years they dropped off, sometimes there was an entry only every two or three months.'

Except for when her son was born up until his death ...

Bella and Robert Latham had a son who died! Shock at this news mingled with a degree of humiliation that she had failed to uncover this fact.

'Maybe she was busy with her son?'

He considered this. 'Yes. But given that Henry died when he was two and she had no more children that would only account for a short period of time. And, of course, one must remember that she had staff. Mary Kelly in particular.'

She was still trying to absorb the news of the child. *Henry.* 'What did the death certificate say?'

Hart got up and went over to another notebook. He read: 'Pneumonia. He was twenty-two months old. Born in 1901 and died in 1903.'

'And Robert Latham left two years later.' The two events had to be connected.

Hart was reading his notebook. 'I did a timeline. Mary Kelly fol-lowed Bella from Selton Park. When Bella died in 1953 Mary stayed on in the house until her death in 1964.' He consulted his notebook. 'She was eighty-two.'

Sally was only half-listening. Her mind was still on the baby. She needed to get serious and, as the librarian had pointed out, go back to the original sources.

She realised Hart had stopped talking. She wondered if this Mary Kelly might be significant. 'So the family looked after Mary Kelly until she died.'

He raised an eyebrow. 'In this instance, yes. Of course, the position of most domestic servants in the Victorian period was appalling. Low wages, long hours and instant dismissal for the least offence.'

Hart's passionate radicalism was curiously attractive. It was such a world away from the dull playgroup talk she had become accustomed to.

'Were there other staff?'

'Mary's the only member of staff mentioned in the diaries. But I presume Bella would have expected more than one maid. A cook? Nanny? My guess is that either there were other servants or money was tight and they were managing with one or two. The Duke would have been their sole source of income. There's no evidence that Latham succeeded in publishing anything. If I had to, I'd opt for the theory that they were short of money.'

It was wonderful to talk like this with someone who was interested in the Lathams in the same heartfelt way that she was. Mutley had fallen asleep on her lap while she absent-mindedly rubbed his ears. 'Bella and Mary Kelly must have been close. They lived together for more than fifty years.'

'And for most of that time it was just the two of them.'

It was the question that consumed her. Why did Robert Latham leave for America and never return? Why, in fact, did Robert Latham sail away from his perfect marriage? And now there seemed another mystery to solve – how could he leave his grieving wife in her hour of need? Did she blame him in some way for the death of the child?

'What did you think about Robert Latham's disappearance?'

He shrugged. 'In her diary Bella says that he was going to work for Wakemont at an iron works in Cincinnati.'

'Oh.' She wasn't totally sure where that was. Somewhere in the middle of the States?

'But as for precisely why he went I don't know. Whatever the reason, Robert Latham got on a boat to America and he never came back.'

'I wonder if the Duke wanted him out of the way?'

She was gratified to see that he nodded at her suggestion.

'It's a possibility. Or maybe the Duke decided to call in a favour – he had allowed the marriage but now he wanted something in return? At any rate, Latham sailed on the RMS *Lucania* in April 1905 from Liverpool to New York. I had the passenger lists checked out.'

'And there's no record of him returning?'

'There's no record of his death in the archive and the family never made any statutory declaration of a presumed death.'

She could understand that. Bella would not have given up hope. Did she ever go to search for him?

'I've ordered Irvine,' she volunteered and was gratified to see him cast her an approving nod.

Hart sat back down. 'I'll be interested to hear your opinion.'

She couldn't remember the last time anyone had said that to her. She felt lifted by Hart's apparent confidence in her. She spoke slowly, thinking aloud. 'I can't believe that it's a coincidence that Bella married so soon after her father brought his new wife and her daughters into their home. And there must be a connection between the baby's death and Robert Latham's departure. Do you remember anything from the diaries about Henry's death?'

There was a pause as Hart looked for the entry. He read, 'We feel his loss very much and Robert suffers greatly. "Thy will be done" we utter and pray for our little one in heaven.'

'Is that all?'

Hart was reading intently. 'I believe so.'

It seemed such a brief and emotionless entry. 'And is there anything from Robert once he leaves?'

'No, which, now you come to mention it, is strange.' He looked thoughtful. 'Given that they appear to have had the perfect marriage?'

'Is there such a thing?' Immediately she was astounded at herself. Hastily she backtracked. 'I mean, you wouldn't expect romantic declarations after five years of marriage.'

Hart's response was polite. 'No. Absolutely right.'

There was an awkward pause. He cleared his throat and began turning the pages of the notebook. 'This is where she writes about Robert leaving to work for the Duke. She says, "Father has provided us with a marvellous opportunity and I must not think selfishly of binding my husband to me. We are blessed ..."'

Listening to Hart one thing Sally knew for sure was that Bella

Latham was not the flighty, indulged girl depicted by the BBC drama department. If anything, Bella's diary entries seemed to veer between social notes and pious exclamations.

'So, where do you think I should go from here?'

He had clearly already considered that question. 'For the time being I would switch to the secondary sources. It's like chasing a big story when the subject doesn't want to talk – you go to the friends and the family, neighbours and work colleagues. See if you can uncover contemporary sources who might refer to the Lathams.'

'OK.'

'See if you can find anything out about Mary Kelly. It's a long shot. Unfortunately it's a very common name.'

He put down his notebook.

'Refill?'

She knew that she ought to get going. 'Yes, please.' Vickie could manage Louis for an hour or two longer.

It was just so thrilling to have an adult conversation about a subject that captivated her. Bella's life, and her own ignorance of it, fascinated and frustrated her in equal measure.

Hart gathered up the mugs and she followed him down into the kitchen.

'Do you still write?'

There was a delay while the coffee grinder made all conversation impossible.

'Yep. Reviewing mainly. I do the opera CD reviews for the *Observer* and some freelance television reviewing for the *Guardian*. And every time there's bad news out of Ireland I get a call to write about it.'

'To go and investigate?'

He laughed. 'No. I write comment pieces. Historical background mainly. I don't get around as well as I used to. My days of leaping out of cars and chasing ne'er-do-wells are long gone.'

'Do you miss that?'

His face was unreadable. 'Sometimes.'

'Even though ...' she searched for the right words, 'it was so dangerous?'

He shrugged. 'Sometimes you have to know when to play and when to fold. Let's just say that it became clear it was time for me to leave the table.'

He poured two cups of coffee. 'Come on. Let's sit somewhere more comfortable.' He led her into the back room. 'As you can see, this is a late Victorian cottage, designed for the lower middle classes employed in the City of London. Kitchen, parlour at the back and front room "for best".'

'I think it's lovely.' She looked around. It still had the original grooved cornice, a cast-iron fireplace tiled with tulip-design tiles and a sash window overlooking the garden.

Hart sat down. 'Most people knock the kitchen and back room in to one.'

'I like it as it is.'

'So do I.'

He cast her a questioning look. 'So why the interest in Bella Latham and her disappearing husband?'

It was strange. She felt so relaxed with Hart. Maybe it was a trait that these journalists developed, the ability to make their subjects feel at ease while disclosing their darkest secrets. But somehow she knew that was not the case with Hart.

'I want to know *why* she married him. Why did she risk so much to marry this man – to leave the luxury of Selton Park to go and live in the suburbs, to be cut off from her family, to turn her back on everything that was familiar and safe? And I want to know whether she had any regrets.'

'Regrets?'

'Yes. Because I think it is possible to go into a situation aware of the bald facts and yet to be blind to the effect of that.' Pia came to mind. Sally paused to collect her thoughts. 'I think one can have a roman-ticised view. Bella knew that Robert Latham was impoverished, that he was looked down on by many of her friends, that she was literally a class above him. But did she know what that would mean for their marriage?'

She stopped. But Hart did not jump in to comment. She was em-boldened to continue. 'And I know that I may never find out. But I want to try. It almost feels as though I need to.' And then she couldn't help herself. 'The Lathams are a symbol of romantic love – the idea that two people who are soulmates can overcome all the odds and then prosper. I want to know if that is true. Yes, I believe in true love – in a moment, for a time. But can true love endure lasting hardship?

Can it even survive the monotony of daily living – or is it ground away to …?' She stopped herself. 'To something different?'

Had she really mean to say *nothingness?*

'And have you reached any conclusions?'

'I think … I think that I would like to be convinced.'

And he gave her a smile that was surprisingly warm. 'Yes. I think I would like to be convinced, too.'

Later, on the tube travelling back to Wimbledon, surrounded by tired commuters and a sprinkling of early tourists, Sally closed her eyes and adjusted her mind to a new set of facts. Hart's revelations had only served to deepen the mystery of Bella Latham. Go back to the friends and family, Hart had suggested. Tantalisingly, she realised that there was a woman who would have watched every scene, known every secret, likely been privy to every confidence: Mary Kelly. But she was not going to entertain false hopes that Mary's story could be uncovered. Working-class women rarely left neat accounts of their lives. They were too busy living them, working and surviving. She dismissed from her mind the hope that any record of Mary's life would exist. After all, who would have thought the story of a working-class maid, one of thousands of such women, worth paying attention to?

'Now, it's all very well you sitting there with your list of questions but we'll get on better if you let me get my thoughts straight. Don't be inter-rupting me all the time. I've heard that's what you lot do. You may have a fancy education but that doesn't mean you've got manners.

I suppose you want to know about Selton Park. Mrs Morrow – she was the matron at the Destitute – sent me there. Mrs Morrow knew the housekeeper at Selton and sent a girl down every couple of years. She trained me up for it and when I turned fourteen it was time to go.

When I say the Destitute I mean the Liverpool Orphanage for Des-titute Children. That's the proper name. They closed it after the war. Aren't you going to write that down? What are you going to do if your recorder machine packs up?

Mrs Morrow took me to the station. She didn't do that with everyone. She pinned the ticket to my coat. Then she pulled me close to her and told me to be a good girl and to trust in the Lord. I was excited then. Me,

Mary Kelly, off on my big adventure. That was before I arrived. Before I left I told Joseph, my little brother, that I'd be back to see him very soon. And I thought I would.

All I had was a tweed bag with my nightclothes and my washing things. They sent a trap to collect me from the station at Henley. It was George, the footman, who came to get me. That boy was no better than he should be. He took the dirt drive at the back and set me down at kitchen door. It was snowing and I slid in my big boots. I nearly fell carrying that bag. That would have been a good start! So, in I went to the kitchen. It was spotless, with a big wooden table running down the middle and the huge shining range with a kettle boiling. There was Cook sitting in the corner drinking her tea. I'm saying Cook now but it was always Mrs Briggs to her face. Yes, Mrs Briggs. No, Mrs Briggs. And I thought, This is all right! Warm and quiet. Little did I know what was in store for me. It was me who was going to be polishing that range and everything else besides. The family was away in London for New Year and when they were away was about the only time we weren't working our fingers to the bone.

Cook shouted for Jenny to show me to my room. I thought the Destitute was big but, oh my goodness, that house! I thought we would never get wherever we were going and if we did I should never find my way back. Corridors and stairs and then more corridors and stairs. It was stone floors on the ground floor, bare wooden stairs and strips of linoleum on the floors upstairs. These were the staff stairs, of course. There's Jenny ahead of me nattering on, she never stopped talking, and all I'm trying to do is work out how I'm not going to get lost for ever in that house. "Is that all you brought with you?" she said, looking at my little bag. At last we got there. It was an attic room. There were three of us. Me, Jenny and Mabel. They were both kitchen maids so they thought they were a cut above me because I was just the scullery maid.

We each had an iron bed and a chair and a washstand with a basin on it. There was a fireplace in the bedroom but it was never lit. In the winter it used to get so cold that the water in the basin got ice on the top. Jenny had a fancy extra blanket on her bed. Her mother had sent it with her. 'You should get your mother to send you one,' she said all sly. As if she didn't know. But I didn't let on. I knew that from the Destitute – if they saw you well up it just made them bait you worse. On her chair she had a novel with a little crochet bookmark tucked in it. A novel! She showed it to me. 'Look, I'm halfway through!' she said. She was very full of herself. As if reading novels would do you any good.

Mrs Morrow told me that I could better myself if I was a good girl and worked hard. "Mary," she used to say, "do all things without murmurings and disputings." No murmurings and disputings, that's what she told me. Do you know that quote? I don't suppose you would. It's from the Bible.'

Chapter 8

Anna sat on Nina's cream leather sofa and began to make a list. First, sketch out the script for the voiceover. Then call the removal company who had left a message asking about access and parking in Wimbledon. Next, call Tim and confirm arrangements for tonight. He was bringing the ingredients for a 'last supper' at the flat. He had promised to help her with the move: Fridays were quiet for Tim, another journalist wrote the Saturday leader, and he usually scheduled a lunch in the West End and rolled home afterwards. Tomorrow he was lunching the Education Secretary. So he had assured her he would be in Wimbledon, though not necessarily sober, by mid-afternoon.

Last on the list – make a television programme. There had been no option that morning but to hand the removers her house keys, show them where the tea and coffee were kept and ask them to post the keys back through the letter box when they had finished. Today they were packing, tomorrow they would come back, load up and drive to Wimbledon. Meanwhile, she had headed off to Bracknell for the second filming session with Nina and Rob Ramsey. Rick had announced that he needed some footage as soon as possible to show the foreign networks.

They had arrived at 8.00 a.m. to an ultimatum from Nina.

'We're not willing to continue unless certain conditions are met.'

Swiftly she had taken Nina aside.

Nina had been resolute 'We've discussed it and we want the next counselling session to be private. There are certain … sensitive issues that we don't want on film.'

Anna had thought quickly. 'Absolutely. No problem.' Now that filming was underway the key was to stop them pulling out. 'Nina, we don't want to lose you. Any of the other couples but not you.'

'No?'

'Nina, you're an inspiration. So many women at home will relate to your struggles. You offer them hope.'

Nina had looked shocked. 'Really? Do you think so?'

'Yes. Who knows what you might set in motion?' This at least was true.

So they had started late, filming Nina baking a cake to show her domestic side.

From the kitchen Anna could hear the voices of Ethne and Nina washing up and Harry the cameraman joking with them. Ethne was getting on her nerves. She might need to replace her as production assistant. She was green, that was to be expected, but insufficiently deferential and with the kind of looks, willowy blonde, that were a hopeless distraction for Harry. Anna had a headache. She needed an aspirin, a good night's sleep and a holiday.

She put down her list and sat thinking about Nina's earlier announcement. She hated being caught unawares almost as much as she loathed being outmanoeuvred. She certainly wasn't going to be dictated to by Nina. Besides, wasn't the whole point of *Marriage Menders* that private issues became public? Then the solution came to her: Nina might not be willing to do what she was told but Rob would be.

She made a swift decision – she would come back tomorrow to film him on his own while Nina was at work. It would be just her and Rob and the camera. She'd do it like a video diary piece in which Rob would confide his innermost thoughts.

Unfortunately, this meant that Ethne would have to supervise the removal men. Ethne wouldn't be her ideal choice to place in charge of all her possessions but work had to come first. She felt a surge of adrenaline, the thrill of rearranging the pieces and players to get what she wanted.

She shouted for Ethne. Nothing. She shouted for Ethne again.

Ethne appeared. In one hand she held her mobile phone. The other hand was stuck in the back pocket of her jeans. Her voice and pose were nonchalant.

'Yeah.'

Anna felt a shock of irritation. She flipped through her notebook and found a clean page. 'I need you to organise my house move tomorrow.'

Ethne said nothing but her mouth turned down. 'I have the Zarkosky work to do.'

Anna ignored her. 'These are the addresses. It's Shepherd's Bush to Wimbledon.'

Ethne sounded surprised, now comprehending that Anna was serious. 'What about the Zarkoskys? I'm scheduled to do another interview with them tomorrow.' She meant another background interview prior to the next film session.

'They can wait. Do them over the weekend—'

Ethne interrupted. 'I'm going to Newbury.'

Something snapped. Ethne was apparently always 'going' somewhere. Anna had read her CV. As a teenager Ethne had attended Besant House, an Islington girls' state school populated almost entirely by the daughters of liberal cabinet ministers and right-on media executives. As a student she had gone to Georgetown University in Washington, DC. Ethne went to all the right places and knew all the right people. Her father was someone in the City. Her mother was the owner of Caldicott's, a chic Islington restaurant. One of the referees listed on Ethne's CV was the current chairman of the Tate Modern. Ethne possessed all the contacts, advantages and introductions that Anna had never had.

But right now Ethne was going where Anna told her to.

Anna looked up. 'No, you're going to Beaconsfield. After you do my house move.'

Ethne could not stare her down. She looked at the floor and said, almost wilfully, 'That's not my job.'

Anna stood up. Slowly she walked over to the living-room door and closed it. It was gratifying, as she turned round, to see Ethne instinctively take a step backwards until she was almost touching the wall.

Anna was angry but not to any degree that could not be controlled. Actually, it was rather pleasant. All the irritations of the past week peaked at that moment: the stupidity of the woman at the removal firm; the delay waiting for someone to answer the telephone at each of the utility call centres; the bureaucratic slowness of the Wimbledon residents parking permit department. Added to these irritations was the frustration she felt at all the things she had not had time to do before the house move – all the clutter she had meant to throw out; the new furniture she had meant to order; the dry-cleaning she still hadn't collected after two months.

She went over to Ethne, stood too close, and let it all go. 'When I started – with a degree and a reputation before I even got to work – I did what I was told. I did what was needed. And I didn't question why or how or whether it was in my job description.' She felt that she was not quite shouting. 'I did it. I got coffee, I fetched sandwiches, and I took them back again when there wasn't the right kind of fucking mayonnaise on them. And that's why I'm at the top of my profession now.'

Ethne looked stunned.

'Take these keys. Go to my house. Meet the movers tomorrow at 7.30 a.m. and move my house contents. Is that clear?'

Ethne blinked. She looked as if she was going to cry. Anna stood back a little.

It was clear that all Ethne's confidence had deserted her. Her cheeks were bright red and her eyes flooded with tears. 'Yes.'

Anna relented a little. 'Look, you don't have to do anything, the movers do it all. All you have to do is let them in, watch them load up and lock up. Then do it in reverse at the other end. There's nothing to it. And get some milk and stuff for the fridge and some tea and biscuits for the removal men. And make sure the phone's working.'

Ethne nodded. 'OK.'

'And the wireless internet connection. I need that this weekend. Oh, and Ethne, if you don't want to do it, that's fine. There are a thousand people out there who will. In fact, probably ten thousand media graduates who'd die for a job at 7–24. And work every weekend.' She could have added, *Like I do,* because there was always someone younger and fresher snapping at her heels with a hungry eye on her job. She paused. 'You need to remember that.'

It was a clear threat. Ethne looked up. Their eyes locked and Anna read Ethne's resentment of her and she knew then that she would have to sack her because Ethne wasn't going to forgive this.

It had been a disappointment when Sally tore open the padded envelope and pulled out E.D. Irvine's book. It was more a pamphlet than a book, the cover consisting of a torn and worn piece of thickened pale blue paper. The title had been typed in block capitals: *A History of the Wakemont Family.*

The booklet numbered thirty pages and was published by the Berkshire Historical Society in 1965. The Foreword, by the Secretary of the Society, explained that the manuscript was discovered by E.D. Irvine's daughter in his private papers after his death. Undated, but assumed to be in the late 1920s, it had not previously been published.

Seated at the kitchen table, Sally ran over in her mind what he had written – and what he hadn't. There was a good deal about the Duke's good works, the charities and committees and the building of schools and almshouses. And plenty about the opulence of Selton Park and the lavish refurbishment that the second Duchess had set in motion: new frescos commissioned, the formal garden torn up and replanted, the interior of the Pineapple ripped out and replaced with new seating and wallpaper – the whole place turned upside down, in fact. Bella was mentioned only in passing, Robert Latham not at all. E.D. Irvine only seemed interested in the men of the family.

From upstairs she could just make out the vague thumps and muffled shouts of Louis's bedtime. Edward's willingness to bath and read to Louis on the days when he was home in time from work had come as a slight surprise. Before Louis was born she had prepared herself for the possibility that Edward, an older, second-time-round father, might not be as hands-on as a younger man. Not for the first time he had confounded her expectations. 'Actually, I'm first time round. Pia did it all when Hope and Dan were babies.'

At the sound of Edward descending the stairs she got up and took the shoulder of lamb out of the oven. It was one of her stalwart recipes, thrown together in five minutes, the lamb cooked in red wine, tomatoes, celery and onions.

Edward, coming into the kitchen with his sleeves rolled up, took the open bottle of red off the counter. He cast her a concerned glance. 'Everything all right?'

'Oh. Yes.' Reluctantly she pulled herself back to the moment. 'I was thinking about the Irvine pamphlet.' She gestured at the table. 'It arrived today.'

Edward was reaching into the cupboard for two wineglasses. 'More Famous Faces?'

'No. That's Iain Braden.'

'So who's Irwin?'

'Irvine. He was a local schoolteacher who wrote a history of the Wakemonts.'

Edward was rooting around in the cupboard, presumably in search of something to eat. He seized on a pack of Louis's mini cheddars.

She covered the lamb with foil to let it rest while she waited for the rice to cook. 'This is nearly ready.'

'I'm starving. Missed lunch. The Far East Planning Team did a preliminary presentation in the boardroom.' He handed her a glass of wine. 'Anyway, you couldn't feed a hamster off one of these packets.'

She considered asking him about the Far East presentation and quickly decided not to. Edward had become something of a zealot in his promotion of all things Chinese.

He sat down at the table and pulled the pamphlet towards him. 'Is it any good?'

'Yes.' She should make an effort to update him. She could explain that Irvine's description implied that the second Duchess was a force to be reckoned with. She could describe how, within the space of two years, Bella had lost her mother, gained a stepmother and watched as her home was occupied by three new sisters. She could share her own theory that for Bella marriage to Robert Latham had in reality been an escape route from a now unhappy home.

'I think Bella married Robert Latham to escape from her home life.'

Edward was clearly making an effort to pay attention. 'Hmm. Maybe Irvine would be worth interviewing?' he suggested brightly. 'Maybe your journalist contact could get you an introduction?'

She tried not to sound dismissive. 'Irvine's dead, actually.' She turned away to face the cooker. As for her journalist friend she had led Edward to believe that he was a retired cardigan-and-slippers-character on whom she had paid a brief and uneventful visit.

No, he doesn't work for a newspaper any more. I think he writes the occasional piece. Just to keep his hand in.

Edward put down the pamphlet and picked up the *Evening Standard*. 'Oh.' He turned to the sports pages. 'Pity.' There was a pause while he turned the pages until he found the coverage of the weekend's England vs. Scotland Calcutta Cup match at Murrayfield. 'How about writing to the Duke?' he said absentmindedly. 'You could appeal to his better nature.'

She took a deep breath. 'I don't think he'll agree.'

It was not Edward's fault, she knew that. There was only one other person who understood the dynamics of the Wakemonts; one other person who was familiar with the trail; one other person who shared her enthusiasm and growing determination to uncover the truth about the past – about Bella Latham and Mary Kelly, two women who had lived in this house for fifty years, each with a story to be told.

'I've just told you about my early life. Do you mean Ireland? Why would you want to know about Ireland? I knew the Duke of Wakemont! And he knew the Queen.

Oh, all right. I was born in County Wicklow in 1882. You wouldn't understand what it was like. There were no pretty workers' cottages in County Wicklow. I suppose you think a cottage has got a thatched roof and a nice old fire burning in the grate. We had a cabin with a mud floor and a roof made of peat. Towards the end my father sent me up to the big house to ask for something to eat. The woman said I was the third girl to come begging that day and if I wanted leavings I should have come earlier. Then she shut the door in my face. So I wasn't sorry to leave Ireland. If my father had been a sober man we'd have sold up years earlier. But he was a stubborn drunk. So by the end we had nothing.

My father decided to try his luck in Liverpool. Oh, he was full of it, like it was going to be the promised land. I was only a young one but I knew it was all a lot of hot air. Anyway, he had a cousin who got him a place in the docks. Well, whatever luck he did find there got poured down his throat by Sunday. On Monday my mother would tell me to get the blankets off the beds and fold them up. She took them down the pawn shop to get something for the week. You had to be careful when you went out. One day I came out in the morning and there was a sailor lying dead in the street. He'd had his throat cut for his wages.

There were seven of us in two rooms down from the Albert Dock. Two other families lived in the same house. My mother went to work in a laundry and I was left to look after the others. You didn't get any choice about it. I hear these mothers now talking to their children: "Would you like this, would you like that?" Back then you did what you were told.

My older brother Tom was working as an apprentice to a bricklayer and between him and my mother we got by. He was thirteen but he said he was older and no one cared in those days. Children were expected to work. When he was flush Tom slipped me a farthing to go down the Salvation Army for breakfast. Oh, I loved it there! It was warm. They gave you tea and a slice of bread and jam. One day my father didn't come home at all and I can't pretend I shed a tear. I suppose you think that's a wicked thing to say. Well, you didn't know the man. He was a brute. But it broke my mother's heart. She was what you'd call sensitive. Her nerves weren't good. Six months after he left she had Joseph and two years later she was dead, dead of a broken heart and overwork, and the four of us were taken into the Destitute. Me, my two sisters and my baby brother Joseph. My brother Tom couldn't keep us all, though he tried for a little while. They split us up, girls on one side and boys on the other. I was eleven then.

We had lessons – I liked those and helping the teachers. I was there for three Christmases. On Christmas Eve morning the ladies from the Society came in to sing. It was the Society for the Children of the Destitute, that's what they called it. They stood on the stairs. They must have sung for a little while. "Silent Night" and "The Holly and the Ivy". I'd never heard proper singing before. Then they gave us a present. I got a tin of pencils the first year, some wool the second year and then a book of Bible stories. When I left I gave the pencils and the book to Joseph. The ladies were beautiful. One of them had a black hat. It was velvet with red silk roses all round the edge and a huge white ostrich feather at the side. She wore that hat every year. I suppose it was her charity hat! I couldn't take my eyes off it and I said to myself, one day I'll have a hat like that.'

Chapter 9

Sally hoped that the girl standing on the middle of her garden would not see her staring. Her best guess was that she was the new owner's sister. She was very thin, with highlighted shoulder-length hair, wearing a white ski jacket and tight jeans tucked into black leather boots. The girl was smoking a cigarette and talking very loudly on her mobile so that Sally could hear her voice but not many of the words. But Sally caught 'removers' and 'really late' several times. She wished the girl would move off their lawn onto her allotted garden area, a square of patio with steps leading up to the main lawn. The woman and her boyfriend had also stood on their garden. And doubtless all their friends would, too, when they had parties.

So the time had come to share the house. As if to distract herself from this unwelcome thought, Sally turned away from the window, took the spatula and spooned cake mixture into the square cake tin, then put it on the centre shelf of the oven. She set the timer for fifty minutes. Louis's birthday cake was to depict the Seven Dwarfs asleep in bed. Tomorrow she would add a layer of jam and marzipan and ice it. The marzipan was bought but delicious. It had been a mistake to taste it; all those stolen little pieces had left quite a dent in the marzipan brick. She had got on a chair and moved it to the top shelf behind the Tupperware containers she never used.

The sponge would form the bed. Each dwarf would comprise a Kit Kat finger covered with icing. Blue for the bedspread, red for their hats, white for their hands, feet and face. Piped yellow for their beards. She had bought the icing, sheets of white fondant that had to be dyed with food colouring. She would do the rest of the party food on the day. Brickie was coming to help.

Maybe she should invite her new neighbours to Louis's party? She was just considering this when Louis barged past her and, with his toy JCB, began banging on the glass of the French window.

'Girl! Girl!' He sounded ecstatic. Clearly neither of them had enough excitement in their lives.

The girl turned round, startled. Sally gave a limp wave.

'Louis!' She had no choice but to unlock the door and wrestle Louis back. She restrained him long enough to pull red Wellingtons onto his sock-less feet. He shot off towards the girl who took a step back. Sally hurried after him.

'Welcome. Welcome to North Walk, I'm Sally,' she said formally, extending her hand before noticing that her nails were caked in flour.

The girl laughed. 'Oh, I'm not moving in. My boss owns the flat. I'm Ethne.'

She shook hands very briefly.

'Your boss?'

'She's on a shoot. So I'm here. Except the fucking removal men are stuck on Parkside.'

Ethne looked down at Louis who was gazing up at her cigarette, enraptured. 'Oh. Sorry.'

Louis seemed oblivious. Sally wanted to ask if the woman on the shoot was married to the man.

To hell with it. 'Is she married?'

Ethne gave a hollow laugh. 'No. She's moving in on her own.'

'She's a film director?'

'Television producer. For 7–24.'

'Gosh.'

'And I need to get to Newbury. I mean Beaconsfield. For work.' She looked at Sally as if she was contemplating asking her something. Louis wandered up closer to the girl and tried to stretch his hands to grab the edge of her jacket. She stepped away.

'Cute,' the girl said distractedly, in the uninterested tone that Sally would have used at her age. Sally realised how dull she must look to Ethne, dressed as she was in a Crew sweatshirt from three years ago and a pair of grey tracksuit bottoms. Her feet, which were freezing, needed a pedicure. Maybe Ethne was thinking, I'll never let myself go like that.

Then Ethne turned away and stubbed her cigarette out on their lawn.

But there was no alternative really. 'Would you like to come in for a coffee?'

Ethne took a moment to consider this. She really was quite rude. 'Actually, I have to do some work.' She added as an afterthought, 'Thanks, though.'

And then her mobile rang and she answered it without further explanation.

'Tash!'

Their brief conversation appeared to be at an end, unless Sally wanted to stand lamely listening to Ethne talking to Tash about 'the guys driving up from Cirencester'. So she pulled a protesting Louis inside.

Soon it would be time for lunch and then a walk. It was the same every day. In the early days it had been better. The girls from the antenatal class had met up at each other's houses to trade war stories and drink coffee. But gradually, one by one, they had drifted back to work until only she, Vickie and Juliette were meeting regularly. Then Juliette's husband, who worked for a German bank, was transferred to Frankfurt at the end of last year.

Now Sally watched from the kitchen as the girl flicked her telephone closed and stubbed out another cigarette on the lawn. Louis wriggled loose and padded off. She could hear him decanting cars from his car basket in the living room. She stayed motionless before stealing a look at the clock. In five minutes it would be an hour since she had last checked her email. She ought to clean up the kitchen first. Instead, she rinsed her hands under the kitchen tap and dashed upstairs to Edward's office.

It was there.

RE: E.D. Irvine
Dear Sally

I agree. E.D. would have taken notes and these might have survived. It's a long shot but worth trying. Is the school still in existence? The office might be a good place to start, both for information about Irvine himself or leads on surviving local Irvines. Some of my best informants have been school secretaries. Let me know how you get on.

Good Luck, H

She loved that he began and ended the email properly, just like she did. He was so enthusiastic and encouraging, but grounded and practical at the same time. He was businesslike but he had a light touch. She imagined school secretaries all over the country breaking into archive files in their haste to help out Hart. And he clearly wanted to continue their association. *Let me know how you get on.* She felt revived and energised. The encounter with the girl in the garden vanished from her mind. Her concerns about the cake-icing faded into insignificance. Even the prospect of facing Pia tomorrow night at Hope's party no longer seemed to matter.

She clicked on the internet and began the search for Selton School.

Anna had anticipated that Rob would have second thoughts. 'Why don't we just sit down, have a chat, run the camera?' she said casually. 'If you don't feel comfortable we can pack up,' she added brightly.

Rob shifted uneasily, his gaze drawn to the living-room window as if frightened that at any minute Nina might appear.

He sounded doubtful. 'I don't know ...'

Anna set up the camera. Ordinarily she would have brought a runner but on balance the inconvenience of setting up on her own was offset by the advantage of it being just the two of them.

'Rob, you can say as much or as little as you like. It's you speaking to the viewer with no distractions.'

She gestured to the sofa and he sat down uneasily.

She decided to bowl him an easy one. 'So, what did you first notice about Nina?'

'Oh.' He looked out of the window again. 'She was ... nice. You know. She always made me a cup of tea. Some people act like you're not there. Nina's not like that. She's generous. She gave her PA a car for their tenth anniversary.'

Anna would not have expected that.

'And her dad. He's in a nursing home. But it's a private one. Nina pays for all that.'

'So you were attracted to Nina's generous spirit?'

'Yeah. *Spirit.* That's a good word, Anna.'

'And yet things aren't right between you ...'

He looked down. There was a silence, which she had the sense not to break. 'It's like … like I'm an outsider. Like I don't belong. I keep thinking … she's gonna wake up one day and dump me. I get all tense like.'

Intuitively Anna understood then – but it would be better if he could come out with it on his own.

'Tense?'

He hesitated. 'In the bedroom. And Nina wanting a baby and all that. It causes … problems. And she won't talk about it because she says everyone will say it's because of her being older.'

'Is it?'

'No! Nina's got an ace bod … It's not her. It's me. I feel all pressurised.'

He looked up at her.

'You don't know what that feels like, Anna. Feeling like you don't belong, like you're not good enough, like everyone's looking down their noses at you.'

He sat back and exhaled, looking up at the ceiling – which was fine as long as he didn't move from his seat, she was shooting in close-up.

'Have you told Nina?'

He shrugged. 'That's why I wanted to do the programme. Like it would make me feel better. Like I was someone. Nina wants me to go to college. She says I need to be proactive.' His tone was anything but.

'Why don't you then?'

He looked away. 'You need … qualifications.'

'And you don't have those?'

He looked uneasy. 'No.'

'Rob, lots of people don't. More than you would imagine.' She thought back to a short film she had made for *Read Freak*, a programme for teenagers who had failed to read in primary school. 'I mean some people can't even read.' She laughed.

And then she read his face, the flicker of his eyes, and she felt horribly embarrassed in a way that she thought she had become immune to.

'Is that it, Rob?' She said softly. She tried to phrase it delicately. 'Is reading a problem?'

He nodded. 'I can't read,' he said eventually.

'Does Nina know?'

He nodded again. 'She says I'm dyslexic.' Then he shook his head disconsolately. 'Anna, I don't think I'm dyslexic. I just never paid attention.'

She forgot the camera. 'Rob, it doesn't have to hold you back.'

It was uncomfortably ironic. Wasn't Rob precisely the type of voiceless, hidden person she had gone into television to film?

'I don't want this on the film.'

'Of course,' she said impatiently, caught up in the moment. 'I could help you. I could help you find a tutor.'

'And no one would know?'

'Yes, of course.'

'I don't want Nina's friends finding out.' She was about to interrupt but he cut her off. 'And don't tell me it's nothing to be ashamed of because it is. It makes me feel like a loser.' He looked up at her. His expression was resigned. 'But you don't know what that feels like. You've been to university. You've got a cool job. I bet you feel great inside, Anna. Really great!'

Ethne had been getting ready to go out into the garden for another cigarette and a further chat with Tash when the doorbell had sounded. It was really loud. The removers. At bloody last. She had flung open the door of the flat. She was faced by a man holding a laptop computer and a huge bouquet of flowers. They looked at each other as though each were the impostor.

'I'm looking for Anna,' he said.

'She's not here. I'm Ethne. I'm her PA.'

He looked relieved. 'Of course. Sorry. I'm Tim Meah. I'm a friend of hers.'

She opened the door to let him in. She knew who he was, Anna had mentioned his name, and after that, when she was still at the stage of wanting to impress Anna, she had gone off and read a couple of his articles. They were all about politics, which didn't interest her much, but they were witty and even quite funny. Her father, who was the Chairman of a firm of City stockbrokers, knew his editor.

'The removers have got stuck, but they're on their way,' she added, anxious to reassure him and pre-empt any call to Anna. God knows what she would say if she knew it was three o'clock and they were still not here.

He seemed unconcerned. He was surprisingly good-looking. She had supposed any boyfriend of Anna's would be a dork.

'Shall I put those in water for you?' she asked.

'Thanks.'

There was no container of any kind so she ran water into the sink and put them in there.

'It's a lovely flat,' she said politely.

'Yes. My lunch was cancelled,' he said by way of explanation. 'So I thought I'd come and surprise Anna.'

She performed some mental calculations. If she left now she could be in Beaconsfield by 4.00 p.m., speed-interview Mrs Zarkosky and be out of the door by 5.30. She had no idea how long it would take to get to Newbury, she was vague as to geography west of Chiswick, but it was bound to be in time for the party, which was the important thing.

All she needed to do now was to persuade Tim to cover for her.

She assumed a slightly anxious expression and looked at her watch.

'Is there a problem?' he asked.

'Oh. Well …' She hesitated. 'I really ought to be getting some research work done for Anna. She needs it for Monday. But—'

It was easy peasy. He interrupted. 'There's no point in you staying now I'm here.'

She looked uncertain. She had to be careful here. 'I don't know … There's the parking permit to organise as well. All the documents are ready.' She showed him an A4 envelope.

'Don't worry about it. As soon as the removers arrive I'll nip down and take care of it.'

'Would you? The foreman's super, you don't have anything to do. Anna found the best firm.' God knows if this was true but it made it all easier.

He looked relaxed. 'Fine. I'll make some calls, do some work.'

She picked up her bag. It would be good to get out before he discovered that there was no mobile reception inside the flat, no phone line until Monday and no wireless until next Wednesday.

He was already unpacking his laptop.

'Bye, then!'

'Oh, goodbye. And thanks for all your help.'

Now she looked around the Zarkoskys' living room. It was like a museum, incredibly still and silent. No cars had passed along the private Beaconsfield road since she had arrived. It was an Edwardian house located in Beaconsfield's Millionaires' Row; the roads marked 'Private', Jaguars and Range Rovers parked in the driveways alongside landscaped gardens that stretched back hundreds of feet.

The drawing-room furniture was dark wood, she guessed mahogany, and there was too much of it. China ornaments were massed on every surface: nuns in prayer poses or glancing heavenward. Her mother would have pulled a face.

'You're looking for what hasn't been said,' Anna had told her condescendingly. 'For what lies below the surface.'

Everyone had warned Ethne that television wasn't remotely glamorous and now, watching Mrs Zarkosky shuffle forward holding an enormous tray, she was beginning to believe it. Mrs Zarkosky wasn't what you would call photogenic. She was thickset and her clothes made her look heavier, pleated plum-coloured trousers and a heavy-knit cardigan.

Ethne was stumped for what to say next. Before she had a chance to ask her first question Mrs Zarkosky passed her the plate of buttered malt loaf.

It would be rude to refuse. She took a mouthful. Even though she was hungry she couldn't believe anyone would buy this stuff. It was like sticky fruitcake that someone had baked all the flavour out of.

'Very nice,' she said between mouthfuls.

Mentally she cursed her lack of preparation. She pulled out a notebook from her bag.

For no other reason than something to do, Ethne turned over the blank page onto another blank one. She needed to be precise.

'Are there any regular activities that you participate in?' she asked solemnly.

At last Mrs Zarkosky sat down and appeared to be thinking.

'Well, Church, of course. But you know all about that. And we used to play golf but we gave that up a little while ago. Peter's back,' she added by way of explanation.

Ethne couldn't see that there would be much viewer interest in Peter's back.

'So you're involved in the Church?'

Mrs Zarkosky shifted. 'Yes.'

'Could you tell me a little about the Church work you do?' Ethne pressed her.

This question released a flood of uninteresting information about the Holy Communion programme and the old people's lunch. Ethne gave up trying to write it all down.

She was beginning to appreciate Anna's qualities. Anna would have had no difficulty asking the type of personal and probing questions that were required and which she was completely useless at framing. And they hadn't even broached the subject of her marriage. Or the mistress. Anna had been very specific about that.

We need to know how much she knew about the other woman.

'Your husband works long hours?'

'Peter started the business with my late father. Thirty years ago.'

'He makes clothing?'

'Yes.'

Mrs Zarkosky seemed reluctant to say more.

Ethne had a moment of inspiration. 'Whose idea was it to participate in *Marriage Menders*?'

Anna had taught her to say 'participate' not 'be filmed'. It made them seem less like zoo animals, Anna had explained.

'Oh, it was a mutual decision. Peter and I think we have a lot to offer.'

Ethne wrote this down. 'Mutual decision'.

She knew she had to ask about the mistress but she just couldn't bring herself to do it just yet.

'How long have you lived here?'

God, she was so lame.

'Fifteen years, dear. We moved here when the children were teenagers. My mother had just died so my father came to live with us in the annexe.'

She wrote down 'Polish Family Values'.

'And we wanted more space for the children. Then we put the pool in.'

Good. An opening to see the house. Anna would expect her to

report back on places where they could film. 'I'd love to see the house.'

Mrs Zarkosky got up. Oh God! She didn't mean right now. She hadn't even got close to the mistress questions. She had no option but to follow Mrs Z. out of the room and into the parquet-covered hallway to the stairs.

After an excruciating tour, during which all Ethne could think of to say was 'Very nice,' they stopped in the hallway.

Mrs Zarkosky reached for a fur-trimmed anorak hanging on the hall coat stand. 'Well, I have to get going, dear. Evening service.'

Mrs Zarkosky's tone of voice assumed that Ethne would know this.

'Of course. I'll just get my things …'

She went into the living room. Her notebook lay open. She had barely a page of notes. Never mind. It would be fine. She would think of something. Call her! Yes, she would telephone Mrs Zarkosky and ask the mistress question. Difficult conversations were always easier over the phone.

Chapter 10

Under the circumstances, Sally thought that she was managing pretty well. She had ironed Edward's shirt, written Hope's birthday card and wrapped Hope's present – a pair of gold knot earrings. She had restrained herself from asking how much the earrings cost when Edward brought them home last night. But now, as the door slammed behind Edward, the house seemed horribly quiet and the hours until the evening very long. In front of her stood the square sponge cake waiting to be decorated. It had sunk in the middle and was not as tall as the one in the picture. Her cakes never were.

Edward had had to leave ridiculously early. He was taking the train so that she would have the car. Wimbledon to Gerrards Cross was an awkward train journey, which necessitated crossing town to get to Marylebone. Pia would be collecting him at the station.

'At the station! Why can't you all meet at the restaurant?' she had asked Edward irritably last night.

'I don't know. I don't make the plans. Pia wants everyone to meet at the house, have a drink and go on together.'

So they would be in the car together and at the house together – just like old times – and then sitting side by side at the restaurant for hours. Together.

Half an hour after Edward left she was regretting not putting her foot down and making him insist on her inclusion. She kept looking at the kitchen clock to calculate where Edward was right now. Why had behaving in a mature and generous manner made her feel so bloody miserable? Like an angry doormat. She turned her attention to the Seven Dwarfs, beginning by cutting a slice of marzipan from the end of the brick and eating it. She needed to roll it out quickly before it was further eroded. Louis appeared.

'Tom-mus!'

So she rinsed her hands and went to put on *Thomas* for the second time that morning, returning to eat another slice off the end. Then she rolled the marzipan a little thinner so that when it was draped over the top of the cake there would be some pieces to eat. She was starving because she had missed breakfast. Tonight she had to fit into her one smart outfit, a black jersey dress, which she had bought for Louis's christening.

Gently she lifted the marzipan, at which point it tore down the middle so she hurriedly flung it on the cake and nudged the edges together. She was getting irritated. This type of project required a serene state of mind. And she hadn't even started on the dwarfs. Two Kit Kats sat on the counter. There were seven dwarfs so it was safe to eat one finger. Pia would have probably thrown the spare away.

Her friends had tired of her obsession with Pia. She stopped talking about it to Vickie and Juliette when she saw them exchange glances. Their expressions said *here we go again.* Brickie had stayed the course but their conversations had a tendency to become diverted onto a discussion of Brickie's married man who owned a classic car dealership near Maidenhead. Her mother would not understand her obsession with Pia.

'But he married *you*, Sally,' she would say. 'He wouldn't have done that if he didn't want to be with you.'

But then her mother was ignorant of the truth. She had told her parents, when she finally got round to telling them that Edward had become more than just her boss, that she had started working for him when he was in the process of getting divorced.

'So he was getting divorced when you met him?' her mother had asked carefully.

'Yes.' It was not exactly a lie: they were definitely separated.

The obsession with Pia had got better. In the early days Sally was a regular visitor to the Fleet Street branch of Waterstone's where she would look at the photograph of Pia reproduced on the back cover of the paperback (2nd edition) of *Smart Women, Smart Choices.* She would pore over her features, try to assess her weight, wonder if the photograph was current or touched up or whether she really did look that good. Thick brunette hair, classic features and a full mouth. Pia's expression, serious with the hint of a smile, promised the reader wise counsel. Eventually Sally had been forced to purchase the book, reading it on the train home in the evenings. It was unexpectedly old-fashioned and slightly school-marmish in tone.

Eating out at lunchtime is an extravagance. Substitute a thermos flask of soup and a nutritious homemade packed lunch.

She did not always seek Pia out. Sometimes Pia found her, rearing up unexpectedly, usually at the hairdresser's when she would turn the page of a magazine and find a Pia Kirwan-Hughes article.

Stop spending, starting saving: 10 tips from the experts
For Richer or Poorer – Do YOU need a pre-nuptial agreement?

But most of the time Sally was simply plagued by the comparisons in her own head. Did she cook, clean, converse, dress and have sex as well as Pia did? Edward met her occasional queries with incomprehension.

'Where does she buy her clothes? No idea ...'

She had met Pia for the first time at Dan's Welton Prize-Giving, held at the end of the summer term. It felt like Pia's home ground. Welton, situated in the Buckinghamshire countryside, was an ugly Victorian brick building with a large 1950s extension to the rear, the Chapel to one side and the Founders' Hall to the other. Edward had parked in a field, from where they tramped to the main entrance where younger boys in the Welton uniform of black trousers, grey blazer and crested tie were handing out programmes. It was a sweltering July day and the boys must have been close to boiling point.

Immediately, on seeing the mothers, Sally realised that she had worn the wrong thing, despite weeks of agonised procrastination. She had settled on her best Porter Stone outfit, a navy blue suit with a cropped jacket, the skirt falling just below the knee. She looked like a chic headmistress. Inside, they were met by the institutional smell of disinfectant and floor polish, the sound of echoing footsteps and the sight of high walls decorated with wooden plates inscribed in black copperplate lettering with the names of past Heads of House, scholarship winners and the holders of sporting records.

On their way into the school an elderly teacher, later identified as

Mr Stookey, Dan's Latin teacher, had greeted Edward warmly and then addressed Sally.

'You have a clever son there. But he needs to apply himself.'

Edward cleared his throat. 'Let me introduce you.' He gestured towards Sally. 'This is Sally, Dan's stepmother.'

Mr Stookey had looked embarrassed but he needn't have been. She was used to it. Edward's mother regularly slipped up and called her Pia.

They had encountered Pia in the entrance lobby to the Founders' Hall where the prize-giving was taking place. Sally was so familiar with her photograph that it was as if Pia's image had suddenly come alive, though her hair was cut dramatically short now and her face looked thinner. Pia had got it just right in a white linen skirt suit and navy pumps, worn with a scoop-necked T-shirt that showed off her tan. Pia was with Roger. She and Pia had simultaneously smiled at each other. To an outsider the scene was that of two exes now neatly re-paired and with no hard feelings on either side. It felt excruciatingly false.

Edward was curiously diffident introducing her. She was determined to look Pia in the eye but she had the feeling that Edward could not. 'Pia, this is Sally.'

Pia gave a gracious smile. 'And this is Roger.' Edward had given Roger, who was tall and wearing a well-cut summer suit, the briefest of handshakes.

There had been an awkward pause. Then Edward and Roger spoke together.

'Lovely day for it ...'

'Terrible traffic coming out of London ...'

Pia rallied. Turning to Sally, looking her straight in the eye, she told her warmly that the PTA did a fabulous tea afterwards. Then Roger asked Edward what sports Dan had opted to do next year – which later Sally realised was generous of him because he saw more of Dan than Edward did and must have already known. It felt as though Pia and Roger were scoring A+ while she and Edward were barely scraping a C.

And then there had been no option but to sit together. The high windows had been opened but with close to a thousand people present it was hot and crushed, the hard wooden chairs pushed close together,

They had taken their places in a row: Pia, Roger, Sally, Edward. She had chatted to Roger while Pia read the programme. She had glanced at Pia's hands; she wore two enormous diamond rings. She wondered if and when Edward had given them to her.

Roger was very good company. He asked no personal questions. Instead, he filled her in on Welton.

'My son came here. Spent most of his time running bootleg cigarettes.'

'What does he do now?'

'Funnily enough he's a commodities trader in the City.'

Ten minutes late it had started. The boys trooped in, then the teachers in gowns mounted the stage and finally the headmaster took the lectern.

'We're off!' whispered Roger.

After the guest speaker, an Old Boy who was now a Fellow of the Royal Academy of Arts, had gone on for ages about his area of expertise – research into tectonic plate movement – the Head Boy gave a nervous vote of thanks. Then came the prize-giving, which went on for ever, the applause becoming ever more desultory. Dan didn't win anything. Afterwards at tea, however, this did not matter. Dan had proved a welcome distraction. The four of them arranged themselves around him, directing their questions and observations at him. Dan had looked at the floor and given one-word answers and eventually Pia had said, 'Why don't you go and rejoin your friends, darling?'

Once he was gone she addressed the three of them. 'I really think we've turned the corner.' Then to Sally, 'He was horribly homesick when he first arrived. All normal, of course. But now he's made a couple of friends ...'

All in all it had not been too bad. So next year, emboldened, Sally had gone again with a lighter heart. But this time Roger was not there. In his place stood Pia's mother, Evelyn, a neat woman in a beige trouser suit with the trouser crease stitched in. She smelt slightly of cigarette smoke. And this time there had been plenty of personal questions.

'Do you work, Sally?'

'Yes.'

'What do you do?'

'I work at Porter Stone.'

'Oh yes. Of course you do.'

At least this time Dan won a prize – Best Improver in Junior Hockey. By then Dan was coming to stay with them for weekends and then for a week or so in the holidays. In the beginning he had been terribly easy. Most of all he had wanted to eat. She was inspired by his appreciation and huge appetite to start cooking. She made him steamed syrup sponge and cherry cheesecake; apple crumble and brownies. Pregnant by then and permanently hungry she ate with him watching Monty Python reruns. He didn't say much. At the weekends Edward took him out, swimming or to the cinema.

But lately Dan had visited less frequently. He said he wanted to be with his friends, especially Pascoe, whom Edward had said was something of a concern on account of his one-week suspension from Welton for smoking cigarettes. Edward, true to form, hadn't said anything but she'd known that he was hurt by Dan's decision.

Now the fondant-icing headboard had collapsed. Try as she might she could not get the thing to stand up straight, let alone form an elegant curve at the top. So she abandoned it, deciding that a headboard wasn't essential, and began mixing blue colouring into two-thirds of the fondant icing to make the bedspread. It was as she was rolling out the bedspread that she heard the voices. There had been bumps and shuffles from the flat below but no voices or sightings of Anna Miller. But now she could hear the voice of a man and a woman. The man's voice was the louder of the two. He seemed to be shouting. She strained to hear. Yes, he was definitely shouting and, although quieter, the woman's voice sounded pretty angry too.

'Why don't you commission Seven-Fucking-Twenty-Four to make a film about me? *Tim Meah: The curious case of his invisible girlfriend.* Then we might get to spend some time together.'

'We will,' Anna insisted. She sat on the bed, a towel pulled around her. She had emerged from the shower to find Tim packing his overnight bag in the bedroom.

He had looked up and said curtly, 'I'm leaving.'

She felt confused. 'Why?"

He gave a half-smile and a shake of his head. 'You just don't get it, do you?'

So, he was cross that she had to work tomorrow. She played for time. 'Well, why don't you tell me?'

She could see that he was angrier than she had ever known him but also knew that his natural sense of fair play would prevail.

'Anna, I'm sick of your obsession with work.'

What a ridiculous exaggeration. 'It's not an obsession!'

'Isn't it?' He stood up straight from where he had been bending over his bag. He began counting off points on his fingers. 'You're either at work or thinking about work or recovering from work. You never switch off. Even when we're out having dinner you're preoccupied. It's like being with someone who isn't there.'

'That's not true!'

'Yes, it is. I took you to the Ivy for your birthday, asked you what you were thinking and you said – quote – *I'm wondering how I would set up the lighting in this room if I was filming in here.* Unquote.'

'I don't recall that,' she lied. 'Anyhow, I don't think it's an obsession,' she added sullenly. 'And I think you need to be more understanding of my situation. I've just started a new job, I'm making a six-episode series—'

'And 7–24 is just about to go public and this is their autumn flag-ship series.' He finished her sentence for her. 'Anna, I've heard it all before. It was the same when you were at the BBC.'

Leaving the BBC was supposed to have given her more time. It hadn't quite worked out like that, if anything she was busier than ever. He went into the bathroom and returned with his wash bag. She had never known him be like this. At least not with such severity. In the past when he'd been irritated she had always been able to pacify him. She had had no idea that he would overreact like this when she told him about Penny, Peter Zarkosky's bit on the side. She had tried to be as considerate as possible – arranging to go and see Penny on Sunday when really she would have liked to have gone today. But Tim wanted to go and have breakfast in the Village and then show her the Buddhist Temple in Calonne Road.

Admittedly she had been late getting here last night. After filming Rob she had gone back to the office to clear her desk for the weekend. The Friday-night traffic through Wandsworth had been close to a standstill all the way up West Hill on account of a burst water main. But eight o'clock could hardly be called late.

And the fact was that the Zarkosky filming was justifiably her top priority at the moment. She felt uneasy about the Zarkoskys: confused by their motives and suspicious that Peter Zarkosky had not told her the whole truth. She hated the feeling that there was something she wasn't being told. Yesterday's telephone conversation with Penny had only served to deepen her doubts.

So when Tim had woken up that morning and they had lain in bed discussing their plans for the weekend, she had hardly thought that her meeting with Penny would pose a problem.

'I have to do an interview tomorrow … Not until the afternoon,' she added hastily.

His voice was resigned. 'Why?'

She loved talking to him about work. 'It's the Zarkoskys. The Polish couple,' she prompted him.

'How could I forget?' he observed drily. 'These people are like a family to me.'

'Well, I tracked down the other woman, Penny. And I'm going to get the truth out of her.'

He lay back on the pillow and exhaled.

'Tim, I have to see her.'

'Of course.'

He hadn't said any more. She had got up and had a shower.

Now she watched as he zipped up his bag.

'Anna, I've heard it all before. After my parents' wedding anniversary lunch – you didn't make that at all …'

She had a good idea of what was coming next.

'… and what about the other night with David Stratford? I had no idea if you were going to turn up or not.'

'I was filming! I couldn't help the traffic back from Bracknell,' she protested.

He stopped what he was doing for a moment and shot her an exasperated glance. 'How about allowing for the fact that rush-hour traffic will lengthen the duration of your journey? Why does that fact always cause you so much surprise? Anna, here's a suggestion: how about wrapping up earlier?'

'It's just not always possible!'

He raised his voice in frustration. 'Anna, how about managing your time? Christ, I know cabinet ministers who find the time to run marathons and write books. Look at the Education Secretary. He's just written a biography of Lord Salisbury!'

She raised hers, too. 'He has support! Staff—'

'So do you. But you never use them. If you can get Ethne to move house for you, why can't you get people to help you with the work?'

'I do! I've sent her to do the background research on the Zarko-skys.'

'Good. Give her some more things to do.'

'I can't do that. I can't hand over editorial control!'

Finally, he looked up and caught her eye. 'That's what it's all about – control. Anna, you're an amazing girl. And you have a fabulous future ahead of you. But I can't spend my life waiting for you to come home from a film set.'

He was making her mad now. 'So, what do you want? Some little wifey sitting at home baking cakes and ironing your shirts?' Unbidden, the image of Ethne came into her mind. How long had they spent together? Was all this just a coincidence? 'Or some airhead bimbo?'

He threw her the look that one would give a tantruming child. 'No. I don't want that. I want you and the creative successful person you are. I think I've always supported you?'

He had, but she could not bring herself in the heat of the argument to concede that.

'I want us to be like a normal couple. I don't want to be wondering all the time how late you are going to be and what sort of mood you're going to be in when you finally arrive.'

'Mood?' she said uncomprehendingly.

'Yes. Will it be "the day has gone well" so Anna is elated. Or will it be "the day has gone badly" so Anna will barely say a word.'

'Where are you going?'

'Home.'

Pride stopped her asking him if she would see him again.

He moved towards the door. 'Anna, do you know what normal people do at the weekend? They have friends over. They read the papers. They go for a walk. They relax. I don't think you know how to do any of those things. I guess there was a time I thought I could show you ...'

He turned, as if to say something else, then wordlessly went up the hallway. She almost could not believe it when she heard the door slam.

She lay back on the bed. Hot tears came into her eyes. She looked at the clock. Perhaps he would go into the Village, have a coffee, come back again. She pulled the duvet up over her, moving over to his side of the bed, and felt an aching for him. Hoping against hope that he was coming back but knowing that he wasn't.

It felt as though she were lying on the floor. There had not been time to assemble the bed so they had found sheets and put them on the mattress and made do. Around her stood furniture in the wrong places and books and tapes that should be in the second bedroom designated as her office.

Last night, when she saw that the bed was not assembled, she had snapped at Tim, 'Why didn't you get the removers to assemble the bed?'

'Because they didn't get here until after three o'clock,' Tim said evenly. 'And they worked really hard until past seven carrying every-thing in and unpacking ninety per cent of it – while I helped them. So I let them go. Wrong call, obviously.'

She had not said anything to that. She was annoyed that they hadn't finished the job – she would have stayed until it was all done in their situation. Instead, she and Tim had gone out to eat. Over dinner she had told him about Rob.

'He's an innocent, really. He isn't stupid and he didn't marry Nina for her money. He loves her, Tim, he just needs some bloody confidence.' And then she felt sad, in a way that she hadn't for so long, that so many people had failed Rob. 'His parents and the school system failed him, and then Nina came along and believed in him.' She still found Nina irritating but she wasn't going to stitch them up. If someone had to be the villain of the programme it was looking increasingly like Peter Zarkosky.

It was second nature to her now: the participants in programmes were characters to be scripted and filmed to her specifications. As a child, growing up in a family that was short on money and empty of ambition, she had dreamed of the time when she would be able to change her world and the people in it.

Tim had looked thoughtful. 'Can you work that into the film?'

'What?'

'The situation of people like Rob – stuck in dead-end jobs because they haven't got the right qualifications.'

She had been dismissive. 'Tim, it's not that type of film. It's about personalities not politics.'

'I'm not suggesting a diatribe. I mean just focusing on that.'

She shrugged. 'That's not what I do.'

And then she had changed the subject and told him about Penny. 'Peter Zarkosky portrayed it as some kind of innocent dalliance, an infatuation on her part. It turns out it was a full-blown affair and it's still going on.'

Now, in the cold light of day, she recognised all the warning signs that she had missed and cringed at all the things she hadn't said. She had ignored the flowers, the amount that had been unpacked, and raised a cursory 'thanks' when Tim pointed out the parking permit that he had collected. Instead, she had poured out a glass of wine, the corkscrew had already been conveniently put away in a drawer, and watched as Tim pieced together her Ikea bookcases. She hadn't thanked him for that either.

She was beginning to feel a cold dawning of the reality of her situation. She was like some overworked, stressed-out corporate man whose wife had spent years trying to get him to hear her complaints until finally, much to his amazement, she walked out. In magazine articles about workaholic spouses it was invariably the husband she could identify with, men so wrung out by work that they had nothing left to give when they got home. She did all the things that the wives complained about: she took files, her mobile and her laptop on holiday, checking her email five times a day. Increasingly she found it hard to relax at the end of the day without a glass of red wine in her hand. And she loved, above all other topics, to talk about work.

The advice to these couples was always for the man to ease up and set aside more time for his wife. And she could see that that might be possible at some vague time in the future, when she was commissioning programmes instead of making them and she was assisted by a handpicked team of professional staff instead of Ethne. It was the same vague time that she planned to have a baby. But right now she knew that if she dropped behind she would never catch up. And these were the crucial years, her mid-thirties, the years that would determine whether she would scale the heights or settle for second place. She thought of Rick Roth, possessed of the media essentials: a Range Rover, a second home in Somerset and an ex-wife. Susie, his current wife, had come to the office Christmas party, cast sideways glances at the stunning reception staff and, after a few glasses of champagne, declared loudly that this was the longest period she and Rick had spent together all year.

Perhaps she should marry someone who worked in television. They could get out their diaries and schedule time together. But even as she had the thought, she realised that she wanted Tim. She could telephone him and tell him that she had cancelled her meeting with Penny. They could go riding instead. Or walk up to the Windmill and have afternoon tea afterwards. But even as she had this thought she felt a stab of anxiety – that would mean going the whole weekend not knowing what was the real story behind Peter Zarkosky's relationship with Penny. Maybe it would be better to let Tim cool off and, in the meantime, get all her work out of the way so that they could spend lots of time together next weekend. It wasn't as if he had ended it.

The shock of the row with Tim began to recede, overlaid by thoughts of the best way to approach Penny. It was always that way. Work was her solace, her place where everything was reliable and predictable, where effort equalled reward, where she was respected and admired, if not always liked, where an underlying order prevailed.

And at a deeper level, work was the only thing that made the fear go away, not that it ever entirely went away, even in the good times. It was a fear she could not name or assuage or reason away. It was best described as the apprehension that one day she was destined to be unmasked. On that day all her success would be revealed to be an illusion, all the prizes judged to have been awarded in error and all her possessions taken from her. Some malevolent force was out there waiting patiently for the right moment to take her down. She lived with a sense of impending loss.

She had tried describing it but people didn't understand.

'But you're so good at what you do,' they would assure her.

Tim had come the closest to understanding. 'You have to have a bit of faith in yourself. And you have to trust that everything will be OK ...'

She tried. But most of the time the only way to make it go away was to check and to double-check and work so hard that she could issue herself a daily insurance policy against failure.

And she had never told Tim the rest. She had never told anyone that one day she would fall and when she did there would be no one to catch her. There never had been anyone in her life to save her so how could she believe that one day there would be?

So now, the solution to Tim's departure was clear.

She reached for her Filofax and found Penny's number. On the third ring Penny answered.

'Listen, my schedule's changed. How about if I come down this afternoon …?'

Chapter 11

Pia surveyed the lunch table. She had chosen this particular table, located by the window, on a visit to the Compleat Angler Hotel several months earlier. She had made the reservation and then confirmed it in writing, keeping a copy in the red folder labelled 'Lunch'. Earlier that morning, on her way to collect Edward from the station, she had come by to set out place cards. On no account could her party be given free rein to sit where they pleased. Her brother Gabriel had to be kept apart from Edward's father – ten years after the event the Normandy Holiday Cottage rental venture remained a sore point – and Dan was best separated from Edward until after the lunch was over.

She felt like a West End theatre director directing an amateur company. A few stumbled lines and missed cues, but the play was underway and to the audience of fellow diners they looked like a typical middle-England family celebrating a twenty-first birthday. Dan sat to her right and Edward to her left. Across the table Gabriel, dressed in a well-worn tweed suit, was holding forth to Edward's mother. The topic was his latest business venture, Royal Jelly.

'The fantastic thing is that I'm in on it at the start. I find people who work under me and sell it. Then I get a share of their sales.'

Edward's mother was curt. 'But can't people just buy it at the health food store?'

Pia had made that point to Gabriel herself. She noticed that his glass was close to empty, having only very recently been refilled.

Edward was chatting to Hope. Hope was simply radiant, in a pale pink coat dress, which might have seemed a little old for her had she not been wearing it here in such formal surroundings.

The Compleat Angler was situated on the banks of the River Thames at Marlow. In the summer, the lawns were dotted with elegant tables and chairs shaded by striped parasols beneath which lunch and then afternoon tea was served. Today, an icy wind had cut across the bare lawn as she shepherded her party in from the car park to the warmth of the hotel lobby and down a panelled corridor to the dining room. As they entered the lobby, her father had tentatively suggested a glass of sherry in the bar but she had shooed him on: she had ordered champagne to be brought over once they sat down. The champagne, like the wine, was the best on the list. Their table was at the far corner, chosen for its views of the church, the white ironwork of Marlow Bridge and of the cascading weir, all viewed through delicate leaded windows, decorated with panels of jumping fish over a flowing river.

As Pia had foreseen, it was perfect. Hope was wearing the Cartier watch that Pia had given her for her birthday and the earrings, presumably costing significantly less, that Edward had presented her with earlier. Frankly, it was hard to imagine a cheaper piece of jewellery: the design a plain gold knot, with not so much as a magnifying-glass-sized diamond. And it was Hope's twenty-first! Hope did not seem to mind. She had always been a daddy's girl, a fact tolerated with amused acceptance by Pia who had been just so incredibly grateful to have a baby. To Hope's right, Pia could see that things were a little tense. Edward's father was speaking to her mother Evelyn, her mother's speech still stilted and difficult to follow unless one had acquired an ear for it.

He sounded resolutely positive. 'We have friends in sheltered accommodation. Marvellous! Fabulous facilities, all sorts of activities. Marjorie says she can't wait to get rid of the house and move in to one ourselves!'

Her mother's expression was tight-lipped, her voice laboured. 'Hmm. Activities! You don't have any choice about it … If you don't go … they all talk about you behind your back. It's all very well if you're old.'

Pia observed Edward's father turn to Hope, but Hope was engrossed in conversation with Edward. So he had no option but to continue the conversation with her mother.

'Have you made any friends?' he enquired politely.

She laughed mirthlessly. 'No. I want to be in my own home … I don't need these busybodies … around. The *others* do … but *I* don't.

Sheltered accommodation! They might as well be … honest about it and call it the … Workhouse!'

The truth of it was that Pia's mother didn't actually want to be in her own home. She wanted to be in Pia's home. It was a conversation they had on her daily visit to The Oaks.

'You've got so much space now,' her mother said disapprovingly. 'Don't you think it's selfish living in that big house all by yourself? And I could help you out. You wouldn't need a cleaner.'

Pia didn't agree that keeping the house was selfish. But she did think that it was extravagant. Which was why, after Hope's party was out of the way, she intended to put the house on the market and buy a nice two-bedroom riverside flat in Marlow. No garden. No maintenance. No expenses other than the service charge that covered the porter who could sign for all her internet shopping parcels. Dan would have his own little room and be further away from Pascoe to boot. She would invest the surplus from the sale of the Gerrards Cross house for her retirement. She intended to spend as much of it as possible on a selection of expensive cruises.

She checked on Dan seated securely next to her. He was ploughing through his food, his expression as blank as usual. One would have thought that today of all days he might display some emotion. But she could not think of Dan right now – if she did she would become distracted from the main task, which was to host a flawless lunch. Besides, she was feeling distinctly under the weather. Her stomach hurt, which she supposed must be nerves. The counsellor Edward had found for them had told her that she had a Type A personality – stressed out, in other words.

The idea of a counsellor had been the first of Edward's bomb-shells.

Later, when they had pudding, she might suggest that the men moved round. Two places anticlockwise would give Edward a stint with her mother. Dan would move safely next to Hope and Gabriel would take his place next to her. He was getting drunk, knocking back her carefully pre-selected 1997 Chateau Cissac claret as if it was Sains-bury's Bordeaux. On the downside, shifting the men about would also mean that on her other side she would end up next to Edward's father who was bloody boring, patronising to the staff and hadn't offered to pay anything towards the lunch. Edward's parents had probably been told that she had got quite enough in the divorce. Maybe that was what Miss Moneypenny had told them? It would make perfect sense, too, if she was the one who had chosen those cheap earrings, Edward had been keen enough to delegate his entire life to her. Pia's friends had laughed when she had told them the unexpected news, the ink barely dry on the decree absolute. Marion had been contemptuous.

Marrying his secretary! What a cliché!

Marion was a tower of strength, her oldest and closest friend, but then she didn't have that many. Marion, whose own husband was no saint, had urged her to take Edward for every penny. Sometimes Marion had seemed more angry at Edward than Pia herself did.

Prior to the divorce being finalised he hadn't mentioned that there was anyone else. The bombshells were going off thick and fast by then. Pia had assumed his lawyer was just being efficient in pushing things through so quickly. She put that thought out of her mind as well. Right now Sally and the baby did not exist.

To be fair, which was always an effort where Edward was concerned, he had offered to pay for the lunch. He had leaned over to her earlier as he had passed back the wine list to the sommelier.

'I'll take care of this.'

In retrospect she should have been more gracious. 'That's not necessary.'

He had been curt. 'I'd like to.'

It was a familiar feeling, one of simmering resentment towards him that did not dissipate even when he did what she wanted. It had been that way for much of their married life. His opinions, choices and tastes made her angry. He brought home a Flymo; she wanted a rotary mower. He was loyal to British cars; she liked German. He would take ice cream straight from the freezer and hack away at it; she let it stand for ten minutes. He loved real Christmas trees; she hated all the mess.

Finally she had understood that she did not resent the things he did – she resented *him*. At the end, in one of the dark kitchen rows late at night fuelled by too much red wine, he had shouted, 'What the hell do you want from me?'

And then, in a headlong rush, she had shouted back, 'I want you to go.'

In the morning they had talked. They would embark on a period of separation. They agreed that they had married too young, been through too much and that a period of reflection was needed.

When he left she began making changes to the house. She bought an entirely different set of Sunday papers, selected flowers she had never purchased before and went into boutiques she had never frequented.

Dan had been angry. 'Why are you changing everything?'

The counsellor had been puzzled. 'But you could make those changes with Edward in the house?'

She could think of no reply to this because it was true. He wouldn't have stopped her. Christ, he probably wouldn't have even noticed.

The indigestion pain was creeping up on her more severely. The dived scallop and foie gras she had chosen to start with had obviously been a mistake. She refused more wine.

'Just some more water, please.'

She felt awfully thirsty. And hot. One would have thought that this type of restaurant could control the heating.

Edward turned to her. Quietly he said, 'Are you OK?'

'Yes!' she snapped. Actually, she was beginning to feel worse. It must be food poisoning. She thought back to what she had eaten the night before – Marks and Spencer mushroom risotto and a glass of wine. It had seemed perfectly OK. It couldn't be breakfast, two cups of coffee and two cigarettes was normal for her.

But whatever the cause, the indigestion located in her solar plexus was getting worse. And the pain was beginning to travel up her spine. She arched her back. Perhaps if she stood up it would ease?

She whispered to Edward, 'I'm going to the bathroom ...'

She stood up. Immediately she realised that this was a mistake. She could feel her face cold and clammy. She reached out and took hold of the side of the table.

'Pia!'

She was looking down at the table so she could not read Edward's expression. But she heard the note of fear and panic in his voice. It was so unusual – Edward was nothing if not calm – and it made her afraid. The pain had surged up now so that it was across her shoulders. And then with a shocking suddenness it was in her arm and then, in a split second, it was really so bad that there was no alternative but to let her knees give way and to fall to the carpet.

'Pia!' It was Edward's voice again. And then she heard him shout to some unseen person, 'Dial 999! Call an ambulance!'

And with an awful clarity she remembered the last time she had heard his voice say almost those exact words.

'It's OK. It's going to be fine. I'm going to call 999 and get an ambulance.'

It had been twenty-two years ago. The day they lost the baby.

Mummy was fine, Daddy had everything under control and the National Health Service had been brilliant. Hope ran these thoughts through her mind like a mantra as they sat, now silent, in the waiting room. Uncle Gabriel had gone off to get a coffee; Granny and Dan sat wordlessly on either side of her on plastic seats; Daddy had stayed with Mummy, waiting for the doctor. There were posters telling you to stop smoking and to eat five portions of fruit and vegetables a day, lots of signs telling you to switch off your mobile phone and multi-lingual directions to the coffee machine on the first floor.

While they had waited for the ambulance – which Hope had feared would take for ever but didn't – the restaurant manager had fluttered around and suggested moving Mummy. It would have been useful if there had been a doctor having lunch that day but there wasn't.

Daddy had said no. 'Keep her where she is.'

He had been talking to Mummy, keeping Granny calm and dealing with the bill.

'Hope, here's my wallet. Take the Amex card and get them to run it through.'

Mummy kept on mumbling about the party that evening. 'Some of the guests have already left home by now...'

'We'll deal with it all,' Daddy had said firmly.

Next he had addressed Grandpa and Grandma. 'Dad, can you go to the house and hold the fort there?'

Mummy wouldn't stop trying to talk. 'The flowers are arriving at four o'clock … check that they've done twelve table arrangements not—'

Daddy cut Mummy off: 'That's enough.'

Then the paramedics had arrived and Mummy and Daddy had gone off in the ambulance, she had followed behind, driving Mummy's car with Dan, Uncle Gabriel and Granny who wouldn't stop crying. They had assembled in the waiting area of Slough hospital. Granny had been beside herself. 'Hope, can you find out what's happening? Ask that nurse ...'

It was useless to trouble the staff yet again, she had asked several times already.

'Granny, as soon as they know anything they'll tell us. We just have to wait here.'

Granny started running through all manner of possibilities. 'If it's a hernia they'll have to operate. I just hope it isn't appendicitis because if you don't catch that it turns into peritonitis – that's blood poisoning – very nasty.' Then she had started crying again. 'And then there's you-know-what.' Granny was superstitious and would never say the word 'cancer'. 'She's lost a lot of weight recently and they say you have to catch it early to have the best chance. You would have thought they could find a cure by now. They can put rockets into space ...'

'Why don't I get you a cup of tea?' Perhaps she could catch a minute to call Jo?

'Oh, I don't like those machines. Your grandfather had a heart attack but she's too young for that.'

Hope looked up and saw her father coming towards them, Gabriel bringing up the rear with a plastic cup of coffee in his hand. She noticed that Daddy had loosened his tie. He sat down next to them and they leaned in towards him. Even before he spoke Hope felt herself relax slightly, his presence itself reassuring. Characteristically he got straight to the point.

'Mummy's had a heart attack. A mild one – the type they call a warning heart attack. She's absolutely fine.'

'Nonsense,' said Granny.

'I think we should get a second opinion,' said Uncle Gabriel.

'Are they sure?' Hope asked.

'Frankly, she ought to be in a London Hospital. A teaching one,' Uncle Gabriel continued.

Granny was thinking out loud. 'Maybe they got her notes mixed up with someone else. She's too young for a heart attack.'

Daddy was very patient. 'It's true, I'm afraid.'

Hope was aghast. 'But that can't be right? She's not fat. She eats healthily.'

Daddy sighed. 'Actually, she has many of the risk factors. She smokes. She has a family history of heart disease. And she's permanently stressed out.'

Granny spoke up. 'She never used to have all that stress. Not until the divorce.'

Gabriel nodded sagely. 'She's had a tough time – on her own.'

Daddy ignored them both.

Dan spoke up. 'What's going to happen?'

'They're going to keep her in. Run some tests.'

Hope had, until that point, entertained the idea that she would be home that day. 'When will she be out?'

'No idea. She needs to see the cardiologist …' He sighed. 'And in the meantime, she's adamant that the party has to go on.'

Hope was aghast. 'No!'

'She made me promise. And she's right. The fact is the caterers are there and there are so many people en route that cancelling it would be more work than having it. So it's going to go ahead,' he said in a tone that allowed for no further debate. 'I'll stay overnight at the house and we'll do the breakfast in the morning just like Mummy planned.'

'Can we see her?'

'I'll ask the nurse.'

He was gone for ages. Granny was crying and saying over and over again that it must be a mistake and Uncle Gabriel was telling her to calm down.

She saw that Dan looked bereft. 'Do you think she'll die?' he asked quietly.

'No!' Hope shook his shoulder gently. 'Look, in a way it's a good thing.' He looked startled at that. She backtracked. 'I mean not a good thing exactly. I mean it's better to have a little warning one rather than a huge big one. This way they can give her drugs and make her stop smoking and rest a lot. Dan, it'll be fine.'

He moved closer to her so that Granny and Uncle Gabriel, who had picked up *Woman's Own*, couldn't hear. 'And what about school?'

She had forgotten about that. She whispered back, 'You'll just have to tell Daddy.'

He looked panicked. 'I can't! Mummy was going to tell him. Later, after the party.'

She knew what he wanted her to do. She rolled her eyes. ' I'll tell him.'

'Do I have to be there?'

'No. I'll go and find him.' She took her purse out of her handbag. 'Here,' she handed him a note. 'Go and buy a newspaper and get a hot chocolate from the machine. And bring back the change!'

She ended up walking for what felt like miles. First to the cardiac ward, which was in a brand-new building with fountains outside and a huge foyer with a glass ceiling and sculptures dotted round a reception desk like a hotel. Mummy wasn't on their computer yet so they had had to call the Accident Department and locate her ward. But when she got to the ward the nurse said Daddy had gone outside – and she couldn't see Mummy yet because she was with the cardiac nurse – so she retraced her steps until finally she located her father back where she had started, outside the main entrance to the hospital. He was talking on the mobile. She guessed that he was talking to Sally. He sounded stressed out.

'Look, just come down. We'll work it out from there ...'

There was a long pause while Sally was talking. *I've been looking for you,* he mouthed at her.

She was about to reply but he held up his hand. He spoke into the mobile. 'Believe me, I've considered all the alternatives. The fact is the caterers are already there and the guests are on their way. Some people have flown in from overseas for this, we have to think of them ...'

There was another pause.

'Look, we can talk about this later. The first thing is for you to get down here ...'

There was another pause. Then Daddy said, 'I *have* thought about that. I'll take Dan back to Welton on Sunday and then come on for Louis's party.'

Oh God, Hope had to let him know. She mouthed, *Dan,* and shook her head at him. He frowned. She pulled her finger across her neck in cut-throat fashion.

What? he mouthed silently. Then he spoke into the phone. 'I can hire a car. Sally, we'll work it out. We just need to take one thing at a time ...'

She shook her head urgently. Then in a stage whisper she said, 'Dad! Dan's not going back to Welton ...'

'Hold on,' he said to the phone. Then he turned to Hope confused. 'But term hasn't ended?'

'I know. But Dan's been expelled.'

Sally was straining to catch what Edward was saying. She could hear cars pulling away, doors slamming and, in the background, Hope's voice. And then Edward came back on the line.

'Change of plan. It appears that Dan is not going back to Welton.'

It was difficult to absorb. Edward, who according to schedule should be en route to Pia's house from the Compleat Angler, was instead standing outside the Accident and Emergency Department of Slough General Hospital. Pia, having keeled over from a heart attack, had decreed that the party would go on. And Edward, now appointed Pia's party planner, seemed to have totally forgotten that Louis's party was tomorrow. In front of her on the kitchen table the Seven Dwarfs slept soundly, as if blissfully unaware that their future as the party centrepiece was in peril. It looked as if there might not be a party for Louis at all.

Edward's voice sounded heavy. 'It appears that Dan's been expelled.'

'*Expelled!* What for?'

'What for?' she heard Edward ask Hope.

Then Hope's voice in the background. 'Smoking dope.'

'Smoking marijuana,' relayed Edward.

She could hear Hope launch into a breathless explanation. 'Mummy didn't want to tell you until after the lunch. She thought it would spoil things. And she's trying to work something out with the school. But they have a zero-tolerance policy. It's an automatic expulsion. He has to go to counselling and the counsellor has to recommend if he can come back. And they'll only take him back if he passes a drugs test.'

Edward came back on the line. 'They have a zero-tolerance policy, apparently. It's an automatic—'

Sally cut across him. 'I heard.' She thought quickly. 'When's Pia coming home?'

'No idea. We'll know more later. They have to see how much damage has been done to the heart and see how she responds to the medications. They're giving her blood-thinning medication.'

She imagined that they would have her up and out as soon as possible, her bed already earmarked for some unfortunate currently stationed on a trolley on the corridor. Or so one could only hope.

'But she'll be out soon?' she said, as much to herself as Edward.

He sighed. 'Actually, I think they'll keep her in. Apparently the hospital has been marked out as a Cardiac Centre of Excellence. Sony has just given them several million for a new operating complex.'

Their voices were drowned out by the sound of an ambulance driving up. With what she detected was a note of relief, Edward said, 'Look, I have to go. Just get down here and we'll have to wing it. Bring an overnight bag for both of us.'

'You want me to stay there? At the house? ' she asked incredulously.

'Well, what's the alternative?' he said. 'Some of Hope's friends are staying over. I can't leave umpteen youngsters on their own in the house. And I definitely can't leave Dan.'

She knew he was right. But their goodbyes were curt and she slammed the phone down with unnecessary force. What next? He would probably see nothing wrong in her sleeping in Pia's bed. Borrowing her nightdress? Using her moisturiser? Maybe it would be better if she went to stay in a hotel. It just felt wrong somehow for her to be there, in a place she didn't belong, in some ghastly collision of Edward's old and new lives.

As she packed she was shocked to acknowledge how much she didn't want to go. She thought about Hope and the brittle politeness that characterised their relationship; then about Pia's mother and her barbed asides; then Edward's parents who appeared still to struggle to remember her name. Not to mention Gabriel who ostentatiously ignored her. As for Dan she couldn't even begin to think about that – or the influence a drug-addicted teenager would have on Louis.

There had been a time when she wanted to spend every moment of the rest of her life at Edward's side. Those were the days when it was enough to be married, caught up in the pleasure of just being together. Those moments were less and less frequent. Tonight she could almost say to Pia, Hope and Dan, 'Here. Have him. Have your husband and your father back …' And then it would just be her and Louis and she would never have to see any of them ever again.

*

It was a testament to her powers of organisation. Even from her hospital bed and in her absence the party would go on.

Pia addressed Edward. 'On my desk there is a blue plastic folder labelled "Evening Party". On the top there is a spreadsheet with an hour-by-hour schedule for today. Underneath that you'll find tomorrow's schedule.'

Hope had looked desperate. 'Mummy, we have to cancel the party!'

'Why ever would we do that, darling?'

Hope sounded anguished. 'Because you'll be here! And I don't want to have it without you …'

What good would be achieved by talking like that? It was defeatist. 'Nonsense, I'll be fine. It's only four o'clock – there's ample time to regroup. Anyway, the Grandpops are coming back to visit this evening.' The Grandpops was the collective noun by which they referred to her mother and Edward's parents.

Her mother was in a state of voluble anxiety. In the circumstances they had agreed it was the best thing for Edward's parents to take her home.

She turned to Dan. 'And I want you to help Daddy.'

Dan nodded mournfully.

She caught Edward's eye. She could tell that he knew. As much to pre-empt any conversation about Dan she yawned.

Hope jumped in. 'Mummy, you must get some rest.'

Edward was thus gratifyingly outmanoeuvred – any conversation about Dan and the expulsion was postponed. Eventually, after Hope had reassured herself more than once that she had water and the call button for the nurse safely to hand, they left.

Alone now, Pia felt physically exhausted and curiously carefree. All the tedious details of the party that had caused her so much anxiety to date – the arrangement of the table flowers, the colour of the napkins, the number of tiny lights to be suspended from the marquee ceiling – now seemed so very insignificant. Hope was going to have a wonderful surprise when she saw the menu – cold salmon and chicken pies, indeed! She had planned everything – except her heart attack. Funny really.

She looked about the four-bed ward, all the beds occupied but thankfully by women. Presumably the NHS was going through a single-sex phase. An intravenous tube had been inserted in her hand. The nurse had told her when she came up to the ward that they were going to give her 'something to relax you'. She couldn't remember the name of it but whatever it was it very good. Hopefully they would give her some more later. She wasn't hungry and supposed that they wouldn't allow her anything to eat anyway. A menu had been placed at her side – *Healthy Options* – described as a range of low-fat heart-healthy choices. Today's choices were salad and vegetable bake followed by low-fat fruit yoghurt or a piece of fruit. Each had a symbol to the side of a cartoon heart with a smiley face.

Even Dan's future did not overly concern her. For the time being it was Edward's problem. Let him deal with it. It had occurred to her at her meeting with the headmaster yesterday that having a son who smoked dope was one of the few remaining modern-day taboos. Everyone knew it happened but everyone wanted to pretend that it didn't. She had received a call from the headmaster's secretary who refused to say what it was about.

In hindsight it was hopelessly optimistic of her to have suspected that it might be cigarettes. Sometimes she smelt smoke on Dan, he was always making up excuses to go outside, but she had told herself that it was some occasional teenage habit. And as a smoker herself it was hard to take a stand.

She had been ushered into the headmaster's office overlooking the sports pitches at the rear of the school. Already seated were the school nurse and Dan. The headmaster had then shaken her hand, asked her to take a seat and without missing a beat informed her baldly that Dan was being expelled for drug use, having been found late that afternoon smoking marijuana in the amphitheatre with Mark Pascoe. She had been stunned.

The headmaster had done this before because he was word perfect, his hands clasped together, his tone regretful but resolved.

'Frankly, all schools have this problem, whether they want to admit it or not. Drug use is an equal-opportunity problem – no respecter of class or money.'

Clearly he had been to some sort of training session.

He continued, 'We have to balance Dan's needs with that of the school community. In the past, schools have adopted an automatic expulsion policy. Now we try to encourage rehabilitation and reintegration back into the school.'

He went on to explain that Dan would be expelled but there was the possibility of reinstatement if he stayed 'drug-free and co-operated with the counsellor'.

At that point the shock had worn off and she had begun to realise the seriousness of her position.

She crossed her legs and leaned forward. 'Is this really a case for expulsion? I mean, it's a one-off incident. A case of experimentation rather than prolonged usage?'

'I would like to think that. But given that Dan and Mark Pascoe were found with a substantial quantity of marijuana it's not an interpretation that we can follow.'

The mention of Pascoe's name infuriated her. She shifted to look at Dan who was studying the carpet. 'Why did you have to make friends with that boy? I warned you about him. What were you doing in that amphitheatre anyway?'

She turned back to the headmaster. 'What were they doing there? Why are they allowed to go off like that?'

'Actually, it is out of bounds.'

Damn! Dan did not look up. The headmaster intervened.

'Let's try to keep calm. Let me assure you that Mark Pascoe is being dealt with.'

She tried again. 'I just feel that this boy led Dan astray. He's never been in trouble before.'

The headmaster nodded in agreement. 'We do understand the power of peer pressure. We undertake sessions in our Social Education classes, teaching boys appropriate techniques to deal with precisely those issues.'

Since when had the headmasters of English public schools adopted the therapy-speak of daytime television? She would have expected this in the state sector. Not in private education. What they needed was less bloody empathy and more discipline – coupled with total surveillance. An idea for an article came unbidden to mind: *The Rise of the Counselling Culture – Time for some Boundaries?*

The headmaster pushed some papers towards her one by one. 'This is a copy of our drug and alcohol policy. This is a paper stating that we are releasing Dan into your care. And this sheet lists the names of counsellors who we have worked with in the past. There are two copies. If you could sign each of them and retain one copy for yourself.'

She felt overwhelmed with a hopeless anger. There was no alternative but to agree to the headmaster's policy if there was to be any hope of reinstating Dan. But given Dan's continued antipathy to Welton it was difficult to see that he would have any incentive to co-operate with a policy that would return him here. If the school secretary, when she had phoned to ask her to come in, had told her what this was about she would have called Edward.

Welton was supposed to have helped him and to have pre-empted just such behaviour. It was a very expensive insurance policy against a broken home, an absent father and a new brother whom she knew Dan must resent. Not to mention Miss Moneypenny. Where had it all gone wrong? God, it was so easy when they were little! Mothers of young children thought they had it rough. They had it made! That was the easy bit – when you could control their movements, monitor their every activity and conduct background checks on their friends. But before you knew it they were catching buses and talking on the phone and going to sleepovers. Sleepovers should be made illegal. Your children assured you that *of course* the parents were going to be there, *of course* there was no alcohol and there was definitely no need to check. All lies.

Now, facing the headmaster, she felt a conflicting rush of blame and failure directed at herself, Edward, the school – and Dan himself.

During the marriage guidance sessions the counsellor had asked them about Dan.

'He's taken this very hard,' Edward said quickly, referring to the separation.

The counsellor had looked at her to see if she agreed. Pia had spoken slowly, choosing her words with care.

'Dan is nine. He's very young. It's difficult for him to understand ...'

'I think he understands more than you give him credit for,' Edward said.

The counsellor, Frances, a willowy woman with elegantly styled greying hair, had made a pencilled note.

Pia turned to Edward. 'What are you saying? That we should stay together for the sake of the children?'

'I think we should at least try for the sake of the children,' he said evenly. 'Until we can try for ourselves.'

'Whatever happens I will make sure Dan is OK,' she had said resentfully.

In a subsequent session Frances had wanted them to talk about the baby.

'I was pregnant when we got married,' Pia explained. She could almost feel Edward wince beside her. It was a fact that Edward hated to acknowledge.

'It was a register office wedding.' Edward's mother had been horrified. There had been talk for a while that she would not attend.

'We met at Loughner's – they own Porter Stone now. I had joined after school. I'd worked there for three years. I was hoping to get on the fast-track programme. Edward joined after university ...' She could feel Edward shift next to her. Her short-lived time at the bank was well-worn ground between them. 'And then two weeks after we got married I lost the baby at five months. We were at home. It was very sudden.'

'What happened?'

'Nothing! It was different then. No funeral. No photographs or hand prints or all the things they do today.' She could feel bitter about that sometimes, the way she had been treated by the hospital. She took a deep breath. 'They just told you to get pregnant again. And to give up work to be on the safe side. So I did.'

The counsellor had consulted her notes. 'That's your daughter, Hope?'

'Yes. Hope.'

She had told herself at the time that the name was an affirmation of life, a retort to fate's dealings with her. Now she realised it was as much a comment on her marriage.

There was more that she could have told the counsellor but didn't. After she lost the baby she wanted to travel. Or run away? She fantasised about getting an inter-rail ticket and going round Europe and then Asia, followed by a few months in Australia. But those were the days when she had been young and overawed by the doctors and the nurses so she had done as she was advised.

'I was told that the best thing was to try for another baby and so we did. I had to do as little as possible during the pregnancy.'

Edward's job with the bank allowed them a cheap mortgage. He was keen to buy a house. So she spent her pregnancy like an invalid, watching daytime television and reading library books, in a 1930s semi in Twickenham while Edward, marked as a high-flier, went to work in the bank's head office and got sent on training conferences to the bank's country house training centre in Hampshire. It even had an indoor swimming pool, he reported back. In the evenings and at weekends he studied for his banking examinations. But once Hope was born it was easier – for a while. She had her reward for doing nothing for nine months – a healthy, full-term baby to take home to the newly decorated nursery. She had devoted herself to Hope.

Seven years later they had moved to the first Gerrards Cross house.

'Hope was at school and I had begun writing,' she had explained. 'At first, small pieces in the local paper. Then a regular column for the *Bucks Free Press* on finance issues for women.' She surprised herself with how much she knew. The editor said she was a natural. She had begun to investigate the possibility of going to university to study journalism. Dan, if not quite an unplanned pregnancy then a careless one, put a stop to all that. She stepped up the pace of her work to make up for her lack of a degree, employed a succession of incompetent au pairs and appointed Hope her 'Little Helper'.

Dan's pre-school years were fitted in between deadlines and her new money management column for *Good Housekeeping*. In the meantime, Edward's career went from strength to strength. The bank had taken over Porter Stone by then. He was part of the new management team, enjoying a succession of better paid and more interesting assignments. When Dan was two years old he was seconded to the Porter Stone's Paris office for six months, coming home at weekends. He could not understand her resentment.

'It's good for *us*, Pia! I'm doing this for us? It's a sign that I'm going to get promoted. It means more money. Why can't you be pleased about that?'

After the Paris assignment he had indeed been promoted and they had bought the present Gerrards Cross house. She had thought it might bring them closer together as a shared project. The house, built in the 1970s, was large, on a good-sized plot, but dated. They ended up arguing over everything from the colour of the stair carpet to the choice of fruit trees to be planted at the end of the garden. Every weekend seemed to be spent in awkward silences in Homebase. She was spoiling for a fight. Granite or corian? Hardwood or tile? Blinds or curtains? Whatever the question she would find an alternative answer to that favoured by Edward. She could not help herself.

They were worn down to a state of existence: never anything less than polite in public and permanently distanced in private, making love when they were both drunk. Edward was uncomprehending.

'What do you *want*?' he would ask her.

The answer, unvoiced, was that she wanted her life back. She wanted space and spontaneity. She wanted the years that she had never had.

Frances the counsellor was nice enough, though she did seem to side with Edward. At the end of one session, the last but one, she leaned forward and said earnestly to Pia that Edward was not responsible for the way she felt. Privately, Pia did not agree: if Edward wasn't the problem then what else could it be? So next time she made her excuses and stopped going. Her idea was for them to live apart for a while and, for want of a better word, for things to drift on like that. But Edward had had other ideas. He dropped another bombshell – divorce. She had imagined that she would be the one to make that decision. It had all happened so very quickly – and unexpectedly. Sometimes it was hard to dislodge the enduring sense of resentment that Edward should have given her a little more time. And space. After all, she had given him so much time, so very many years – it was the least she deserved. If anyone was going to make the final call on their marriage it should have been her.

Chapter 12

It was difficult for Sally to decide what exactly had been the low point of the evening. The conversation with Gabriel – though to be accurate it could hardly be called a conversation, more a monologue – had been unpleasant. But it was not, in retrospect, wholly surprising that one of Pia's family would take it upon themselves to represent Pia in her enforced absence. Predictable, too, was Hope's chilly politeness towards her; the way several of Pia's friends had cut her dead and the news that Dan was to return home to Wimbledon to stay with them while Pia was recuperating. What had been truly shocking had been her discovery of the receipt for the lunch at the Compleat Angler, Edward's signature at the bottom of the counterfoil of an American Express credit card receipt. The discovery was worse than having to sleep in the spare room of Pia's house – worse, even, than having to watch Edward make the speech of the evening, in a house that he had formerly occupied, applauded by an audience largely comprised of former friends of his and Pia's.

The receipt felt like a shocking betrayal. It was paper evidence that Edward had lied to her about the lunch when he told her clearly that Pia was paying for it. Yes, it was the low point, Sally concluded, sitting alone at the table where she had spent the evening feeling horribly uncomfortable. It was now midnight and there were still three hours to go. The dance floor was full. Pia's blue folder had contained a type-written playlist for the DJ so Sally had known that the dancing would start with Stevie Wonder's 'Happy Birthday' and that the evening would conclude with 'Isn't She Lovely'. The DJ was currently playing 'Come On Eileen' at just the right volume, loud enough to encourage dancers but not so deafening that conversation was impossible. The guests, good-looking twenty-somethings and their well-heeled parents, were dancing or bunched in groups around half-empty bottles of wine and pots of coffee. Edward's parents had departed an hour earlier to go and check on Evelyn. Gabriel was on the dance floor with Teresa, his partner for the night. Teresa, who was best described as a bubbly blonde, appeared to be a recent acquaintance, judging by the way they smooched their way through dinner. Edward had disappeared to confer with Tony the Chef about the 2.00 a.m. breakfast. Dan was presumably with the younger crowd in the Chill Out Zone. As for Hope, she had presumably slipped away with Jake, whom Pia had secretly flown in from Costa Rica for the weekend.

Pia was full of surprises.

The party, to be totally fair, was nothing short of sensational. In his sparse descriptions of Pia's plans, Edward had said something vague about a marquee in the garden. Sally had envisaged some sort of small big top affair consisting of a faded round tent rising in the middle, accessed by a flap in the off-white canvas. She had in mind the tents they had at fêtes when she was little. However, in the intervening years marquee technology and decoration had clearly moved on. There was not one marquee but four tented rooms – the largest termed the Main Hall, a rectangular structure with transparent plastic leaded-light windows. The Main Hall was accessed by an entrance area, one wall of which comprised a collage made up of photographs of Hope and the family. Sally had not had a chance to look at it properly. To the side of the Main Hall was the Chill Out Zone, the floor covered with kelims and scattered with oversized soft cushions. Last was a service tent for the caterers.

The Main Hall, where the hundred guests were seated, was neither faded nor even white. It had been lined with an array of exotic colours, the theme Arabian nights. The roof of the marquee had been draped with dark blue silk and covered with hundreds of tiny lights to make a night sky. The walls were hung with burnished red, gold and bronze fabrics. The tables were covered with white tablecloths and set with silver-coloured candelabra and each was finished with a centrepiece arrangement of velvety claret-red roses and wafting white Casablanca lilies, encased in glossy hosta foliage. Beforehand Sally had privately thought that the dress code – black tie and evening dress – was over the top for a family party in a Gerrards Cross garden. Her mother always said that it was better to be underdressed than overdressed.

On this occasion they were both wrong. Sally's three-quarter-length black jersey dress, with the addition of a gold sequined scarf, just didn't cut it.

In this, as in all her other expectations, she had misjudged the class and scale of Pia's arrangements. She was absolutely sure Edward had said it was a sit-down meal and they were starting with cold salmon. In fact, there was a buffet, duplicated in three locations to avoid queues, serving the type of traditional British food that was enjoying a fashionable renaissance: bangers and mash, steak pie with Guinness and a sublime beef wellington; roast chicken and fish pie. It was a top-notch fish pie made with salmon, prawns and scallops, topped with filo pastry. Gabriel informed them over dinner that Tony the Chef had trained at the Savoy before starting his own outside catering business a couple of years ago. The desserts were fabulous, too: sticky toffee pudding, crème brulée and Eton mess, which was a sort of mashed-up strawberry pavlova; chocolate brownies with pecan and maple syrup ice cream and pots au chocolat.

Every detail had been executed in the most perfectly creative form possible. The photographer, Gabriel proclaimed, freelanced for *Harper's*. The places-setting were squat little H-shaped ivory cards, the name of each guest calligraphed on the horizontal. When everyone was seated the ceiling lights were dimmed so that there was a starry roof above and a warm candle-lit glow across each table. Halfway through dinner Sally gave up trying to calculate how much it had all cost.

Sally had arrived at seven o'clock, one hour before the first guests were scheduled. She had packed an overnight case at breakneck speed, grabbed Edward's suit bag containing his tuxedo and shirt, and hurtled off to her parents' house. Louis had toddled off down their hallway without so much as a backwards glance, a reaction far removed from that of Vickie's son who would cling to Vickie screaming mournfully at any threat of separation.

Her mother had been full of concern for Pia. 'Oh dear. Is she going to recover?'

'Yes,' Sally had responded briskly, heaving in the travel cot, which was now too small for Louis. 'She'll be fine.'

'Well, you never know,' her mother retorted. 'Look at your father's hernia. They thought that was heartburn.'

Sally had heard that particular tale of misdiagnosis too many times before.

She handed her mother Louis's bulging baby bag, an over-sized carrier bag of toys and a small holdall with four changes of clothes. Experience had taught her to err on the side of over-supply.

Her father appeared from the kitchen. 'Is Louis coming to live here?' he said cheerfully. It was the same remark he always made when sighting Louis's things.

'Edward's wife's had a heart attack,' her mother announced.

And then Sally had to recount the whole story again to her father. 'So his ex-wife,' she concluded, 'is laid up in the hospital.'

Her mother looked almost anguished. 'And after all that work planning the party she won't be there to see it. The poor woman! Shouldn't it be postponed?'

'Apparently it's too far gone to cancel.'

'These things get a momentum of their own,' observed her father.

'It doesn't seem right to me,' her mother added. 'I feel for her. You must pass our best wishes on to her when you see her.'

Sally had driven nervously on the darkening M25 and then slowly through Gerrards Cross. She was unfamiliar with the area, so that even with Edward's directions she got lost along the exclusive tree-lined roads, all of them looking much the same, the newer houses pillared, gated and landscaped. Eventually she found Pia's house. It was situated in a cul-de-sac of similar houses, 1970s plain brick, set on broad wooded plots. Two large trucks occupied the driveway and the entire garden frontage was filled with vans, so she parked outside the nearest neighbour's house. It felt wrong somehow, even being in the vicinity of this house, just as it felt awkward pushing open the front door of the house, having received no response to her ringing of the bell. She stepped into the small parquet-floored hallway, expecting at any moment someone to discover her and ask what she thought she was doing in Pia's house. She looked into the living room to the left. It was surprisingly dated. She had expected some *Hello*-style interior. Instead, there were two Dralon-covered sofas, a mismatched fawn easy chair and an assortment of worn reproduction tables. The fireplace, in York stone, must be original.

She went back into the hallway and entered the eerily empty kitchen, which she had imagined would be taken over by the caterers.

It was silent, the pale cream worktop bare except for a bunch of dirty coffee mugs piled by the sink. The kitchen was flooded by light from the garden. Through the window she saw Edward. It was dark now but the scene of activity outside was illuminated by floodlights positioned at intervals along the perimeter of the garden. Stepping outside the kitchen side door she heard the hum of unseen generators and as she rounded the back of the house she saw that it was a very large garden, dominated by a rectangular marquee. Staff in white kitchen overalls were going to and fro, sidestepping a team dressed in bottle-green gilets with 'Rufus Swayne Party Planning' embroidered across the backs.

She found Edward standing talking to one of the bottle-green gilet men. Edward was distracted, leafing through a blue folder. 'Hello, darling.' He didn't lean forward to kiss her. 'This is Rufus.'

'How do you do?' Rufus, tall and languid in baggy corduroys and wearing a flecked blue and white fisherman's oiled sweater beneath his gilet, looked and sounded like an ex-army officer from a very good regiment.

There was a lot of talk of logistical planning. Edward and Rufus immediately resumed their conversation. The main concern seemed to be that guests would trip up over the cables on their way to the 'Luxury Lavatories', as Rufus called them, situated in yet another tent reached by a covered walkway. Of course. Pia would hardly want umpteen teenagers and their parents tramping through the house.

Edward, far from appearing inconvenienced by his new responsibilities, was clearly in his element.

'So, we reposition the power lines to the rear of the property ...' Edward had even begun to sound faintly military in tone himself.

'Yep. We'll fix extension cords so we can divert them around the trees.'

'Good.'

'I'll notify the catering staff of a temporary power interruption,' Rufus looked at his watch, 'at nineteen thirty hours.'

It was freezing. But once the challenge of the power lines had been overcome Edward and Rufus strode off further down the garden to confirm the positioning of the 2.30 a.m. Farewell Firework display.

'We like to end on a bang!' Rufus quipped.

Eventually, after Rufus had signed off on the fireworks, agreed the timing for the serving of dessert and introduced them to the Chef – Tony who broke off from icing 'H' onto white china ramekins of pots au chocolat – they made it into the house. So far so good. No one had challenged her or suggested escorting her off the premises. Maybe she could do this after all? What she needed now was to hold Edward and be held by him and take a moment for themselves.

Edward picked up their bags. 'I'll lead the way.'

And then she followed him up the stairs of her predecessor's house.

Her birthday was turning into a horrible nightmare. Her mother was in hospital, the Wicked Witch had just landed on her broomstick and Jake currently had his hand halfway inside her shirt, fiddling with the back of her bra strap. How in God's name was she going to explain any of this to Jo?

They were standing in her bedroom, where Hope was attempting to have a serious talk with Jake. It was nearly seven o'clock and she needed to get changed into her party dress as a matter of urgency.

'Jake, we need to talk …'

'Baby, we need to fuck.'

Baby. How had she ever thought that Jake was cool? To be accurate his hands were clammy, his breath was sour and he had a red rash round his neck where he had shaved too close. And she was sure he'd had blond highlights, though he insisted it was just the sun. If only her mother had warned her! There were times when even though Mummy was amazingly capable and really generous that it would be better if she stayed out of things. At Welton Jake had been so inspirational. He was captain of cricket and Head of House. He'd been to 10 Downing Street and to Christmas drinks with the Foreign Secretary, thanks to his dad who was the Deputy Ambassador to Buenos Aires. Jake had spent his childhood in boarding school so he was as at ease in the corridors of Welton as he was in his bedroom at home, more so, in fact, because his father's postings meant that his bedroom changed on average every three years. When Jake had embraced her in his muscular arms at the Christmas sixth-form dance she had swooned like a Victorian heroine. They made the school's hottest couple.

However, when Jake had appeared on the doorstep that afternoon, she had felt an emotion approximate to horror. If only she had known that he was coming! It would have been so much easier to send him an email telling him that she had met someone else.

Jo had proved the antidote to Jake. Jo didn't think that talking about herself constituted a conversation and when she asked what Hope wanted in bed she actually meant it. Jo never watched football on TV or indeed any sport at all. Jo, to celebrate their first time in bed together, had got up and made them ice-cream sundaes, which she described as her signature blend of vanilla ice cream, a blob of peanut butter, a splurge of chocolate fudge sauce and a broken-up bar of Cadbury's Dairy Milk, all piled in a bowl and microwaved for thirty seconds. As Hope had sucked on a half-melted chocolate chunk she realised what a fool she had been to hanker after Jake. Or any boy at all. After so long fighting it, after so many months of wondering why time spent with Jo was so much better than with anyone else, one embrace had ended all the years of never feeling right, of always feel-ing different, of doing things with Jake and with other boys because it was expected. She had told herself that in time she would feel normal like everyone else seemed to do. But she never had ... until she met Jo.

Now Jake was trying to kiss her neck. 'No!' she said firmly. There was the sound of someone coming in the back door. 'My dad's down-stairs.'

She had to tell him. Jo would be arriving any minute now. And once she told him she needed to move the place cards. Mummy had put her next to Jake and put Jo next to Alexis, her old room-mate at Welton, who had enormous boobs and worked at Sotheby's. It was all wrong.

Your twenty-first was supposed to be the most wonderful day of your life. Or the second. The best was your wedding. Or was it the day your first baby got born? At any rate, she was beginning to realise why all those brides got so stressed out. Jake was reaching for her waistband.

'Baby, you have such a great ass ...'

When had he learned these ridiculous lines? From an American girl, obviously.

She pushed him away.

'Please ...'

'*Please,*' he repeated suggestively. 'Are you begging for it?'

It was hopeless. Mummy would have known what to do in this situation. Mummy was good at difficult conversations, like complaining in restaurants and taking things back to shops. But Mummy wasn't here. It was all Hope could do to straighten her clothes, grab her handbag and bolt for the door. It was as she was out of the door and on the landing that she saw Daddy and The Moose coming up the stairs. Oh God! Not now. Not now for the stiff exchange of hollow pleasantries that constituted her conversations with Sally. Later she would make an effort. So for now she raised her best smile and said 'Hi' as brightly as she could before bolting down the stairs in search of Jo and a plan of action.

As they ascended the stairs Hope hurtled past them, a boy in tow. Sally could hardly dare look at Edward's face. Hope looked flushed, the boy looked dishevelled and it would require a parent to go beyond psychological denial into the realms of a coma not to deduce exactly what they had been doing before they burst out of Hope's room. She felt a surge of justified anger as her stepdaughter raised barely a cursory 'Hi' in her direction. Edward, who thought Hope had the character of an angel and the private life of a saint, could hardly excuse such blatant rudeness.

As Edward pushed open the door to the spare bedroom and fumbled for the light switch she said, 'I think Hope could have said hello. And introduced that boy.'

He paused. 'That's Jake. It's a big night for her. She's bound to be preoccupied.'

Apparently it didn't require a coma to be blind to the bloody obvious. But before she could respond Edward moved swiftly across the room, tossed his jacket onto the bed and opened the far door.

'We added the shower room when we extended the kitchen.'

It was a typical spare bedroom. Furnished with G-plan veneer, carpeted in faded blue, wallpapered in large pink roses.

'Laura Ashley,' she guessed out loud.

'Sanderson.' His voice could be heard from the bathroom.

Of course, he probably papered it himself. She opened the wardrobe and hung up his tuxedo, dress shirt and her dress from the suit bag. Then she sat down on the squishy double bed. Edward had emerged and appeared preoccupied with the tasks at hand.

'OK. I need to take a shower and change. And work out what I'm going to say tonight.'

'Say tonight?' she repeated, confused.

'I have to make the speech,' he explained, rifling through their overnight case for his wash bag. 'Pia wrote it. She says there's a copy in the blue folder.' He gestured to the file now lying on the spare room bed.

'Pia wrote a speech for you?' she said, stunned.

'Yes,' Edward confirmed distractedly.

'Why did you ask Pia? Why didn't you ask me to do it?' she protested.

He sighed. 'I didn't ask Pia. She took it upon herself. Anyway,' he continued reasonably, 'I haven't got time to write anything else so we may as well use it. What does it say?'

Unbidden, some residual professional impulse took over. She began looking through the folder. There were pages and pages of spreadsheets and timetables; menus; the playlist of music for the evening; contact telephone numbers; lists of hotels that guests were staying in; and names and numbers of the taxi firms that had been booked for 3.00 a.m. Sally saw to her dismay that Pia had placed her between Evelyn and Gabriel.

She located the speech.

It was typed and double-spaced. She picked it up nervously as if Pia's disembodied voice might suddenly emerge from its pages. *Put That Down!*

At the top Pia had written a pencilled note to herself.

Check that Rufus is in position to pull cord on panel.

'What's the panel?' she asked Edward.

'Oh, there's a fake panel at the back of the Main Hall. After the speech it falls away to reveal the dance floor. It's a surprise,' he added unnecessarily.

'Do you want to hear the speech?' she asked.

'Yep.'

'OK.' She cleared her throat. 'Months of planning, weeks of preparations and twenty-one years have led up to this evening. And every one of those twenty-one years have been a blessing to us. Every parent thinks that their child is wonderful. Well, we know that she is!

'Hope, you look beautiful tonight. But those of us who have had the pleasure and the privilege to watch you grow up know that your beauty is both inside and out. You are a loving daughter, a watchful sister, a dutiful granddaughter and a true friend to so many here tonight.

'You are our shining star.'

Abruptly, reading that sentence, Sally realised that she could not imagine Pia writing the equivalent speech about Dan. On the couple of occasions she had seen them together they appeared so distanced from each other. She read on.

'I want to share a story that says so much about you, Hope.'

She put the paper down. It was hopeless to concentrate. 'Edward, I really don't want to sit on the top table. In fact ...'

He looked up. His voice was curt. 'Look, I want you there. Why not? Anyhow, it's not a top table. It's a round one just like all the others. Pia thought a top table was too stuffy.'

When had Edward and Pia discussed all this?

'Besides, we're two people down,' he continued, 'Pia's mother's not coming either.'

At last – some good news. The absence of Pia's mother was some small, secret relief. 'Are you sure Evelyn's not coming?'

'No. Apparently she's taken a Valium and she's flat out.'

She wished Edward would sit down. It was one thing to be there with Pia – quite another to be there without her. She felt like a usurper, stepping publicly into the shoes of her incapacitated predecessor, the villain of the piece. It was almost Shakespearian. She pictured herself, dagger in hand, sitting at the feast table, Pia's ghost floating about the newly revealed dance floor.

The nagging thought that had been growing in her mind since she walked into the house grew louder. Why didn't she just leave? Get up, take her bag and go? There were no rules in this situation, no precedent or convention that governed conduct by a second wife in the event of a first wife's heart attack. Edward could manage perfectly well alone; Hope would obviously be happier without her; no one would even notice let alone regret her absence.

She continued, 'And I really think I should just drive home afterwards.' She took a breath. 'Or even before. Soon. Now.'

'You're my wife,' Edward responded. 'I want you here.'

'It doesn't feel right!' she protested. 'What will people say?'

Edward was dismissive. 'To hell with them. Let them say what they like. It's none of their business. What does the rest of the speech say?'

She turned over the neatly typed double-spaced page.

He was still searching through the wash bag. 'I can't find my studs.'

'I gave them to you before you left. I put them in your jacket pocket so they wouldn't get lost.'

It was always this way. No conversation between them could be concluded these days. Louis would start whining or the telephone would ring or Edward would be making a dash for the door lest his missed his train or plane or meeting. They lived in a permanent state of interrupted speech.

She reached over and took the wallet from his suit jacket. Perhaps the studs had become embedded in that? As she unfolded the wallet a slip of paper floated to the ground.

Edward saw it and stepped forward to grasp it.

'What's that?' she asked.

'Nothing.' He was folding it now.

It was so unlike him. He looked distinctly shifty. 'Edward. What is it?'

'It's just a receipt,' he said quickly.

'What for?'

'Nothing.'

Now he was being ridiculous. 'So you paid for nothing.'

'It's not important.'

'So tell me what it is!'

'Look, it doesn't matter.'

She was getting really irritated now. They were going round and round in circles. It was like talking to Louis.

She took it out of his hand. Short of fighting her for it he had no choice but to let it go. She saw first the name at the top – The Compleat Angler – and then the amount below. She was at first unable to believe the evidence in her hand. 'You paid this! You told me Pia was paying for it!'

'She was …' His voice trailed off.

It was inexplicable. 'So why did you pay?'

'She was hardly in a position to do anything ...'

Sally relaxed. 'So she's going to pay you back?'

He said nothing.

'Edward?'

'Look, it's not that much. Not in the scale of things. I think I should make a contribution.'

I should? She was dumbfounded. 'It's a *huge* amount. It's virtually a month's mortgage payment.'

'That's how much any decent meal out costs these days. Three courses with wine – and there were eight of us,' Edward added as if by way of mitigation.

She looked again at the receipt. Thoughts of what the money could buy them flooded her mind. First and foremost a holiday. Maybe not abroad but an off-season cottage by the coast for a week. Definitely a decent haircut, proper highlights and some bloody clothes. 'It's a fortune! Why did you have to offer?'

He looked rattled. 'What did you want me to do? Sit there in front of my children and my parents, sitting on my hands while my ex-wife paid for lunch. It's humiliating. '

She had never felt so angry with him. 'So your pride is more important than our financial future! What about me and Louis?'

'Sally, we'll be fine.' Why did he have to sound so blasé?

'It's not fair,' she ran on, smarting. 'If you were going to pay then you should have chosen the restaurant.' She was livid now as the implications hit home. 'And I should have been invited.'

Edward turned away. 'Look, do we have to discuss this now? I need to get downstairs.'

His attempt to end the discussion infuriated her. 'Oh yes. To run Pia's party for her. Why don't you call her and ask her if there's any-thing else she needs doing?' Why had this conversation led her to plumbing the depths of bitter sarcasm? Whatever the reason, she just couldn't help herself. 'Maybe the gutters on the house need clearing out? Or the oil on her car needs changing? She could make you a list of jobs.' It was as if years of pent-up jealousy and frustration had been released.

She took her dress out of the wardrobe.

'What are you doing?' he asked.

'What does it look like?' she fumed.

Home beckoned, with the comforts of her own bed, a bar of Dairy Milk and E.D. Irvine.

Edward moved over to her and put his hand on her arm. 'Sally, you knew I had a family when you married me.' Clearly he had decided to shift the ground.

But she had not known the full implications of that. She knew that Edward had a wife and family. She had thought, vaguely and naively, that there would be a limited amount of contact on specified occasions for set periods of time: Speech Day, Christmas Eve and Father's Day, for example.

He turned away and she knew he wanted to leave it there. And usually she would have complied. But today she was beside herself. She attached her dress back into the suit carrier.

'And you knew that we would have a family, too,' she countered. 'What are we – the Number Two Family?'

'Of course not.'

'Well, that's how it feels.' Her voice rose impassioned. 'Why should you feel guilty? Why do you have to be the one to put it all right? Pia wanted the separation. What were you supposed to do? Wait in the wings while she decided if she wanted to be married or not?'

'I know,' he said quietly. 'Look, can't we just leave this for now and pull together for Hope's sake?'

She could not help herself. 'As if she appreciates it.'

She could almost see him bristle. She had crossed the line. Edward would never entertain a word against Hope.

But a burning sense of injustice fuelled her words. 'She barely acknowledged me when I came in today. And what about Louis's party? I sent an invitation to Hope and I haven't even had a reply.'

Edward shrugged. 'She's a student. All kids are unreliable like that. She has a lot of work to do.'

'You'll find any excuse! There's no reason why Hope can't come to Louis's party and you know it. The truth is she doesn't want to.'

'It's not surprising that she feels awkward,' said Edward stiffly. 'She didn't ask for any of this.'

She saw Edward's mouth set in a hard line. They had reached an impasse. She zipped up the suit carrier.

His voice contained a note of bewilderment that she had never heard before. 'I thought you liked Hope.'

Did she? The reality was that she hardly knew her. Her whole relationship with Hope felt fake – every interaction mannered and calculated, every word and gesture carefully considered.

She tried to sound sincere. 'Of course I do …'

'Then what's the problem?' Edward sat down on the bed. He sounded genuinely confused. 'Why do you care so much about what everyone thinks? So what if they don't think you should be here? To hell with them.' He looked up at her. 'You're my wife, I love you. I want you here. Why isn't that enough?'

And she realised then that he was genuinely baffled.

He stared at her, his uncomprehending expression indicating that this was her problem. And in that moment she knew it *was* her problem, not in the sense that she had invented it – rather that this was something that they could never share because their perspective was so irreconcilably different. Edward could move effortlessly between his two families, bound to Pia, Hope and Dan by ties of blood and history stretching back more than two decades. Whereas Sally was destined to be the perpetual outsider, the imagined destroyer of all that had gone before, at best tolerated and at worst despised. How could he understand her reaction of fear, suspicion and outright jealousy towards those he had loved for so long?

She sat down next to him. 'I don't belong here, Edward. And what's more, no one wants me here.'

'That's nonsense.'

'No. It's not. I'm here because I'm married to you – and you're here because this is your family. You're the common factor – that's why you feel comfortable with all of us.'

Her words hung in the air.

'Can't you be friends at least? With Hope?' He ran a hand through his hair and said as if to himself, 'And God knows, Dan needs someone.'

'I'm not sure Hope even wants that.'

There was a protracted pause. She felt her stomach form a knot. Then he said sadly, 'Maybe not.'

It wasn't much. It was the faintest acknowledgement that he had ever made of the truth. But it was a faint crack in the façade he had maintained for the duration of their marriage and it was enough for her to look at her husband, to see the tiredness in his face and to lose all resistance in the face of his next words.

'Please, Sally. Please don't go. I need you.'

She got up, reached for the suit bag and unzipped it to take out her dress.

The garage was cold but it was safer than going to his bedroom and not as cold as the garden. Pascoe passed Dan the joint. He gave Dan a sly smile. 'So, I get to come to the party after all.'

It gave them a buzz. Pascoe, having been banned by his mother, was now under her roof smoking dope and eating pilfered chocolate brownies. Dan inhaled, moving away from the closed door to the kitchen in case some of the smoke wafted under the doorway. It was all a joke. One big joke. A flashy party to show everyone what a great family they were. The truth of it was that they weren't a family at all.

Pascoe had told him that he came from a fucked-up family. His dad had a secret girlfriend and his mum took prescription painkillers she bought from a woman she met up with at a multi-storey car park in High Wycombe. Sometimes she took Pascoe in the car with her. Now, the more he thought about it, Dan realised that his family was fucked up, too. They were just a bunch of hypocrites. They never told you anything – and when they finally did tell you something they lied about it. And they acted like they were so much better than everyone else.

His mum told him that Roger was 'just a friend' long after he had found the condoms in her bedside drawer. She had promised him after his dad left that 'nothing was going to change'. It did. He would be going to Welton two years earlier than planned.

'In the Lower School, darling. So you have time to make more friends.'

So much for her promises. And now she was hiding her plans to sell the house. He'd found the estate agents' valuations in her desk drawer.

She'd even lied about the heart attack. 'Illness is all in the mind,' she always said. 'I don't allow myself to get ill.' Clearly that strategy had stopped working. In the last couple of years he'd stopped listening to half of what she said anyway. Like when she lit up. 'Now don't you start smoking! If I'd known then what I know now I would never have started. Of course, we didn't know the risks then.'

They were all just a bloody bunch of liars. Except Hope. Hope was like him, pretending to have a good time tonight even though Jake was pissed off at having flown back for nothing and there was no time to change the seating so they had to sit next to each other. There had nearly been a bust up in the Chill Out Zone.

'Have a nice life, Hope,' Jake had spat at her and Jo looked like she wanted to hit him. Hope had been close to tears. He had pulled her to one side and she had wept onto his shoulder.

'I just wish Mummy had *told* me. And I wish she was *here*! Instead of *her*.'

He'd given her a brotherly hug and then asked her if she had any money and she had given him enough to buy some ciggies off one of the waiters.

But Hope was wrong about Sally. Sally was no problem. Sally was a pushover. Sally could barely keep tabs on a two-year-old. In fact, going back to Wimbledon with her and Dad could turn out to be the best thing that had happened to him for a long time.

As she sat alone at the table, Sally saw out of the corner of her eye a woman in a very tight long evening dress advancing purposefully towards her. Instinctively she hoped she would go away. The table was deserted, Gabriel and his friend on the dance floor and Edward nowhere to be seen. He had got up half an hour ago. 'I'll just check on the fireworks. Back in five minutes.'

The woman came up to her and held out her hand. 'I'm Marion. You must be Sally.'

Sally's expression must have shown her confusion.

'Pia and I go back a long way.' Something in Marion's tone said that this was code for a role as Pia's confidante.

Sally's heart sank. 'Oh.'

Marion looked out into the room. 'Fabulous, isn't it?'

It was impossible not to agree because it *was* fabulous. The caterers were starting to set up the breakfast. Testament to the success of the party was the fact that at nearly 2.00 a.m. barely anyone had left.

Marion sat down and lit a cigarette.

'Pia told Hope that it was cold salmon to start and then chicken pies.' Marion gave a hoot of laughter and took a sip of wine. 'Can you imagine! *Boring!*' Sally guessed that Marion must spend an awful lot of time in the gym, interspersed with sessions on a sun bed, because the strapless ice-blue dress she wore showed admirably slim and toned arms. She felt like a frog sitting next to a princess.

'Poor Pia,' Marion continued. 'Still, it must be a bit of a relief to you really.'

'A relief?'

'Oh, come on!' said Marion, rolling her eyes. 'You don't have to pretend. It must be awkward.'

'I just hope Pia gets well as soon as possible.' This was true, too.

Marion's expression was one of amused disbelief. 'I suppose it takes some guts to be here. I'm not sure that I would have shown my face. Still, times have moved on, I suppose – easy come, easy go.'

It was an echo of Gabriel's words to her as they had mingled before dinner.

I think in your position I might have passed on this one. Better for all concerned ... She had caught the draught of alcohol on his breath. *It is, after all, Pia's party.*

Later she wondered why she had not thought to correct him and say that surely it was Hope's party. Unless it was because he was right? He had gone on patronisingly to advise her to *keep a low profile* and *be aware of the sensitivities.*

Sally was not going to be caught again in the same conversation. She stood up. 'You'll have to excuse me.'

Marion looked contrite. 'I'm sorry. Really. Have I offended you?' She got up, too. 'There's no need to bolt.'

'I'm not *bolting*. I'm going to find my husband.'

Marion laughed. 'Well, you need to keep an eye on him.'

'That's isn't what I meant.'

God Almighty, if she wasn't careful this woman was going to provoke a scene.

'You'll have to excuse me.'

She walked away as briskly as she could past the clutter of chairs towards the entrance and through the reception area. People were gathered around the photo collage, glasses in hand, admiring the pictures of Hope – by a sandcastle, on a pony, in a tutu. Edward was pictured with his arm round her on a beach somewhere. At least there were no pictures of the four of them. Marion kept a determined pace at her side. Her voice was low and conversational. 'Why don't we stop and look at the photos? They're printed onto the canvas – so clever.'

'I know.'

'The family looks so happy!'

She resisted pointing out that Pia was hardly likely to have selected shots depicting them looking bloody miserable.

Where on earth was Edward? She wasn't sure exactly where she was going. She contemplated heading off down the garden in search of him. But some instinct steered her away from venturing into the cold darkness with Marion at her heels. She could go to the loo – but that risked being stuck in a confined space with her or, worse still, overheard. Marion was still at her shoulder. Surely she wouldn't follow her into the house?

'Goodbye,' she said with as much finality as she could muster, pushing open the kitchen door.

Marion followed. She found herself alone with Marion in the kitchen.

She was unnerved. 'What do you want?'

Marion squared up to her. 'Let me speak plainly, Sally. Don't you feel ashamed?'

'Ashamed?'

'Yes. Stepping into the shoes of a critically ill woman. Poor Pia! She could be dying as we speak.'

Either Marion was drunk or she was high on melodrama.

'From what I understand her condition is stable.'

'From what you understand?' mimicked Marion. 'But you don't *know* that, do you? And given that you don't know how Pia is, the proper thing would have been to stay away.'

She had had quite enough of Marion and Gabriel, of Hope and Pia. It was time to take a stand.

'No. I think the proper thing is to support my husband. And not to be attacked for doing so.'

Marion gave a hollow laugh. 'What did you expect? A fanfare? You've brought this on yourself. Edward was married to Pia when you started seeing him – if "seeing" is the right word – I can think of other words for what you did.'

The woman was outrageous. 'Look, I don't know who you are

or why you think you have any right to speak to me like that. My marriage is none of your business.'

'A pity you didn't take the same attitude with Pia and Edward.'

'They were separated when I met Edward,' Sally shot back.

'They would have got back together.'

'No, I don't think so,' she insisted, though she had thought exactly that, many times.

'Of course you don't. You'd have to live with the guilt. Look at poor Dan – that boy is a lost soul.'

Sally was incredulous. 'Surely you're not trying to blame me for that?'

Marion looked unfazed. 'Do you think that would have happened if his parents hadn't broken up? They were getting professional help. They were working through their issues. Pia just wanted a break. Well of course, like a typical man Edward couldn't bear to be by himself. So he turned to the nearest soft place to land.'

Sally wanted to slap her. She knew she should walk away. Even though she knew that Marion was oblivious to any opinion but her own she was compelled to defend herself. 'But she asked him to leave the house!'

'Yes,' Marion said matter-of-factly. 'Because she needed some space. Look, there's clearly something you need to know. Before Edward slipped between the sheets with you there was never any talk of divorce. None at all! Until you appeared and in a puff of smoke Edward was off. It was very sudden and very ill-considered.' Marion waved her hand around the kitchen. 'Look at this. This is a shared life, Sally. This is the result of years and years together – friendships. Holidays. A life. Look how Edward has just come in tonight and taken over. That's because he used to live here, this was his home. It's as if he never left.'

The woman was awful. But Sally had had all the same thoughts herself.

Marion was unstoppable now. 'Sometimes the truth hurts. Well, the fact is Edward was always devoted to Pia – until you came along. And why wouldn't he be? She's an amazing woman. She's organised all of this, single-handedly – and paid for it. She's the perfect wife.'

'If that were true they'd still be together.'

'If he hadn't met you they would be,' Marion concluded. 'I know both of them. I've known them for over twenty years. And let me tell you this: I've seen more than one couple rush to get divorced – and then remarry when they come to their senses.'

Marion strode to the kitchen door. She opened it slightly then turned. 'Why don't you just slip away? Don't worry – no one would notice that you had gone.'

And then, having secured the last word, she went back into the garden, slamming the door behind her.

In the darkened kitchen, Sally could hear the sounds of the music from the disco and raised boisterous voices from the garden. If Marion hadn't suggested slipping away then she probably would have done just that. But she was damned if she was going to let the woman run her off. From upstairs she could hear muffled thumps and she thought she could hear voices coming from the garage, presumably teenagers sneaking off from their parents.

Never had she felt more acutely her position as an outsider. She ful-filled no role at Hope's party beyond that of consort to her husband.

Then, in the still surroundings of Pia's house, she suddenly under-stood that this powerless position was how it had always been for Bella Latham. First the dutiful daughter; next the sidelined stepdaughter; then the submissive Victorian wife?

God, what if she and Hope had to live together? She could almost wince at how oppressive it would be for the two of them to find themselves in the same circumstances as Bella and the new Duchess: forced to live under the same roof, in a house formerly occupied by a first wife, and confined in the country for days and weeks on end. No wonder the new Duchess set about changing everything; she needed to erase the reminders of her predecessor. But for Bella it must have been still worse: a forceful new stepmother and three new sisters.

Who, in such an unhappy domestic situation, wouldn't seek out a confidante – an ally – a correspondent, so that at least a letter or even a visit would serve to break the loneliness of the day? And how easy it would be to imagine a better life with that person …

But you knew what you were getting yourself into. Her mother had said that once, with a trace of criticism in her voice, when they had been boxing up wedding cake and Sally had complained about Hope's tight-lipped expression throughout the wedding and the fact that neither Hope nor Dan had given them a wedding present. But she hadn't known, not really, and she suspected that Bella hadn't either. Now, in Pia's kitchen, it was almost as if Sally could summon up Bella's growing disillusionment. The more she thought about it, the more certain she felt that Hart was right – *Letters* was a load of old tosh. The real story between Bella and Robert was harsher; their supposed love story was a convenient escape for each of them; it was an arrangement born of need and circumstance.

'No one worked as hard as me at Selton Park. That's the life of a scullery maid, you see. Now the copper pans, they were the devil. You used soft soap, water and sand for the insides. If there was a party you could be up until all hours doing those pans with the water running cold. But even if you went to bed at four you still had to be up at six to light the range and God help you if Cook didn't get her cup of tea on a tray at seven sharp. In the afternoons Cook set me sharpening the kitchen knives and cleaning the blades. You used emery board for that. I did her boots, too. You girls don't have the foggiest how to clean.

The new Duchess? Well, that set tongues wagging. The Duke married again and the old Duchess scarcely cold in her grave. But that's the rich for you. They're a law unto themselves. It meant more work. She brought her three daughters with her so there were three more to feed every day. And then she started up the house parties every weekend. Actresses and high-ups came and it all had to be just so.

The Duchess brought her own Cook and Housekeeper. She wanted everything changed, you see. That ruffled some feathers. Some of the old staff gave their notice. But the new housekeeper, Mrs Lyndon, took a shine to me. She could see I was a worker and she moved me up to work in the house. I was made an under housemaid.

I remember that first day. The second housemaid took me with her to clean the morning room. Don't touch anything, she said. How was I sup-posed to clean without touching anything? She made me get down and sweep the carpets. In those days all we had were tea leaves, you spread them out to catch the dust and swept them up. That was the first time I saw the India painting! Oh, it was lovely! There were elephants and mountains, officers on horses and little dark boys in white tunics carry-ing baskets of fruit and stone jars. I thought the jars would be filled with wine. Everything was beautiful. The carpets were peacock blue and the curtains; I can see them today, matching blue silk with yellow trim. There were two big glass doors leading out into the conservatory. She opened them and oh, you can't imagine! The scent of those lilies, wafting in.

She was never happy. Always chopping and changing and decorating perfectly good rooms. And the money she spent! She had Mr Jackson the artist come down from London and I had to clean up after him, too. More sweeping and dusting and all the regular work to do as well. That's when I met John. He was assistant to Mr Jackson.

They were there for three months painting the conservatory. The Duchess wanted an Italian scene. If she could have done she would have had the India Panel whitewashed. It reminded her of the first Duchess. So she did the next best thing and had her own painting done. John painted all the balcony – the balustrade, that's the proper name for it – and the trees and the steamship. But he never got any credit for it. John was an artist. If he'd had an education he could have done paintings in frames and sold them. But you had to have money in those days to get anywhere.

Where was I? Oh, yes. The cleaning. In the afternoon you had to get all the bedrooms straight and the fires lit by five o'clock so it was warmed up for them to change for dinner. But I was used to it by then. I was always eager to learn. But you couldn't show that you knew anything at all. If you got a reputation for being clever they'd decide you were a trouble-maker. Then they'd find some excuse to get rid of you.

One day John brought me some raspberries left over from Mr Jackson's lunch tray. Mr Jackson liked to eat on a tray in the conservatory so he could look at what he'd done. Mr Jackson wasn't much of a talker; he walked around with his head in the clouds. They were in a proper little crystal bowl. He hadn't touched them. We sat on the kitchen step and ate them. God knows how, I was always working, but we must have found a minute. It was a nice little sun-trap on that step. George the footman saw us and told the butler. The butler called me in and made me stand in front of his desk and told me how I could get the sack over that. In their book it was stealing. I said sorry, acting all humble like. But I didn't mean it. He was miffed he didn't get them for himself!

But most of the time I kept myself to myself. Mrs Morrow had told me to keep my head down and that is what I did. In the second year I went to see Joseph. If I could have taken him away I would. But where would we have gone? So I sent Mrs Morrow what I could and she made sure he had some extras.'

Chapter 13

Edward and Dan arrived home at six o'clock, half an hour after the last of Louis's birthday party guests had departed. There had been four and a half guests: her parents; Vickie and Rory; and Anna the neighbour. Edward had sworn to her last night that he would make it back with Dan. Edward's parents had called earlier in the day to say that yesterday had been 'very tiring' and they wouldn't be coming after all. Two of the playgroup mothers called to cancel – full-blown tonsillitis and a chicken pox scare respectively. Brickie was delayed in Wiltshire at a house party. Hope never did RSVP.

Edward had telephoned intermittently, distractedly saying on each occasion that he hoped to leave soon. But clearly not soon enough.

Anna had been drafted in at the last minute. Sally had gone down to the basement flat and knocked on the door. Quickly Anna had flung open the door and for a split second her face had fallen. Sally had the distinct impression that Anna, dressed at 11 a.m. in expensive-looking silky pink pyjamas with red piping, had been hoping to open the door to someone else.

So it had been a surprise when Anna had accepted the invitation after an initial hesitation. 'I may need to work ... No! Forget that. I'd love to come. Do I need to bring a present?'

'God, no.' Sally had felt embarrassed. She had scarcely given Anna any notice. 'Just bring yourself. That's all that matters,' she said truthfully.

Anna had arrived on the dot, holding two large wrapped presents and a card in a bright red envelope, which opened to reveal a pop-up dinosaur. The present was a plastic Pirate Ship and an accompanying Castle.

'I ran down to Tesco,' Anna explained. 'I wasn't sure which one was better so I got both. If they're no good I can give you the receipt.'

'No! They're perfect. And very generous.'

The pirate ship was an instant hit with Louis. He abandoned Vickie's present, a hand-painted wooden xylophone, and turned his attention to lining up pirates. Anna, in turn, had been a hit with her father as soon as he found out that she used to make films for *The Holiday Programme*. They had discussed motoring holidays through the South of France whilst sitting together on the living-room floor assembling the ship and castle.

'I saw the Carcassonne one,' he exclaimed. 'Fancy that. You must be a very clever girl.'

If Anna minded being referred to like this she didn't show it.

'So what's Natasha Webster really like?' cut in her mother.

Vickie struck the only note of discord when she was alone with Sally in the kitchen setting out the birthday tea. 'Two presents! Don't you think it's a little over the top?' she whispered as she watched Sally turn out a red jelly in the shape of a rabbit. 'It's almost as if she's got something to prove. I think single girls get like that after a certain age. They need to compensate for not having a man.'

Sally did not respond. She was just grateful for Anna's presence. Before Anna's arrival she had felt self-conscious and awkward, holding the fort single-handedly. Anna and her BBC anecdotes were a welcome diversion.

'I don't think Edward's going to make it,' she confided to Vickie. Vickie pursed her lips disapprovingly. At Rory's party, Vickie's husband had patrolled with a camcorder and then donned a Scooby-Doo outfit to hand out party bags.

Later, over tea, Vickie had talked for too long about her old job as an account manager for a national newspaper. It had been a relief when she and a grizzling Rory got up to leave. Anna left soon after and then it was just her parents. They sat in the living room; her parents on the sofa and Sally on the armchair, arranged in a worshipful arc watching Louis play with his ship.

'It's a shame Edward isn't here,' said her mother for the second time.

'Yes. It is.'

They had left shortly before Edward's eventual arrival, which was heralded by the sound of Dan crashing through the door, tossing his holdall carelessly down so that it thumped against the wall, marking a faint black line on the paintwork. Louis looked up and hurtled up the hall ecstatically.

Edward swept him up. He could not fail to notice the deliberate chill with which Sally greeted him but affected not to notice. 'Have you made up the bed in the spare room?'

'Yes,' she said coldly. Clearly it was no longer to be known as her future office.

While Edward went upstairs with Dan, she stayed downstairs to clear away the party food. Louis was playing with the red fire engine given to him by her parents. He made a noise that was an approximation of a siren, *Heeee Heeee*, as he pushed it along the floor. Most of the cake and the jelly remained. She'd given an entire plate of egg mayonnaise sandwiches to her parents to take home. The second roll of camera film she had optimistically purchased sat unopened. There were only so many photographs one could take of five adults and two children.

Eventually Edward came down.

She was surprised to realise that she didn't even feel angry any more. Just resigned to the situation. 'Where were you?'

'I'm sorry.' He didn't sound it. He poured himself a glass of wine. 'It just took longer than I expected.'

It felt as though they were going through the motions. 'Well, why?'

He sighed. 'We had breakfast and then the caterers had to pack up. Rufus turned up at noon for the marquee – it takes time to take all that down, you can imagine. Then I had to get them all out of the house and get it cleaned up.'

Even though she knew that was what had happened, hearing it from Edward still irritated her. 'Cleaned up?'

'Yes. Can you imagine what it looked like after ten teenagers had camped out? And then we had to go to see Pia.'

That was the limit.

'You mean you were with her this afternoon?'

'Yes. Hope and Dan wanted to see her.'

'And you had to go too?'

'Yes. I had to bring them back afterwards. There's next to no public transport on a Sunday.'

'Why couldn't your parents take them?'

'Because they're babysitting Evelyn. She's not coping very well and she's threatening to leave the old people's home and install herself at Pia's.'

'And what about us? What about Louis's party?'

'Look, I'm sorry. Really. But there was absolutely nothing that I could do about it. Besides, it's not as if Louis noticed.'

'That's not the point,' she protested. 'The point is you were supposed to be here. With me!'

'I know. What did you expect me to do?'

She knew that was what he would say. This time she was prepared. 'Couldn't you delegate? Surely someone else could have dealt with this. What about Pia's friends? What about Gabriel?'

'Gabriel! Gabriel couldn't pack a suitcase. And actually Marion was there. She helped with the clean-up.'

It was like a pack of cards falling. How much worse could this get?

'What did she say?'

He looked perplexed. 'Say?'

'Yes. Say!'

Louis looked up.

'Look, keep your voice down. She didn't say anything. Just forget about her.'

It was exactly what Edward had said the night before when, at 4.00 a.m., they had got into Pia's spare bed and she had reported her encounter with Marion. 'Forget about her. She's a nutter,' he'd said dismissively before falling asleep almost instantaneously.

'Sal, we were working! Picking up rubbish, hoovering, clearing up. It was a clean-up not a party.'

'No,' she said cuttingly. 'The party was here.'

'I'm sorry,' he said angrily. 'Hell, what do you want me to do?'

'I want you to be here …' she snapped, raising her voice in response, ' … when you say you're going to be. I want to be able to rely on you.'

'You can rely on me,' he protested. 'This is hardly normal. It's a one-off crisis.'

That fact appeared to ignore Dan installed upstairs.

'And that's another thing,' she added, lowering her voice. 'We need to talk about Dan. Have you spoken to him?'

'Yes. And I've made it very clear that we won't tolerate any drug use. He's got to keep his head down and toe the line. Anyway, it's not as if he knows anyone around here. He was getting this stuff from Pascoe. Now that they're separated hopefully the problem will resolve itself.'

'Maybe it will,' she said not totally convinced. 'When is Pia going to be home?'

'She sees the consultant tomorrow. I'm sure he'll discharge her.'

'So she seemed better?'

He shrugged. 'She insists there's nothing wrong with her. But none of the staff are prepared to say anything until she sees the consultant. Then they'll make a decision.'

'But they're bound to discharge her?'

They had to discharge her. Dan needed to go home, too. And she wanted her husband back. For once, NHS bed shortages seemed like a good thing. Not that she actually wanted Pia to suffer. Far from it, she wanted her up and about and restored to full health in Gerrards Cross with her children around her.

'Good.' She tried to sound upbeat. But it was hard not to feel that this weekend represented a watershed in their marriage, the first time they had been challenged and failed to stand shoulder to shoulder, their reactions dictated by differing perspectives and loyalties. With hindsight, she regretted staying for Hope's party. It had depleted her. What had seemed at the time a magnanimous gesture now appeared to her foolish weakness. It did not feel as though Edward appreciated her sacrifice. On the contrary, by his non-appearance at Louis's party he had come close to humiliating her. At that moment she could not see how the tensions between them arising from the legacy of his first marriage would ever be healed. It was a depressing thought.

Edward moved towards her, putting down his glass on the kitchen counter. 'What are you thinking?'

'Nothing.' She looked deliberately at her watch. As he came to stand in front of her she anticipated his embrace and sidestepped it. 'It's late. I need to give Louis his bath.' And she walked past him, avoiding his gaze.

Dan crept back upstairs. Sally and his dad were talking in low, urgent voices in the kitchen. Pascoe said that was always a good time to get under the radar – when your parents were debating the best way to deal with you – like in the army, attacking when your enemy was facing the other way.

Dan pulled out his mobile. Bugger! There was no reception. Now he recalled his dad saying that his mobile didn't work in the house.

He thought for a moment, then picked up the extension phone. It was riskier than the mobile but there wasn't any choice.

Pascoe's mother answered.

She sounded distracted. 'I'll get him for you.' Then a trace of suspicion entered her voice. 'Who shall I say is calling?'

'Johnny.'

Contact between them had been forbidden. Hence a code was necessary. Dan was Johnny. Pascoe was Sid.

'I'll just get him for you.'

There was a delay while she shouted for Pascoe and he retrieved the phone, taking it up to his bedroom. A door closed and Dan could hear music in the background.

'Hey, Johnny.' Pascoe sounded as cool as ever. 'How's it going?' There was a click as Pascoe's mother replaced her handset. Pascoe had warned him ages ago to wait for that. It was why they preferred using the mobiles but Pascoe's had been confiscated. As if that would make any difference.

'It's going—'

'Woof, woof.'

It was their private joke, one of many. Pascoe said they had been quarantined like a pair of dogs.

'Can you get there?'

'Yeah. No problem.' His dad would be at work and Sally wouldn't notice if he was beamed up in a space ship.

'OK. Twelve o'clock. By the Starbucks at the front of Victoria Station.'

Dan couldn't hear the voices any more. 'I've got to go.'

'Don't be late. Oh and Johnny – don't forget your pocket money.'

Her neighbour's birthday party had been a revelation. It had been fun. It was proof that she was not the workaholic killjoy of Tim's imagination. Sally was friendly, her parents were really genuine and Louis was sweet. Vickie was a bit of a bore but that was how these stay-at-home mothers could be – they lost their social skills after a while. It had, nonetheless, been a disappointment to return to her flat and find that Tim had not called. But Anna was damned if she would call him. Look where that kind of weakness had got Penny! The woman was a walking warning to single women everywhere. Tim had walked out and so, on principle, he should walk back in again. Besides which it was a very good thing that Anna had ignored his advice and gone down to see Penny. She had learned a lot. Now the only question on her mind was whether at five o'clock on a Sunday afternoon she should go down to Beaconsfield to see the Zarkoskys herself. But they would probably be at church or visiting the sick? She pulled out her mobile to call Ethne before remembering that she didn't have any reception so she pulled on her coat and walked out of the flat to try and find a signal.

Penny Anderson had cast things in a different light to that portrayed by Peter Zarkosky and was very possibly one of the most deluded individuals Anna had ever encountered in her career in television – and there was a long list to choose from, most of them directors. After eight years, it was clear that Penny was still clinging to the hope that Peter would one day leave his family.

Her flat was bright. Anna took in the blue and white curtains with tie-backs, the neat sofa, the flat-screen television, the assortment of souvenirs and candles. All in all it was a scaled-down low-budget version of Rob and Nina Ramsey's house. Photographs of Peter and Penny were dotted around.

Anna bent over to look at one of them. 'Where was this taken?'

'Warsaw. Peter was negotiating some manufacturing contracts out there.'

Penny herself was the type of woman that everyone looked at and said, surprised, *He left his wife for her?* She was simply nondescript: thirty-something, with shoulder-length brown hair, a slim build and brown eyes. She was dressed in jeans and a pink and purple striped V-neck sweater.

Penny had got straight to the point. 'Peter is very ... vulnerable. He's a man caught by his circumstances.'

'His circumstances?' Anna repeated blithely.

'His family are very strict Catholics. It would have been impossible for him not to marry a good Catholic girl. Actually make that a good

Polish Catholic girl. It was virtually an arranged marriage.'

Penny seemed anxious to convey her side of the story to Anna.

'Do you think that he'll ever leave?' Anna asked.

'Oh, yes. Once the girls have finished college. That will give him time to turn the business around.'

Anna wanted to shake her. It seemed inevitable that they would be having the same conversation in ten years' time.

Do you think that he'll ever leave?

I think he could. Once the grandchildren have started school. And if he can sort out his pension provision.

'Are you seeing him at the moment?'

Penny looked surprised. 'Oh yes. Once or twice a week. Peter comes over here. He says we have to lay low for a while.'

So Penny was prepared to settle for that. No weekends together, no two-week holidays, no Sundays spent wandering along the riverbank. These thoughts brought Tim to mind. Anna pushed them away.

'How did you feel when Peter asked you to leave your job?'

Penny shrugged. 'It was nice working together. But what was the alternative ...?' Her voice trailed off.

'Once Mrs Zarkosky found out?'

Penny grimaced. 'Actually, it was his daughter Basia who found out. A friend of hers saw us together. She gave her father an ultimatum – either he stopped seeing me or she would tell her mother.'

Anna looked up. 'You mean Mrs Zarkosky didn't know?'

'I mean she still doesn't know. Not really. She suspected something and when I left he had to come up with some explanation. Peter made up some story that he had "feelings" for me and it was better that I left before he acted on them.'

Thank God she had had the presence of mind to tell Ethne to find out what Mrs Zarkosky knew before letting the cat out of the bag.

Penny continued. 'He said he was putting himself out of temptation's way.'

Listening to Penny, Anna hated the feeling that Peter Zarkosky thought he could play her for a fool. He was clearly masterminding this whole operation: Penny thought he was leaving; his wife believed that he was staying, and he'd all but denied an actual affair to Anna. It would be intriguing to know what he was planning to tell the counsellor. It was a damned shame that this wasn't a cable show. Then Anna could arrange an intervention-style surprise meeting with Penny and the Zarkoskys.

'Did he tell you about the programme?' Anna asked.

Anna was half-listening now.

'We want to do things properly. Peter wants to get the business sorted out so that he can take care of me.'

She nodded attentively at Penny while she tried to recall her meetings with Peter. Had he admitted to an affair? She had thought so. But in retrospect she couldn't be certain that he had actually used that word. What had he said? Mistake? Indiscretion? Dalliance! That was it. *Dalliance.*

As soon as she got in the car she had called Ethne's mobile. It rang and then went onto answer machine.

'Ethne. This is Anna. I need to speak to you *urgently* about the Zarkoskys and what Mrs Zarkosky said about the affair. It turns out it's rather more than a dalliance. As we suspected it's been going on for years. I need to know e*xactly* what she said. Call me as soon as you get this.'

Since then she had called Ethne umpteen times but the phone never got answered. Now, seeing that she had a signal in the High Street, she tried again.

'Ethne! Call me as soon as you get this message.'

She closed the phone, seething with frustration. Ethne should have been in regular contact while she was at the Zarkoskys and have reported back without delay on leaving. She should have gone herself! But Tim had gone on and on about her delegating. She resolved instead that when she saw Ethne she would debrief her and then suggest that she would benefit from a spell in accounts. Anna walked back along the High Street, past the shops and wine bars, navigating a sea of couples window-shopping arm in arm. Apparently she was the lone single person adrift on a Sunday afternoon. She began to feel self-conscious. Maybe Tim was feeling the same way and would call tonight. They could go out to dinner. In the meantime, she reacted as she always did in periods of free time by formulating a plan of action: first, stop off at Space NK for some Kiehls supplies; second, pick up the Sunday papers; third, head home to complete the unpacking.

Ethne pulled out her mobile from her back pocket and saw just in time that it was Anna's number. No way was she answering that! It was the hundredth call that weekend! Miles was playing Tash's dad's Creedence Clearwater Revival album at full blast and Zak was hauling in firewood. Tash, meanwhile, was on the phone to the Peking Garden Chinese restaurant. And Ethne herself had just snorted a couple of lines of coke procured that afternoon from Druggie Dave in the car park of the Rose and Crown in the village. The four of them were planning a night in watching Channel 4's *Top One Hundred Break-up Songs*. Zak was pretty cool. He was an agricultural student at Cirencester with great abs and a BMW 3 series. Plus his parents had a cottage in Rock, which would be fun for the summer. And he was good in bed. She might see him again.

Zak lit a match and began blowing on the kindling. He turned round and grinned at her. 'Come on, baby, light my fire ...'

She got up and sauntered over to him. He reached up and pulled her down to him, his hands spanning her waist. Then he kissed her, his hands working their way up to skim over her breasts.

She pushed him away. 'Later ...'

He ignored her, kissing her neck until Tash came in.

'Break it up, guys.'

Zak pulled away and added a log to the burning kindling. And then Ethne reached over for her Marlboro lights and a bottle of Cobra, pausing to switch off her mobile phone with a satisfied push. Anna Miller could wait until tomorrow. She'd left a zillion messages but those could wait too: it was important to achieve a work–life balance. Besides, she was beginning to formulate other plans. Zak had told her that he knew a bloke who ran a restaurant down in Rock. And Mummy knew all about running restaurants, right? The obvious thing was to go down for the summer! Zak said there were amazing beach parties. Ethne thought about bossy Anna Miller and her boring job – all that writing and listening – not to mention having to get up early every single day and go on the disgusting Northern Line. It was stupid. She might just chuck her crappy job and go and hang out in Cornwall.

She turned to Zak and said conversationally, 'So, how big is your parents' cottage?'

Chapter 14

Anna loved the early morning. The first light of sunrise was veiled by morning mist, while the muted chill of the March air held the vague promise of spring. At seven o'clock there was enough traffic along the King's Road to feel that the City was coming to life but not so much that she would not be at her desk, cappuccino to one side, by seven thirty. After five hours' sleep she felt buzzed and ready to go. As she drove westward, the antique shops and galleries of the Lots Road end gave way to upmarket boutiques and expensive restaurants. Just before Sloane Square the traffic slowed. She avoided looking to her right at the site of the old Duke of York barracks, now converted into a modern-day square, lined with designer shops and chic cafés. The Patisserie Valerie had been a Sunday-morning favourite when she was with Tim, the setting for newspapers, bacon and eggs and a basket of brioche, croissants and mini pain au chocolat.

He had not called last night.

She concentrated on the traffic. She was following a Porsche, probably headed for the City. Behind her a white builder's van edged too close. She was used to that. Small, expensive, red BMW sports cars had that effect on some men.

Rick had given her a key to the building when she started. Yesterday evening it had been deserted. At eight o'clock in the evening, after two hours of unpacking, she had cracked and driven into work. She would have expected a researcher at least, but she had remained undisturbed in the seclusion of the basement editing suite. It was known as 'The Edit', a small room where she worked the computer screens and viewed her work on the television monitor. She liked it that way, in the semi-darkness, alone with the images and voices. At first she played with them, flipping and cutting until her experimentation took form and then the laborious process of getting it perfect began and the hours passed. It was an offline edit, the pictures not of broadcast quality, but it held the narrative. She had put in a voiceover herself. Maybe it would persuade Rick that a woman's voice could be used after all.

It had been past midnight by the time she had left but she was wide awake and hyped up on a creative high. She had deliberately left her phone in the car, it was too much of a distraction, and when she came out she had hoped that there might be a message from Tim. There was not. Nor had there been one at home. As a result of her efforts spent in the editing suite, Rick would find the first episode of *Marriage Menders* on his desk when he arrived at work today. It needed polishing but it was good. The Michaels, all kids and banter, provided the warmth and light relief. Rob and Nina were the lifestyle choice. And the Zarkoskys were set up for a fall. On the tape Peter Zarkosky did most of the talking. They were pictured in their spacious Beaconsfield kitchen. Peter was talking about his family.

'Without family a man has nothing.' He had spread his hands open at that point. She had cut then to Mrs Zarkosky washing up some cups and saucers. Then back to Peter now in the lounge, appearing simultaneously to read a newspaper. She commented on the voiceover.

'The Zarkoskys have opted for a traditional marriage in which Mrs Zarkosky does all the housework, cooking and cleaning ...'

All that remained was for her to make a decision about Rob. The tape of their private session lay in the editing suite. She had played and cut it over and over. It was compelling. Unscripted, raw and honest. And yet when she played it Tim's voice came into her head.

Can you work that into the film? The situation of people like Rob – stuck in dead-end jobs because they haven't got the right qualifications.

There was something about Rob that was fundamentally innocent. For all his laddishness, he was ignorant of the ways of the world. Her experience told her that his taped admission would make powerful television. And yet she resisted pushing the set of buttons that would clip and slot Rob into place. It was odd that of all the *Marriage Menders* participants it was Rob that she felt closest too.

She parked the car in the tight spot at the rear of the building, locked it and went off to get a cappuccino and a Danish from the Italian café round the corner. She felt energised, even though she had skipped her morning run. She would compensate with a gym session that night. There was another reason to feel good today. Once Rick had viewed the tape she intended to extract a reward for all her hard work. She wanted a new researcher, handpicked and extracted from the BBC. The more she had thought about it the more she wanted Ethne out of her office and, furthermore, out of the company. The girl was a dilettante, a waste of space and money, and she would make that very clear to Rick.

The time had come to exercise a little power at 7–24.

'Knock, knock.'

The woman, newly arrived at the bottom of Pia's bed, tapped at an imaginary door.

Before Pia had a chance to say 'Come in,' the woman came and sat down next to her at the top of the bed. She was wearing a navy blue shirt and trouser uniform but Pia had no idea what the colour signified. Next to her she put down a large laminated Liberty print shopping bag.

She greeted Pia enthusiastically. 'Pia! I'm Nurse Carole. I'm the Smoking Co-ordinator.'

There seemed to be no option but to turn off the small rented television system suspended over the bed by a metal arm.

Carole took out a file. 'Now. Mr Nicholls has referred you to us.' She looked at Pia, seeking confirmation.

'Yes.'

'How do you feel?'

She felt desperate for a cigarette. 'Much better, thank you.'

'Good!'

Pia was not going to say anything that might prolong her stay. The ward had grown much noisier since Saturday. Her serenity had worn off along with the sedatives – she would kill for a cigarette, and a glass of wine would be nice later, too. The events of Saturday lunchtime seemed a very long way away and her hospitalisation felt like a massive overreaction. She needed to get back to work. No sooner had one edition of *Smart Women* hit the shelves than it was time to get working on next year's edition. Plus there was a feature piece overdue

– a beginner's guide to investing in the stock market – and a proposal for a new column for a magazine aimed at the over-fifties. And there were all the final payments to make for the party.

'And Mr Nicholls wants you to stay another day or so for observation.'

'Yes.'

'Good!'

Nurse Carole put down her notes and began rooting in her shopping bag. Didn't they have some medical-issue bags? She handed her a small booklet.

'This is your Quit Diary.'

The cover had a cartoon man stubbing out a cigarette. A morose waft of smoke trailed from its dying embers. He looked elated. Pia, on the other hand, would like to have retrieved the cartoon stub from under his little round foot and had a good drag on it.

'It has information on quitting at the front and a daily diary for the first thirty days at the back. Write down every time you feel like a cigarette.' Carole opened up the pamphlet and held it open towards Pia. She began pointing. 'There are three columns. One for time. The second for place. The third for feelings.'

She would be writing all the time then.

Carole closed it up. 'Then you bring it along to the group – Thursdays at 7.00 p.m. in the new wing – and share your experiences. You help each other!'

The best way to get her to go away was to nod and say yes.

'The Smoking Support Group is led by an ex-smoker.' Carole said this in a tone suggestive of a combat veteran. 'And Mr Nicholls does expect his patients to attend.'

Pia nodded. Fuck Mr Nicholls. God, she hated all this God-doctor stuff. She was definitely going to write an article about it.

Carry On Doctor? The NHS may talk the talk of a service-based client culture. But down on the wards the culture of the 1950s survives to this day.

Mr Nicholls' visit to her bedside at 8.00 a.m. that morning had been a short and mannered affair. To one side stood a nurse and to the other a junior doctor. In an outer circle stood a conclave of silent and anxious-looking medical students. She had been sleepy and confidently expecting to be discharged. So she had been caught unawares when he had reviewed her chart, adjusted her medication and told her that they were going to do a Stress Test to check the condition of her arteries. Before she had had a chance to object he had disappeared though the curtain.

Nurse Carole was rooting in her shopping bag again. 'Mr Nicholls has put you down for nicotine replacement. You can have the patch, the gum or the inhaler.'

She couldn't stop herself. 'Don't they give you a bag for all that stuff?'

'No, dear. My hubby got me this for Christmas.'

Pia softened towards Carole. She reminded her of Lucille, one of the cleaners, who had confided that she brought in her own rubber gloves because the hospital issue ones were so huge they were impossible to work in.

'Patch, gum or inhaler?' Carole repeated.

Well, she wasn't wearing a bloody sticky patch. And she had fought years of battles with her children against gum.

'The inhaler, please.'

Carole took out a little white inhaler and began unscrewing it. 'You put the little cartridge in here, click and you're good to go!'

She couldn't believe that Carole had ever smoked herself. Carole assumed that Mr Nicholls' command would be enough to stop her. Carole hadn't asked her the single most important question – *do you want to stop*? And the answer to that would have been yes, of course – apparently I've just had a heart attack – but I'm not sure that I can.

'Call me if you have any questions. Make sure you don't run low on cartridges for the inhaler.'

Carole handed her a card. 'Call me if you need a chat. I work Mondays and Wednesdays from nine till two and Fridays from nine till one.'

It was unclear what Pia was supposed to do if she craved a cigarette outside of these hours. Carole began filling in a form on a clipboard.

Pia picked up the Quit Diary.

You didn't learn to smoke in a day. So don't be surprised if quitting takes time! But the health benefits are immediate. After one hour ...

The writers of health education pamphlets, she had noticed, were heavily reliant on exclamation marks. She turned the page.

Many people find it helpful to set a 'Stop Date' in advance. In the box write down your Stop Date. Mark it on a calendar. It's an important anniversary! And stopping smoking is the best present you can give yourself! Make sure you tell family, friends and co-workers about your Stop Day. Invite them to be members of your personal Quit Team. In the box make a list of your Quit Team members ...

Who were her potential Quit Team members? Hope sprang to mind. Dan and her mother were presumably disqualified by the fact that they were smokers themselves. She could ask Marion but couldn't imagine her taking it at all seriously. Roger would have been a member. So would Edward – once. She closed up the pamphlet.

Her divorce from Edward had not come as a surprise to her mother. She had listened to Pia's complaints for years. But her mother was aghast at the news of her break-up with Roger. 'Pia, at your age it's a buyer's market. Men your age want someone younger.'

She had gone out with Roger for close to nine months. The first three had been the best. Then, for her birthday, he had taken her away for a surprise weekend to a country hotel in Dorset. It would not have been her choice of hotel, which he would have known if he had checked with her before booking it. It was decorated in an English country house style, with small chintzy rooms, a library and a tiny restaurant with a very limited menu. It was five star but she would have preferred something more glitzy with a spa. That was when the first irritations had crept in: Roger's habit of draping his clothes over the back of the armchair; the way he left his shoes outside the wardrobe; the clutter he left in the bathroom. She liked things put away in their proper place. At dinner he always asked for Flora in-stead of butter, though with the benefit of hindsight she wasn't on the strongest ground with this particular criticism. Roger liked to lie in on a Sunday whereas she liked to be up and about. She was reminded, as she looked at his possessions scattered around the hotel room, of all the reasons she had left Edward.

After that she found it impossible to hold back with her criticisms. She suggested that he upgrade from a Jaguar to a Mercedes, everyone knew they had a better resale value, and she told him he was crazy not to move some of his money held on long-term deposit into the stock market. It was so obviously the sensible thing to do. The final straw had come when he had missed the opportunity to extend the gallery and set up a gift shop. She had been on at him for months to add more space by taking the lease of an adjacent shop that was falling vacant.

'You'd make a fortune from a gift shop in that location. Have you any idea of the profit to be made from birthday cards? In time you could even add a restaurant. People love to come and shop and eat at the same place.'

They were sitting in Burgers in Marlow having coffee on a Saturday morning. It was an old-fashioned beamed tea-room. Roger liked to stop off there after a walk along the river bank.

Roger looked unenthusiastic. 'God, the gallery is enough of a tie. I already have to go in this afternoon because I can't get the staff. Think what a headache a bloody restaurant would be.'

'But it would be so lucrative!' she insisted. 'Why not do it if you can?'

Roger raised an eyebrow. 'Because I don't need to?' He took a bite of a chocolate ganache cake. 'Anyhow, the lease has been taken.'

She was aghast. 'By whom?'

'Some coffee bar place.'

She could not conceal her irritation at his apathy. 'I think you've missed a fabulous opportunity. Why didn't you take it?'

'Because there's more to life than work?'

She ignored the edge in his voice. 'But it's so … pedestrian to keep on doing the same thing.'

Too late she realised that with this last comment she had over-stepped the mark. Roger looked furious. 'So, I'm pedestrian? Christ, Pia, is there anything that I do to your satisfaction?'

There was a protracted silence before she had the last word. 'I'm just being sensible, that's all.'

They had finished their coffee without speaking and did not linger over the hand-made chocolates and decorated cakes in the shop. Usually Pia liked to buy a box of assorted milk chocolates to give to Hope. That was the last day they spent together. Roger called her to say that he thought they ought to take a break. He had not called again. Marion had assured her that the worst thing she could do would be to chase after him and there were plenty of better men out there. But so far, nearly a year later, she had not been on a single date. It was as well that she had her children and her mother. Otherwise, at times, she would have felt totally alone.

RE: E.D. Irvine

Bad luck! Who decided that a basement would be a great place to store vital historical records? I wouldn't give up on the LEA. Some official bodies are diligent in keeping records (of course others regularly toss top-secret files on rubbish tips). Let me know how you get on with the local records.

I'm off to Belfast for a couple of days. The *Guardian* want a piece on the anniversary of the Good Friday Peace Agreement, so I'm going to do some background interviews.

H

Below Hart's replay, Sally re-read her original email. She was concerned that it sounded downbeat. She had written it trying to conceal her disappointment with the Secretary of the Berkshire Historical Society.

RE: E.D. Irvine

The trail has gone cold. The current secretary of the Berkshire Historical Society called this morning to say that all their pre-war records were transferred to the Henley library in 1940. Unfortunately the basement where they stored them was flooded in 1948. So if E.D. Irvine did leave any notes they're lost. As for Selton School, it closed in 1951. All the records were transferred to the Local Education Authority. I'm following that up with them.

Hopefully, the Wimbledon records will be more revealing. I'll let you know how I get on.

Sally

It was a white lie when she wrote that the secretary had called her. Actually, she had called him. By ten o'clock she could not conceal her impatience any more. She had left a message on Friday morning and he still hadn't called her back. Like the archivist at Selton Park, the secretary demonstrated no sense of urgency about events that occurred over one hundred years ago. He had been nice enough but quite clear about the fate of the records.

Now, putting a notebook and pen in her handbag, she could hear thuds from upstairs. It was the sounds of Dan getting up. She felt a twinge of concern about leaving him on his own. As he came down the stairs she came out of the study to meet him.

He looked half-asleep. He raised a hand in greeting.

Ordinarily she would have offered to make him breakfast but she was anxious to drop Louis at her mother's and get to Morden where the local births, deaths and marriages records for Wimbledon Village were kept. The news that Hart was flying to Belfast made her all the more determined to do some investigating herself.

'I've got to go out. Will you be OK on your own?'

'Yeah. No probs.'

She hesitated. It felt awkward questioning him. 'Have you got any plans?'

He shrugged. 'Don't know.'

She looked at her watch. 'Well, you know where everything is. If you go out, take the spare key from the kitchen drawer. Make sure you double lock the front door.'

'Yeah.'

'Maybe you could go to the library?' she suggested.

He looked up at her. 'The library?' It was as if she had suggested visiting the Galapagos Islands.

'Yes! They have a teen fiction section.'

He gazed at her. 'Oh. All right.'

She thought out loud. 'Maybe we could go somewhere this after-noon?' She paused. 'The local history museum?'

Dan's expression told her all she needed to know. 'No.' She thought again. Then she had a moment of inspiration. 'Bowling! Let's go to Kingston and go bowling.'

Dan's features lightened. He smiled so rarely. 'Yeah. OK.'

And then he was gone, thumping heavily down the stairs, presumably in search of food. She made a mental note to stock up on boxes of cereal. And to suggest to Edward that he took Dan to see one of the new film releases this weekend. As she ascended the stairs she felt a new resolve not to give up on Dan, not to succumb to the age-old role of the jealous stepmother, to prove that it was possible to love another woman's child.

'John was so good with his hands. He made Master Henry a train. It was about this long with six wheels and a funnel. The wheels turned and there was a carriage for the people. He painted it red. He was going to make the little people, too, for his next birthday.

We all loved him.

Miss Bella took Henry's death very hard. She was never the same after that. Of course, children died more often then. There was no penicillin like there is today. But that didn't make it any easier. He was such a good baby, he didn't fuss. Oh, he liked to be carried though! He was better once he could sit up in his pram. I used to take him down to the pond to see the ducks.

But it doesn't do any good to dwell on it.

You see those rhododendrons – John planted them. He took on the garden here. Oh, you should see them in the spring. They're all ragged now but he got a lovely shape to them. They must be forty years old now but they survived because he knew the right place to put them. They need shade, you know. He didn't have a garden in Fulham. There was just a paved back yard with the privy. After the war they pulled his street down and moved the people out to the flats at the Arndale. Do you know them, the tower blocks? I'm glad John didn't have to see that. He knew Fulham how it used to be, before all these young couples moved in and drove the working people out ... It's the poor who always get the wrong end of it.'

Ethne knew she was lucky to have heard the news while there was still time to make a plan. Blythe, who was Rick's secretary, had told Oliver – who knew everything – who had told Ethne. Thank God Anna was shut up downstairs in the edit so Ethne had told Denny the receptionist that she was slipping out to Starbucks. One hundred yards down Charlotte Street Ethne slipped into an alleyway and called her mother, breathlessly conveying the whole garbled story in a frantic whisper.

'What am I going to do?' she ended. 'I was the last person who spoke to her!'

Saying those words made her feel like the prime suspect.

Mummy sounded businesslike. In the background Ethne could hear the kitchen sounds of the Caldicott outside catering kitchen in Stoke Newington, pans clanging and shouted orders. The council had given Mummy a grant to set up her new kitchen there, so it had hardly cost her anything, and it was nice and close to home. 'You called her?'

'Yes. On Sunday afternoon. They're saying it happened on Sunday night.'

'Wait a moment.' She could hear the sound of footsteps as Mummy went up to her office and then the door closing. 'Well, you are the only two who know what was said in that call. And since this Mrs Zarzinsky—'

'Zarkosky ...'

'Whoever, is in no position to talk to anyone, it's your word that counts.'

'But I was asking her all the questions about Penny, the mistress. I thought she knew!'

'Ethne, you did nothing wrong,' her mother said matter-of-factly. 'You were just checking your facts.'

Was she?

Mummy was sounding serious now. 'Listen carefully, Ethne. This is what you say. Anna Miller asked you interview Mrs Zarzinsky about the mistress. That is what you did. Full stop.'

'But I think I should have called Anna back ... I should have checked—'

Her mother cut in. 'No! You did what you were asked to do. Don't complicate it. You were simply following the instructions that Anna Miller gave you.'

'But ...'

'Ethne!' Her mother's voice grew lower and more urgent. 'This is life and death. Someone is going to pay for this. Someone's name is going to be splashed across the papers. Someone's career is going to be ruined. Do you want that someone to be you?'

Ethne felt chastened. 'No.'

'Then do what I say. Tell them that you went down as instructed to interview this woman. You carried out the interview. Then you called her again on Sunday in order to double-check your facts—'

'But I didn't!' Ethne interrupted. 'I asked her how she felt about her husband having a girlfriend. I was so nervous about asking her that I just blurted it out. . And she said, "What girlfriend?" And I said, "Penny." And then she started asking me all these questions. And I probably said more than I should have. Like how it had been going on for years.'

Ethne thought as hard as she could. She was trying to recall exactly what she had said to Mrs Zarkosky and what she had said in reply. She had been really hung-over and trying to negotiate the Sunday-afternoon traffic back into London. Truth to tell, she hadn't really been listening. 'And I didn't have enough time. Because Anna made me move house for her.'

'Then make sure you tell them that. Make it clear that while you were focused on the job on hand, Anna Miller was distracted by her house move.'

'Well, she was!' Ethne remembered. 'When we were filming in Bracknell the day before she was calling the removers.'

'Good. Tell them that. But in a nice way, Ethne. Say that you were worried about Anna – say that she seemed to be under a lot of stress and you were concerned about whether she was coping. That's why you agreed to help with the house move in order to help her out.'

'OK.'

'She's in charge. She can take the fall. Now,' her mother said briskly, 'go back to the office and act normally. Don't speak to anyone about this. You know nothing. In the meantime, I'm going to call your father. He can deal with Rick.'

'Thanks, Mummy.' Then she had another thought. 'But she kept leaving me messages. What am I going to say if they ask me why I didn't call Anna back?'

Her mother sighed. 'Easy. Listen carefully. Begin by pointing out that it was a Sunday and she had just moved house ...'

'At four o'clock yesterday afternoon your researcher Ethne Caldicott called and spoke to Mrs Zarkosky. She asked her,' Roy Jardine looked up at Anna momentarily, 'on your instructions, a number of questions about her husband's eight-year affair with Penny Anderson.'

How many times did Anna have to repeat herself? 'I never asked her to say that. I told her to find out what Mrs Zarkosky knew. And to speak to me first.'

Anna felt like she was drowning. She had been in Rick's office now for half an hour, hauled out of the edit by Blythe.

'Rick wants to see you.'

'What for?'

Blythe had shrugged. 'Don't know.'

Climbing the stairs to Rick's office Anna had imagined that it would be about *Marriage Menders*. She looked at her watch and worked out that he would have had time to watch the tape. She had felt buoyant.

'It's about *Marriage Menders*,' she said confidently over her shoulder to Blythe who was following behind her. 'I think we've got a winner with that one.'

Even when Blythe showed her in and shut the door and she noticed the stranger, an older, heavy-set man in a suit sitting incongruously at Rick's glass-topped conference table, even then she had not been concerned. Her first thought was that the man worked for a television company. Yes, he was a buyer for an overseas network. Rick had been so impressed by *Marriage Menders* that he had persuaded this man to see it there and then.

Rick had introduced her. 'This is Roy Jardine from Masterson Ryder Jardine.'

She recognised the name. A top-ranked firm of London solicitors. She was surprised. She thought Nina might be angry if she found out about Rob's secret tape. But she didn't think Nina would go to a lawyer.

Then the questions had started.

When did you first meet Mr and Mrs Zarkosky?

Do you have notes of that meeting?

When did you last speak to Mrs Zarkosky?

She had responded as best she could, repeatedly asking, 'What is this all about?'

Roy Jardine had been dismissive. 'We'll come to that.' She had looked at Rick who was not sitting at the conference table. Instead, he was pacing round the room. It was unsettling.

Roy Jardine was relentless. 'But you did tell her to go down and conduct an in-depth interview?'

'Yes.'

'And you knew that her husband was conducting an extra-marital affair?'

'I suspected that—'

'So you told her to go down, spend the day with Mrs Zarkosky and question her about a matter that you knew to be highly sensitive?'

'No! It wasn't like that!' she burst out.

'Before you were in full possession of the facts.' Roy Jardine looked at her as if to say it was exactly like that. He continued, 'Well, apparently Ethne is a diligent young woman who was anxious to double-check her facts.' His voice carried the clear implication that this characteristic was in contrast to Anna's slapdash ways. 'Naturally, even commendably, one might say, Miss Caldicott called again. The news, it turns out, was an absolute surprise to Mrs Zarkosky.'

Now, after repeated cross-examination about the Zarkoskys, starting with her first meeting and ending with the last weekend, the pieces had begun to fall into place.

She asked again, 'Will you please tell me what is going on?'

'We'll come to that.'

She had had enough. 'No! We will come to it now. Or I'm leaving and coming back with my solicitor.' As soon as the words left her mouth she had regretted not saying them earlier. The two men looked at each other as if to confer. Rick shrugged his shoulders.

Anna knew already what he was going to say. Mrs Zarkosky had taken a fatal overdose. That was surely how a woman like Mrs Zarkosky would kill herself – quietly, with as little fuss as possible.

She could not help but hold her head in her hands. Was there some faint chance, some hope against hope, that she was still alive?

With an awful sense of foreboding, she said quietly, 'How is Mrs Zarkosky?'

The lawyer was almost breezy. 'Unrepentant, I gather.'

She looked up. 'What?'

Rick intervened. 'She's saying that she did what any woman in her situation would have done.'

'Tried to kill herself?'

Rick sounded impatient. 'Mrs Zarkosky hasn't topped herself! She went to Penny's flat and shot her with a Second World War German-issue Luger!'

Was he joking? How on earth would Mrs Zarkosky come to own a gun? They were illegal!

There must be some mistake. Some mix-up of identity? Or at least a confusion of some vital fact.

'How would she get hold of a gun?'

Roy Jardine looked up from his notes. 'It belonged to her late father, apparently. The looting of German weaponry by allied forces and the retention of such weapons as souvenirs was quite common then.'

Hell, she hated lawyers.

'How do you know all this?'

'We received a call from an interested party.'

'The first of many, no doubt,' Rick cut in bitterly, looking out of the window at the skyline as if some black-clad journalist might even now be crouching, pen and paper in hand, on an adjacent roof-top. 'We're expecting it to break on the lunchtime news bulletins.'

She looked at her watch. It was only 11.30 a.m.

Neither of them had commented on Penny. 'Is Penny … dead?'

'She's in a critical condition.'

Rick rounded on her. 'And who do you think is going to get the blame if she dies? Christ, can you see the headlines?'

Rick's selfish anger sparked her. 'Mrs Zarkosky I would hope. She pulled the trigger. Christ, you don't give a damn about Penny. Only about saving your own skin.'

Rick was on edge. 'Anna, I don't need lessons from you in how to treat people.'

Roy Jardine raised his hands. 'If we can return to the matter in hand, our present concern is Mrs Zarkosky's state of mind.'

Rick sat down. The lawyer's words had clearly been intended to pull him back on track.

'Yes, state of mind. Like how she found out, Anna?'

She felt resolute. It was very simple. 'Not from me.'

Roy raised his eyebrows. 'I'm not sure that is the correct interpretation. A train of events was set in motion by you that led to the commission of this crime.'

'I've done absolutely nothing wrong. Peter Zarkosky lied to me – to us – and I've got the tape to prove it.'

Rick shot back at her. 'You broke the first rule, Anna. You didn't get your facts straight.'

It was so unfair. 'That's exactly what I was in the process of doing.' She rallied. 'That was what I asked Ethne to do. That was why I asked her to call me back.' Surely they could not find fault with that?

'She says she was unable to reach you. She pointed out that there was no landline telephone at your house and no mobile reception either.'

'But she could have left a message!'

'Miss Caldicott says it was impossible to contact you given the absence of communications occasioned by your house move.'

It seemed most unlikely that Ethne would have said that. It was almost as though he was representing Ethne in her absence, as though Rick and the lawyer were consciously protecting her. Suddenly Anna realised the significance of the fact that they had spoken to Ethne before they spoke to her. Belatedly she realised that there was a game being played here, that she was part of it, but she didn't know the moves or the rules. She was a pawn not a player.

Instinctively she looked for the tape of *Marriage Menders*.

It had gone from Rick's desk.

'Have you watched the tape?'

Rick's eyes flickered away. 'I haven't had time to watch it all. I flicked through them. Briefly.'

He was lying. Rick never flicked through anything. He was like her, able to make a sharp assessment in a short period of time. He may not have watched it in its entirety but he had taken a good, hard professional look.

She played for time. 'And what about Ethne?'

Roy Jardine was impassive. 'Miss Caldicott is not relevant to all this. You are the director. You had overall responsibility.'

Roy and Rick exchanged glances. Then Rick pulled back a chair and finally sat down at the conference table, the two men on one side facing her. He nodded at Roy. Roy continued, 'Which is why you will understand that 7–24 cannot continue your employment.'

Employment?

'I have a contract,' she pointed out. 'You can't just terminate it!'

The lawyer did not seem the least bit put off by this. 'Yes. Mr Roth supplied me with a copy.' If anything he appeared to be hitting his stride. 'And you are in the six-month probationary period of that contract. It allows for termination without notice by either party during that period.' He took a copy and, as if for dramatic effect, pushed it across the table at her. 'Please check for yourself.'

She ignored him. Instead she turned to Rick. 'You bastard. You told me the probationary period was a formality! A standard clause.'

Rick was unabashed. 'It's a term of the contract, Anna. This is business.'

'I've done nothing wrong!'

Roy Jardine sighed. 'You were in charge,' he stated conclusively.

'And what about *Marriage Menders*? Are you going to scrap the series as a mark of respect to Penny?'

Rick said nothing

She laughed. 'Of course you're not! At the end of the day it's absolutely fantastic publicity.'

Roy Jardine intervened. 'I think that's a most tasteless remark.'

'It's a truthful assessment,' she shot back. 'Ask your client yourself. Is he going to abandon *Marriage Menders*?'

In the silence that followed she decided that she wouldn't go down without telling Rick exactly what she thought of him. 'Rick, you'll take full advantage of this situation. I'm the scapegoat – the sacrificial lamb to show the world what a socially responsible company you are while all the time you've got the rights department on the phone right now flogging *Marriage Menders* round the world.'

She could tell that she had hit the mark. Rick got up and walked to his desk.

Roy Jardine continued seamlessly as if he had not heard her last remarks. 'In the circumstances, we will be keeping to the terms of the contract. That is, we will pay your salary to the end of the month. The stock options, naturally, are terminated with your employment. We require the return of all equipment and film belonging to 7–24, which naturally includes all the footage of *Marriage Menders*. We require you to observe the confidentiality clause – that is paragraph three point one in the contract – by which you agreed not to speak about your work at 7–24. If necessary we will take steps to enforce that by means of an injunction and to require payment by you of the legal costs of that action.'

'Oh, shut up.'

She got up. Whatever happened she was going to make damned sure they never saw the footage of Rob. She moved to the office door. Rick, anticipating her move, darted towards it.

'Anna!' There was a new note of urgency in his voice.

He was fast but she was closer. She made it to the handle first. She ran two miles before breakfast so there was no way Rick was going to beat her down the stairs. With a thrill of victory she flung open the door. Immediately in front of her, turning to face her as they were alerted by the motion of the door opening, were two uniformed security guards. In a swift, rehearsed movement they moved together, blocking her path. She was so stunned that she could not speak. As she took in the scene she heard Roy Jardine's voice. It lacked any trace of apology or embarrassment. It was clearly a script he had followed before.

'There is no cause to be alarmed. It's a policy we follow. We find that it avoids any unpleasantness. These gentlemen are employed by my firm. They will escort you downstairs to your car.' He said this in such a way as to imply that they were doing her a favour. 'We will arrange for your personal effects to be packed up and delivered to your home by close of business today.'

It was so catastrophically awful that it was unreal. In less than four hours after she had arrived at work she had been sacked, held responsible for a woman's possible murder and was about to be escorted from the building. Between the shoulders of the two guards she saw Blythe. For a fraction their eyes met until Blythe looked away, her gaze redirected towards papers on her desk, which she began to move purposefully from one pile to another. She was able to picture the scene through Blythe's eyes, her path blocked by two uniformed security guards, Rick at her shoulder, Roy Jardine still standing by the conference table. And her own words before the meeting.

I think we've got a winner with that one.

And then everything happened so quickly.

Roy Jardine was behind her. 'Well, this seems an appropriate moment to proceed downstairs.'

The two guards broke apart, arranging themselves so that one preceded her and one followed behind. Never could she remember feeling so powerless, so robbed of her autonomy. Never had five flights of stairs seemed such a very long and daunting walk. There was no alternative but to walk to the stairs. She was in that state whereby she understood what was happening and yet she could not believe it. At the top of the stairs she was suddenly fearful that she might stumble and fall. She grasped the handrail. She made up her mind to look at the back of the head of the guard in front of her. If they met anyone she would ignore them. The third floor was quiet. On the second they ran into a man from Xerox repairing the photocopier. His toolbox and the insides of the photocopier blocked the narrow corridor. They were forced to halt.

Rick's voice was tense. 'Can you move it out of the way, mate?' For the first time she realised that Rick was feeling the pressure.

They stood in a line while the insides of the machine were moved to one side.

It took an age, or felt like one, for the man to allow them to pass. And then they were at the top of the stairs leading to the ground floor. Here the walls were showier, lined with stills from 7–24 productions. Children in an inner-city playground. A celebrity model pictured leaving as the winner of a reality survival programme. One day there would be a still from *Marriage Menders* and probably an award to stand in Rick's office or a certificate to hang in the lobby or a magazine profile of Rick. She felt robbed. And then they reached the lobby. She allowed herself to breathe. The office appeared to be hard at work. The unpleasant thought came to her that perhaps they had been warned to keep out of the way. Everything seemed to have been so carefully worked out.

And then she saw the basket. The willow basket that fitted on the frame of the sit-up-and-beg bicycle ridden by Allegra who brought the sandwiches from Too Good To Eat. As she descended the next step she saw Allegra, unmistakable in her red beret and navy gilet. Next to her, with his hand outstretched to pay, she saw Oliver. With each step more was revealed. Behind Oliver stood Harry the cameraman. And the old bloke who worked in accounts. Next the New Zealand computer man. The whole bloody office seemed to be assembled in the lobby. Then Matt and Caroline the researchers. And then Ethne.

The first guard reached the bottom of the stairs just as Allegra looked round.

'Hey, Anna! I've saved a coronation chicken for you!' Her voice rang out. In the silence that had descended as everyone took in the scene Allegra's voice echoed in the most ghastly way. It was more than an embarrassed silence. It was the silence that greeted the outsider, the outcast, the one who has been shunned. And then Oliver pulled at Allegra's arm. Anna looked away. And even though she knew that she had to keep her head high, even though every instinct of survival told her that she needed to meet Ethne's eye, when she reached the last stair and she was parallel with Ethne, it was then that her last ounce of resilience deserted her. The tears began to fall and the doorway beckoned and it was with a gasping relief that she made it onto the pavement.

Chapter 15

It was not very nice to think of a person in the same way that one would a stray dog or cat but the brutal fact was that for the past two weeks Anna Miller had turned up on Sally's kitchen doorstep every day at approximately half past twelve, a time when Sally felt she had to offer her some lunch. Anna then sat on the sofa all afternoon, either watching television or playing PlayStation with Dan, often until Edward's return from work. That was the cue for Anna to get up, announce that it was time for her to go to the gym and head off home.

Sally handed Anna a cheese and mushroom omelette and turned to make a smaller one for Louis. Anna was not an ungrateful lunch guest. She always helped wash up and she usually brought a contribution. First a bottle of olive oil, then a jar of Carluccio's sun-dried tomatoes and most recently a tin of Fortnum and Mason chocolate chip cookies. Aside from the gifts, Anna's presence had spurred Sally to make more effort. Louis's standard lunch was either a boiled egg with bread and butter soldiers or a cheese and tomato sandwich. Today with the omelettes she made a side salad.

Anna appeared to have undergone a personality transformation. The confident persona of Louis's party had vanished when, two weeks earlier, Sally encountered her emerging from her car just as Sally was about to open her front door. Ahead of her, pushing to get in first, was Louis. They were back from a trip to Sainsbury's. Sally's attention had been caught by the sound of sharp braking. She had turned to see Anna's car, which was parked at an odd angle, the back jutting out. Anna had stumbled out.

'Is everything all right?' Sally had called down. It clearly wasn't. She had ascended the three steps from her front door.

Anna gave a mirthless laugh. 'Oh yes. A woman's dying, I've been fired and Rick Roth's about to make a fortune off my back.' Now Sally could see that her eyes were reddened and the hand that held her car keys was shaking.

'Oh, how awful.' It was the only response that came immediately to mind. Louis had been tugging at her hand and in the other she held two bags of shopping. 'Would you like to come in? Have a cup of tea?'

Unexpectedly, Anna had nodded. She had declined a sandwich but nodded yes to a piece of birthday cake. Sally had cut it from the top so that it included a dwarf's head in order to supply her with extra sugar, which she recalled from her school Red Cross training was good for shock. Louis was playing up, wanting cake, too. Fortunately Anna had wanted to go and watch the television news, giving Sally time to negotiate with Louis and unpack the shopping.

'She couldn't even fix up the television. I've got no satellite for a week! And she wants to work in the media!' Sally had presumed that Anna meant the girl in the garden whose name now escaped her. Anna offered no more explanation, heading off with her plate of cake to the living room where she had stayed for the afternoon watching satellite twenty-four-hour news. The next day she had returned and the first of many narrations of the previous day's events had commenced. In the days that followed Anna updated the story with fresh details, painstaking analysis of crucial conversations and colourful character profiles of the main players.

'So,' Anna continued, attacking the omelette, 'the fact is that legally there's nothing I can do. The contract's solid.'

Sally was not surprised. She was now familiar with every clause of Anna's contract of employment and much else besides. The Zarkoskys' marriage. Anna's finances. The company history and accounts of 7–24. Then there were Penny's surgeries, one to remove the bullets and the second to reset her fractured shoulder – and Mrs Zarkosky's fate as she awaited trial for attempted murder while remanded in custody in a women's prison in North Kent. But Anna's most passionate accounts were reserved for the backstabbing, social-climbing arch-manipulator who was Rick Roth – and his traitorous accomplice, Ethne Caldicott.

Anna got up and went over and put the kettle on. She liked to have a cup of coffee directly after the main course.

'So, what are you going to do?'

'Nothing for a while. My lawyer said the best thing was to keep a low profile until Penny gets out of hospital. Then I'll try to get some freelance work. There's no way anyone will hire me at the moment. My best hope is that Mrs Zarkosky pleads guilty and there's no trial.'

From what Sally had heard of Mrs Zarkosky that seemed unlikely.

Anna put down her fork. 'I just can't believe it. After all the trouble she's caused the bimbo gets off scot-free.'

Sally was used to Anna's abrupt non-sequiturs. She knew what was coming next.

'...Tim said that Ethne's father is definitely the one who's handling the 7–24 share issue. He asked one of the journalists on the City desk. Her father's Mark Caldicott. As in *Caldicott and Wilson*.'

'I think you've mentioned him ...' Tim, despite being a very recent ex, appeared to have rowed in on Anna's behalf, making discreet enquiries. Privately, Sally wasn't too sure that Anna's strategy of letting Tim cool off – whilst calling him frequently to vent her fury at her ill-treatment at the hands of Rick Roth – was the best way to win him back.

And then Anna was off. 'It's the establishment! We live in the twenty-first century, in a modern industrialised economy. But at the end of the day it's who you know and where you went to school that still counts. It's unbelievable!'

Louis pottered in the corner. He was lining up his cars to make a car park. He would then transport them down the hallway to the front room where his Fisher Price petrol station, complete with upper-level parking, was kept. It would be no surprise if his next words were 'breach of contract'.

Sally had learned that the best thing was just to let Anna rant on.

Anna put down her fork. 'I never had a chance! And now the bimbo's leaving anyhow! She's going down to spend the summer in Cornwall.' Anna rolled her eyes. 'With all the other rich brainless bimbos.'

'How did you find this out?'

'Harry the cameraman.'

Harry? The hard-drinking, fast-talking womaniser. Not to be confused with Boff the Computer Man or Oliver the Post or any one of the cast of 7–24 employees with whom Sally was now acquainted.

'But they weren't going to sack her. Not the killer bimbo.'

Louis's omelette was almost cooked. Sally prised him away from his traffic jam and lifted him into his booster seat. She could almost hear her lower back muscles complaining. When Edward was at home Sally called on him to extract Louis from where he was wedged into place. Lately Anna had taken more interest in Louis. Not a great deal but enough to play cars with him for a while – Anna liked the cars in neat, straight lines too – and watch afternoon BBC children's television. Once Sally overheard her commenting on the camerawork to Louis.

'Look. Now it's zooming in. Now it's zooming out!'

And she was fabulous with Dan. Anna not only talked about 'youth culture' but actually knew what it was. At Anna's suggestion, Sally had taken Dan to the IMAX cinema and enrolled him in a Saturday-morning theatre workshop. Afterwards, Dan had got in the car holding a sheaf of papers. For the first time ever, Sally had caught a note of genuine enthusiasm in his voice.

'I've got to write a scene and perform it next week.'

Now, Sally fastened Louis's bib. He looked up at her. She anticipated his next words – *drink!* But before she had time to turn to the kitchen counter, scanning for where she had put it down, Louis's face broke into a broad grin.

'Bim-Bo!' he shouted, chortling. 'Bim-Bo!'

Jo's face wore the expression of hurt and incomprehension that Hope had first seen on the night of the party. Since then Jo had grown less tolerant of their secret, her features now displaying an added element of growing impatience.

'Why don't you just tell them? This isn't going to go away, Hope!'

Jo waved her hand around the room from where she sat on Hope's bed. She was wearing Hope's old Welton netball team T-shirt. 'We're a couple, aren't we?'

And beneath the belligerence of Jo's tone, Hope caught the undercurrent of insecurity. She turned from where she was sitting at her desk, finishing off an essay on her laptop.

'Yes! Of course we are. This isn't about us.'

'Of course it's about us!'

Hope got up. 'No. It's about me. About my parents. It's just not that easy.'

Jo didn't understand. Jo's father was a university professor at Cambridge teaching international relations; her mother, who was fifty but looked about thirty-five, was a special needs teacher. They were the type of people who marched for peace, reclaimed the night and told you so with bumper stickers. Her father, over a dinner in the kitchen, the dining room was a paper-strewn annexe to his office, had explained to Hope how he was organising a scheme whereby several thousand environmentalists would purchase square-foot portions of a field in order to frustrate the sale to developers.

Jo's parents had let them share a room in their ramshackle Victorian villa and the next day, when they went for a pub lunch, Jo's mother had introduced Hope to the landlord as Jo's partner. They seemed to know everyone in the pub. Her mother was only on a nodding acquaintance with their neighbours in Gerrards Cross. Jo told Hope how, when she had come out at the age of eighteen, her mother had embraced her and said that they loved her and her father had asked if there was anything they could do to support her. Somehow, Hope knew those wouldn't be her parents' first choice of words.

Jo was not about to be put off. She had seized on the occasion.

'It is that easy, Hope. Tell him next time you have lunch together.'

'In Pret a Manger?'

Jo's voice slowed. 'Just call him and arrange to meet for lunch. It isn't going to be a complete surprise to him. Surely he must have picked up on something at the party?'

Hope wasn't so sure. Her father, if he did pick up on things, appeared then to wilfully ignore them. He still, after four years, acted as though everything was great between her and Sally. And as for Dan's dope habit and expulsion, it appeared to have come as a bolt from the blue. And he asked those toe-curling questions about Jake.

Hope shrugged.

Jo leaned across. 'Hope, I know it's hard. But in the long run it would make things so much easier. We wouldn't have to lie. The Jake thing wouldn't have happened if your mother had known.'

'Don't remind me.'

The memory was still raw: Jake's anger, her fear that he would guess her secret, the terror that he might drunkenly denounce her at her twenty-first. He had not. Fortunately he was by nature too self-absorbed to dwell on her motives for rejecting him. By the end of the evening he was deep in tactile conversation with Alexis from Sotheby's.

She smiled weakly. The party seemed like such a very long time ago. It had been her mother's party: full of her mother's friends who were people she barely knew and might never see again; all of it conceived and organised to her mother's taste and specifications. It was wonderful, of course. Creative, elegant and perfect. But Hope would have preferred to have gone for dinner with a few friends, maybe one or two from school, but mostly the people she mixed with at university. School seemed such a very long time ago. It had been hard, after the swapping of notes on current courses and job plans, to find much to say to her old sixth-form compatriots. Thinking about it made her quite miserable and then she felt immediately guilty because the strain of organising the party must have contributed to her mother's heart attack. And as soon as she thought of her mother in hospital, worse still collapsing at lunch, she found herself back where she started, her resolve replaced by a lacklustre state of miserable guilt.

Her birthday had been hard on Jo. First there had been her exclusion from the lunch. When her mother had first suggested the lunch idea Hope had tried to get her invited but her mother had been matter-of-fact: lunch was for family; the evening was for friends. But in the evening Jo was marooned on a faraway table, her proper place at Hope's side taken by an increasingly drunk Jake. Much later, finally reunited in Hope's bedroom, Jo had cried.

'Is this real for you, Hope? Or is it just a phase?'

Hope had cradled her. 'It is real. You're the most real, alive, honest person I have ever met. Jo, I love you ...'

The last three words had been instinctive. Until she heard herself speak them she had no idea that they had formulated in her mind. And then she was filled with a pure happiness that the biggest party, the most expensive present, all the fireworks and lights and music in the world in the world could not produce. They had pushed her old three-drawer dresser to block the door and climbed into bed.

Afterwards, in the morning, Jo had observed quietly, 'Hope, your mother never actually asked you if you wanted the party, did she?'

On the two occasions Hope had subsequently seen her mother – in hospital and then newly returned home – her words had failed her. It had been hard to get a word in edgeways.

I'm back on track and it's full speed ahead!

So, she had taken to avoiding her mother's calls. Meanwhile the burden of her secret grew larger.

Now Jo reached over and began caressing her hand. 'Your dad seems so nice. And reasonable. What's he going to do? Disinherit you in the middle of Starbucks?'

Hope's gaze was downcast. 'I don't think he'd understand.'

She could hear that Jo was making an effort to keep her frustration in check. 'Hope! There's nothing to *understand*. It's a question of *acceptance*. This is the way you are. The way you've always been. You're still you. You haven't metamorphosed into another person. It's just telling them about a part of you that has always existed.'

Hope got up and began putting papers in her backpack for her afternoon tutorial.

Jo's voice followed her. 'Hope, it's going to come out some time. Isn't it better that it's at a time and place that you choose?'

As Jo finished speaking, throwing herself melodramatically back onto the pillow, Hope wondered if perhaps in some undefined way that was what she wanted: that the knowledge would quietly seep out, entering her parents' consciousness, an unspoken but accepted fact. And as she pondered this the realisation came to her that that was how all that was uncomfortable was always dealt with in her family. The first baby who died and was never mentioned; her mother's moods; her parents' rows. God, the list went on and on. Dan's dope smoking; Dad leaving; Sally and Louis; Roger. None of it was ever discussed. The reason she wasn't having a conversation with either of her parents was because she had no clue where to begin. Her family dealt with issues by ignoring them.

She turned to Jo. 'I will tell him.'

Jo sat up, resting her head on one arm. 'You promise?'

'I'll try. I really will.'

'So, how old is this guy?' Edward's sleepy voice nonetheless contained a newly suspicious edge.

'Oh. I don't know. He's semi-retired.' Neither of these statements was untrue exactly. Working freelance was virtually the same thing as being semi-retired, after all.

Edward's hand moved onto her thigh. She shifted slightly away from him. Hopefully he would fall asleep soon. Currently she was preoccupied with trying to work out when she would have time to get back to the Wimbledon local records office let alone Christ Church College, Oxford, where the Duke of Wakemont's state papers were lodged. Hart had found a way to get her in there. Earlier today, distracted by thoughts of the 1901 national census, she had absent-mindedly offered Louis her coffee mug in place of his beaker of juice.

Edward's hand stayed in situ. 'Just so long as he doesn't get any ideas.'

But would she like him to? Sally thought she most probably would. Not that she would actually have an affair. Sally was clear in her mind, the more she went over it, that she loved Edward, that her current sense of distance was a reaction to recent circumstances and that she would do nothing to break up her marriage. Her relationship with Hart would be strictly a romantic affair, appropriately Victorian in nature, in which their mutual passion would be held in check by the constraints of duty and morality. But they could talk and go on investigative trips, perhaps exchange gifts and letters – or rather emails – which they now did two or three times a day. The emails were reports of Sally's research at the library. Hart talked about his work.

Good news! Tony Harris – the ex-journo Prof at CC – called. He put in a word to the College librarian and they'll give you access on the side. Just call ahead to let him know when you're coming and Tony will meet you there. H

That's fantastic. Thanks so much! I'll get down as soon as I can. How's Carmen?

Very passionate, thank you. She'll be in the Saturday Arts Review. How's Mary?

Still working hard at North Walk. No other sightings to report.

It had been a mistake to relay the Christ Church development to Edward. She realised belatedly that she would make a hopeless double agent. It would be impossible to keep track of what fact she was supposed to tell to which person.

Edward was not to be put off. 'He seems to be pulling out the stops for you.'

Privately she agreed. It was flattering and exciting all at once.

'It's professional,' she said firmly.

'Professional relationships can turn personal,' retorted Edward. 'You of all people should know that.'

'It's just research.' She pulled the duvet around her, intending this as a signal that she was preparing for sleep. 'Goodnight.' After a few seconds she felt Edward pull away.

As she lay awake the image of a jar of peas came to mind. Brickie had told her about the jar of peas theory.

'Every time you have sex before you get married you put a pea in a jar. A dried pea, obviously. And every time you have sex after you get married you take one out. Apparently you'll still have peas in the jar five years later. Or is it ten? I can't remember ...'

It was easy to blame the arrival of Louis for the slow decline of their sex life. But she was not sure the well-worn new-baby explanation was true in their case. She recalled having sex quite a bit in the months after his birth, at a time when no one else in the post-natal class gave any clue that they were doing it at all. It was more recently that their sex life had dropped off. Now, thinking about it more clearly, she realised that the decline coincided with the move to North Walk. And to be exact it was not an indefinite decline at all but rather a withdrawal on her part. Edward was as keen as ever. She was the one who had pulled away. At the time she had barely thought about it and when she did so she put it down to tiredness. But now she realised that the purchase of their first home had in one way marked an end rather than a beginning. It had depressed her. It was the end of the carefree, rather reckless life she and Edward had lived to date. Now their life was carefully preplanned and budgeted. It wasn't just the mortgage. There were all the bills that single people never noticed like life assurance and the extended warranties for domestic appliances. When you owned your own home you felt obliged to send Christmas cards to the neighbours and agree to watch their houses when they went away. As for going away themselves, Edward said that a holiday with young children was a contradiction in terms.

It was wonderful of course to have their own house. She was grateful for that. But it was also very grown up. She could see the years stretching ahead, in time the birth of another child, with each school-run day very much like the last. They would end up booking two weeks in July at the same cottage in Devon because, as Vickie said, it's easy and you know what you're getting. Sometimes she wanted *not* to know what she was getting. On occasions she regretted not making more of her trip to India when she had the chance. She felt an intermittent but insistent craving for the unpredictability and surprises in her life that had gone before. She was a married woman, she certainly looked like one, but there was a part of her not so deep inside that was still a single girl. When she was with Hart she felt ten years younger and an immeasurable remove away from her life as a wife and mother. And she decided that she needed that feeling. Not to replace being a wife and mother – or to endanger it – but as an expression of the part of her that was just *her*. All that was required was a little more care in the execution of her new dual existence.

'Now, Jenny didn't like it when I was sent upstairs. She was still in the kitchen. Oh, she was sour about it all!

When you start off you think to yourself, I'll never survive this. But you do. So one day Mrs Lyndon calls for me. Mary, she says, Miss Bella is leaving to get married and she needs a maid. I'd never spoken to him but it was all they talked about below stairs – Miss Bella's fancy man and how Mr Latham had ideas above his station. Of course, Miss Bella didn't see it, not then. She always thought the best of everyone.

Where was I? I was telling you about Mrs Lyndon. Miss Bella needs a maid, she says. Well, that started warning bells ringing. What about the cook, and the butler and the housekeeper and the other maids? I heard stories about girls who were the only maid. The mistress made a slave of you. Mrs Lyndon said there would be a cook engaged and other staff to follow. So I agreed. They were getting a bargain. I could cook – two years in the kitchen and I'd picked up enough – and clean and they only had to pay me an under housemaid's wages. Not that the cooks taught me anything. They were both bad-tempered. A good cook never shared her recipes.

When we got to Wimbledon Miss Bella hired a cook and a kitchen maid and we took on a daily boy to run errands. The cook had her own room and I shared with the kitchen maid. There was no room for anyone else. Miss Bella could have afforded twenty staff if she'd wanted to and a proper house. The Duke never kept her short of anything. She was his favourite. She could wind him round her little finger. But she said to me, "Mary, we want to live the simple life." That's exactly what she said. "Mary, we want to live the simple life." But if you want the truth of it he was no gentleman. Not when you scratched the surface. He wasn't brought up with servants. We made him feel uncomfortable. So Miss Bella gave in to him on that like she gave in to him on everything else and got rid of all of them. Except me, of course.

That's why they lived in this little house. He wanted it that way. And to think she could have had any man she wanted.

After I left, Jenny married one of the gardener's boys. He left the Hall and joined the army. They sent him to South Africa. He got the malaria and died out there. So there she was left with two babies and only a widow's pension. They would have been better off staying at the Hall and holding out for a gardener's cottage. So you see, all her airs and graces didn't get her very far. We lost touch after that ...'

The routine ran out at eleven o'clock at night. That was the most dangerous time. That was when it was too late to call her lawyer, call a friend, run on the treadmill at the gym, go shopping – or rather window shopping – scan the media jobs pages of the *Guardian* or any of the other activities that Anna was currently relying on to get through each day. On the third night she had got up and gone to Tesco at 2.45 a.m. Anywhere rather than to be alone. After that she had made an appointment to see her doctor.

I have a very demanding job. And I'm working on a high-pressure project. I'm finding it really hard to sleep.

Suicidal thoughts? No! I'm not the type. It's just stress ...

The pills made her sleep late. When she woke up there was no reprieve. There was none of the few seconds' grace she had read about in people who had suffered a bereavement. No, she remembered straight away that she had been fired. She recalled immediately the police interviews and the obvious disdain of the investigating officer at Beaconsfield Police Station for what he termed 'London media types' and their 'shenanigans'.

She had to impose on Sally. Without Sally's house – the warm kitchen, the comfortable front room, the feeling throughout of safety and shelter – she would have nowhere else to go. Her mother appeared to take a sly delight at the turn of events. 'That's what happens when you fly too close to the sun. You get your wings burnt.' Her BBC friends were sympathetic but busy. Sally was the only person she knew who was at home during the day. Besides, there was nowhere else she wanted to go. She liked Sally. She loved the slow way she moved through the routine of her life. Sally listened in a way that no one at work did: carefully and patiently. Sally did not listen with an ear to interrupting and putting forward her opinion. Sally didn't try to tell her what to do. There was something very serene about Sally.

At eleven o'clock there was only the television to watch. Edward, she had deduced, took a glass of water to bed with him, from the quick faint sound of the tap running and his heavy footfall at about this time. That was her cue. Anna got up and went over to her handbag. She pulled out the sleeping pills and took out one, swallowing it with the last of the small bottle of Evian she had taken to the gym.

She took some deep breaths. She reminded herself that if she followed the routine closely enough she would be OK. Next she would brush her teeth. Then she would return to the sofa and stay there, watching television while she waited for the pills to take hold. Then she would stumble from the sofa to her bed and fall asleep almost immediately. Or stay on the sofa all night, waking briefly at three or four to the television showing Italian league football.

The alternative was to allow the thoughts and then the anxiety to take hold, gripping her, circling in her mind, pulling her down so that the fear would come and she would imagine herself broken, shamed, homeless and permanently unemployable.

It was not so far-fetched. She had enough in the bank for the next two months' mortgage payments. But that was not the worst of it. There were the questions she now asked herself about all that she had hitherto held as certainties: was it possible that hard work was not rewarded, that talent did not always win out, that you could give your all and be kicked out without a second glance?

And was it true? In the darkest moments, when she allowed herself to look past Rick Roth's betrayal and replace it with a replay of Roy Jardine's relentless interrogation, she asked herself was it true that her actions almost got Penny killed?

If so, she had lost her touch, her judgement, and above all her nerve, so that she could never do this work again. How could she push it to the edge, take the risks that made her the very best, now that she knew the consequences? She understood now that it wasn't a game.

Tonight she would stay on the sofa. Sometimes going to bed alone was just too hard. She would think of Tim, hugging a second pillow to her chest, imagining his voice and his touch. He had agreed to meet her for lunch. Not for a couple of weeks, he was off to the States to interview the British Ambassador. But that was fine. That gave her time to prepare, to work out what she needed to say to persuade him to try again. If nothing else, she could grasp a second chance with Tim.

Chapter 16

The Acorns was situated in a red-brick terraced house in Southfields. Large signs attached to the brick wall enclosing the small pocket of front garden asked parents not to double park when dropping their children. The road, narrow and lined with cars in residents' permit spaces, was currently blocked by a Volvo estate and a black Golf GTi.

'Look. Everyone stops outside,' said Edward coming to a halt. 'We can run in.'

'No!' Sally protested. 'It might take ages.'

Edward didn't seem to have any sense of occasion. It was, after all, Louis's first day at nursery school. Or that was how she thought of it, though the Acorns described itself as a 'Day Care Provider'. That would explain why she was wearing make-up and a new pair of jeans under her best black cashmere-mix winter coat. Whether it was the stress of the party – or thoughts of Hart – or forgetting to eat while preoccupied by the Bella Latham story, she had lost five pounds without trying.

She was still in two minds about Louis going at all. Two seemed so young. Dorothea, the owner and earth mother type, who had shown her round, had been very understanding, whilst pointing out that some of the children stayed all day. Dorothea – her grey hair in a plait, dressed in layers of peasant-style cotton and a thick woollen cardigan – had shown her the room for naps. It had little mats on the floor and the ceiling was painted in blue with clouds. Sally couldn't imagine Louis going in there willingly. He had to be in a state of miserable semi-consciousness these days before he would agree to an afternoon nap. So, she had registered for nine to twelve and now even those three hours seemed too long. She felt horribly nervous. Louis, on the other hand, had been running around shouting 'skool, skool' for days. It was as if he was desperate to get out of the house.

They parked, paid for a ticket, the cost of which Edward said was outrageous, and walked Louis along the pavement. There ought to be a soundtrack playing: 'I'm Walking On Sunshine'?

When they arrived at the Acorns Dorothea answered the door smiling, took Louis's coat and shook hands with Edward. Dorothea bent down to talk to Louis.

'Would you like to play with the sand and the water? Or would you like to do some painting?'

There was no hesitation. 'Paint!'

She reached up to a row of pegs, each with a painted animal face. 'This is your coverall, Louis.' He started gyrating excitedly. 'Stand still, sweetie.' He stood still.

'Some of the mothers embroider these with their names,' Dorothea continued, looking up at Sally. 'But you don't have to.'

Edward stepped forward to pat him on the back.

'Say bye bye to Mummy and Daddy,' Dorothea said.

Louis was standing looking over the safety gate. 'Bye Bye Bye Bye Bye.' Why was he suddenly so obedient? And then Dorothea unlatched the wooden safety gate and Louis was off before she had even had a chance to kiss him, hurrying towards the paint table.

They stood excluded.

She heard Edward's quiet voice. 'We ought to go.'

She didn't want to go. She wanted to stay – jump the gate and sit down at the paint table and watch over him. 'What if he needs me?'

She felt Edward's hand on her shoulder. Gently, he said, 'Come on. He's fine.'

And he was fine. He hadn't clung for dear life to the bars of the safety gate or wailed for his mummy or screamed to go home. Vickie had explained, several times, how it was when Rory started nursery: he pleaded for her not to leave; an hour later the owner called her to say please would she come back in because he was still crying inconsolably; he was so much happier now at home with her.

Louis was holding his brush like a hammer, slapping it into a saucer of green paint and making splodges on a large piece of red paper. He appeared to have forgotten the existence of his parents.

'It feels like … it feels like the beginning of him growing up.'

'No. He still needs you. He'll always need you. Even when he's twenty-one and bringing his laundry home.'

And then Edward steered her down the hallway. 'He'll be coming home before you know it. Why don't you go and have a coffee? Ring a friend.'

There was nothing she could think of to say to this.

They stood on the pavement. He glanced at his watch. 'I need to get going.'

He kissed her on both cheeks. 'It's good for him, you know, to be with other children. You're doing the right thing. It makes starting school easier.'

'Does it?'

'Yes.' He looked hesitant. 'Look, Pia hardly let Hope leave the house when she was little. When she started school it was a nightmare. She didn't know how to play. Pia barely ever invited other kids round.'

'Why?'

'I think she was scared of them spreading germs.'

It was an almighty shock. She had imagined that Pia would have been the Queen of the Playgroup, marshalling the mothers with spreadsheet-driven efficiency.

'We learned the lesson. I put my foot down and insisted that Dan do more activities. Of course, that may have been a mistake, too ...' His voiced trailed off. 'Look, I really have to go.'

She watched Edward stride off down the street in the direction of Southfields tube station, pulling his mobile out of his pocket, already focused on business. She had three hours until it was time to collect Louis. It was clear that neither her husband nor her son was going to miss her. Even Dan was preoccupied, revising his theatre scene, which had been chosen as one of three to be performed at an end-of-term show. The residual feelings of doubt and guilt that she entertained about her morning plans ebbed away. Why should she feel guilty anyhow? Hart was passing through on his way to a meeting in London. Meanwhile, Sally had lots to report. What could be more natural – and sensible – than for them to meet as arranged in the Wimbledon Starbucks?

*

Pascoe sounded really angry. 'What? I thought it was sorted.'

Dan lowered his voice, as if he was afraid of being overheard. 'There's nothing I can do. I can't go out.'

This was not true. The house was deserted and the front-door key was in its usual place in the kitchen drawer. He just didn't feel like going after last time.

'Can't you slip out? Just go!' demanded Pascoe. 'Just walk out of the door. What's she going to do? Wrestle you?'

'I can't. Listen,' he lowered his voice still further, 'someone's coming. I've got to go.' He slammed down the receiver.

The house stood silent around him. Pascoe was all right – as long as he got his own way. Which meant going where Pascoe wanted to go and hanging out at the back of Victoria Station with Pascoe's new friends. They said dope was for beginners. They made Dan feel like a little kid.

Besides, it was cold out. And Sally had said that she would be back at lunchtime and they would have a special lunch for Louis's first day at school. Risotto with something. Sally might even make a cake. Hopefully, Anna would come round, too. He could show her the changes to his scene. Then they could play PlayStation or watch a film. Anna called them 'movies'. She had thousands of DVDs. Last week they had watched all three of the *Godfather* episodes, one a day. Anna told him things as they were watching. 'Look at the lighting. See how the characters' faces are lit up against the darkness.' She didn't go on and on through the entire film like his mother did. She just made the occasional comment, pointing out the way the director told the story. 'It's not just in what the characters say. It's how they treat each other ...'

Afterwards, she asked him questions: 'What do you think about the music?' or 'Why do you think Michael changes so much?'

Then she actually listened to what he said.

Anna had said that she would show him how to use a camera. Anna knew other things too. One day, after he'd gone for a walk on the Common and had just a tiny spliff, she'd bumped into him in the hallway as she was coming out of the living room. Straightaway, he could tell that she'd smelt it on him. But she didn't go all psycho like his mother would have. She just said quietly, so that Sally couldn't hear, 'I've seen a lot of very talented people go to hell with that stuff.'

Then she paused and gently shook his shoulder. 'Dan, I think you're talented too.'

Anna and Sally were always saying nice things like that. Sally told him yesterday morning that he made great scrambled eggs. And she said he should do art classes because he was really good at making things with Louis's Playdough. Anna said he should keep a diary as a 'creative exercise' because he was really good with words. And Louis, who'd got a lot better overall, followed him everywhere shouting his name. 'Dan ... Dan ...'

Even his dad had chilled a bit. Last weekend they'd gone to the rugby at Twickenham because his dad had got tickets from someone rich at the bank.

Basically, what would be really good would be if he could live here, go to school here and visit his mother once a month. He was due to go down to Gerrards Cross next week. There was no avoiding that. He would definitely have to see Pascoe before then to get some supplies. It was the only way he could drown out his mother. But here, at North Walk, it was easy and sort of ... normal. It wouldn't be like that in Gerrards Cross.

Hart had secured them a table for two by the window looking out onto George Street. The Starbucks in Wimbledon town, across from the railway station, was always busy. Sally made her way past the collection of tables and expensive, parked pushchairs to where Hart was sitting.

He looked up. 'Hi! I ordered you a coffee. But I can get you something else if you'd prefer.'

'No. Thank you. Coffee's fine.'

'You take milk?'

'Yes.' He'd remembered.

She put down her folder and slipped off her coat. 'How long have you got?'

'I have to be there at noon.'

'At Channel Four?'

'Yes. I know the interviewer. There are going to be three of us. I'm the impartial academic.'

'Is it live?'

'Yes,' he said matter-of-factly. It sounded desperately glamorous.

She made a mental note that it was one o'clock. That would give her ample time to collect Louis and get home to sit switch on the television.

'So. What did you find out?' He really had the most attractive brown eyes.

She cleared her throat. 'OK. First the bad news. The woman at the LEA finally got back to me and they've no idea where the Selton School records are and they haven't got anyone who could look for them.'

Hart gave a resigned nod. 'That's the way it goes sometimes ...'

'But there's lots of good news. I went through the electoral register.' She tried to keep the excitement out of her voice. 'I was working on what you said we should do next – look for the secondary players. Who else was living at North Walk between 1900 and 1905 when Robert Latham left? Well, I found Latham listed from 1900 to 1905. He was qualified to vote because he occupied a freehold property—'

She was interrupted at this point by a woman trying to exit the sofa area with a double buggy. She stood up to make way. She sat down and continued. 'The problem with the register is that during this period only a very few woman were able to vote – and then in parish elections, not for MPs. So it wouldn't give us a comprehensive picture of who was living in the North Walk houses at the time.'

Sally reached for her handbag and took out her notebook. She gave Hart a half-smile. 'But fortunately in 1901 there was a national census. It's all on microfiche. It took me a while but I found North Walk. The Lathams were living there with three servants. A cook and two maids. Henry's listed, too.'

She had Hart's attention. 'How much information does it give?'

'Quite a bit. Robert Latham is listed as the head of the household, born in 1870 in Streatham, his occupation is given as "gentleman".'

'Not journalist, then?'

'No. Interesting, isn't it?' She looked at the first page of her notes. 'Bella doesn't have an occupation at all. Then there's Henry. Born 1901.'

'What about the servants?'

'Well, Mary's listed. Born 1882 in Ireland. Listed as a general servant. Her age is given as nineteen. Then there's another servant, Winifred

Rolfe born in Wimbledon. And a cook, Jean MacKinnon also born in Wimbledon.'

'So they were recruited locally.'

'I imagine so. But this is the interesting point. Ten years later, in 1921, there's only Bella and Mary. No listing for a cook or another servant.'

'And after that?'

Sally shrugged. 'You can't find out. The census returns are sealed after that. But they are both listed on the electoral register until they die. Bella in 1953 and Mary in 1964.'

Hart sat back. 'Frustrating about the census. OK. Well, what do we have?'

Sally jumped in. 'Given Bella's background and the way that she was used to living, I'm backing your theory of money troubles. Why else would she reduce her staff? I'm hoping that the Duke's papers might shed some light on that.'

Hart made a jotted note to himself. 'I think the next stage is for me to go right back, line by line, through my notebooks. Let me see if Bella's journal has any clues that we've missed. I'll look for anything she writes about money. Maybe Latham was supposed to be sending her money from America?'

'I wondered about that. Isn't that the most likely scenario? That he got over there, met someone else and effectively deserted her?'

'Which would make *Letters* look like a load of hot air.'

'And explain why Sandy Wakemont doesn't want to open up that archive. Maybe he knows that it all went sour.'

Hart gave her a broad smile. 'Hey, you've got the beginnings of a conspiracy theory there. I love it.'

And even though she knew he was teasing her, she laughed. 'It's just a theory. I want to believe that they lived happily ever after. But if you look at it rationally, the odds were against them. Bella rushed into this marriage in the aftermath of her mother's death and her father's remarriage. She had a stepmother and three new sisters living at Selton Park and it's clear from Irvine that the new Duchess wasn't the shy and retiring type. She didn't waste any time in turning the Hall upside down. Within a year or so the life that Bella had known was erased. And I think Bella was close to her mother. I think she went to Italy with her mother willingly. So she fell into Robert Latham's arms at a time when she was vulnerable. But then she had to live with the reality of marriage outside her class and social circle.'

'And Henry's death proved the final straw.'

'Very possibly. We're assuming that the Duke pushed Robert into taking a job for him in the States. But who knows? He may have volunteered to go to escape a collapsing marriage.'

Hart nodded. 'At any rate, we've identified the questions. Now we need to look for the answers.' He looked down at his watch. 'Have you got time for another coffee?'

She checked hers. She couldn't risk being late.

'I ought to go.' She reached back for her coat. There was so much more to be said, as she had known there would be. Which was why she had days ago formulated the suggestion in her mind. She had even planned the menu: lamb cutlets, French beans and roast potatoes in olive oil and rosemary followed by pears poached in red wine.

She hoped she was looking cool because her heart was racing. She tried to sound as nonchalant as possible. 'Would you like to come to lunch? I could show you the photocopies?'

He nodded. 'Sure.'

She wanted to jump up like a delirious teenager. Instead, she reached for her handbag and put away her notebook in what she hoped was a businesslike action. 'How about next Tuesday?'

Hope sat in the Fleet Street branch of Pret a Manger waiting for her father. In her hand she held the draft notes of her Easter assignment, which asked her to discuss, with reference to contemporary sources, why the French Revolution of 1789 had not been replicated in England.

The knot of fear in her stomach grew tighter still with every minute past noon as she scanned the approaching office crowd for the figure of her father.

How could it be that the possible sentences she had framed in her mind, each one short and succinct, so very rehearsed, could be so difficult to choose from?

Daddy. Jo and I are more than just friends. Jo's my girlfriend.

Daddy. I'm gay.

Daddy. I'm in love with Jo.

Her father's hand on her shoulder made her start with surprise.

'Daddy!'

He looked taken aback. 'Only me!' He looked at her quizzically. 'Is something the matter?'

'No! No. Nothing at all.' She slid off her seat. 'I didn't see you come in.'

It was a pity she had said 'nothing at all', although to come out with it there and then would not have been the best timing. Her father, hungry and already moving towards the fast-lengthening lunchtime queue, was expecting a sandwich, a brownie and a coke – not a proclamation of his daughter's sexuality.

She joined him by the cabinets where the sandwiches were lined up. He rubbed his hands together. 'Let's get something to eat? The usual?'

She hesitated. Then, 'Yes, the usual.'

Now, as she sat down with her father, she felt miserably on edge. She assessed each point in the conversation to see whether it was a possible opening.

'So, what are your plans for Easter?'

'I'm going home. But I want to spend some time with Jo.'

Her father frowned. 'Which one's Jo?'

'She was at the party. She's very slim with short blonde hair?'

He father shook his head. 'No. I can't bring her to mind.'

'But I introduced you,' she prompted him. 'She's very pretty.'

'Not as pretty as you. How's your mother?'

'Fine. They did the Stress Test and they want to try some different pills. I'll stay for as long as I can.' She paused. 'Before I go to see Jo.'

'Any plans for surgery?'

'Not right now. I think they're going to see how the pills work.'

'Is she smoking?'

'No.' It was an easy lie. Her mother had sworn her to secrecy.

I'm trying so hard, darling. And I've cut right down. I'm just getting myself mentally psyched up to stop.

He seemed to accept this. He nudged her. 'Eat up! You've hardly touched your sandwich. Are you eating properly?'

'Yes!' Hope pressed on. 'Jo's parents live in Cambridge. Her father's a university professor.'

'Good.' He pulled out his wallet. 'Here. Take this.'

'Dad …'

'Unless you'd rather have an Easter egg?'

'No!' She put down her sandwich and pushed the notes into the back pocket of her jeans. 'Thanks.'

'Now.' His face grew serious. 'I have a request. I want you to come to Sunday lunch. Two weeks' time. Both of us do,' he corrected himself.

An excuse began to formulate in her mind. 'Term ends then,' she said, trying to sound regretful. 'I'll be in Gerrards Cross. I don't know if—'

Her father cut across her. 'I want you and Sally to get on. I want you to spend some time together. You could help her cook lunch.'

'Can I let you know?'

'I'm giving you plenty of notice. I'm sure you can work something out.' She had a glimpse in the determined edge that had entered his voice of how he must be at work. 'I want you to be there. Besides, Dan wants to see you.'

'OK,' she said reluctantly. How had the conversation become diverted from the subject of Jo to a wholly unwelcome cooking session with her stepmother? Jo would be furious. And then she had an idea. It wouldn't be the same as telling him there and then. But at least it would placate Jo and get Daddy used to the idea of Jo. Maybe he would even guess?

'Daddy?' she said tentatively. 'Can I bring Jo?'

'Bring whoever you like,' he said, unconcerned. 'Just don't be late.'

Chapter 17

Sally felt compelled to double-check. 'You're absolutely sure there are no diaries before that date?'

Hart nodded. 'Definitely. There are none in the archive. Bella started keeping a diary after she got married. In fact, she says as much.'

Hart leaned forward and ran his finger down the three notebooks that were stacked on Sally's kitchen table, extracting the bottom one. Sally took the opportunity to move the white oval Wedgwood serving dish containing the last of the poached pears from the table. They had been very good. Just soft and spicy enough. As for the lamb cutlets, they had been close to perfect. Hart had complimented her on the honey and mustard glaze. He had brought a bottle of Bordeaux and none remained.

The house was still, just as she had planned. Edward was fully occupied: it was the day of the bi-monthly Far East Planning Team meeting. On this occasion, Edward had informed her, it was to be presided over by the Chairman himself. Edward had asked her three times to make sure she collected his grey chalkstripe from the drycleaner's. Then he was taking the afternoon off work to go down to Welton for a meeting with the headmaster, Dan and Pia. Dan was spending a week in Gerrards Cross with his mother.

Louis kept saying, 'Dan?'

'He'll be back very soon.'

That morning, dressing for work in their bedroom, Edward had been in reluctant agreement with Pia's plan. 'Pia wants him to go back to Welton for another term. She says he hasn't given it a proper try.'

Sally spoke carefully. 'What do you think?"

'I think it would at least buy us some time to find somewhere else.'

She had to speak up. 'I don't think he wants to go.'

Edward had looked resigned. 'I know. But he has to go to school.'

She would miss Dan if he went back to Welton. She no longer regarded him as the wayward drug-addict of her early fears. He was, as every mother said – and why shouldn't that include a stepmother? – a good boy who'd got into the wrong company.

Louis, meanwhile, had happily toddled off with Anna. The weather forecast was predicting a dry day, so Anna could take him down to Cottenham Park or out to tea at Wombles, the café just off the High Street with the chocolate chip cookies Louis loved.

'Three o'clock then,' Sally had repeated to Anna.

'Yep. Three, no problem.' And Anna had turned to wave. 'Wave bye bye, Louis.'

Now, as Sally moved the side plates and glasses from the table to the kitchen counter, she felt at the perfect pitch of relaxed companionship. 'More coffee?'

'Thanks,' Hart said, thumbing the pages of the selected notebook.

There was no residue of stiff politeness left between them now. It was as if they had known each other for ever. She got up to boil the kettle and make a second cafetiere of Colombian coffee, fresh ground and specially purchased from Starbucks in Wimbledon Village yesterday.

'Here. Bella writes at the beginning of the diary in 1900 that she wants to record an account of her new life. "Robert agrees that my little journal is an excellent idea, a record of all the fun we shall have and something for all our children ..."'

Hart put down the notebook. He leaned back in the kitchen chair and put his hands behind his head. 'But ultimately I don't think the diaries are revealing. It's all about social visits and shopping.'

She cut in. 'We know Robert's career in journalism was going nowhere. We know they had to let staff go. Therefore, the Duke must have been helping them financially. I think in exchange he made Robert Latham run an errand to Cincinnati. Except he didn't come back.'

'Which leaves us searching every death record in the USA for a Robert Latham over a period of about fifty years ...' Hart's voice trailed off.

' I know,' Sally said resignedly. 'There must be thousands of Robert

Lathams. It's hopeless. I'm still going to check the Christ Church records, just in case there're details of the Duke's personal finances.' She pre-empted Hart. 'But that's a long shot ...'

She put two cups of coffee on the kitchen table and sat down. For lunch she had dressed, after agonised forethought, in a long – and therefore slimming – dark red skirt in mock suede and a cream merino polo-neck, which itched round the neck but, coupled with the padded bra, made her breasts look bigger.

Hart leaned forward conspiratorially. 'Which leaves us with our last option: breaking into the Wakemont Family Archive by dead of night ...'

She looked up. The prospect of breaking into a stately home with Hart was irresistibly exciting.

'Unfortunately,' he said sitting back again, 'we couldn't use any information we gained as a result. It would be deemed to be stolen.'

Sally knew that they had reached an impasse. But she could not bring herself to say so.

Instead, trying to keep her voice light, she said, 'Do you think you've got enough for an article?'

From his expression she could see that she had clearly been considering just this. 'I think we've fallen short,' he said slowly. 'There are too many questions. We know Robert left in 1905 from the *Lucania* shipping records. We've got absolutely no leads on where he went after that. To all intents and purposes, Robert Latham disappeared off the face of the earth after 1905.'

She was not about to admit to Hart that she had been looking on the internet at the price of flights to the middle of Ohio. And hotels. And from there she had fallen into a recurrent daydream in which she and Hart slipped away for a few days to solve the mystery of Robert Latham and write a book that would become the basis for a multi-million-dollar Hollywood screenplay.

She knew he was right.

Reluctantly she took up the thread of Hart's last comments. 'And if Robert was sent to do the Duke's dirty work ...'

'There wouldn't be any record of it,' Hart concluded.

She sighed. 'It's just so hard to accept that we'll never know.'

Hart smiled. 'Maybe you should become a journalist. You have that tenacious streak.'

He jolted her. It was one of so many of the things he liked about him. *You should.* Not you should *have* in the tense that implied her life was all but over. She never had conversations like this with Edward these days, or conversations at all – unless the subject was China and the bank's new office in Shanghai.

In the easy familiarity that had settled between them, she ventured, 'Are you thinking about Ireland? When you nearly got killed?'

He shook his head. 'I got beaten up. The people I was dealing with kill with bullets. If they had wanted me dead they would have made sure I was. They just wanted me – and anyone like me – to go away.'

He paused and when he resumed speaking it was to anticipate her next question.

'And it worked. I was in no state to go anywhere. By the time I got back on my feet the cell had closed down and set up elsewhere. The trail went cold.' He looked up at her and gave her a rueful smile. 'So you see the journalist doesn't always get the story.'

There were a hundred questions she wanted to ask him and too many facts that she wanted to forget. She was married, she was a mother and yet, sitting here in her kitchen, she felt younger than she had … for years. She felt happy, vibrantly alive, energetic and purposeful. She might not be any the wiser about Robert Latham but she had met Hart and now she could no longer deny to herself her motivation in pursuing the project with him. Hart inspired her. He lifted her from the ordinary repetitiveness of her life. And he elevated her also from the obsessions that had made her so miserable. Edward's meeting with Pia would have tormented her in the past. Now she barely gave it a second thought. She was not sure why but felt better somehow – more confident, less defensive. Altogether more capable.

She wanted this time together to go and on. It would be unbearable if, after today, the trail went cold and they never met again.

'Perhaps,' she ventured, 'it would be worth researching some of the other members of the family. Bella's two brothers and Camilla?' It was a weak lead and she knew it but she wasn't about to give up.

Hart looked doubtful. 'But their papers are kept in the Selton Archive?'

As she was working out a response to this, a second line of attack, the doorbell rang.

She glanced up at the clock. It had to be wrong. It could not be quarter past three.

But it was – and Anna wasn't early, she was late.

Sally got up, feeling suddenly weighed down, and as she did so Hart glanced at his watch.

'I ought to get going.'

He began putting his papers away in his briefcase.

A feeling akin to panic flooded her.

'Are you sure? Please don't feel you have to hurry off.'

She wanted to add something more persuasive but she had no choice but to go to answer the door. As she opened it to Anna and Louis a cold blast of air entered the hallway.

'Sorry we're late.'

'Late!' chimed in Louis. He began struggling out of his coat.

'But we had lunch. And went to the library. And then we went to the park and made our film …'

'Fim! Made a fim …'

'And then we went and had a biscuit and some hot chocolate. How was your meeting?'

'Mummy, fim!'

'Oh, we're just going over some of the details.'

Would Anna take the hint and leave?

'I'll let you get on with it then.' She leaned down and spoke to Louis cheerfully. 'Bye Bye. I'll make the film and I'll bring it round tomorrow.'

Louis's face creased into angry disappointment. 'Fim! Look at fim!'

A note of dangerous petulance had entered his voice and he began tugging at the camcorder case. His coat was hanging off one arm.

'He wants to see it on the television,' explained Anna. She bent down again. 'You saw it on the little camera screen, didn't you?'

She looked back up at Sally. 'Of course I need to edit it. I'll do it on the computer and bring it round tomorrow.'

Louis began to cry. 'See fim. Now!'

Hart appeared in the kitchen doorway, presumably alerted by the commotion.

'This is my friend, Anna,' Sally attempted to explain above the wailing. 'And this is my son, Louis. Anna, this is Hart Rutherford.'

Sally thought Hart said 'hello' but it was difficult to tell above the noise. Sally had to make a split-second decision. Either she could get Anna out of the door and be left with a tired and tantruming Louis or she could give in, let Louis see the film and hope Anna would leave them to it while Louis took a nap. The frustrated desire to be alone with Hart for just a little longer was close to unbearable.

Louis was getting ear-splittingly loud.

Sally put on her brightest voice. 'Let's see the film!' She grabbed Louis's hand and tugged him into the living room. 'We're going to see the film. See the film.'

He sniffed and sank to the floor. Anna followed, unzipping her coat, an unglamorous parka-style jacket in combat green, presumably purchased for work. Underneath, however, she wore figure-hugging brown cords and a short waist-skimming muted-pink sweatshirt with a skateboard logo. Hart stood awkwardly in the living-room doorway, his expression indicating that he was considering bolting. Sally felt suddenly anxious. She looked over her shoulder from where she sat on the floor taking off Louis's shoes. 'Come and join us!'

'It jumps about,' Anna explained apologetically, taking the camera out of its black carrying case. 'I need to edit it. And add a soundtrack.'

'A soundtrack?' asked Hart quizzically, still standing in the doorway.

'I thought Oasis,' said Anna.

'Oasis?' repeated Sally bewildered, unclear how this would relate to a children's playground.

Hart shot Anna a second glance.

'Yep,' Anna said confidently. 'I thought "Roll With It". It goes like this ...' She started humming.

'Yes. From *Morning Glory*. I know it,' Hart said, a touch curtly.

That stopped Anna dead in her tracks. For a moment she looked almost wrong-footed.

Hart nodded towards the camera. 'You do this professionally?'

'I used to. Until I got fired. One of my interviewees got shot.'

'Tell me more.' Hart ambled into the living room and sat down on the sofa.

Anna pulled a cord from the camcorder bag and deftly hooked up the camera to the television. Then she sat on the sofa next to Hart.

The film began to play. Louis sat enraptured, pointing at himself. But this was no home video. Even without editing it was good. Very good. Louis was in perpetual motion. Sliding, circling, swinging. Then swooping after a flock of pigeons. Somehow Anna had managed to tell a story of an everyday trip to the park. There was the tentative friendship with another child. The hit-and-miss kicking of a ball. But the best part was the exploration of the climbing frame. First it showed Louis wandering through the lower bars. Then the perspective changed. Anna had gone onto the climbing frame herself and shot a segment as if from Louis's eye-view, so that the viewer could see what he saw as the camera weaved through the bars, Anna shooting so that the heights looked enormous and the ground very far away.

'I like it,' said Hart, obviously impressed.

Anna shrugged. 'I enjoy doing it. Making films is what I always wanted to do.'

She knelt down and began to unhook the camera. As she did so her short pink sweatshirt rode up slightly to reveal the pale flawless skin of her back and her narrow waist.

'With the BBC?' asked Hart.

'Yep. Graduate-training programme. Actually I started in BBC radio.' Anna put the camera back in the case. Sally decided to take this as a sign that Anna was getting ready to leave. Good. Then she would offer Hart a cup of tea and a slice of cake.

Anna sat back on the sofa. 'Then I went over to television and ended up making programmes for the BBC1 Saturday-night early-evening slot.'

'So you must know Anne Bayliss?' asked Hart.

'Yes. She was appointed a year after I went over to BBC1.'

Who was Anne Bayliss? Neither of them bothered to explain.

'I know her husband. He's a sub on the *Guardian*.'

'Colin? Yes, I met him at her summer party.'

And then they were off, swapping names, dates and piecing together the network of media types they knew in common. Anne Bayliss, it turned out, was the Controller of BBC1. Sally, who had been instructed by Louis to push his cars up to the upper level parking, sat not so much excluded as totally forgotten.

Then Anna explained the whole 7–24 saga. Hart was clearly fascinated.

'And then they marched me out of the building.'

'Hey, they did that to me, too. When I got sacked from the *Express*.'

'You were sacked!' Anna exclaimed.

'Yes. I refused to tell the editor my source for a piece on Welsh nationalists. I didn't trust him not to pass it on. His first priority was circulation, closely followed by grabbing a knighthood. So he sacked me. Not that he called it that; those were the days when journalists went on strike. I was made redundant. That was when I moved to the *Guardian*.'

He had never told Sally that story.

Anna stretched out her arms behind her head. Her sweatshirt rode up again, now revealing an inch of flat flawless stomach. 'But you felt more at home there?'

'Actually, no. I always enjoyed being a tabloid journalist. In those days you could chase a story.'

Anna nodded. 'Funny. As soon as I left the BBC I missed it. Even though the money was better at 7–24.'

'And you had more freedom?' he ventured.

'Yes. Freedom to screw it up.'

Sally, now lining up cars in a queue to enter the ground-floor car park, was beginning to feel mutely self-conscious. She had been plotting ways to introduce the subject of Tim into the conversation.

Hart, perhaps you also know Tim Meah, Anna's ex-boyfriend? He's a journalist, too. She's hoping to get back together with him ...

'I saw the news reports of the shooting,' said Hart. 'What's the situation on the court case?'

'The prosecution doesn't want me as a witness. I spoke to one of the police officers – off the record. He said they're trying to downplay the whole involvement of 7–24 and make out that this was a slow-burn type of crime. I think they're going to argue that Mrs Zarkosky had been planning this all along.'

'To avoid a provocation defence?'

'Exactly. The defence may call me but I haven't heard anything.'

'I guess the defence strategy is to portray Mrs Zarkosky as a victim herself.'

Of course, Hart began his career as a crime reporter.

Anna nodded. 'So at the moment I'm just keeping my head down.'

'Are you going to try to get another job?'

'Quite honestly I don't know where to start.'

Hart looked thoughtful. 'I have a friend you might like to speak to. He makes short films for Channel Four. They quite often sub work out.'

'I've done one or two of those before. I did a poetry series. Short, two-minute films.'

'My friend's name is Sean Doyle.'

'Sean! I know Sean. He was a judge for the London Uni Student Filmmaker's competition.'

Sally could already feel Hart's next question. Sure enough it came.

'You were a prize winner?'

'It was a long time ago,' Anna said modestly.

'Row-da-bout,' ordered Louis. He wanted her to make a round-about.

'Not that long,' countered Hart gallantly.

'Row-da-bout.'

Sally just couldn't take any more.

'In a minute, Louis.' She got up from the floor. Her foot had gone numb and she staggered slightly. 'Would you like a cup of tea?'

Anna and Hart looked up simultaneously.

'Yes, please.'

They made no sign to get up from where they were now sitting side by side on the sofa, deep in conversation. Even Louis stayed put, presumably wanting to remain in the living room at the centre of the action.

In the kitchen, where the sad remains of lunch lay spread out across the kitchen countertop, Sally put on the kettle and got out her large wooden-handled tray. She had made a cake. Now, taking it out of its Tupperware container, she felt ridiculous. How long had she spent looking through recipes, dismissing one as too rich, another as to complicated, before settling on a classic Victoria sponge sandwiched with strawberry jam and buttercream. She never made anything like that for Edward these days. The top was coated with icing sugar that she had carefully dusted through her finest sieve. Hot, foolish tears of disappointment welled up. She blinked them back furiously. What had she expected? From the living room she could hear Hart laughing. The fantasy and the reality of her relationship were colliding, the truth achingly apparent that it was no more than an innocent friendship based on a common interest. Only in her dreams, or more accurately delusions, had it been something more. Did she want to go to bed with Hart? Maybe. But more than that she wanted attention, excitement, romance. She wanted a day in her life that was not exactly the same as the last.

And today, for a short while, it had been just such a day.

The best that could be hoped for now was to serve them tea and hope that Anna would leave for the gym as soon as possible. Maybe she could suggest that?

But when she went back in she found Anna and Hart deep in conversation.

'So the next stop was the census and the electoral register,' Hart was explaining.

'Hey,' Anna looked up brightly. 'Hart's been telling me about the Lathams.'

Sally put down the tray. She didn't want to talk about it. 'Yes. We seem to have reached a dead end, unfortunately.'

Hopefully they would be distracted by the Victoria sponge standing imperiously on a white china cake stand. But neither of them appeared to have noticed it.

She felt like the housekeeper. And she looked like one, too. Set against Anna's look, her red skirt and the polo didn't look smart or chic as she had envisaged – just frumpy.

She cut a small slice for Louis.

Without waiting to be asked Anna said, 'Yes, please.'

Hart raised a hand. 'Not for me. But it looks delicious.'

'So,' Anna said enthusiastically, 'what are you going to do next on the search for Robert Latham?'

Hart shrugged. 'All ideas gratefully received ...'

Anna took a bite of cake. 'This is delicious.' She turned to Hart. 'You really should try this.'

'Well, if you say so.' He leaned forward and took a plate.

Sally wanted to scream. It was *her* cake, not Anna's. It was *their* project, not Anna's. And Hart was *her* friend! She felt a surge of anger at his betrayal. She gave a tight smile, not trusting herself to speak. She handed Hart the plate without catching his eye. He didn't appear to notice anything amiss. He was too busy filling Anna in on all the details of Sally's research.

'The census returns were a real breakthrough.'

Anna nodded. 'That sort of standard research can still bring in the results.'

Sally was beginning to feel a new sympathy for Rick Roth. Perhaps Rick had felt miserably insecure around Anna, too. Maybe he was sitting right now in his penthouse office, twirling in a big leather chair, happy and relaxed, enjoying not being made to feel inadequate in every way.

Hart was leaving no stone unturned, filling Anna in on the shipping records and the diary entries.

'But as Sally says, we've reached a dead end,' he concluded.

'It's a shame,' said Anna. 'If you were interested in the later history of the house there's the sound archive. But that doesn't start until the 1960s.'

Hart looked up. 'What sound archive?'

Anna was casual. 'I told Sally. It's the reason I moved here.'

What on earth was Anna talking about?

Anna looked over at Sally. 'I told you I started in radio.' She turned back to Hart. 'Well, my first assignment was assessing some of the old sound archive material to see if it could be reissued. Either for programme use or for sale direct to the public on cassettes and CDs.'

'It must be a fabulous collection.'

'It is. There's so much that the public doesn't get to hear. Anyway, in the 1960s the BBC and the University of London collaborated on an oral history project. It was groundbreaking at the time. They wanted to go out and record the voices of ordinary people. There are other oral history projects but the early ones tend to focus on famous people or women like the suffragettes. This was more wide ranging. They took three areas – Kensington, Bethnal Green and Wimbledon.'

'Wimbledon was chosen as the middle-class suburb?' Hart asked.

'Exactly.'

'So, there are hundreds of hours of tapes. It was impossible to listen to them all. I just reviewed as much as I could. Anyhow, one of the rows of houses covered was in North Walk.'

Hart cast a glance at Sally and unless she was imagining it there was a trace of condemnation in his eyes. 'This could be really useful.'

Before Sally had a chance to defend herself Anna cut in. 'It was pretty famous at the time. It was called the Berner Project, after Professor Alfred Berner. He was a social scientist. It was his brainchild.'

Sally rallied. 'But how much help is it going to be if the interviews took place in the 1960s?'

Anna considered this. 'It's possible that contemporaries of the Lathams would still be alive. Someone who was aged twenty in 1900 would be eighty in 1960.'

Hart followed on. 'And some of the neighbour's children would probably still be around, for example.'

'It's the idea of a collective memory,' explained Anna. 'Stories get passed down from generation to generation.'

Sally was about to point out that she knew what 'collective memory' meant because she had a history degree but before she could speak Hart turned enthusiastically to Anna. 'Is it possible to get access to the tapes? I have a press pass.'

Anna got up. 'I'll make a call.' She turned to Sally. 'Can I use your phone?'

And then it all happened in a matter of moments. Anna called the BBC, got straight through, and chatted amicably with the archivist with whom she was on first-name terms.

Hart moved closer to Sally. He whispered, 'You never know. It might just crack this open.'

Sally could not help herself. Whispering still more quietly she said, 'It's a long shot.'

At that, Hart cast her a look that was difficult to read.

Anna put the phone down. 'OK. The librarian is going to pull the North Walk tapes and send them out to BBC Centre. I've arranged to go and pick them up tomorrow from the front desk.'

'We can take them out?' said Hart, surprised.

Anna gave him a half smile. 'Let's just say that the librarian assumed I was still at the BBC and I forgot to tell her that I'd left. Of course, we'll need the right tape deck. But I can probably locate one of those tomorrow.'

'Fantastic!' said Hart

'But I don't know exactly what we've got,' warned Anna frowning. *We've?*

'They're just labelled "North Walk",' she continued. 'We'll have to look at the individual tapes.'

We'll?

'Even then they might not be labelled. Lots of the tapes never got edited. They're pretty much in the same state as they were in the 1960s.'

'Good. I prefer original sources.' Hart sounded like the journalist he was.

Anna continued. 'Anyway, I'll drop them off tomorrow.' She looked up at Sally. 'I'll leave you the tape player as well.'

'Thanks.' It was all she could muster. But at least Anna appeared to be backing out. Better still, Anna was reaching for her handbag. 'I ought to get going. Sally, thanks for the cake. It was fabulous.'

She stood up.

So did Hart.

And then Hart reached into his inside jacket pocket. It all happened so quickly, after that. It was like being a passenger in a car and knowing you were going to hit the car in front. You knew exactly what was going to happen but you were utterly powerless to stop it. Hart pulled out a pen.

'Anna, let me take your number. I'll get Sean to give you a call.'

All that remained was for Sally to clear away the tray, demoted now from housekeeper to maid.

'Who told you that? I thought this was a proper enquiry! I don't know anything about that. I was just the maid. I wasn't family. Listening to idle gossip isn't very scientific, is it? Who told you that?

He was a charmer, I'll say that for him. But very moody. He spent his time locked up in that bedroom writing his novel. How was I supposed to clean? It was coal fires back then. Oh, the soot! You had to clean everyday. She made that bedroom a picture – a proper four poster with the curtains and a dressing table with her boxes and brushes, all silver. I kept those polished up and all the brass, too. She had a statue she'd brought back from Italy, she had it next to the fireplace. Marble it was, a lady with a shawl wrapped round her. Some Italian goddess.

Anyway, she'd come down and tell me I had to be quiet because he was working. What about my work! You try cleaning without making a sound.

They kept themselves to themselves. That's what you have to under-

stand. It's not true to say we didn't have callers. We didn't have many of them, that's all.

But I got out and about, off to the butcher and the shops on the High Street every day. I saved up and the next year I got myself a bicycle and on a Sunday I'd cycle down to Ewell and Epsom. The roads were empty in those days. South of the Worple Road there were hardly any houses. It was lovely, miles of cornfields and bluebell woods. It's all built on now and as for Wimbledon it's all gone. Flats, that's what they want now. I got every Sunday afternoon off and the first year I got a week off. I went to see my brother Joseph. My sisters were working then in the cotton mill at Burnley and Tom had got married. He got a house off Allerton Road. But Joseph was still at the Destitute.

Joseph left when he was fourteen. You had to leave then. He went to work in the brewery. It wouldn't be around today. All the small breweries got bought up after the war. It was hard work. But it was better than the mines and better than going into service, come to that. I would never have let that happen. Joseph did very well for himself. Very well. He was a clever boy and not afraid of hard work.

After Miss Bella died people said I should take that bedroom for myself. But I never did. It wouldn't have been right. There's nothing wrong with knowing your place – but I don't suppose you'd understand that.

Well, go on then. What's your next question?'

The headmaster cleared his throat. 'So, as you can appreciate, we will not be able to offer Dan a place next term.'

He replaced the thin white paper on which Dan's drug test analysis was printed in a dark green folder on his desk.

Dan watched as his mother spoke up. 'But the counsellor was very positive. If we assume that Dan will pass the next test, surely he could come back in the meantime?'

The headmaster smiled blithely. 'I'm afraid we can't base our decisions on contingencies.'

His mother played for time. 'If you could just show me the counsellor's report again.' The headmaster wordlessly took it out of the file. She scanned it. 'Here!' she said triumphantly. 'It says, "Daniel has co-operated fully with the process and answered honestly."'

The headmaster was unmoved. 'I understand that. But we must have a clear test.'

His voice carried a note of finality.

Dan saw his father touch his mother gently on the arm. 'Pia, let's talk outside.'

But, predictably, she would not be put off. She carried on reading. 'With early-stage professional support and on-going family intervention there is a good chance of a positive outcome ...'

In the end, his father had to take hold of her arm and lever her out of the chair.

Outside, his parents started on each other straight away.

'Edward, how could you let this happen? Do I have to do everything?'

'I think I've gone beyond the call of duty.'

'And all this in my state of health.'

His father sounded bewildered. 'You were saying earlier that it was a fuss about nothing, that they weren't going to do anything except put you on medication.'

'That's beside the point!'

They moved away from him, but seconds later their voices rose and Dan could hear them quite clearly.

'Shanghai!' his mother screeched.

'Look, I only found out this morning. I haven't even told Sally. It's a three-year posting.'

'Very convenient,' snapped Pia. 'How old's the baby?' She never referred to Louis by name.

'Louis is two,' his father said testily.

'So your other son can start school when he's five. But what about Dan?'

His father sounded exasperated. 'Look, I thought he'd get back in here.' He waved his hand around the entrance hall to indicate Welton. 'I had no idea he was smoking dope.'

'Well, you should have supervised him better!'

'I'm at work!'

'Well, Sally should then.'

His father sounded startled. 'She's got Louis to look after.'

The pace was really heating up now. His mother fired back. 'I had two children. I managed them both. And I worked!'

'Don't be ridiculous! You can't expect Sally to monitor Dan twenty-four hours a day.'

'Don't call me ridiculous! It's a reasonable suggestion! How difficult is it to ask him what he's doing?'

'Clearly very difficult. We thought he was at the bloody library!'

His father ran a hand through his hair. 'Look, we'll just have to work out an alternative. There must be a day school near you that would take him.'

They made him sound like a stray. Perhaps he would end up in a kennel at Battersea.

'That's right,' his mother hissed. 'Foist the problem on to me while you head out East!'

'I am not foisting anything on to you. Christ, you can't have it both ways. You want maintenance, you expect me to pay for all of this and then you break my balls when I have to go to work to pay for it.'

'You don't have to go to Shanghai,' his mother said petulantly.

At that point a door swung open and Mrs Spencer, whom Dan recognised as the scary Bursar's secretary, poked her head out. 'Will you keep your voices down!'

'Sorry,' his parents mumbled simultaneously. His father indicated that they should all go outside.

They walked into the late-afternoon sunshine. Dan looked over at the chapel and out to the playing fields. He didn't miss Welton at all.

His parents began walking to the car park. They were still arguing.

'You should stay here and face up to your responsibilities,' said his mother. 'You can't just duck out now.'

'I am not ducking out,' protested his father. 'This is my career, Pia. Be reasonable.'

'Career! And what about my career? I had to juggle my job with bringing up two children. You were never there! Now you know how it feels.'

Suddenly his father stopped short and swung round.

'Dan!'

He was startled. He had assumed that they had forgotten he was there. No one had said anything to him since the headmaster delivered the fateful news to his stunned parents.

The test is positive.

Pascoe had said that when that happened he should say that the tests weren't 100 per cent accurate but his father had cut him off when he tried to explain that. *Shut Up!*

Now, his father was walking back towards him, his mother following. He began to feel alarmed. His father was looking at him strangely. The one thing he feared, US Military School, loomed large in his mind. Pascoe wasn't worried about that, his mum was soft.

His father stopped dead in front of him. 'Now listen, Dan. Listen very carefully. I'm going to ask you a question. There is no right answer and no wrong answer. All you have to do is be honest. Can you do that? No one is going to be upset by what you say, but we have to know so that we can do the best thing for you. Do you understand?'

Dan had no idea what was going on. The important thing was to anticipate any question that might lead to US Military School.

Where is your passport?

Can you run one mile?

His father paused. 'Dan, do you want to live with me? Or do you want to live with your mother?'

'What?'

'Do you want to live with me? Or do you want to live with your mother? Once we know that we can start looking for a school for you.'

'A school nearby?'

His father looked at him with forced patience. 'Yes. Obviously.'

He was about to answer but his father cut him off. 'Dan, you mustn't feel that you are choosing between us. You mustn't feel responsible for our feelings. Or guilty. We both love you. All we want is the best for you.' He turned to his mother. 'Isn't that right?'

'That's right!'

'We want what's best for you. That – is – all – that – matters,' His father concluded ponderously.

'That's all that matters,' repeated his mother.

Dan didn't feel responsible or guilty. 'I want to live with Sally.'

'You mean you want to live with your father?' his mother said, confused.

He stared at the ground. The thing was Dad thought Sally would be going to Shanghai with him. But would she? Sally really liked the new house. She liked her friends, Anna and Hart. Plus, Louis really liked his new school. And Sally had her important history project to finish.

Dan knew he had to be clear. He looked up. 'No. I mean *Sally*. I want to live with her.'

Chapter 18

'She stole my husband and now she's stolen my son,' Pia declaimed.

Hope, whilst no cheerleader for Sally's cause, wasn't sure that either of these two statements concerning her stepmother was fair or even accurate. Her mother pulled a pack of low-tar menthol cigarettes from her handbag.

'Mummy!'

Her mother looked defiant. 'They're French, darling. All the French women smoke them – and they're not keeling over. Marion brought me back some from Calais.'

'She should be encouraging you to stop – not helping you.'

'She is, darling.'

'By buying you cigarettes! She was supposed to be part of your Quit Team.' Her mother had told Hope all about the Quit Team concept and the Thursday-night hospital meetings. She had gone for a couple of weeks before announcing that the team leader was an idiot and the other participants were nice enough but not the sort of people one would choose to spend an evening with.

'Why don't you have a biscuit instead?' Hope suggested. Her mother was looking very thin. She wore a navy blue trouser suit she had owned for years and a cream silk blouse. The jacket hung off her shoulders and her hands appeared large and bony.

'I'll have one later.' Her mother lit up. 'It was a huge shock. My own son abandoning me for *her*.'

Hope did not point out that her mother had been smoking before Dan's alleged betrayal. What was the point? Her mother would do exactly as she pleased. She had turned up at Hope's flat on her way back from a publicity planning meeting at her publishers and for the past hour had sat in the kitchen drinking tea and recounting the events of the previous day at Welton. Her mother had called Hope from her mobile ten minutes prior to her arrival.

'Where are you, darling?'

'At the flat.' Too late she realised her error.

'I'm on my way!'

'Mummy … I'm in the middle of an essay crisis.'

'I understand. I won't stay long.'

Hope sat down at the kitchen table, having made a second pot of tea. 'I don't think Dan has abandoned you. It sounds like he just wants to go to day school.'

'Sally probably indulges him. No! It's *obvious* she indulges him. God, some of these women go out and buy pot for teenagers. Pot or worse. They do it to make them easier to handle. Do you think she does that?'

'No.'

'She's like Cruella De Vil – snatching up everything she wants.'

'He'll probably get tired of living there and want to come home soon.'

'Why?' her mother said loudly. 'Why would he get tired of being able to do exactly as he pleases?'

Hope felt overwhelmed. There was the French Revolution essay to research before she left for the holidays, two books she had ordered for the weekend to collect from the university library and tonight she and Jo were going to the National to see the new production of *King Lear*. And on Sunday they had to go to Wimbledon for Sunday lunch, which meant she would lose nearly the whole day. She wasn't sure whether to tell her mother about the trip to Wimbledon. Maybe after it had happened?

Her mother inhaled deeply. 'Frankly, Dan is a lost soul.' She said this more in anger than in sadness. 'I have absolutely no clue what goes on in his head. And I don't think that counsellor knows anything either. That whole report was a bunch of strung-together clichés.'

'What exactly did it say?'

Her mother did not answer this. Instead she said, 'Your father should have known that he was going to fail the drug test. Instead of that, we went into that meeting like lambs to the slaughter.'

Before Hope could reply they were interrupted by Jo walking in with a clutch of Sainsbury's bags.

'Hi!' There was a momentary hiatus. Jo didn't know what to call Pia so ended up calling her nothing. 'How are you feeling?'

'Much better, thank you,' Pia said briskly. 'All a storm in a tea cup.'

Jo turned, surprised, from where she had put the bags down next to the fridge. Hope could tell that Jo was about to say something in response. Hope shook her head at her. Her mother now claimed that she hadn't had a real heart attack at all, just a spell of temporary exhaustion, which the doctors were over-reacting to because they had found out she was a journalist and they were scared of getting written about in the newspapers.

'Mummy,' she said gently, 'aren't you supposed to be taking it easy?'

'I am! We've postponed Manchester and Leeds. I'm just doing the publicity events in London.'

'I know but … what about resting? Didn't the doctor suggest more exercise—'

Her mother cut her off. 'I'm fine. I'm popping umpteen pills a day and I'm due to see the consultant in a fortnight. Everything is under control. If only the same could be said for Dan.' Her mother took a puff of her cigarette.

'Dan's decided to live with my dad for a while,' Hope explained to Jo.

'Cool,' said Jo. 'So we'll see him on Sunday.'

'Sunday?' her mother barked, swinging round at Jo.

Hope cut in. 'We're going to down to Wimbledon for lunch.'

'Wimbledon?' Then comprehension showed itself on her mother's face. 'Oh, I see.'

'Daddy invited us.' That was the best way to present it. Her mother was happy enough for her to see her father. Several times she had made comments about 'not letting him forget us'. But seeing Sally always made Hope feel disloyal, probably on account of the tight-lipped fake smile her mother assumed on the two or three occasions she had found out that such a visit had occurred.

'Well, I'm sure you'll all have a nice time.'

'Thanks,' said Jo baldly. 'Hope says the shops are fabulous.'

'Well, I wouldn't know about that. It's not my neck of the woods. Hope obviously knows the area better than I do.'

Hope got the conversation back on track. 'Have you tried talking to Dan?'

'I've tried. All that comes back in an assortment of shrugs, grunts and *dunnos*. It's exasperating. Girls are so much easier.' She reached over and took Hope's hand. 'Thank God I have you, darling. We'll have such fun at the Easter vac!' Hope smiled weakly. Jo's presence made Hope aware of how the scene must look to her girlfriend's eyes. Her mother's presence suddenly felt suffocating. A change of subject was needed. But with her mother there was only one safe topic of conversation.

'So how is the book going?'

Her mother brightened. 'Very sound. And I've got some good news! I've just been offered a column for a new mag for the over-fifties.'

Jo's voice emerged from the cupboard under the sink. 'The grey pound is really important.'

'I think silver pound is the term,' Pia said curtly.

Jo looked up at Hope and grinned unabashed. 'Whatever.' She was the only person Hope had ever met who wasn't overawed by her mother.

'What are you going to write about?' Hope asked quickly.

'I thought something light to start with. It's a July publication date so probably holiday insurance.'

'Hey,' Jo turned round, 'we could do with some advice on that.'

'Oh?' her mother ignored Jo and turned to Hope, frowning.

Hope felt a knot forming in her stomach. 'We were thinking of going away for the summer. Well, part of the summer,' she corrected herself. 'Not the whole summer. To Greece. We thought it would be fun to go island hopping.'

Her mother shook her head, as if to dismiss the idea out of hand. 'Greece is ghastly in the summer. Very hot, very crowded and it's hell catching the ferries.'

Jo cut in. 'I've been before. There are ways to avoid the crowds – leaving in the early morning, for example.'

Her mother continued to address Hope. 'Well, is this a definite plan?'

Jo and her mother were simultaneously fixing her with hard stares.

'Yes. Yes, it is.'

Her mother paused. 'You must let me know the dates you plan to be away.'

'I will. Of course.' Why did she feel so guilty?

'I'm not sure that we'll have definite dates,' Jo added. 'We may head on afterwards.'

'Head on?' said her mother querulously.

'We were thinking of diverting to Istanbul,' explained Jo.

It really would be better if Jo just shut up.

The problem was Jo didn't understand that all conversations with her mother involved careful navigation around sensitive areas. These subjects, Hope understood, were age, singledom, Sally, Dan, her father, Roger, money and Hope's plans for the summer holidays. Her mother had already started planning a schedule for the two of them, beginning with a week in a cottage in Stow-on-the-Wold and thereafter sunbathing in the back garden at Gerrards Cross. The schedule did not feature Istanbul. This, moreover, was not a comprehensive list of risky topics. At times, when they had had a spat, Marion joined the list. Health topics were always risky. The heart attack, Hope could tell, was fast becoming taboo. One also had to be very careful around hair, make-up and clothes. Once, when he was six or seven, Dan had accompanied Pia to the hairdresser's. When he got home he had remarked to Granny, 'My mummy makes her hair a different colour.'

Her mother had swung round. 'Dan, talking about the way someone looks is very rude. You mustn't do it.'

Her father had also got chewed up one Friday night in the Beaconsfield Pizza Express for saying innocently that a pair of her mother's hipster jeans were 'very trendy'.

'Are you saying they're too young?' her mother had snapped back. The people at the other table had looked round at them and Hope, aged twelve at the time, had wanted to dive under the table.

It was safer not to say much at all.

Jo began assembling ingredients for a stir-fry. 'You're welcome to join us,' she said.

'No. Thank you. I must be going.'

'Yeah, we have to get off soon. Did Hope tell you? We've got tickets for *King Lear*.'

Pia had taken her lipstick out of her handbag and was applying it with the use of a compact mirror. 'At the National?'

'Yes.'

'Jo went and queued this morning for student standby,' Hope explained.

'How clever of her.' Her mother stood up. 'Goodbye, Jo,' she said coolly. 'Have a nice evening.'

'Thanks!'

'Hope! Let's walk down to the car.' She clicked out into the hallway in her navy kitten heels. Her mother loathed 'flats' as she called them.

They ascended the concrete staircase. 'I didn't like to say anything back there, but how are things with Jake?'

'Jake. Oh.' Hope looked away. 'Fine. He's very busy.'

'I had thought the flame might have been reignited?'

'No. I don't think so.'

They walked towards the car. 'And tonight. Is it a foursome?'

'A foursome?'

'At the theatre.'

'Oh. No. Just the two of us.'

'And Jo. Does she have a boyfriend?'

'No.'

Her mother reached into her handbag for her car keys. 'To be frank, I'm not surprised. She's very … forthright.'

'I think she's just honest.'

'You're always so generous in your assessments.' Her mother made this sound like a character defect. 'Darling, please don't take this the wrong way. And please don't say that I'm interfering. But you mustn't let her *use* you. She might not have a boyfriend but you could get one tomorrow! You're too young to be going round with her – like a pair of old maids. The theatre's all very well, darling. But what about a party? A nightclub? Somewhere that you can mingle?'

'I like going out with Jo.'

'I'm sure you do. But my suggestion is only go out with Jo on a weekday. Save the weekends for the boys.' Her mother held her hand up. 'I know. You think it's all different now and I don't know what I'm talking about. Hope, nothing really changes. Trust me.'

Hope should tell her. It was the perfect opportunity. Her mother had brought up the subject of Jo, the excessive amount of time that they were spending together and the alternative of boys. How much easier could it get?

Her mother peered at her. 'Darling, don't look so woebegone. It might never happen!'

Hope was seven years old again.

Darling, I know you think you like the purple dress but the pink one is much nicer …

Darling, the stabilisers don't slow down the bicycle. You just think they do. Leave them on a little bit longer …

In the end her father had taken a wrench and without reference to her mother removed the stabilisers from her bicycle and taught her to ride without them in a morning. She had been the last girl in the street to have them removed.

Now Hope nodded dumbly at her mother just as she had done then.

Her mother bent forward and kissed her lightly. She smelt of face powder, Calvin Klein Eternity and cigarettes. She used to wear Chanel Number 5 but threw the bottle out after Daddy left.

Her mother unlocked the car door and got in. She started the engine and wound down the window.

'I don't want you to think that I'm some interfering old trout. It's just my opinion. Take it or leave it. I won't say another word!'

That was how it always was.

It's your decision but …

It's just my opinion but …

Do what you like! But remember this …

Her mother was winding up the window. 'Call me. And we'll talk about the holidays.'

And then she was gone, having safely and reliably secured the last word. Hope walked slowly up the stairs to the flat. Jo was at the kitchen table reading the *Evening Standard*.

She closed the newspaper as Hope walked in. 'I'll make the stir-fry.'

'Thanks.'

Jo grinned. 'Don't tell me. She's confiscated your passport?'

'Believe me, that is a real possibility.'

Hope sat down at the kitchen table. She felt miserably drained. 'Jo, I can't go on like this,' she murmured. 'I have to tell them.'

And for the first time Hope meant it.

*

'So you see, I'm beginning to believe that every cloud really does have a silver lining!'

Tim nodded. 'That's great, Anna. Really great.'

The waiter came with two plates, a small filet of beef for Tim and baked herbed salmon for Anna. Tim had opted to skip a first course so she had followed suit, even though she loved the mozzarella here and would have liked the salad. They were seated in the basement dining room of Orso's in Covent Garden. It was early and the dining room was still largely empty. The time, seven o'clock, and the venue had been Tim's suggestion. She had been to Orso's before, for work lunches, but not in the evening and never with Tim.

'Sean Doyle needs a piece on City Churches for Channel 4.' She broke off a piece of bread. 'He wants to talk about the idea of the Church as central to the community. So it covers all the people who use the Church for different reasons – community groups, toddler playgroups and all the religious stuff.'

The waiter returned and refilled their glasses with Orvieto.

'How much does it pay?' Tim said politely.

She shrugged. 'Not much. But at least it'll keep me afloat. I'm probably going to get rid of the car.'

For the first time since they had sat down she seemed to have caught his attention. 'Your pride and joy?'

She shrugged. She hated the idea but was working hard to convince herself that it was a sensible economy. 'I hardly use it. I certainly don't need it. I can take the tube most of the time. And if I do need a car it's cheaper to hire one for the day and charge it to the job.'

Tim looked thoughtful. 'Are you going to stay in the flat?'

'Not if I keep making short films for Channel 4. But if I get more work in I should be OK. I've still got some shares and some savings that I can cash in.'

Some of that money had gone towards her outfit for the evening, a jersey wrap dress in dark red, which was a sassy departure from her usual casual style. Tim was wearing his office clothes, black 501s and an open-neck Oxford shirt.

He looked unsure of what to say next. 'You seem to be handling it very well.'

Was she? If she wasn't then it was not the time to show that to Tim. The memory of the anguished calls she had made to him in the

223

aftermath of the sacking made her cringe. Recalling her behaviour before she got sacked was still worse.

Her purpose tonight was to open a door and to show Tim that she really had changed. She wasn't expecting him to fall into her arms, haul her into a cab and take her home. Of course not. These things take time. She would have to regain his trust.

She said keenly, 'But that's enough about me. So how's your work? What are you writing at the moment?'

'Nothing very exciting, I'm afraid. I'm going to Brussels next week for a couple of days. The European Commission is taking a group of journalists out for a freebie.'

Her stomach lurched. Would there be women present? French interpreters? Italian diplomats? Journalists of all complexions?

'Great!'

'And then once I get back it will be the final stages of the Tory leadership contest.'

'Who are you backing to win?'

'I think Butler will hold on. I don't think there will be any upsets. It's about the right of the party flexing its muscle. So there won't be a change of leader but he may need to make concessions to the right in terms of shadow cabinet positions. Stratford's lobbying for shadow Home Secretary.'

Tim spoke with the knowledgeable assurance of a man speaking from facts not opinion. He made it his business to get out of the newspaper's Canary Wharf offices and mix with people from all parts of the political spectrum. In the short time she had known Tim, Anna had been amazed by how many people he knew.

There was a pause in the conversation. The mention of David Stratford's name had evoked the uncomfortable memory of the theatre trip.

Then Tim spoke. 'Have you met your neighbours?'

There was something polite about this and every other question he had asked. It was as if he was tiptoeing very carefully to avoid any of the common territory that they had shared.

'Yes. Sally and Edward. And Dan, he's Edward's son. And their little boy, Louis. I took him to the park, actually. She had a meeting.'

Tim could not keep the note of surprise from his voice. 'Gosh. How did that go?'

'Really well. There's nothing to it. We made a film.'

Tim's eyebrow shot up.

'Just a fun one,' she backtracked. 'Something for Sally and Edward to keep.' This was partially true. She had given a copy to Sally. But it had also occurred to her that the film she had made of Louis was also the basis for an idea she could put to Sean Doyle – a proposal for a series of two-minute films looking at the everyday lives of children from different places and social backgrounds. The working title was *Child's Eye*. There might be some children who, in contrast to a middle-class child like Louis, hardly ever left their high-rise flats? It would be fascinating to film their perspective of the world.

There was another pause in the conversation.

'And you?' she ventured. 'Have you been anywhere interesting lately?'

Oh God, it was the desperate question of a failing first date.

But Tim did not appear to have noticed this. 'Hmm. I saw the new Ridley Scott last week.'

But that film was not yet out on general release. 'Last week?' she said puzzled.

'Yep. I went to the premiere.'

'Lucky.'

'A friend had tickets.'

Anna was old enough to know that when a man's eyes flicked away from you at the same time he uttered the words 'a friend' then there was only one interpretation. However, a nameless friend was much better than a named friend. A nameless friend could be a girl from the office, a first date and no more than a platonic blip.

'Anyone I know?' she said, as casually as she could manage.

Tim stared resolutely at his steak. 'Yes. Natasha.'

'Oh.' She relaxed. Well, that was a good thing. Natasha, her old friend, at whose party she and Tim had first met.

'Good film,' he said absently. 'I enjoyed it, even though it's not really my sort of thing.'

She knew that. He didn't need to point it out. They had been together long enough for her to know that Tim liked political thrillers.

There was another pause.

She realised that she needed to try to break through this mannered exchange.

She put down her fork and leaned forward. 'Tim, I want to say that I'm sorry. I want to say that I behaved really badly. And when I said earlier that every cloud has a silver lining, I meant it. I meant that getting sacked wasn't all a bad thing.' She wasn't quite sure if this was true but she needed to believe it. Otherwise she would never rouse herself off the sofa. 'It hasn't ended my career. It's just taken it in another direction.'

Tim looked as though he was considering saying something but no words came forth.

'Tim, I have to be philosophical about it – to see it as an opportunity. And I think it's an opportunity – a second chance – in more ways than one.'

Tim now put his knife and fork down. He cut in. 'Anna, I think before you say any more that there's something you need to know …'

'I do know! I know that you can't just be expected to take my word for that. I understand it would take time to prove …'

'It's not that.'

'It's not?' He could at least give her a chance.

'Natasha and I are seeing each other.'

Seeing each other. Was there possibly some ambiguity about that?

'Seeing each other?' she repeated.

'We've become more than just friends.'

'But …'

A hundred questions flooded her mind. First and foremost, '*When?*'

He looked blank. 'What do you mean?'

'You know exactly what I mean!' she hissed.

Far from being defensive or, as she had every right to expect, apologetic, he sounded very sure of himself. 'Nothing happened until after we split up. I wouldn't do that to you.'

She believed him, but it didn't appear to make any difference to the way she felt, which was boiling angry. Bizarrely, the recollection of David Stratford's invitation to his new country house came to mind. Natasha would be going with Tim now – and it should be her!

'Well, you didn't waste any time, did you?' Her thoughts veered towards Natasha's role. 'Why didn't either of you tell me before?'

'I'm telling you now. I'm trying to do the right thing.'

'What does Natasha say about it?'

'It was her idea that I came here tonight. She felt it was important that I told you directly. And she still wants to be your friend …'

'Having stolen my boyfriend!'

Tim assumed that tone again. 'No one stole anyone. We'd split up. You'd made it very clear that I was a dispensable part of your life.'

'I thought we'd get back together again! I didn't realise it was permanent.'

'You didn't even pick up the phone!'

'I was having a work crisis!'

He rolled his eyes and almost laughed. 'Your whole life is a work crisis!'

'Not any more,' she countered petulantly. 'I'm unemployed. Virtually.'

Tim looked at her for the first time that evening with some real affection. It was awful. 'Look, Anna, you are a fabulous person. You're beautiful. Intelligent. And you're great fun to be with. But soon you'll get another terrifically high-powered job and you'll give it your all. There's nothing wrong with that. You can't change your personality – and it would be wrong of me to try to make you someone that you're not. And I can't change mine. We want different things, Anna.'

'But surely you can see that I've changed?'

Tim looked again as if he was about to say something then changed his mind.

'What?' she demanded angrily.

'It doesn't matter …'

'I think you should let me be the judge of whether it matters!'

He was clearly choosing his words carefully. 'I think the whole 7–24 thing has implications beyond the loss of your job. I know that getting fired must be horrendous. But,' he hesitated, 'if it had been me I think I would have been asking myself questions about the ethics of—'

'Ethics?' Anna interrupted, annoyed. She had taken an undergraduate philosophy course that had a class in ethics but she couldn't remember much about it. 'Yours or mine?' she snapped.

He held his hands up in mock surrender. 'You asked me what I was thinking.'

She had no reply to that because it was true. But she was in no frame of mind to dissect her disastrous working life at the same time as what remained of her personal life had collapsed.

Eventually Tim said, 'Look, it's probably better if we skip the coffee.'

Her voice was stony. 'Yes.'

He turned and caught the waiter's eye. Then he said softly, 'Let's not end it like this, OK. Let's just accept that it wasn't meant to be.'

The waiter arrived. 'Dessert? More wine?'

'Just the bill, please.'

'We have some excellent tiramisu tonight. Can I tempt the lady?'

She felt wretched. 'No. You can't.'

Tim spoke up. 'Thank you. Just the bill.'

Silence fell between them in the age it appeared to take for the waiter to bring them the bill.

He pulled out his credit card. Anna reached for her handbag.

'I'll get this,' said Tim, surprised.

'No. I'll pay half.' That made her feel a little better for some reason.

The waiter went off with their respective Amex cards.

Tim said quietly, 'I'm sorry. Your career is none of my business.'

'It's OK.'

'Anna, you need someone … to complement you. Someone who's just as passionate about their work as you are. Someone who doesn't mind the hours you work. Someone who can give you the support you need.' He shrugged. 'I know it's a cliché but I'd like us to be—'

'Please don't say it!'

Tim gave a weak smile. 'Fair enough.'

There were two voices on the tape. The first was young and well modulated.

'This is Judith Grant, research assistant, and I am interviewing Miss Mary Kelly of 12 North Walk, Wimbledon, London SW19, in her home on 7 June 1962 for the University of London Working People's Oral History project led by Professor Alfred Berner.'

At times, Judith's Grant's voice fell so low it almost could not be heard. In contrast, Mary Kelly's voice rang out sharply, each word carefully articulated and overlaid by an Irish accent that Sally had expected to be stronger. Mary took the lead. It was some minutes before Judith Grant was able to ask her first question. She was clearly reading from a prepared list.

'*Can you tell me where and when you were born and something about your early life?*

'*I've just told you about my early life. Ireland? Why would you want to know about Ireland? I knew the Duke of Wakemont! And he knew the Queen. Oh all right. I was born in County Wicklow in 1882.*'

So Mary was eighty years of age at the time the Berner tapes were made. She sounded younger. The impression Sally gained by the time she had finished listening to the tape was of an active woman, living alone without any apparent assistance.

With occasional questions from Judith Grant, Mary's narrative continued largely uninterrupted. It was a life contained in an hour of audiotape. Towards the end it was clear that Mary, her voice confident to the point of being overbearing, still had plenty to say.

'*Let me tell you a secret. If you go to the Conservatory at Selton and you look very closely you'll find a shamrock. A shamrock! In an Italian garden. It was supposed to be a painting of an Italian garden looking out onto the Mediterranean Sea. Mr Jackson was a stickler. He made sure that all the plants and trees were Italian ones. Authentic, that's the word. But if you look closely in the bottom right-hand corner you'll find a shamrock. John put it there for me. "It's your Shamrock, Mary," he said. It was our little joke. All the gentry admiring it and none of them noticing there's a shamrock growing in the middle of Italy!*'

'*I'll make sure that I look for it,*' said Judith Grant politely. But as she spoke there was a rustling of papers. Didn't the girl have any sense of romance? Sally wondered.

'*Thank you very much, Miss Kelly. That has been very helpful.*'

'*Is that all you want? There's plenty more I can tell you.*'

'*Thank you. I think that's everything we need.*'

'*When is it going to be broadcast?*'

'*Broadcast? Oh, that's for Professor Berner to decide. He's in charge of the project.*'

'*When will I meet him?*'

The young woman was clearly caught off guard at that point. '*I'm afraid I can't say.*'

And then there was silence. After a few moments Sally switched off the tape recorder.

Sally had listened to it twice. The kitchen had grown cold. Edward must have fallen asleep upstairs. She looked around the kitchen. Mary would have known it as the dining room. Perhaps they conducted the interview in this very room. They must have done for Mary to have pointed out rhododendrons planted in the shade. Questions flooded her mind. Was it Mary and John, separated by circumstance, yet friends for twenty-five years, whose story was the true love affair left immortalised in a shamrock that would never wither in the Selton Park conservatory? Sally wound the tape back.

'Marriage! No. John had his mother and sisters to look after and I had Miss Bella. In those days you did your duty. But on a Sunday he'd come over from Fulham and we'd cycle out. Oh, we cycled for miles! We used to go over to Richmond and he'd set up his easel at the top of the Hill and sketch the river on the bend. One time, on my birthday, he took me for a proper watercress tea at the Star and Garter Hotel. John was an artist. He was just as good as Mr Jackson, but of course the high-ups want to deal with their own sort. He was a damned sight better! Excuse my language, but it makes me cross when I think about it. After his mother died he took to having his Sunday dinner here. In the kitchen, of course. Not in the dining room. I bought us two deckchairs and in the summer we'd sit out afterwards. John died in 1929. He had a growth. By the time they found it there was nothing they could do. It was in his bones. Of course there was no health service back then. You got what you could afford. They sent him home and I wish I could tell you he didn't suffer but he did. He's buried at Mortlake. Before he passed he told me to make sure I wore a hat with an ostrich feather. I promised him I would. I went up to the Army and Navy and bought a black velvet hat with a big white feather. Oh, there was ever such a lot of people at the funeral. His sister did a tea afterwards and we all went back for that. Of course, she hadn't been in service so it wasn't up to much. There's a bus stop by the gates. I go over there on his birthday.'

Most intriguingly of all, what was the local piece of gossip that had made Mary get so angry with her interviewer?

The young woman had hesitated slightly before asking. *'There was talk of a … a matter that may have caused Mr Latham to leave the country. Do you know anything about that?'*

Mary snapped back: '*Who told you that? I thought this was a proper enquiry! I don't know anything about that. I was just the maid. I wasn't family. Listening to idle gossip isn't very scientific, is it? Who told you that?*'

Was he in trouble with the police? The family? With Bella herself? Mary was infuriatingly vague at times. Sally rewound the tape to listen once again to her comments about Henry's death.

'*Miss Bella took it very hard. She was never the same after that. Of course, children died more often then. There was no penicillin like there is today. But that didn't make it any easier.*'

And that was all. Miss Grant moved on. Sally had begun to foster increasing feelings of resentment towards Miss Grant, who seemed to be ticking questions off her sheet and barely responding to the answers. So many of Mary's replies begged a second or third question. If the gossip about Robert Latham was untrue then what was the real reason he had left? Why didn't they have any more children? How did Bella survive the loss of her only son and then the disappearance of her husband? But Miss Grant left these most obvious questions unasked. And then there was Mary's younger brother Joseph, the brother she was so anxious should not follow her into domestic service, the only member of her family she appeared to have cared about. There was no clue as to his fate after he left the orphanage for his first job in a brewery.

It was past one o'clock in the morning. There were two other tapes from North Walk. She got up and stacked the tape player on the counter top safely out of Louis's reach. Tomorrow she would listen to those. As she turned out the kitchen light Mary's voice continued to echo in her mind. It was as if Mary was back home again.

'*Miss Bella never came down to the kitchen! Why would she help? I didn't need any help, thank you very much. What you have to understand is that Miss Bella was a lady. She was brought up with servants to do everything for her. She didn't know any different. Back then people were brought up to know their place. You weren't supposed to get ideas above your station. And most people were happier for it.*

'*Right after the war I got pneumonia. It was a devil of a job keeping the house warm, coal was rationed then. I got a cold and it went onto my chest. Oh, it was bitter, that winter of 'forty-seven! I was laid up under a pile of blankets and she was dressed up in her coat, in and out* of my bedroom, asking me this and that. "Mary, the fire's gone out … Mary, there's no milk …" It was all she could do to butter a bit of bread and put a bit of spam on it. There was rationing then, of course, but Miss Camilla used to give her something, pork ribs or a bit of liver. One Christmas we got a nice side of ham. Her husband's family owned land down in Kent so they were never short. The rich and the farmers, they never went hungry.

'Girls nowadays think all they need to do is open a tin. Where's the goodness in that? I've always made my own of everything. Marmalade, jam, pies, everything. I don't suppose you can pickle an onion, can you? That's the trouble these days – people think they know better. They think rushing about is going to make them happier. They need to be more content with what they've got. You should write that down.'

Chapter 19

The night before, it had occurred to Sally, when Anna turned up on her doorstep at nine o'clock at night, dressed up to the nines alone after her make-up dinner with Tim, that Anna was the sister she had never had. Infuriating, demanding – now in unconscious competition for the same man – but nonetheless impossible to turn away.

So it was that Anna had collapsed into Sally's arms on the sofa where, just a few days earlier, she had stolen Hart's attentions. And yet Sally had been unable to do anything other than embrace her and hold her as Anna cried like a child.

'I have just made a complete and utter fool of myself,' Anna wept. 'My life is a series of fucking enormous humiliations that I never see coming. I am always the last to know.'

'So you didn't get back together?' Sally felt it safe to venture.

Anna flung herself back on the sofa. 'He's going out with Natasha!'

'Natasha? Your friend Natasha. The TV presenter.'

Anna reached for a tissue. 'Yes. They swear it didn't start until Tim left that day.'

It was a tricky call. 'What do you think?'

'I believe him. That's one of the reasons I loved Tim. He's completely straight. He's got … ethics.'

Sally was at a loss to know what to say next. So she improvised. 'Anna, you'll be fine. I know it's horrible and awful but you will get over it and soon you'll meet someone else.'

'I don't want someone else. I want Tim.' Anna began crying again. 'It was unbelievably awful. I got all dressed up and he turned up in his old Levis and it looked as if I'd made tons of effort and he'd made zero. And the waiters kept treating us like we were on a date. And Tim was really, really professional. Talking to me like we work together.'

'Are you going to speak to Natasha?'

'I have done. She called me in the car on the way home. She said she was really sorry and she felt awful about it and she really thought it was over between Tim and me. And then she offered to stop seeing him.'

'Gosh.'

'Yeah, I know.'

'What did you say?'

'What could I say? I said of course not, they should carry on. But what I wanted to say was no, no, no! And by the way I think you should move to New Zealand.' Anna choked. 'How can I compete with Natasha anyway? She looks like a model and she acts like a saint. She's just spent three months in an Ethiopian village, for God's sake!'

Anna had stayed for a couple of hours and got through a fair amount of Edward's whisky. It would have seemed churlish not to invite her to Sunday lunch.

Now, as Sally took the beef out of the oven, Anna took hold of Louis and began showing him *The Very Hungry Caterpillar*. He had been fractious and difficult from the moment he woke up.

Edward appeared. 'Something smells good! Hi, Anna.' Then he added hopefully, 'Oh, Louis looks very settled. Shall I skip the park?'

Sally ignored this. 'If he doesn't go for a walk he'll be hyped up all through lunch.'

She marched out of the kitchen to get Louis's coat. Then, as if to a small dog, she bent down and said enticingly, 'Would you like to go for a lovely walk to the park, Louis?'

He dived off Anna's lap. She reached over and began scanning the Sunday papers.

Sally turned back to Edward. 'While you're out could you get some horseradish sauce? Oh, and can you wake Dan up?'

'Fine,' Edward said resignedly. 'See you later, girls.'

Sally put the batter for the Yorkshire pudding to one side and started peeling a bag of apples. To the side sat the bottle of good red burgundy Anna had brought, already uncorked to let it breathe.

From the hallway a dreary whining could be heard as Edward negotiated with Louis about his coat. 'Good! Now let's try the other arm.'

'Well, there's nothing about Tim and Natasha.' Anna put the papers down.

'Maybe it won't last,' Sally said comfortingly.

'I think it will,' said Anna. 'I've got a premonition that Tim and Natasha will end up getting married and it won't be long.' Anna watched as Sally worked through the pile of enormous Bramley apples, quartering them and cutting them deftly into slices. 'They both want the same things: children, a warm kitchen – and apple pie. They want what you have.'

Sally half turned. 'Not pie, crumble. I was going to do pastry but it's too hot in here.'

'Too hot?'

'Cold in the making, hot in the baking. That's the rule for pastry.' She had got into the habit of passing on cooking hints to Anna. 'We're hardly the model family.'

'I think you do OK. Edward's devoted to you.'

Was he? It was hard to tell these days. They were running on parallel lines, both apparently in the same direction, sharing the same house and bed, yet her thoughts lay with Hart and Bella and now coming to terms with the cold truth that the trail was running cold.

She had called Hart to report back on the tapes.

She had given him a quick précis of Mary's story. 'So obviously there was some rumour going round about the Lathams. But Mary didn't give anything away, I checked the tapes from the other two houses. Twice.'

'So what's the next move?'

'I need to go down to see the Duke's papers at Oxford.' Goodness knows when she would do this. Louis's nursery schedule left little time for academic jaunts. It was the last remaining decent lead.

Hart had sounded a cool note. 'I'm not sure how useful we can expect them to be on something that was clearly very personal. Aren't they state papers? Relating to the Duke and the government?'

'Yes. But I want to rule out the possibility of any personal correspondence that might have been included.'

His tone had been lukewarm. 'Well, let me know if you come up with anything.'

Now, in response to Anna's last comment, Sally said automatically, 'Yes. He is. I'm very lucky.'

'But if they do get married I will draw the line at being a bloody bridesmaid!'

Sally pulled herself back to the moment. 'Why don't we have a glass of that wine?' She nodded at the burgundy.

'Good idea.' Anna got up and reached for two glasses.

She passed a glass to Sally who was chopping up pecans into little pieces.

'What are those for?'

'Crumble topping. Something to make it more interesting. I'm going to add some cinnamon, too.'

'Don't tell me, Edward loves it.'

Sally rolled her eyes. 'Yes. He and Louis like the same food. But I've done a fruit compote as well, so there's something lighter.'

She brushed her fingers on her apron. 'We ought to lay the table. Now,' she counted on her fingers, 'we've got Hope and Jo, you and me, Edward and Dan. And Louis. So there are six adults and Louis.'

Sally began laying out the orchid placemats, a wedding present from Mad Auntie Mary, printed with reproductions of Victorian botanical drawings.

Sally chose the moment. As casually as she could manage and without looking at Anna she said, 'Have you heard anything from Hart?'

'No.' Anna's voice was firm. 'Nothing.'

It was incredible how quickly her mood lifted. So Hart had not rushed to desert her! Better still, Anna did not appear to be dwelling on Hart. 'So, fill me on the lunch guests.'

'OK. So there's Hope. Edward seems to think that this will be a new beginning.'

'Any reason for that?'

'Other than his wishful thinking? No.' Sally rooted through the top drawer in search of serving spoons. One day they had promised themselves a proper canteen of silver cutlery. For now they had Ikea stainless steel and a drawer of mismatched oddments. 'Poor Edward. He just wants us all to get along as if nothing had happened.'

'But Hope resents you and feels loyal to her mother.'

Sally looked up surprised. 'Yes. In a nutshell.'

'I did a programme on stepfamilies. Think about it. Two – or three women if you count Hope's mother – all competing for the attention of one man. No wonder it gets tricky.'

'So what was the moral of your programme?'

'I'm not sure there was one. Probably that you have to work at it.'

Sally paused. 'I think I've probably given up.' It felt that after the twenty-first birthday she had more than paid her dues. 'I don't think Hope wants to see me, either. And Hope is bringing her friend Jo. It feels like she's got back-up with Jo coming.'

'Have you met her?'

'Briefly. She shares a flat with Hope and she was at the twenty-first party. They shared Hope's room. Edward says they're planning a holiday together this summer.'

'Gosh. They're never apart.'

Sally considered this. 'I've never really thought about it. I know so little about Hope's life.' She searched her memory to recall where Edward had said they were going. 'Mykonos and the Greek Islands. That's where they're going on holiday.'

Anna looked up. 'So are they friends or girlfriends?'

She was caught off guard. Girlfriends? Why ever would Anna think that? 'No, just friends. It's not like that. Hope had a boyfriend, Jake.'

Anna sounded curious. 'It seems a shame. You and Hope both studied history, live ten miles apart and yet you don't ever do anything together.'

'I know. I mean, in the beginning I did. I asked her out for lunch a couple of times and once we went to the theatre. But it was always false. As though she was there because she had to be and she couldn't wait to get away.' Sally paused. 'It's that thing about me breaking up the marriage. I know that's what she thinks – that if I hadn't come along then maybe the separation would have been temporary and they would have got back together.' Sally looked up. 'Oh God, it's a bit like you and Natasha.'

Anna shook her head. 'I think you could have come along years later and it wouldn't have made much difference to the way you and Hope get on. It's daddies and their daughters, isn't it? I mean, you don't have any problems with Dan, do you?'

'No.' Sally leaned forward and whispered across the kitchen table. 'In fact, he's said he wants to live with us permanently. He told Edward and Pia when they went down to the school.'

'And will he?'

Sally nodded. 'I think so. With some ground rules. He's got to come off the dope. Totally. But he's no trouble.' Dan was more than that. He was company, a presence in the house.

Sally went over and opened the fridge door, taking out the vegetarian roast. She read the cooking directions then looked up. 'So you see, that's why we're having lunch. It was Edward's idea.' She threw Anna an ironic smile. 'To show that we can all get along like one big happy family.'

'Won't you even try going back to Welton for a term?' asked Hope encouragingly.

'They don't want me back,' said Dan blankly, reaching over for his third portion of roast potatoes.

The potatoes were very good. Maybe Daddy had married her for her cooking. Jo and Sally were getting on really well, too. It was odd. Why did she never manage to have those conversations with Sally? They were discussing Victorian social reform. Sally was talking, surprisingly knowledgeably, about the Victorian Liberal Party.

'I did my second-year paper on Gladstone and the Evangelical movement. So then in my final year I decided to do my thesis on Victorian voluntary organisations. Mainly the Charity Organisation Society.' That was news to Hope.

Jo was enthused. 'So did I! Well, almost the same. I looked at the whole concept of the deserving and the undeserving poor.'

'What's that?' asked Dan.

He was sitting next to Sally. He seemed so incredibly at home in this all-new spacious kitchen. It was so different from Gerrards Cross. Seeing him with Sally, watching him pass her vegetables and help her cut up Louis's food, it felt as though her mother was right in saying he had joined the other side. It made Hope furious with him.

Jo took up his question. 'It's the idea that some of the poor deserve help and others, who were thought to be idle or morally corrupt, didn't. That was why the workhouses were so awful ...'

'Of course, there were more enlightened reformers,' added Sally. 'But they were in the minority.'

Hope tuned out. But to her other side her father was deep in conversation with Anna the Neighbour.

'So you see, it isn't just the market that China itself presents. It's also the fact that China is a gateway to the Far East ...'

Anna nodded politely.

Hope concentrated on her Yorkshire pudding. It was pretty good, too. Light and crispy on the edges. Her mother never made it, though she had bought the frozen ones once. Hope had arrived as late as possible with Jo. Her father had answered the door. It was still a shock, seeing him open the door of this terraced Wimbledon house, wearing a shirt she had never seen before, with Louis in his arms, a broad gold wedding ring on his finger. He had not worn one when he was married to her mother. He had ushered them in and called for Sally, and Hope had felt the tight knot in her stomach as they exchanged a stiff embrace. She introduced Jo, proffered chocolates, cooed over Louis. It was all so fucking staged. It made her want to scream.

Somehow it had been easier when Daddy and Sally were renting a flat together. The small, hopeful thought had been allowed to flourish in the back of her mind that maybe Sally, like the lease on the flat, was a temporary commitment. But now they owned this house. More so than the wedding, the house seemed to indicate permanence. It didn't smell or feel or look like home, though. She felt like a visitor. As Edward ushered them into the living room Hope immediately recognised the few things that he had taken from their old house. In a corner stood the antique Chinese lacquer cabinet inherited from his godmother. Next, she spotted the pair of delicate nineteenth-century silver candelabra that used to stand on the hall bookcases, then the prints of the harbour at Honfleur that used to hang in his study. In their new settings – the prints over the sofa, the candelabra on the mantelpiece – they looked newly transplanted.

For a little while she, Jo and Daddy had been alone. Sally and Anna went off to finish lunch. That would have been the time to tell him.

There had been several openings.

So, girls, tell me about your holiday plans …

But she had stalled, afraid of having to sit through lunch newly, openly gay. It would definitely be better to wait until after lunch when, depending on his reaction, they could stay a while longer or bolt.

She had thought lunch would consist of dull conversation interspersed with protracted silences. But all around her it was zipping along.

She nudged Dan. 'Mummy says you could do the drug test again.'

There was a delay while Dan passed Louis a piece of roast potato, which the toddler crammed into his mouth with his fat little fingers.

Dan shrugged. 'It's fine for you, you liked Welton.'

Hope was genuinely surprised. 'No, I didn't!'

'Yes, you did. You were in the sixth form.'

'That doesn't mean I liked it.'

'Then why did you stay?'

'Because that was what Mummy and Daddy thought was best.' Too late she realised how priggish this sounded. Jo looked up at her in surprise.

'Well, it just shows that we can always learn more about each other. Even those closest to us,' cut in Jo smoothly.

Hope took a large gulp of wine. 'I just think you should give it a go.'

'I did!' Dan protested. He looked wounded. 'And it didn't make any difference.'

Jo spoke up quickly. 'What do you like to do at the weekends, Dan?'

Hope knew that Jo was trying to change the subject. Louis was straining forward to try to get at the one remaining potato. Dan gave him half, taking the other for himself.

'Play football,' said Dan.

But Hope wasn't ready to let it go yet. 'Well, you could do that at Welton. You could have a kick-around with the other boys.'

Dan rolled his eyes. 'They play hockey and cricket. And having a kick-around isn't the same as being in a team. With a coach. In a league.' His voice was dismissive.

Then Sally spoke up. 'I think he wants to play in a school team.'

'I understand that,' Hope snapped. God, that was a bit sharp. She ought to say sorry. She glanced at her father to see if he had noticed, but he had resumed his conversation with Anna.

Sally got up. As soon as Sally's back was turned Jo mouthed at her across the table, *Just leave it.* And Jo accompanied her words with a silent tapping of her own wineglass. Behind her, Sally was taking something out of the oven.

'I think he's acting very hastily,' said Hope, 'that's all.' It felt impossible to back down, say sorry or shut up.

What had got into her? Whatever it was, it wasn't letting go. She felt searingly irritable and steadily more drunk. She was spoiling for a fight. She took another gulp of wine, emptying her glass.

Jo frowned at Hope. Then Jo said to Dan, 'But in the meantime have you thought about day schools?'

'Yeah. Sally's found two. We're going to see them next week.'

'Just for an informal look around,' Sally added hastily from behind her.

No wonder her mother felt usurped. Sally had taken Daddy, packed him up and brought him back here. Then she had come back for Dan and unwrapped him, too. But they didn't belong here!

Jo had changed the subject, seizing on the subject of schools to introduce her time spent teaching English as a foreign language on her gap year in India.

Sally had returned to the table. They were discussing the Taj Mahal. Sally had seen it at sunrise, Jo at sunset.

'You could really see how the pollution had affected the marble,' commented Jo.

'Did you go to Pushkar?' asked Sally. 'We went after we left the Taj Mahal.'

Who had Sally travelled with and when? Hope had no idea, any more than she had known that Sally had visited India. They were all but strangers to each other.

Meanwhile, her father had finally exhausted the subject of the Chinese economy and was listening to Anna talk about her early days in Radio 1.

'I was out on the road, mainly listening to new bands, hitting the festivals …'

Dan got up and began loading the dishwasher. He never did that at home. All the conversation merged into a hum of voices. She gave herself up to the wine and the heat of the kitchen.

How could this be? How could the life that Hope had known with her parents, a life she had believed as a child would never change, just disappear? Things hadn't been perfect. The rows, the silences, the feuds and her mother's scorecard of petty resentments. But she was used to that. Those things had always been there. But this – this house and Sally and Louis – who were they and where had they come from and why did she have to have them in her life when she didn't want them? She looked down at the flower placemats and the cheap cutlery, up at the blue saucepans hanging from the wall and the cookbooks on the shelf. All unfamiliar and alien and not part of her life at all. Yet all she did was smile and nod in tacit acceptance. Why did she spend so much of her time doing and saying things she didn't believe in?

Jo had commented on this in the early days. 'You're always taking care of your mum and your dad. Worrying about what they think. You need to have a teenage rebellion, girl.'

Maybe that was it. Perhaps her twenty-first birthday had triggered some delayed rebellion. Because that was how she felt. Dan had had one. Why couldn't she?

'Hope. Hope!'

Jo was talking to her.

'Oh. Sorry.'

'I was just telling Sally about our Greek trip, about Mykonos. She said we should go to Tinos. Apparently it's very small and there's a beautiful church there.'

It was the cue for Hope's customary polite response. 'Good idea. When did you go?'

Sally was looking at her appraisingly. 'When I first started work. I went with a girl from the office.' Sally pushed her chair back to get up.

Hope couldn't help herself. 'Was that at Porter Stone?' Some voice was emerging from inside her over which she had no control.

Sally cast her a hard look. Then she said evenly, 'No. It was a PR firm in Soho. I didn't stay for long. The boss was brilliant but mad.'

Hope turned to Jo. 'Sally met my father at Porter Stone. She was his secretary.' She was having difficulty forming her words. She slurred the 's' of secretary slightly. She slowed her speech to articulate the words more carefully. 'But then their professional relationship became personal.'

Jo gave her a dramatic frown and shook her head.

Hope responded with a wide-eyed look of innocence. 'I'm just telling you what happened.'

Jo was looking anxious. 'Why don't you have some water?' She looked over at Dan, still loading the dishwasher. 'Can you get Hope some water?'

Sally cut in. 'There's only tap water now.'

Behind her Hope heard a cupboard open and Dan's voice. 'No problem.' Then the sound of the tap running.

She didn't want any water!

Then Edward called out, 'Hope! Why don't you help Sally with clearing the table?'

And in that moment, listening to her father's jovial voice, seeing the complacent expression on his face, everything changed. For a fraction, time stopped. She wasn't irritated any more or worried or depressed. In that moment a red-hot clarity gripped her. She saw her father in a new light. She had been so good, tried so hard; done everything right from her first ballet class to the day she got her university acceptance letter. And given her all at every school play and concert, every Brownie camp and family gathering in between. She had been sweet, polite, helpful, pretty, perfect Hope. And this was how he had repaid her. He had left. He didn't care how she felt. He didn't give a damn about Mummy. He had allowed a complete stranger to come and tear up their lives like a piece of paper.

'Why should I?'

Edward looked stunned. As well he might. Hope had never spoken to him like that. For a moment he was clearly at a loss for words. But he quickly recovered.

'Because Sally has put a great deal of effort into lunch and it's a common courtesy to help.' His tone was horribly patronising. But she was no longer five years old and he had no basis of moral authority.

'Leave it, Edward. It's fine,' Sally said quietly.

'No. It's not fine.' He sounded cross now.

Jo was trying to appeal to her, her hand outstretched across the table. 'Hope!'

Hope ignored it. She looked her father in the eye. 'No. It's not *fine*. What about Mummy?'

Her father looked bewildered. So did Anna, sitting next to him, who belatedly put down her glass.

Edward spoke. 'This has nothing to do with your mother.'

'Yes it does! She's alone in Gerrards Cross and we're all here and now she's losing Dan.' She swung round on Dan. 'Because you've decided to live here.'

'She sent me away to boarding school!' Dan protested.

Edward was recovering himself now. 'Hope, your mother is not alone. She has her own family and, until recently, a boyfriend.'

'That's not what I mean! I mean you leaving! Walking out on us. And running off with her.' She just couldn't utter Sally's name.

She had to give him credit. He didn't miss a beat. 'I hardly think that is a fair or even an approximately accurate interpretation of what happened. Since you have raised the subject it was your mother who asked for a separation.'

'Yes, a separation. Not an affair.'

He raised his voice to silence her. 'Hope, that's enough!'

But Hope was on a rollercoaster, gathering momentum, unable to stop the flow of words. 'Oh. It's enough now – now we're getting to the truth. That's how this family operates. Everything's perfect until the truth comes out.'

It was beyond her power to stop. Some rage had overtaken her. Her words were streaming out.

'You didn't even *try*. Mummy just needed some time. Everything would have been OK. But you met her and it all fell apart.'

She saw her father turn to Anna. 'Please accept my apologies.'

'No problem.'

'Hope,' her father said tolerantly, 'that is simply not true. I think you've had too much to drink.'

'Yes, it is true!' She was screaming for someone to listen to her, as she had been screaming inwardly for so many years now. 'Yes, it is! You even went to Paris together.'

'Hope …' her father said hesitantly.

'No, we didn't,' said Sally.

'You liar!' In that moment Hope understood how people killed in rage. 'That's a *lie*. Mummy found the hotel receipt in Daddy's flat.'

Sally's reaction was to cast a triumphant glance in her father's direction. 'I *told* you she went through your things!'

She turned back to Hope. 'Your father did go to Paris but it wasn't with me. It was with a woman called Louise Winter.' Sally downed some wine and gave Edward a pretty unpleasant look at that point.

'Is it necessary to go into details?' he called out belatedly.

Sally was unrepentant. 'Hope wants the truth. Now she's got it.'

Hope was stunned. She looked at her father anew. How many women had there been?

'Hope, why don't you have some coffee?' said Sally, more gently now.

'I don't want any fucking coffee.'

'Hope!' her father bellowed. It was incredibly loud. 'Louis is in the room.'

Louis began wailing. Dan sprinted forward and grabbed hold of him. 'I'll take him, Dad.'

Hope was incensed. '*Louis!* It's always about Louis. All your time, all your attention, everything's about Louis and her. What about us? What about Dan and me?'

Her father looked defensive. 'I see you as much as I can. We have lunch …'

'You're always dashing off.'

'That's because of the job I have.'

'You think you can just throw money at me and that makes it all OK. Well, it doesn't.'

'Money?' Sally burst out. 'What money?'

Edward had no chance to reply to this. Hope had been watching as Dan hoisted Louis from his booster seat, intent in using him as a hostage in his getaway strategy. He wasn't going to escape that easily.

Hope rounded on him. 'And as for you, Dan. How could you just leave Mummy? She says you want to live with Sally! Have you any idea how hurtful that is for her? Couldn't you have said you wanted to live with Daddy?'

Dan was far from defensive. 'Because I don't want to live in Shanghai!' Dan said this as if it was self-evident.

There was a hiatus as a short, stunned silence engulfed the room. Dan reddened slightly. He looked at his father. 'Sorry, Dad.' Then he grabbed Louis and made a dash for the living room.

Sally's startled voice rang out. 'Shanghai! What are you talking about?'

Hope wasn't about to give up the floor. 'We're talking about my family …'

'Shut up!' It was a shock. Hope had no idea Sally could shout. Sally had fixed Edward with a killer glare. 'What about Shanghai?'

Edward held up his hands as if in surrender. 'Darling, it's all good!'

'Good? What is?'

'I wanted to tell you at an appropriate time.'

'Tell me what?'

'Darling, let's talk about this later.'

More evasions, lies and deceits. Hope was sick of it. 'Daddy's been offered a job in Shanghai. He told my mother.'

Sally looked at Edward. 'You told Pia! You told *Pia* before you told me!'

'No. Yes. In the context of Dan's school plans. I didn't *tell* her as such. It was incidental.'

Sally was shouting now. 'Well, maybe you could have told me too – incidentally. Given that I'm your wife.'

'I was trying to. I was waiting for the right time … The bank has offered me a directorship – Director of Far Eastern Business. Based in Shanghai.'

'Shanghai?' Sally repeated horrified.

'It's only for three years. Well, a maximum of five.'

'Five!'

Even Anna looked aghast. Dan reappeared at the kitchen door. 'Sally, I think Louis wants you.'

'Give him some Wotsits and put *Thomas* on,' instructed Sally curtly, not taking her eye off Edward. 'Well, when does this start?'

'Early next year.'

Hope was steaming. 'Does anyone around here ever tell the truth?'

No one answered. A silence had fallen on the table.

Her father and Sally were looking at each other like strangers. Anna had begun to clear away the scattered remains of Louis's lunch. Jo had sunk back in her chair.

Finally, Sally spoke. 'Would any one like pudding?'

No one answered.

'Yes, just a small piece,' Edward said as if out of loyalty.

Sally got up and carried over an apple crumble to the table. Then she went to open the fridge door. She put cream and a berry dessert on the table. There was the sound of the kettle filling. From the living room, the faint sounds of *Thomas* could be heard. There was no sign of Dan. Anna got up. 'I'll go and check on Dan and Louis.' No one responded.

And then, very quietly, Jo spoke.

'Why don't you begin, Hope? Why don't you tell the truth?'

Hope looked across at Jo. Around her, she could feel all eyes upon them.

How many times had she rehearsed this moment, practising and discarding every possible variation of words? She felt terrified and resigned all at once.

She looked across at Jo, into her eyes, and found that it was Jo she was speaking to. 'Jo's my girlfriend,' she said quietly. 'We love each other.'

No one knew what to say next. From the living room came the sounds of Louis's voice. And then something totally unexpected happened.

Sally spoke. 'Good. It's good that you have someone in your life.'

It was so different from what she had feared. There were no questions or demands for explanations or hysterical outbursts. It was nothing like talking to her mother. Sally was so calm. Right then she grasped one reason why her father had married Sally: he wanted a bit of peace and quiet.

Hope looked up at Sally and saw that she was holding Edward's gaze. She understood that Sally's words were as much directed at him as her. Sally was telling him what to say. And Hope was suddenly grateful. She looked from Sally to her father.

'Yes,' her father said uncertainly. 'Yes. Absolutely.' He looked from Sally to Hope and back again. 'Shall we have coffee?'

Jo reached across and took Hope's hand, which prompted Edward to cough and get up to help Sally. God knows what they would all talk about over coffee. They needed a change of subject to lighten the atmosphere but though Hope tried to think of something suitably non-contentious her brain had frozen solid. When Sally and her father returned to the table, as Hope has predicted, silence fell again. But it was only for a fraction.

Then Sally smiled brightly, turned to Jo and said, 'How would you two girls like to take a day trip? All expenses paid.'

'All expenses paid?' queried Edward, confused.

'Well, we don't have Dan's school fees to pay any more, do we?' Sally said cheerfully. 'All expenses paid,' she repeated.

'Where to?' asked Jo.

'It's in connection with a little project I'm working on. I could do with some help. It means going to Oxford. Christ Church College library to be exact.'

Chapter 20

Anna and Hart sat by the window of the Coach and Horses on Wimbledon Village High Street. Outside, a thin drizzle fell, the roads busy with cars, couples and families returning to London from weekends away. Inside, it was already crowded. Anna was unsure if this was a date but she had decided to plan for all eventualities. She had spent nearly an hour going through her wardrobe, trying to match up something glamorous but casual. It was the type of thing Natasha pulled off effortlessly. She pushed that thought away. Eventually she had picked out jeans, suede boots, a J. Crew pink striped shirt she had bought on her last trip to New York and a Jigsaw jacket from last winter in claret velvet. She had added an argyle scarf, taken it off and put it on again. She was useless at this! When she was rich and famous she would employ a personal stylist. Sometime never? It was another unwelcome thought to be put at the back of her mind. She had reminded herself as she picked up her handbag, straightened the papers, put the washing-up in the dishwasher – not that she had any intention of inviting Hart back – that the mortgage was paid for this month.

'So, how's the mystery of Number Twelve North Walk? Have you solved it?'

Hart shook his head. 'No. And we're not going to either, I'm afraid.'

'But you've done so much research!'

'Yes. But research and answers aren't the same thing.'

Anna had lied to Sally about hearing from Hart but not in a premeditated way. It just came out like that. Somehow, without Sally saying so, Anna had known that Sally wouldn't like to hear that she was meeting Hart for a drink. There had been something in Sally's tone when she asked the question – *have you heard anything from*

Hart? – that had belatedly alerted Anna to a potential conflict of interests. Afterwards, as she got ready for her drink with Hart, some of the pieces had fallen into place, the largest of which was that Sally wasn't as happily married as Anna had thought. She recalled the day Sally had shooed her and Louis out of the door to finish cooking what, in hindsight, was a very elaborate lunch for Hart.

Watching Hope lose it over lunch at Sally's that afternoon had depressed Anna. Ordinarily she would have sat, a detached observer, contemplating how she would film this. People having arguments were tricky because they moved about. But when she had seen the anger and hurt in Sally's eyes and the resentment and fear in Hope's she had felt engaged, shocked and ultimately disillusioned. She had thought Sally had it all.

She wondered how Sally would feel if Hart lost interest in the Lathams. 'Are you going to write about it?'

Hart sounded unenthusiastic. 'We could probably stretch it to a "What the maid saw" type piece. I know Sally would like to carry on.'

It was the perfect opening. 'Will you do it together?'

'I think I'll probably back out. It's always been her project. I don't feel like writing up what we've got.'

She understood his lack of excitement. 'Because it would feel like settling for second best?'

He looked up at her. 'Exactly. Most people don't get that. They say – why don't you write what's easy, what's in front of you?'

'Oh, I get it. I always want to push it. My ex-boyfriend said I needed to acquire a set of ethics.'

Good God, what was she doing breaking one of the cardinal rules of first dates – make no mention of the ex?

But Hart looked unfazed. 'Was he right?'

'Probably.' She hesitated. 'You see, the irony of *Marriage Menders* is that I did trample over someone. But it wasn't Mrs Zarkosky.'

Hart said nothing. Perhaps he was counting up the number of first date rules she was breaking. Number Two – making an intimate confession of a grievous error of professional judgement.

At last he spoke. 'Well, who was it then?'

'His name is Rob. He's one of those people who thinks that exposing his private life on television is a good idea. He had no conception that you can't take it back.'

'And what's Rob's secret?'

'He confessed to me, on camera, that he couldn't read.'

'He knew he was being filmed?'

'Yes.'

'Then I'm not clear what the problem is.'

'The problem is Rob. I manipulated him into being filmed without his wife – who is the brains of the partnership – and encouraged him to open up and led him further and further in until he forgot there was a camera at all.'

'Gosh. Sounds pretty skilled work.'

'I do it all the time,' she said with mock modesty. 'And that's the point. Because I thought I could control it. I wasn't even sure that I would use it. When I was in the edit I got gripped by some residual flicker of conscience and I left it out.'

'There you are, then.'

'But now 7–24 have the film and I know they won't leave it out. They'll probably use that segment for the trailer.'

'Does he know?'

'Who?'

'Rob.'

'No.'

'Then why don't you tell him?'

She was stunned for a moment. 'Tell him?'

Hart leaned back. 'Yes. Presumably he has given consent for the filming. Well, he can withdraw it.'

'But that would mean I had to go and confess to trying to set him up.'

Hart grinned. 'Hmm. That's the tough part about ethics.'

It was so simple. Why hadn't she thought about that? 'I'm not sure if there's time. They may have finished filming.'

'Well, there's always time before it's broadcast. And given that it can't be broadcast before the Zarkosky trial because it would be *sub judice,* you should be fine.' Hart took a sip of his drink. 'Anna, it's your call. No one can tell you what to do.'

'Is that the journalist talking?'

'No, the part of me that's a human being – the two being exclusive, naturally. Another drink?'

'Yes, please.'

She watched as Hart went over to the bar. Even on a Sunday the pub was full. They had been lucky to get a window table.

When he came back he looked thoughtful. 'Personally I think you can argue it either way. Yes, you led him on. But he's an adult and he consented to be filmed. Some people would say it's not your problem.'

'I feel I have to save him from himself. He's hopelessly naïve.'

'Then go.' Hart paused. 'You have to go by gut instinct. Of course, it can get you into trouble.'

'Has it got you into trouble? Do you mean getting beaten up? I remember that, you were in the papers.'

Hart looked away, then back again. 'To be honest, the real trouble was on the home front. My wife never forgave me for going back to Ireland that last time. She wanted me to sit in London, nab a cosy column to write, do a bit of sedate film reviewing here and there, and come home for dinner at six. Frankly, she was pretty pissed off with me that I got myself beaten up. Everyone else was proclaiming me to be a hero and she was sitting by my hospital bed telling me it was all my own arrogant fault.'

'That was pretty harsh!'

Hart shrugged. 'She was right. I was off work for a long time. Meanwhile, she had to work full time, she was a teacher, then come home and look after an invalid. I was in physical rehab for about a year.'

'So what happened?'

'She had an affair with her Head of Department, left me and married him. They're still together, now they've got two kids. She sends me a Christmas card.'

'I'm sorry. Did you have any children together?'

'No. Which people say is a good thing.' He paused for a fraction. 'And you – have you ever been married?'

'No.'

So it *was* a date. Now, as the pub filled and the noise levels rose, Hart looked at his watch. She was startled to feel a stab of disappointment that he was preparing to leave. They had been there barely an hour.

He leaned towards her. 'Have you eaten?'

And then the disappointment died. She knew exactly what he was going to say next. And even though she wasn't remotely hungry she said innocently, 'No. No, I haven't.'

'Then shall we have dinner?'

'I'm sorry, Edward. But I don't see how I can go with you.' Sally was faltering now. Earlier she had been adamant – *I'm not going*. But now, as they sat on either side of the bed, she felt herself weakening.

'So what are you saying?' Edward's voice was growing bewildered. 'Are you saying I should turn down the directorship?'

'No! Of course not. I mean, I just don't think we have to go with you.'

Edward ran his hand through his hair. 'It's ridiculous! Why not? I understand what you've said about not wanting to sell this house. But we don't have to sell the house. We can rent it out. We'll be back in three years.'

'Or five.'

'At the outside.'

They had been over the same ground countless times. Now they spoke in urgent but low voices, both aware of Louis and Dan sleeping. It was midnight.

'Edward. That is such a long time …' Her voice trailed off. It would be so easy to give in, to keep the peace, to make Edward happy.

Edward looked bereft. 'Is it so much to ask that you come with me?'

She found that she could not answer him directly. 'Edward, I have a life here. Friends, family, the house. I have my history research.' As she said this she felt a pang of regret. 'And I'd like to go back to work.' As soon as she said it she realised that this was not her best argument, given her inaction to date.

'You wouldn't need to,' he countered. 'We'd have more than enough money. We'd have my living allowance out there and the rent from the house here. It would set us up financially. I thought that was what you wanted.'

'I know,' she conceded. And she understood that for Edward this was the opportunity he craved to recover financially from his divorce. And hadn't she wished aloud, countless times, for their situation to improve? 'But we could visit.'

'Visit! How can that be a good thing? It's an insane amount of travel for Louis. Don't you think he needs me?'

'Yes.' Now there was no hesitation.

Belatedly Edward seemed to realise that Louis was his strongest card. 'And he needs me all the time. Christ, if I learned anything today it's that you have very little idea what your children are doing at the best of times. Besides which, I think it's a fabulous opportunity for him. And the Chinese love children. We'd be able to afford for you to have some help in the house.'

She was incapable of lying. *Help in the house!* She felt exhausted from a day of cooking, clearing up and relentless toddler taming. And there was a good chance that at five thirty – in less than six hours' time – Louis would be awake again. She felt wiped out. A mirage floated before her eyes in which her liberal principles were jettisoned and replaced by the image of a gentle, smiling, ever-patient Chinese nanny teaching elementary mathematics to her now dutiful and obedient son.

'Really?'

He took advantage of this implied concession to push on. 'Sally, there is a huge English-speaking community out there. You could learn the language – but you'd have English-speaking friends, too. My God, there is so much to see and do out there. There's the Old City and the French area and the shops are fantastic.'

'But I'd be living on a compound for foreigners,' she objected.

'It's a compound not a prison. To be accurate, it's a gated development. Hell, Surrey's peppered with them. What's the difference? You'd adjust in no time. There are fabulous facilities. The sports club has an Olympic-size pool and a gym with a climbing wall.'

'You told me.'

Edward didn't miss a beat. 'You'd meet other mothers. All these places have a social calendar for the ex-pats. It's the chance of a lifetime! And your parents could visit.'

'What about Dan?'

'He can come with us.'

'I don't think Pia's going to agree to that.'

'I'm not sure she has a choice unless she can find a day school in Gerrards Cross that will take him.' Edward had clearly thought this out. 'There are umpteen international schools out there.' And he had done the research, too.

They had been arguing intermittently since Jo and Hope left. Anna had disappeared directly after lunch, doubtless grateful to flee the scene before the curtain went up on any more family secrets and betrayals. Then Edward had summoned Hope into the living room. Sally had washed up, assisted by Jo. Louis and Dan had gone upstairs for a nap. Edward had been vague about what had been said but as they left Hope had embraced her and said sorry for spoiling lunch and Sally had surprised herself by suggesting they meet for coffee next week.

But the calm had been short-lived. As soon as the front door had closed she rounded on Edward.

'How could you tell Pia before you told me? How could you?'

'I didn't mean to! I was just waiting for the right time ...'

His denial of any wrongdoing had made her still angrier. On and on they went in a circular argument until finally Edward did what he should have done at the start. He took her in his arms.

'Sally, I'm sorry. I truly am. You didn't deserve to hear it that way. And I will do everything I can to make it up to you. Please – just hear me out.'

And then it had started, Edward portraying China as the promised land, Sally fighting to stand her ground as he chipped away at each successive objection. In between times she asked him about Hope. But he had been reluctant to discuss it.

She was surprised to find herself anxious on Hope's behalf. 'You didn't say anything ... harsh, did you?'

'No. I just ... Hell, Sally. It was a bloody big shock. And maybe I'm supposed to "get with the programme" as all these young people say, whatever that means. But ...' Edward's voice trailed off inconclusively.

'So what did you say?'

'I told her she was my daughter and I loved her ...' He petered out again.

'And?'

'And that she shouldn't make any hasty decisions.'

'Decisions?'

'I mean commitments. I mean, it could just be a phase, couldn't it?'

Talking to Jo as they had cleared up together, Sally had learned that so far this was no flight of fancy . 'I think you have to be open-minded about it, whichever way it turns out.'

'Hmm. Well, I don't think that's how her mother's going to react. Pia will probably try to persuade Hope to have a shot of electricity through the temples ...'

Sally had been taken aback. 'Surely she won't have a problem with it?'

Edward had given a mirthless laugh. 'She has a problem with any deviation from her Master Plan of Life. Hope is supposed to get married – to a man, preferably a doctor – after she's established her career as a journalist and then have two children, one boy and one girl, bringing them up in a nice house in Marlow.'

'Oh.'

'And Dan's supposed to be a barrister.' Edward sighed. 'It doesn't look like any of that is going to happen.'

Now, Edward moved across the bed and took her in his arms. It was ages since they had lain close to each other like this. 'Look,' Edward said reasonably, kissing her neck, 'why don't you come with me on my next trip? Leave Louis with your parents and come out and have a look around.' He opened his hands expansively. 'I haven't got anything to hide. If it was truly awful I'd make us sell the house, get you out there and hide your passport.' His hand settled on her hip bone. This was the old, irresistible Edward at work. 'All I'm saying is be open to the idea. Isn't it what we've always wanted? To travel? To do something out of the ordinary? To have a little excitement?' His hand began to caress her as she felt his lips on her neck once more, his kisses more passionate now.

'OK. I'll go for a visit.' But as she said the words she knew, as surely as Edward did, that he had won. The visit was a fiction to ease her defeat. She understood how it would play out. She would go to Shanghai, they would choose a place to live and when she came back she would arrange for letting agents to view the house, school brochures to be sent and set in motion all the vaccinations and removers and visas to be organised.

As she spoke it was as if the image of Hart and the book and the Lathams began to recede, fading until eventually nothing would be left of them except a pile of closely written notebooks. She would remain in the present, living in what was tangible.

Edward pushed her gently onto her back, shifting so that he was looking down on her. His hand caressed her face.

'Sally, I'm sorry about today, about the way it came out. You mean so much to me. Everything. I don't want anything to happen that would make you unhappy.'

She believed him. Edward was a good man, a kind father: a man she could live her life with.

'So you don't have any regrets?' she said tentatively.

'Regrets?' He looked puzzled.

'At Hope's party Marion said that you and Pia would have got back together.'

She saw a spark of anger cross his face. 'Marion is a trouble-maker. She likes to stir things up. It was Marion who was always pushing Pia to leave me.'

'Oh.'

Looking at his face she saw that there was something he was holding back.

A part of the puzzle slotted into place. 'Did she ever ... make a pass at you?'

He did not reply immediately. 'Once. We were in the kitchen. Her husband was in the garden with Pia. He's a corporate lawyer. He spends the week at a flat in the City. You can guess the rest. She suggested that she could come up to London one day and we could have dinner.'

'What did you say?'

'I said that she should ask Pia to join us. As you can imagine, that didn't go down very well. That's when I became the bastard in Pia's life who was the cause of all her problems.'

'Did you ever tell Pia?'

'No.' Sally already knew that is what he would say. Edward was an honourable man. He continued, 'Marion is an unhappy woman and she wants every other woman in Gerrards Cross to be unhappy with her.'

'So why is Pia friends with her?'

'Pia doesn't know how to read people. She's ...' he hesitated, 'she's not a people person. She's good with words and numbers. But people confuse her. That's why she needs to boss everyone about. And when she can't she lashes out.'

'So you never think about going back?'

'Are you crazy!' It was impossible to mistake the genuine amazement in his voice. 'Sally, I've told you. I love you. I married you. Why isn't that enough? You've got to stop this. It doesn't make any sense.'

It didn't. Her obsession with Pia and Hope had achieved nothing except to make her miserable. It had been so easy to criticise Hope for being distant and unsociable when in truth she had been both those things herself. Today, on her home ground, watching Hope run out of control, she had at last seen that Hope was struggling, too.

Edward reached down and began undoing the button of her skirt. She felt awkward. It had been such a long time. She reached over to switch off the light.

'You don't need to do that,' he said.

'I do.' Maybe the Shanghai Racquet Club was just what she needed. There was still that stubborn baby tummy to lose.

'No.' He kissed her deeply. 'You worry too much.'

His hands ran over her body, shifting up her skirt. Feeling him touch her then move inside her, she pushed her face into the warmth of his neck. As they moved together she felt a surge of love for him.

'I love you,' she whispered. 'I love you, I love you, I love you.'

'I love you, too,' he murmured. And suddenly it all seemed so simple, to live in the moment and appreciate that Edward was with her and Louis was asleep upstairs. Afterwards, she lay in Edward's arms. She listened as Edward's breathing grew heavy and regular. Gently she pulled away and eased herself out of bed. There was one more thing that she needed to do today.

She went silently down to the kitchen. From the top kitchen shelf, stowed safely out of Louis's sticky reach, she pulled down the borrowed BBC tape recorder and put on the headphones. It was time to say goodbye to Mary Kelly and the Lathams and to accept that there were some mysteries that would never be solved.

It was time to honestly acknowledge that she had gone as far as possible.

Mary Kelly's voice spoke to her.

John put it there for me. "It's your Shamrock, Mary," he said. It was our little joke. All the gentry admiring it and none of them noticing there's a shamrock growing in the middle of Italy!'

She sat still, silently, and began to cry. She could not bring herself to take off the headphones for the last time: to leave Mary and Bella here in this house with their secrets.

She knew the tape so well now. There were parts that she could recite word for word.

'In the afternoons Cook set me sharpening the kitchen knives and cleaning the blades. You used emery board for that. I did her boots, too. You girls don't have the foggiest how to clean.'

Mary's voice was always confident and often opinionated. She was a woman of strong feelings and, it appeared, the holder of grudges that she nursed for decades. Sally thought back to Mary's comments about Jenny.

'So there she was left with two babies and only a widow's pension. They would have been better off staying at the Hall and holding out for a gardener's cottage. So you see, all her airs and graces didn't get her very far. We lost touch after that.'

Tomorrow she would make a copy of the tape, pack up the recorder and the originals and return them to Anna to go back to the BBC. The concluding words of the tape were playing.

'Thank you. I think that's everything we need.'

'When is it going to be broadcast?'

'Broadcast? Oh, that's for Professor Berner to decide. He's in charge of the project.'

'When will I meet him?'

'I'm afraid I can't say.'

Silence. The tape made a click, click, click sound as it continued to turn. Sally resolved to make an archive of the copies and her notes, purchase a folder and file away her research. She would send Hart a change of address and maybe exchange the occasional email. It was over.

'You told me it would be broadcast!'

It was Mary's voice and she sounded angry.

What on earth was this? She checked the tape. Previously she had shut it off by now, assuming that after Miss Grant's closing sentence the tape had ended.

But there was more.

Miss Grant hesitated. 'It's not my decision. Professor Berner listens to all the tapes and decides what material will be included.'

'*But my tape will be.*' That was Mary! It was that unmistakable note of righteous self-confidence.

There was another hesitation. '*I would hope so. As you can imagine, we have a great deal of material.*'

Did Miss Grant know that the tape was still running? Was this an accidental recording?

'*Well, you tell your Professor Berner that I need to talk to him. Why ever wouldn't he want my story! I knew the Duke of Wakemont!*'

'*I will. I will put your case as strongly as I can.*' Miss Grant hesitated. '*Actually, I think you have a very important story to tell. And now that we're off the record perhaps I could ask you if you ever thought about writing a memoir. An account of your life.*'

'*I know what a memoir is. You don't have to explain that to me.*'

'*I'm sorry. I just meant that your life is so interesting.*'

'*That's as maybe. It wasn't very interesting at the time, I can tell you. It was hard work. Girls nowadays they wouldn't be able to keep up.*'

'*I'm sure.*'

'*Now let me ask you a question. Who told you about Mr Latham? Who told you?*'

'*I really don't know. One of the other researchers mentioned it to me. I don't know who told her.*'

'*Typical! They talk behind your back but none of them will say anything to your face. But I've got a good idea, I can tell you.*'

There was a long pause. Miss Grant appeared to be moving about. Then she spoke: '*Is it true?*'

'*About him having bad blood? Yes.*'

'*And that's why he left?*'

'*Mr Latham left to find a cure. The story was that he went away on business. But he left to find a cure. That's what they did in those days.*'

'*Did it work?*'

'*After a while Miss Bella didn't hear nothing from him.*'

'*But what do you think happened?*'

'*I think he died trying – or he found one of his own sort. After Miss Bella found out, she wouldn't have … relations with him.*'

'*And Henry …?*'

'*Well, she blamed him, and who wouldn't? After Henry died Miss Bella took to sleeping up there in Henry's room. In his little bed. She wouldn't let me touch anything. I used to take a pail of coal up and*

259

make the fire up for her.'

'But did she know about Mr Latham's condition when she got married?'

'No! He kept it well hidden. Like I told you, he was very charming. Of course, when it flared up he swore to her as how he didn't know. His story was he thought it was cured. He'd taken mercury. But it came back. Like I said, there was no penicillin in those days. It stayed in your body and then it got into your brain. Oh, he suffered! He never left the house once it came back. One day he'd be perfectly normal and working on his book. The next he was laid up and crying out with the pain. And once the rumours started, no one came to visit. People were afraid of catching it.'

'But you can't catch it except ...?'

'People were afraid! That's what you have to understand. None of the family came down. Except the Duke. He'd visit of an evening and spend an hour with her. The Duke wouldn't see him, mind you. Mr Latham had to stay in his room when the Duke called. Of course, the Duke had to keep the visits secret from the new Duchess. She wouldn't have liked it. And he would say to me when he left, "You take good care of her, Mary." And I would say, "Yes, Sir," and bob a curtsey and most times he gave me a shilling. He didn't want to lose me, you see.'

'So, Miss Bella saw her father secretly?'

'Oh yes. He gave her money, too. But none of the others would come down. Miss Camilla was the only one who saw her, but she had to keep quiet about it. They all cut her off, that's why Henry's buried at St Mary's. Now that was pure spite. The new Duchess put the Duke up to that, I've no doubt about it. Henry should have been in the family vault at the Hall but she wouldn't have that. She didn't even come to the funeral.'

'And after Mr Latham left? Did Miss Bella's family resume contact with her?'

'No. That's the gentry for you. Once you're out you're out and you can never get back in.'

She lost herself in Mary's voice, in the flow of recollection. Mary was more relaxed now as the layers of the past were revealed for another hour.

'I like to keep busy. I help at the Church, that's the Sacred Heart on Edge Hill. I've been cleaning there since 1905. That's over fifty years!

260

Miss Bella went to St Mary's. She started to go after Master Henry died. They didn't know what to make of her. Some of the women could be funny – there were rumours her husband had run off. But she did the best flowers. They couldn't take that away from her. She was a lady and most of them were nothing more than jumped-up grocers' daughters. You can't buy class. Either you're born with it or you're not.

'When the Duke died, Miss Bella went up to Selton and that was the last time she saw the place. "It's changed, Mary," she said. "I'm glad you didn't have to see it."

'Miss Bella got out a bit more after she met Major Stephen. She met him at St Mary's. In the summer they'd drive out to Brighton on a Sunday. He used to take her to the theatre. She loved that! He'd bring her home afterwards and she'd give me the programme. I always waited up for her, and she'd waltz down that hallway, sparkling like a young girl. Miss Bella kept her figure – that's what a lady does.

'She liked Noel Coward and the musicals. She was ever so good at picking up a tune. The King and I, *that was the last thing they saw. 1953. She came in singing that song. "Shall we dance, tra la la ..." I'll show you the programme. I kept them all.*

'Major Stephen was a gentleman. He was ever so cut up. We weren't expecting it, you see. It was her heart. But there was never any talk of marriage. How could there be? She was still married in the eyes of the law.

'She was very particular about how she wanted things to be. She used to say to me, "Name and dates, Mary. That's all." You see, she didn't want his name on her headstone. I went with Major Stephen to order the headstone – poor man, he wasn't up to it on his own, and I picked out ivy and lilies to go round the edge. That's ivy for remembrance and lilies on account of Selton. We buried her next to Master Henry. That was what she wanted.'

Then there was only the sound of movement. Sally found herself clutching the table. Would Miss Grant take another chance to ask once more the last, most important question? Did Mary know what really happened to Robert Latham?

'Thank you. I must be going. I have another interview at three o'clock.'

She did not.

But Mary had not finished. Her voice was urgent.

'*Sit down a minute. I want to tell you one last thing.*' There was a pause and then Mary's voice could be heard quieter and softer than before.

'*Everything's changed. I think the winters were colder back then. The lake at Wimbledon Park used to freeze over and they'd open it for skating. John persuaded me to go and Miss Bella had skates that she lent me. John had his own pair. There used to be smithies there who'd fix them up for you. They'd take a steel to sharpen them up good and proper so you could go faster. All around the banks of the lake there were huge bonfires and braziers set on wheeled carts, selling roast chestnuts and potatoes. It was what you'd call a spectacle. When it got dark you'd see the flames from the fires reflected on the ice and all the skaters lit up as they whirled round and round.*

'*John was a beautiful skater. So elegant and graceful. I can shut my eyes and I can see him now. He taught me and then we practised skating hand in hand. We went every year. The last winter we went I got so cold out on the ice! I'd fallen earlier and got wet and the cold is a terrible thing when you're wet. So I told him I wanted to go home. He would have liked to have skated some more. "Come on, Mary. One more spin!" But I'd had enough and we left. I wonder if he already knew.*

'*The next summer was when he started to feel bad. He'd had a cough for years. But then the pains started in his back. By then it had spread from his lungs into the bones, you see. I think it was the paints that caused it – all those years mixing paints and breathing in the fumes. He went so quickly, which they say is a blessing. I don't know about that. I used to catch the bus up to Fulham to see him. His sister was looking after him and I helped her out. He died in 1929. Seventeenth October 1929.*

'*Now, when I think back to that day at the lake, I wish we'd stayed to skate. Never mind the damn cold and wet. I wish we'd skated to the end of the day. You have to make the most of it while you can. Life is very short. Remember that.*'

Chapter 21

Anna arrived unannounced. Wimbledon to Bracknell and back would be the last journey for the BMW, albeit a good last one in the June afternoon sun with the top down. Tomorrow she would hand the keys back to the dealership, marking the end of her three-month notice period. She parked outside the Ramseys and pulled out a copy of the *Evening Standard*. She did not have long to wait. Rob's van pulled into the driveway at just past five o'clock as she had anticipated. Fearing that he might not open the front door to her if he went inside, she swiftly got out of the car and ran to greet him.

'Rob.'

He looked pleased to see her. 'Anna! What are you doing down here?'

'I came to see you.'

'Oh?' Now there was a flash of curiosity. 'You'd better come in.'

It was going better than expected. Over the last few weeks she had dithered constantly, observed with amused detachment by Hart. 'What if they refuse to speak to me?' she had said. 'What if they say I'm just making it up because Rick fired me?'

'All you can do is go down to see them. If they don't want to listen then that's their business.'

Whatever confession she had to make to Rob would be far easier without Nina there. But as he entered the house Rob called up the stairs.

'Nina!'

He turned back to Anna. 'She hasn't been well. The doctor told her to take a nap in the afternoon.'

He shouted again. 'There's someone here to see you. Anna from 7–24.'

'Anna?' Nina's faint voice sounded surprised. 'I'll just get dressed.'

Rob escorted Anna back into the Ramseys' familiar living room. 'I'll put the kettle on.'

Nina, when she appeared ten minutes later, looked nothing short of awful, her complexion pale and her hair unkempt. She was dressed in a jade green velour tracksuit.

Nina sat down and turned to Rob questioningly. 'Cup of tea, sweetheart?'

'Sorted. The kettle's boiled.' Rob left the room.

Anna wished he had stayed. She tried to put as much warmth as she could into her voice. 'Nina, how are you?'

'Oh, of course, you don't know.' Nina cast her a look that was difficult to read but contained a spark of pleasure. 'Now that you don't work for 7–24. I'm pregnant. We just found out.'

'Pregnant!' Her first thought was that it would be good for the programme. She recovered herself, however. 'Congratulations!'

'Thank you. And what are you doing now?' Nina enquired coolly.

'Oh, I'm making a film for Channel 4.' It was a pity to begin telling the truth with another lie. But this was not exactly a lie because she soon would be.

'We heard all about it,' said Nina. 'About you getting the sack. Ethne told us. It sounded very dramatic. She said they escorted you from the building.'

'Yes.'

'I liked Ethne,' Nina continued in a tone that drew a clear comparison to her feelings about Anna. 'She was a sweet girl. But she left, too. She got offered a job in Cornwall.'

Anna was starting to regret this whole ethical escapade. Why shouldn't she let Nina go, in full pregnant denial, to her TV fate?

'Really?'

'Yes, she's working in a restaurant. But she persuaded Rick to make a programme about it. Rick's really excited. Ethne and her mother are the stars. Her mother came down and liked the restaurant so much she's going to buy it. It's about mothers and daughters and about cooking. Rick says it's very commercial. They've had a lot of interest from the TV companies in South America.'

Nina seemed very familiar with Rick and his work.

'Have you seen a lot of Rick?' Anna asked.

'Oh yes. He's taken a personal interest. When you left he came down, and he said that from now on he would be micro-managing the whole project. He said 7–24 couldn't afford any more mistakes.'

Doing the right thing was proving increasingly vexing.

Nina was relentless. 'Rick said you left quite a mess for him to sort out.'

Anna had heard enough: Nina clearly didn't want, let alone deserve, her assistance.

They were interrupted by Rob coming in with a tray.

'Actually,' said Anna, 'I was just leaving.'

Rob looked woebegone. 'Oh. Stay for a cup of tea. I made a cake yesterday.'

'A cake?'

'Cinnamon coffee cake. We did a class at Ballymaloe. It's in Ireland.'

'I know.' The cake did look good. 'Yes, please.'

He served both of them a slice.

'Rob's underselling himself,' chipped in Nina. 'He's a natural. He's starting chef school in September and if that goes according to plan we're thinking of starting a restaurant ourselves. Meeting Ethne has really inspired us.'

'Really?'

'So many people criticise reality television, but I have to say that the whole experience has only been a positive one for us. It's made us look at our relationship, it's allowed Rob to explore his potential.' Nina patted her stomach. 'I don't even think this little one would be here without it.'

'What?'

'Rick sat me down one day and he said that he was worried about me. He's a very caring person beneath that hard shell. He was worried that I was so focused on the programme that I was neglecting myself.'

Anna had been about to take a bite of cake but now put down the plate down on the glass-topped coffee table. 'Are you saying that Rick persuaded you to have a baby?'

'No! We were always planning to start a family. Rick just said that it would be something that the viewers could relate to.'

Enough was enough. Anna might not be inspired by Nina's fate but she was damned if she was going to let Rick's behaviour go unchallenged.

'He's even extended the filming schedule to include the baby,' Nina added.

No. Anna knew that he had had to extend the filming schedule until after the trial. 'I think there is something you need to know.'

'Oh?' Nina looked unimpressed. She turned to Rob. 'Lovely cake, sweetheart. But just a teeny weeny bit dry?'

Before Rob had a chance to defend his cake, Anna cut in. 'Rick Roth is not your friend. He doesn't care about you or Rob or the baby. He cares about ratings for *Marriage Menders*.'

Nina shook her head. 'I think you underestimate the man.'

'No. I worked with him. And I have been making television programmes for twelve years. The reason you think *Marriage Menders* has been a success is because it hasn't been broadcast yet.'

'Anna, with all due respect, we know what we're doing,' Nina countered confidently. 'I'm sure Rick does care about his ratings. He's a businessman. But we feel that by making this programme we are giving something back. Life has been good to us. Yes, we've had our struggles, but we want to show people how you can come through difficult times. They can relate to us.'

Weren't these her lines? 'That sounds great, Nina. But that isn't what is going to happen.' She spoke as resolutely as she could. 'Nina, you're being set up.'

Nina looked defensive. 'How do you know?'

'Because I helped to do it.'

'Anna, that's ridiculous! We and Rick are on the same page.'

'No, you're not. He's just telling you that you are.'

'No!' Nina was glaring at her now and her voice had a hard edge to it. 'You are an embittered ex-employee who wants to hurt Rick because he fired you. I think you'd better leave.'

'No.' It was Rob. 'Hear her out.'

Anna seized the moment. 'You're being set up because what you're describing to me isn't good television! A couple with problems that they discuss reasonably and resolve and live happily ever after is not a story! It's not entertaining for the viewer! It lacks the essential ingredient of drama – which is *conflict*. Added to jealousy, resentment, disloyalty and general back-stabbing. That's what gets ratings. Think of any soap opera you can watch. What's the formula?' At least she had caught their attention. Before she lost it she delivered the killer blow. 'And your story is how a successful older woman dominates her younger husband.'

Nina looked astonished. 'But Rick said we'd be thrilled with the results!'

'Rick is lying to you. People lie, especially television people. I know because I did it.'

Rob's voice was quiet. 'Did you lie to us, Anna?'

She took a breath. 'Yes. Yes, I did. I made out that you were doing the world some charitable service when all I was really doing was making the most entertaining film I could.' She didn't want to say the next words but she had to. 'And I filmed you, Rob, saying that you had … issues with literacy.'

'You told her you couldn't read!' screeched Nina at Rob.

Anna interjected. 'But I never put it in. I swear to God, when I did the first edit I left it out. But I don't think Rick will.'

Nina was looking daggers at Rob. 'How could you be so stupid?'

Rob looked crestfallen. 'We were just talking about me and you and your friends. I forgot the camera was running. You do forget it after a while, don't you? Even you've said that, Nina.'

Nina made to get up. 'I'm going to call Rick.'

Anna objected. 'To tell him about the footage? Your best chance is that he just takes my first edit and doesn't review the other footage.'

'And then what will happen?'

'My guess is that it will be shot to make Nina look as bossy as possible. Rob, you're going to look like a wimp. I guarantee Nina will never be shown holding the baby. I never showed you lifting a finger around the house.'

'But I clean all the time!' protested Nina.

'Yes. All I showed was you letting in the cleaning firm and Rob loading the dishwasher. Ninety-nine per cent of your footage is at work, especially having lunch with clients.'

'But that's something I do once a week!'

'Yes. But it looks like you do it every day.'

Nina sounded sullen. 'Well, Anna, what do you suggest we do?'

'OK. First you can ask to see the existing films. Rick won't let you. He'll probably tell you they don't have any ready to show. They do.

Then you can ask for editorial control, which he won't give to you. Then you can pull out.'

'Pull out!'

'Yes. And at the same time withdraw your consent to the broadcast of the existing footage.'

'What about the others? They'll go ahead.'

'Not necessarily. Why don't you speak to them? You could call the Michaels.'

'We don't have their number.' For the first time Nina sounded unsure of herself. 'We keep asking Rick for it and he keeps forgetting to give it to us.'

Anna opened her Filofax. 'Here.' She read it out.

Nina was clearly trying to formulate a plan. 'Why should we believe you? You have a motive to get back at Rick, don't you? '

'Yes, I do. But in the scheme of things this is hardly a revenge plot. Even if *Marriage Menders* doesn't get broadcast, Rick has a stable of other programmes. Like Ethne's.'

'So why are you here?' asked Rob.

'I'm here because I did something unethical. I led Rob into revealing a confidence. And, yes, I agree with you, Nina, it could – hypothetically – be something that might help other people. But I don't think that simply declaring to the world that you have a problem accomplishes anything on its own. You'd have to show Rob dealing with it, getting help and moving on. You would need to have a telephone number at the end of the programme that people with the same problem could call. None of that is going to happen in a programme made by Rick Roth. This is commercial television not a public information broadcast. It will be sensationalised and you will spend the rest of your life associated with it. What about your mother, Rob? Have you thought about the effect on her.' She delivered her final argument with conviction. 'There's a good chance that in the long run the stress of the programme will break up your marriage. Ironic, when you come to think about it.'

'I don't think we should make any hasty decisions,' said Nina.

'I think we should pull out,' said Rob.

'Why?' Nina said, startled.

'Because we've got what we want out of it. We've had a bit of free counselling, I've found out what I want to do and we're having a baby.' He paused and said with a newfound determination, 'I don't want my mum dragged into this.'

Nina sounded reluctant. 'There's no saying your mum will be. Rick may not even have found that tape.'

Rob got up. He looked from Anna to Nina. His voice was uncompromising. 'We're not going to do it.'

Anna did not know who was the more surprised, her or Nina.

Nina started to speak. 'But Rick said—'

He cut her off abruptly. 'I said no!'

Silence. Anna got up. 'I ought to be going.'

Nina was staring at the floor. She did not look up as Rob walked Anna to the front door.

He opened the door and walked to her car with her. 'I'm sorry you lost your job, Anna.'

'I probably deserved to. Mrs Zarkosky nearly killed someone.'

'Nah. Some nutty woman wants to shoot the mistress, that's her business.'

They stood together next to the BMW. 'I'm the one who should be sorry, Rob. I misled you.'

He shrugged. 'Forget it. I never liked that Rick Roth anyway. Always called me "mate", like he was one of the lads.' Rob laughed. 'Yeah, one of the lads in his Range Rover, flashing his Rolex around.' Rob shook her shoulder gently. 'You're better off out of it. Smarmy geezer, isn't he?'

Pia was trying to keep her cool. She reached into her handbag for a cigarette. Was it any wonder with children like hers that it was impossible to give up smoking? She would have expected this from Dan but never from Hope.

She kept her voice low and even. The important thing was to maintain control in spite of the disappointment she felt towards her daughter. 'Let me get this straight. You went to Oxford on Sally's behalf to research a project.' She said the word 'project' as if in speech marks and paused for effect. 'A project that no one has commissioned and for which no one is paying.' She paused again to light her cigarette. 'And now you're planning to interrupt the summer holiday to run off to Liverpool to do even more unpaid research?'

'No. It's not like that.'

'Well, how is it?'

'We want to go to Liverpool. It's a sort of holiday.'

'Holiday! Why can't you have a holiday here?' It was time that Hope realised how selfish she was being. 'Frankly, darling, it's very hurtful. How can you have time for that woman and not for me? It's bad enough Dan eating out of her hand and talking non-stop about Shanghai ...'

'Dan's upstairs!' Hope protested. 'Why do you keep talking as if he's abandoned you?'

'Well, he has!' It was self-evident. 'In less than a month he's leaving his mother to go to the other side of the world. It's as if he's fallen under her spell.'

'He'll be back for the holidays. Anyway, you're the one who sent him away to Welton.'

Pia could scarcely believe her ears. 'Because it was the best thing for him.'

'But he's here, isn't he?' said Hope, her voice thick with irritation. 'He's come to visit before he goes and instead of having a nice time all you do is go on at him about tidying his room and his smoking and Sally and getting expelled.'

'Some things need to be said!' The situation was getting out of hand. Never had she experienced disloyalty of any kind from Hope. Pia attempted to lighten her tone of voice. 'And what about Granny? What is she going to think? She'll be very disappointed if you're not here.'

Pia had planned everything so carefully for the summer vac. She had spring cleaned Hope's room, bought a new rosebud duvet cover and matching pillowcases from Laura Ashley and put fresh flowers on Hope's desk. She had even driven to Marlow to buy chocolates from Burgers. But now, after barely a day at home, Hope had come in to the kitchen and announced that she wanted to take off to Liverpool for three days. With Jo.

Perhaps she should say more about what she had planned? 'I thought we could go to John Lewis at High Wycombe to buy some things for your room. And you know how you like to go shopping in Windsor. I thought we could have lunch at the Castle Hotel ...'

'We can still do all of those things.'

'How? How can we fit in everything I've planned if you go off to Liverpool?'

'I'll be here for nearly two months, Mummy!'

Hope was not giving way as she usually would have done. She had never been difficult like this in the past. They had always been so close. Pia looked at her daughter as if trying to work out what had changed in her.

'Has Sally put you up to this? Is she paying you?'

Hope laughed. 'No! She's just giving us the money for the train fare and the hotel. Mummy, we want to go. It's a really interesting project. We went to Christ Church and now we want to finish off what we've started.'

It was infuriating listening to Hope speaking such nonsense. 'It's not a project, it's a hobby! Researching the history of your house is a *hobby.*' For want of something to do she opened the dishwasher and began unloading it. 'I will not have our family summer holidays ruined by that bloody woman's self-indulgent and ...' She struggled to find words of sufficient force, ' ... and ultimately pointless pet project. If she had a job she wouldn't have time for all this. I had to work.'

Hope was leaning against the fridge, her arms folded. 'Mummy, you *chose* to work.'

Pia could think of nothing to say to that. She was momentarily silenced.

'Look,' said Hope reasonably, 'it's only for three days. I'll be here for most of the summer. We can go after that. How would that be?'

'Before you head off to Greece! And that's assuming you don't decide to divert to China in pursuit of Sally!' Pia added sarcastically.

Hope rolled her eyes. 'No. Why are you being like this?'

Pia felt petulantly confused. 'I just don't understand why you're suddenly great pals with her.'

'I'm not,' said Hope wearily. 'I'm not suddenly great friends with Sally. I just think that it's a difficult situation for everyone and I'm caught in the middle.'

Then you should move to my side, was the unspoken thought that came to mind. Marion had said that Sally was dull as ditchwater. What on earth did Hope think she was doing joining this purposeless expedition to Liverpool and some ghastly back-packing trip to Greece when she could stay here in Gerrards Cross for the whole holiday? 'I understand, darling. I just don't think that you should let her take advantage of you.'

'She isn't taking advantage of me.' Hope sounded exasperated. 'I want to go. So does Jo.'

Pia couldn't help herself. 'Jo! Well, I might have known she would be behind this. That girl dominates you.'

Hope snapped back. 'No, she doesn't! She's a very good friend of mine! Why can't you try to like her?'

'I do, darling. I just think you could do better.' It was time to provide Hope with some wise counsel. 'You go to university to study but also to meet the right sort of people – people who'll make a good circle of friends for the rest of your life. And frankly, I don't think Jo is the type of person you'll want to associate with in a few years' time, once you've matured a little and established yourself in your career. She is rather alternative. And that's great fun at uni but it doesn't go down very well in the real world.'

Hope was unmoved. 'What is the real world? Do you mean your world?'

'Hope!' She had never known Hope be so insolent. 'I mean the world in which bills need to be paid.'

This very reasonable statement provoked the most astounding outburst. 'Jo is my friend and I don't want you to be so horrible about her.'

Pia stood firm, as one would with a small child, saying sharply, 'Sometimes the truth hurts.'

Hope raised her voice. 'The truth! What would you know about the truth? All you do is criticise me and other people and tell yourself it's speaking the truth. It isn't. It's just your opinion.' Hope was very nearly shouting now.

'Hope!'

'Your opinion,' Hope repeated. 'You think you have all the answers and no one else knows anything. I'm sick of being lectured by you.'

They were both shouting now. 'Hope! That is enough!'

Suddenly Dan's voice rang out. 'Why don't you tell her?'

Pia felt a jolt of shock. She rounded on Dan who was standing in the kitchen doorway.

'How long have you been standing there?'

He did not reply. His gaze was fixed on Hope. Hope, when she spoke, sounded oddly disconnected. 'What's the point?'

Pia was feeling unnerved. 'What's going on? Tell me what?' She looked from one to the other. 'Well, one of you tell me!'

Dan stuck his hands in the back pocket of his jeans and leaned against the doorframe, mirroring Hope's pose against the fridge. 'Jo is Hope's girlfriend, Mum. Haven't you guessed that by now?'

The word girlfriend reverberated as Pia turned it over, trying to work out what he meant. 'What do you mean?'

Dan gave a melodramatic sigh. 'I mean, they're girlfriends. You know … gay.'

It was unbelievable. 'You mean they're … lesbians!'

'Yeah. Lesbians.'

She felt a physical shock hit her. She could feel it stun her whole body. Dan moved forward, his expression now one of concern. 'Here. Sit down.' He pulled over a chair.

She looked up at him as a sudden anxious thought occurred to her. 'Not you as well?'

It made him want to laugh. 'No!' He saw the expression on her face. 'No,' he said firmly. 'Hey, Mum. It's no big deal.'

That was the most inappropriate statement of the day.

Her immediate instinct was to challenge Hope. 'Are you sure? Surely it's just a crush? A schoolgirl crush.'

Hope sounded confused. 'I'm not a schoolgirl, Mum.'

Swiftly Pia began to regain her sense of reality. Of course it was not true. 'No. But you're very young. Young girls often have these types of friendships. It's a …' She struggled for the right word. 'It's a pash.'

'A pash?' echoed Hope and Dan simultaneously. Dan was grinning.

'It's not funny!' Pia snapped at him. But his response was silently to mouth *pash* at Hope with his hand on his heart as if swooning. 'Dan! I said it isn't funny.'

'Mum,' he said, 'lighten up.'

'Lighten up! Good God!' Her mind was racing. 'Hope,' she said firmly, 'it's a phase and you'll grow out of it.'

Hope looked at Dan. 'You see. What's the point?'

Dan turned to her. 'Mum, I know it's a shock. Just try to accept it.'

'I can't accept something I know is wrong.' She heard Hope groan. 'Yes, Hope. It's wrong. You've had some quarrel with Jake and Jo has taken advantage of your vulnerable emotional state to tell you that

273

you're … something that you're not. Hope, I'm your mother. I know you. And I'm telling you that you're definitely not gay.'

Hope looked hard at her. 'No. No, you don't know me. And what's more you've never tried to. It's always been about what you want.'

Pia was not standing for that. Hope's ingratitude was astounding. 'It's been about what's best for you.'

'In your judgement. Because no one else's ever counted.'

Hope was being absurd. 'And so you think Jo and Sally know better! Do you think they care more about you than I do? Is that what you're saying?' A thought crossed her mind. 'Have you told your father about this?' She was damned sure Hope hadn't.

'Yes. And he's fine about it.'

It took her a few seconds to recover. 'Well, that'll be her influence. When it comes to immorality the woman's an expert.'

Hope's voice took on a pleading tone. 'Mum, it isn't like that.'

Pia didn't want to hear any more. She got up and went over to her handbag, taking out her cigarettes. 'I'm going to my office.'

Hope was still talking. 'Mummy, I don't do what Sally tells me. I don't. But at least she listens to me.'

Pia walked out of the kitchen. There was simply no point in discussing this any further. It would be a question of letting events run their course until such time as Hope came to her senses: until then she would have to go out and make her own mistakes. Clearly her maternal guidance wasn't wanted. So be it. As Pia went into the hallway she heard Hope raise her voice behind her.

'And she listens to Dad and Dan. At least she's interested in other people and their points of view. Mum, the problem is you always think you're right.'

Chapter 22

'Why did you keep the tape running?'

Miss Grant sighed. 'I know that was wrong. Professor Berner would have been horrified if he had found out. It was unethical to record people without their knowledge or consent. But you see I *knew* Mary Kelly had more to say. But what else could I do? Professor Berner told us off if we deviated from the list of questions. Oh, I was itching to ask more. But that wasn't allowed.' She touched her grey hair, cut layered and fashionably short.

It had taken weeks to track down Judith Grant via the University of London alumni association and from there the secretary of the Old Girl's Association of Haberdashers Aske's who said she couldn't give out an address but she would pass on a message. Miss Grant had called two weeks later.

I'm awfully sorry. I only just got the message.

That had been the day before Sally left for Shanghai, packing her file of hundreds of pages of hand-written notes and photocopied extracts to review while she was away.

On the flight over, as she tried to read, Edward had been irritatingly upbeat. 'The international community in Shanghai is incredibly cosmopolitan.'

She felt herself bridle in response to his unrelenting enthusiasm. 'Why don't we reserve judgement until we get there?'

In retrospect she wondered if she had given in too easily. Edward could after all say no to the promotion. But even as she considered this she understood that refusing this job would stall his career at Porter Stone, consigning him to his present level of seniority – and perhaps causing him to resent her forever?

In the event, on their arrival in Shanghai, there was no more time for introspection. From the moment their taxi sped away from the arrivals hall, they were submerged in the heat and crowds and frantic itinerary of their visit. And despite herself she was entranced: by the people, by the fascinating history of the surviving old narrow streets and the sheer pace of a city that made her life back home seem small in comparison. Edward, on their final evening as they stood on the balcony of their hotel room looking out onto the illuminated night, had asked her what her decision was.

'Yes,' she had said boldly.

Relief had shown on his face. 'Really?'

'Really,' she laughed. She gestured towards the city. 'How could anyone not be won over?'

On the plane back, opening her file again, she realised that she was running out of time in her quest to prove what she suspected.

Sally had arranged to meet Miss Grant in Marks & Spencer, Kensington High Street. Miss Grant was coming up for a theatre visit with her sister. They sat amongst the late-afternoon shoppers at the back in the half-empty café, both drinking chocolate-sprinkled cappuccino.

'I was so excited to get your message,' Miss Grant had exclaimed, sitting down. 'I always wondered if one day someone would call. The project was famous at the time.'

She was no longer Miss Grant but had for the past thirty-two years been Mrs Wright, a teacher of English at a small private girls' school in Littlehampton and the mother of two grown-up sons. She was married to Gerald, a structural engineer. She gave the impression, in her navy pleated skirt and matching jacket-style cardigan, of living a quietly prosperous middle-class life.

'You get a feel for people after a while,' she continued. 'I suppose it's a little bit like being a policeman. We came to Wimbledon after we did Kensington. So I was quite experienced at it by then and you could tell who was speaking the truth and who was all show. Sometimes you would pick up bits of gossip here and there.'

Miss Grant took a sip of her coffee. 'And the fact was, by all accounts, that Mary Kelly ran that house. Bella Latham would have been lost without her. Several of the neighbours alluded to it privately. We weren't allowed to ask those sort of personal questions on the tape.'

'Why not?'

'Professor Berner was very firm. He drilled it into us that our investigations were to be scientific. We weren't to dabble in tittle-tattle. We had to stick to the list of questions.'

Sally was taken aback. 'Even if some of it was the truth?'

'Things were different then. Professor Berner was a pioneer but he believed that the words of ordinary people had to be filtered by experts in order to be of value to the academic community. Professor Berner, like many great men, had no truck with dissenters. Oh no! It was his way or the highway. Most of the girls were terrified of him. But I liked him. When the project ended he chose me to help him review the tapes. I even typed up his results. It was so sad.'

Miss Grant fell silent.

'Sad?'

'He died two years later. An aneurysm.' Miss Grant's voice and her thoughts had drifted away.

'We were speaking about Mary,' Sally prompted her.

'Yes. Mary. Well, for one thing, she volunteered to be interviewed. We were supposed to pick houses at random. But she was so insistent I gave in.'

Sally could feel a small surge of excitement rising in her. 'And what was she really like?'

'Oh my goodness! Well, you have to remember it was a long time ago.' Miss Grant paused as if to consider carefully her choice of words. 'Mary was a person who stays with you. She was tiny. She couldn't have been more than five feet tall. And very sprightly. If you had passed her on the street you would have thought she was in her sixties. She was a very strong woman in every sense. She was happy to talk about what she wanted to talk about and impossible to draw on the rest. The other interviewees were grateful to be accepted and allowed us to direct the interview. With Mary I had the feeling that she was in charge. Actually there was something quite domineering about her.' She took a bite of fruitcake. 'And her memory was very selective. It made me think she had something to hide.'

'And what was that?'

Miss Grant leaned forward. 'Well, obviously Robert Latham's syphilis.'

'So it was syphilis!' Sally exclaimed. 'She doesn't say directly. But she mentions mercury.'

'All the neighbourhood gossips alluded to it. Robert Latham was housebound. At the end he was laid out by attacks of it.'

'And that was why the servants left. And the callers stopped.'

'I've no doubt.'

Sally could hardly conceal her excitement. 'Syphilis would explain so much! I researched it.'

Sally lowered her voice, aware of the bizarre nature of their conversation, conducted as it was in the conventional surroundings of Marks & Spencer. 'Syphilis never goes away. It comes back but often it takes years to do so. In the meantime, the patient feels fine. I think that's the period when Latham met Bella.'

Miss Grant nodded. 'And when it did come back they would have had to hide him away. The poor man would have gone insane.'

'It all fits. Mary mentions his moods. And the callers stopping. People would have been terrified of catching it. Especially once Henry died.'

'Oh that was so sad!' Miss Grant exclaimed. 'The poor woman.'

Sally reached down into her bag. 'I wanted you to have a look at this.' There was a delay as Miss Grant searched in her handbag for her glasses.

'Do you think there's a resemblance? It's a photograph of Joseph Kelly. It was a studio portrait of him. By then he was the owner of a brewery in Cincinnati.'

Miss Grant read the title out loud. '*A History of Germantown Brewing.*'

'It's the central area of Cincinnati.' Sally reached over and opened the bookmarked page.

Miss Grant's features reacted with surprise. 'Oh Yes! Goodness me. Oh yes. The resemblance is striking.' She leaned forward to gaze at the photograph, then up at Sally. 'Gracious! Imagine finding that. Well done!'

'Joseph called his brewery Marys.'

Miss Grant looked up. 'Golly! He did very well for himself. But what has this got to do with Bella Latham?'

'I think that Robert Latham never went to the USA. I think Joseph was sent in his place. To make it look like he had left. I'm not totally sure. It could be that Joseph went anyway. I need to double-check with the orphanage records and the shipping records.'

'Goodness!'

Sally spoke slowly. 'On the tape Mary said that Robert Latham went abroad for a cure.' She tried to frame the question as openly as she could. 'What did you think about that?'

Miss Grant put down her cup. She caught Sally's eye. 'I'm not sure that I believed her.'

'Neither do I!'

'But wherever he went I'm sure Mary knew all about it.'

'I think she knew everything. That's why the family kept her on – because she knew too much. But where exactly did he go?'

Miss Grant shook her head. 'I don't know, my dear.'

Sally felt a churning in her stomach. Miss Grant would be the first person she shared her theory with. 'Because I think he may have been murdered.' She looked at Miss Grant's face, searching for a reaction and fearing that Miss Grant would dismiss the idea out of hand.

But Miss Grant's initial expression of shock was soon replaced by one of thoughtful evaluation. 'Have you got any evidence?'

'To be honest, nothing definite.' Sally paused. 'But I think Bella and Mary had the strongest possible motive. Of course, it's a stretch to say that they were capable of murder.'

'I think you can safely draw some conclusions,' said Miss Grant carefully. Now it was as if she had returned to the persona of the young university researcher she had once been. 'Of course, I didn't meet Bella. But I think you can say that Mary was a hard person. It wasn't her fault. She had lost her parents, then she was sent to an orphanage and at the age of … what was it? Fifteen?'

'Fourteen …'

'Fourteen! Sent to do back-breaking work in a world that must have seemed totally alien to her. Imagine that happening to a child today! You would need to shut down emotionally or you wouldn't survive.'

'But she did more than survive, didn't she?' Sally took up the thread. 'Mary Kelly was the poorest of the poor, Irish and a girl. At the time that put her on the bottom rung of life. But somehow she ended up living in an expensive house in Wimbledon Village until the day she died. That sort of change of fortune doesn't happen by accident. Mary had the ability to use circumstances to her advantage. That's what I noticed all the way through. As she herself said, everything works out for the best.'

'Sally? It's Hope.'

'Hi! Sorry.' There was a yelling in the background. 'I'm trying to get Louis to go upstairs for his bath.'

Hope pressed her mobile to ear to try to hear more clearly. 'Shall I call back?'

'No.' In the background she could hear Sally talking to Louis. 'Go and play with your ship. Mummy needs to talk on the telephone. It's Hope.'

'Hope,' echoed Louis.

Sally came back on the line. 'It's complete chaos here. The removal firm came round today to estimate the boxes we need and two letting agents and, of course, they want tons of things changed.'

'Oh?'

'They say we need an alarm and a waste disposal and they're all being snooty because we've only got one living room. Apparently the best houses have a play room.' There was another interruption. 'Louis, stop it! Sorry, he's pulling at the telephone. He's been really clingy since we got back from Shanghai. Hold on a minute. I'll switch phones.' There was a faint buzzing as Sally presumably switched to the cordless then she came back on the line. 'How's Liverpool?'

'Good.' Hope shifted the papers on the small desk in their room at the Liverpool City Centre Holiday Inn. 'It took a while, but we've found the records for the Kellys.'

'Great!' Sally's next words were drowned out by a sudden wail. 'Sorry. Louis's tired. Hold on. I'm going to switch the television on.'

Hope half-listened as Sally negotiated with Louis. From the bathroom came the sounds of the shower running as Jo got ready to go out. The day trip to Oxford had been fun, especially the bit where Jo kissed her behind a bookcase in the Christ Church library, but Liverpool was tons better because they got to sleep in a double bed in a proper hotel with a mini bar and satellite television. The receptionist had asked them if they wanted twin beds but Jo had said no and the receptionist hadn't batted an eyelid. Sometimes it was all so much easier than Hope would have expected, and at those times she wondered why she had worried about it all so much. Best of all, it felt as though she could breathe after the events back home: her mother vacillated between lofty speeches about how one's children must make their own mistakes and impassioned appeals to see the error of her ways. When she opened her suitcase Hope had found a book entitled *Healing From Relationship Addiction*. Her mother was now locked away for hours in her office surfing the internet. Every so often she called Hope in.

'You must look at this, darling! There's a homosexual conspiracy out there and you need to know about it.'

Her mother had forbidden her from telling Granny or the neighbours. Marion had been told, however. Her mother reported back on their conversation. 'Marion says you're far too pretty for all that. She thinks you're running away from your confidence issue with boys. Why won't you just try talking to someone, a professional?'

Hope had refused and booked a ticket to Liverpool instead. Her mother had insisted on driving her to the station. In the car, her mother had tried everything. 'If you do this I really fear that our relationship will never be the same again. Actions have consequences, Hope.'

It had been such a relief to get on the train and pull away from her mother, standing on the platform, her face clouded with disapproval.

'Sorry,' said Sally. 'I'm in the kitchen now so I can talk. How's it going?'

'Fantastic. Liverpool's amazing. We're staying right in the city centre. And tonight we're going to the Albert Docks.'

'I wish I could be there!'

Hope reached for the tourist brochure, detailing the redevelopment of the former working docks into shops, restaurants and museums. 'And tomorrow we're going back to the Tate and the Beatles Story.' She decided to leave out the fact that they were going clubbing that night as well.

'I envy you,' said Sally with feeling.

Hope began scanning her notes. 'OK. Let me tell you what we found out. We found the orphanage records and the entries for Mary and Joseph and the two sisters. They were called Bridget and Kate. So it all ties in with the dates that you gave us. Mrs Morrow was quite a local celebrity. There's a statue of her outside the orphanage.'

'What does it the orphanage look like?'

'We couldn't get inside. It's council offices now and they wouldn't let us in. It's brick, with really high walls.'

'Did you find the date that Joseph left the orphanage?'

'Yes. Hold on a minute.' Hope began turning the pages of her notes. 'I just need to look it up.'

'Don't tell me!' Sally's voice was excited. 'Let me guess. It was April 1905. The beginning of April.'

Hope could not conceal her surprise. 'How did you know that? It was the fifth of April, actually.'

Sally sounded elated. 'I knew it! I just knew it!'

Hope could not fail to be impressed. 'Wow. But how did you know?'

Sally's voice was full of passion. 'It was when I stopped looking at the facts and started thinking about the people – that's when it all began to make sense. All the time I was looking at Robert Latham. But I needed to look at Joseph Kelly. It was Joseph Kelly who got on the *Lucania*. On the seventh of April 1905.'

Hope interrupted. 'But what about Robert Latham?'

Sally was emphatic. 'He never caught that ship. Joseph Kelly went in his place. It was all a cover-up.'

Hope felt two pieces of the puzzle slot neatly into place. 'And that's why the Christ Church records are important. The Duke bought a steerage ticket for the voyage.'

'Yes. The Duke was helping Bella and Mary all along. He might have remarried the horrible Duchess, but he wasn't going to abandon his favourite daughter. At first I thought he sent Robert Latham third class to be spiteful. But then I realised that they could hardly send Joseph Kelly first class. He'd stick out like a sore thumb.'

'So where do you go from here?'

Sally sighed. 'Shanghai for three years! I'm going to try to find time to research the census records before we leave. But the clock's against me.'

Hope reached for a pen and paper. 'I can help. What do you need?'

Anna felt awkward. 'Are you sure this is a good time?' She had thought that the evening might be a better time to call in on Sally. At least Louis would be in bed. He was, but Sally looked as frantic as she had every day for the past month since her trip to Shanghai. On her kitchen table were spread piles of papers, leaflets and brochures.

'God. How much stuff have you got to do?'

Sally gave a manic laugh. 'Don't ask.'

She reached up and took down two glasses from the cupboard. 'I've got some wine in the fridge and if I don't drink it I'll probably pop.' She poured two glasses. 'I feel I'll never get it all done in time. The removers are coming in a week and then we'll go to a hotel for three days before we fly out.'

No sooner had Sally sat down then she got up again. 'God, it's hot in here. Flaming June!' She flung open the French windows and a delicious evening breeze swept in. 'Can you smell the honeysuckle? We were going to plant wisteria if we'd stayed.' Her voice held a note of regret. 'The lawn looks awful.' They had already had an early summer of hot days and record temperatures. A hosepipe ban had been imposed and television news reports showed Bournemouth beach covered with sunbathers so tightly packed they could barely move.

Anna was trying to find a space to put her glass. There wasn't one so she held it. 'Are you excited to be going?'

'Yes.' Sally sounded resolute. 'I'm excited to be going but I'm sad to be leaving. I feel better now I've been there.' She took a drink. 'Everyone says three years will go in no time. You'd better be here when I get back!'

'I plan to be. Assuming I can pay the mortgage.' At that point, Anna realised that this presented a good opening into discussing Hart. 'It looks like I may be doing a series for Channel 4.'

But Sally cut across her. 'Terrific! Now, the new tenants are coming round on Saturday to measure up, so if you like I can bring them down to meet you. They're from Italy, they're terribly nice, and they're both lawyers. I'm really hoping they'll stay long term.'

'Any children?'

'No. They seem to be into their careers. I don't think they'll take any interest in the garden. But I've found a gardener, so it won't be untidy.'

'Don't worry about it.' Anna still couldn't summon up much enthusiasm for gardening.

Anna's mind turned to Hart and more particularly the awkwardness she felt regarding Sally. Previously, Anna had told Sally that Hart had called her to tell her, off the record, that a contact of his had learned that the prosecution in Mrs Zarkosky's case were prepared to reduce the murder charge to manslaughter in return for a guilty plea. Time spent with their star witness, Penny, had given them cold feet about a trial. Sally had seemed to have no problem with that. Emboldened, a couple of weeks later, Anna had let slip that she had visited Hart in Camberwell and that Hart had invited her to the Summer Exhibition of the Royal Academy. Sally had not said very much in reply. She suspected that Sally already knew that their relationship had taken a romantic turn. Mutley, let out into the garden last weekend, had barked crazily at a squirrel until she ran out in her dressing gown to grab him in. He'd probably given the game away.

'Sorry. I'm a bit obsessed with moving right now.' Sally got up and refilled their glasses. 'What have you been up to?'

Here it was. 'Oh, working. I've been offered this series. A proper documentary.'

'Sorry, you said. Tell me about it.'

'It's for Channel 4. It's a six-parter about life in Northern Ireland.'

Was it her imagination or did a shadow just cross Sally's face? 'Oh?'

'It's about life after the Troubles. Hart's the presenter. It's a fantastic break for him. He's been a print journalist all his life, but this is his chance to get into television.' She was aware that she was talking too quickly. 'He'll write it and present it. There'll be interviews with all sorts of people. The first episode is a historical recap. Then it moves on to the present day.'

She didn't want to stop talking but she had run out of things to say.

'So, you'll be working together?' Sally said slowly.

'Yes. And none of this would have happened without you!'

'Are you going out together?'

'Yes.'

It was awful. Sally was so clearly discomfited and so obviously putting on a brave face. Mutley hadn't been spotted after all. 'I'm really pleased for you.'

'Thanks. And doing the series gets some money coming in, which is a relief. There may also be a book to accompany the series.'

'Is Hart going to write that?'

'Yes. To be honest he could do it standing on his head. Well, not literally.' She gave a laugh.

There was an undeniable tension.

She spoke hesitantly. 'Sally, sometimes it's awkward when you introduce two of your friends and they go off together.' The words *without you* hung unspoken in the air.

'No. It's fine,' said Sally bravely. 'Really. It's wonderful that you've found each other. And you're so compatible!'

And the truth was that they were. Hart had a passion for his work in the same way that Anna had. But he added the ingredient that she had been missing all her life – fun. Hart always checked his facts, perfected his prose and filed his copy on time. But he enjoyed doing it. And in between times he walked Mutley, saw his friends, went to the cinema and made her a fabulous cooked breakfast on a Sunday. Last Sunday he had said smoothly, *I think you should skip your run today*. And she had. Hart had a way of making suggestions so that it never felt that he was telling her what to do. He was calm and peaceful. Just like Sally.

Chapter 23

She had told Hart over the telephone that they needed to hold their final meeting at St Mary's Church. He had sounded surprised.

'Why?'

'There's something I need to show you.'

She locked up the house and walked to Church Road. The morning was still cool, the temperatures for the rest of the day forecast to be scorching. In the village, the streets were already marked with cones and one-way signs in preparation for the Wimbledon tennis championship. In a few days the ramshackle tented village would appear, winding down to the gates of the All England Club, occupied by fans queuing overnight for Centre Court tickets. Vickie had warned her that it would be impossible to drive in the gridlocked village for the two weeks of the tournament.

As Sally walked away from North Walk she could feel that she had begun to detach from the house. It was a slow goodbye that had begun even before she and Edward had gone to Shanghai. When they had returned she had seen North Walk and Wimbledon through newly Eastern eyes. Shanghai was a flash of glittering spires below which the street life of centuries continued. It was a city of silk next to jute. On their return, North Walk and the streets of Wimbledon appeared to her quaintly narrow, and the buildings aged and sedate beneath a muted blue-grey sky. There was something very restrained about the English landscape. Their Shanghai house, located on the outskirts of the city, had been reserved for July. The black-clad, petite Chinese letting agent had warned her that it would be hot and steamy when they returned. Edward had spent the week relentlessly upbeat. 'All the better to sit by the pool!' He did not need to be. She was a late convert to the idea. It was impossible not to be caught up in the excitement of the city, the promise of centuries of history, a clash of cultures and the cosmopolitan character of the international schools. Vickie was already dropping heavy hints about coming to visit. 'I could come with Rory and the baby for a week. You are getting a nanny?'

Sally had opened a file reminiscent of her Porter Stone days to deal with the move. Their possessions were to be listed and insured, export packed and shipped; the house let unfurnished; and in the meantime her two-page list of jobs never shortened, new tasks added as soon as others were crossed off.

And then there had been the last, frantic pieces of the Latham puzzle to be put in place, until she reached a point beyond which it was fruitless to go further.

As she rounded the corner of Church Road she saw Hart waiting outside St Mary's. He raised a hand in greeting. Behind him the tall, slim steeple of the church, designed by the Victorian architect Sir George Gilbert Scott, rose up. When she reached him he gave her a brotherly hug and got straight to the point. 'So – why the mystery tour?'

'Ah-ha. Wait and see.'

They went down the pathway as if towards the main doors of the church but then diverted off to the churchyard. Thick with foliage and overgrown in places, it was crowded with Georgian and Victorian headstones and the once-grand vaults of the families who had owned and built Wimbledon, the stone now worn and weathered.

As they walked she spoke. 'Hart, I think this is what happened – Robert Latham never went to America. In fact, Robert Latham never left the country.'

'But ...'

She paused to gather her thoughts. Slowly she began. 'Mary Kelly grew up in an orphanage in Liverpool. But what happened to her brother Joseph? The last we know of him is the orphanage record. He left aged fourteen to go and work at a Brewery – a brewery whose name Mary claimed not to remember. Let me tell you, Mary Kelly has a very convenient memory. She was caught between proclaiming her pride in Joseph's achievements and yet not remembering anything about them. It didn't make sense until you work in the notion that she needed Joseph – and his whereabouts – to remain forgotten.'

They were nearly there.

'How do you know?'

She drew a breath. 'OK. The more I listened to the tapes, the more suspicious I became. Especially when I found out that Robert Latham had syphilis.'

'Syphilis?'

Now she had Hart's attention.

'Yes. It was obvious that he hadn't gone to work for the Duke. He was too ill. But next I started to question Mary's explanation that he had gone away to find a cure. I couldn't believe that after two or three years he would just disappear without trace.'

They were at the spot it had taken her hours of searching to locate. It was time to show him. 'Here. Look at this.'

Hart bent down to read the faded lettering of the headstone. He touched the worn engraving.

Henry Latham. 1901–1903. Blameless and harmless.

He stood up. 'It doesn't mention the parents.'

'No. I don't think Bella could bear to have her husband's name on the headstone. Hart,' she said urgently, 'I'm convinced that Henry's death gave Bella the motive to kill her husband. She blamed him, thinking he had passed on the illness. And I'm sure Mary was an accomplice. Look at the inscription.'

Hart frowned. 'I'm guessing it's biblical, but I can't place it.'

'It is biblical. It's from Philippians.' She recited from memory. '*Do all things without murmurings and disputings: that ye may be blameless and harmless* … It's the same verse that Mrs Morrow taught Mary in the orphanage. Mary says so on the tapes. She chose the inscription!'

Hart raised his hand. 'So you're saying Bella and Mary acted together to kill Robert Latham, bury him in the garden and send Mary's brother Joseph to the USA in his place?' To her relief he didn't laugh. He seemed to be taking her completely seriously.

'In a nutshell – yes. But not necessarily in the garden. Hart, I'm not just saying it. I can prove it. Well, some of it.' They began to slowly walk away from Henry's headstone. 'In 1905 it was Joseph Kelly, travelling as Robert Latham, who went to America. He travelled on false papers. I went back and double-checked the shipping records. You were right. There was a Robert Latham listed. But there was something that didn't fit – it was a steerage ticket. Robert Latham was a gentleman; he would have travelled first class. Then I realised that Joseph Kelly was a fourteen-year-old Liverpool orphan. They couldn't let him travel first class, as the real Robert Latham would have done. He would have been too conspicuous to the other passengers. That's why the ticket is for steerage. The Duke paid for the ticket. It's listed on the accounts at Christ Church. But there's no record of the name of the ticket-holder.'

'Steerage! Damn.' Hart ran his hand through his hair. 'I should have picked that up.'

They had reached the gate. Hart gestured to a wooden bench to sit down.

She continued. 'But it's not just the ticket. After they discovered the ticket details at Christ Church, I asked Hope and Jo to go and check the orphanage records in Liverpool. Joseph Kelly left, signed out to the care of his sister Mary, on the fifth of April 1905 – two days before the *Lucania* sailed.'

Hart looked stunned.

She tried to keep her voice even. 'It's just too much of a coincidence not to be connected. I think Mary spent two days in Liverpool with Joseph and then she sent him off.' She turned to Hart, impassioned. 'Off to a better life than she had had, away from the drudgery of domestic service or the mines or the brickworks. I think that was her mission in life, the purpose that kept her going through all the hardships of domestic service.'

Hart, paying close attention, said nothing.

'I was determined to find Joseph Kelly. And I did! Actually, Hope did. She went through the Cincinnati census online. In 1920 there was a Joseph Kelly who owned and lived at a brewery called Marys. No apostrophe. And then I found a photograph of him. Miss Grant thought they looked alike!'

She stopped, waiting for Hart's reaction.

He responded slowly, as though formulating his thoughts as he spoke. 'OK. It's a connection but it's not enough. Miss Grant saw Mary a long time ago. And any Joseph Kelly born in Ireland would likely have a sister or a mother called Mary. It isn't proof that this Joseph Kelly is Mary's brother.'

She was ready for him. 'I agree. But there's one last piece of incontrovertible evidence that links Joseph Kelly to Mary Kelly. She left this same Joseph Kelly number twelve North Walk in her will. I checked with the solicitors.'

Hart exhaled. 'Mary owned the house? I assumed the family had let her stay on.'

'It's a reasonable assumption,' Sally said generously. 'But after Bella's death Mary bought the house. I calculated that even if she had saved every penny of her salary she couldn't have afforded it. Joseph must have given her the money.'

'So the will is the solid link between Joseph Kelly of Cincinnati and Mary Kelly of Wimbledon.' Hart paused. 'OK. I'll buy that Joseph went in Latham's place.'

'And there was a cover-up,' Sally interrupted. 'Someone told E.D. Irvine that Robert Latham had sailed on the *Lucania*.'

'Hold on. None of this means that Bella pushed Robert Latham down the stairs or Mary put arsenic in his tea. Where's the proof, Sally? There's no body. No confession. Not any evidence of a murder taking place. Who's to say that Latham was murdered? Much more likely is a scenario whereby the Duke paid him to disappear abroad with a warning never to come back.'

'No.' She was emphatic. 'Joseph sailed precisely so that there was a ticket in Latham's name. Hart, it *was* a cover-up, don't you see? That's why they made up the diary. I think it was all written after Latham was killed.'

'They faked the diary!' For the first time that day Hart looked openly surprised.

'Yes. The diary's obviously a fake,' she said confidently. 'I realised that as soon as I listened to the tapes. The two accounts are totally inconsistent. Like you said, everything was wonderful between the Lathams according to the diary. But it wasn't. We know that from the tapes. The diaries are there to divert attention away from the bloody enormous motive that these two women had to kill Robert Latham. I knew from the start there was something cold and unfeeling about that diary!'

'And the reason for them blaming Latham was his syphilis.'

'Yes. I think Bella killed him because syphilis was thought to be hereditary in those days. Actually, it isn't unless the patient is in the midst of an outbreak. The irony is that Henry probably did die from pneumonia.'

Hart paused. 'But why kill Latham? Why take the risk? Why not just persuade the Duke to pay him off?'

'Because they both hated him by the end. And because it wasn't necessarily pre-planned. I think it's most likely that it was a crime of passion. I've got some ideas about that.'

Hart laughed. 'I'm sure you have! OK, Bella had motive.'

'Bella *and* Mary had motive. I don't think Bella could have acted on her own. As Mary says umpteen times, she was a lady.'

'So where's the body?'

Sally jumped in. 'I'm betting on it being at North Walk. The Duke couldn't risk taking it. He couldn't do anything that would arouse the suspicion of his new wife.'

Hart was frowning. 'And that's why Mary stayed in the house.'

She pre-empted him. 'I know. In itself it's no proof of a body. Joseph may have bought the house for her because she liked it and wanted to stay there. But I think Joseph bought it from the Wakemonts to keep her safe after Bella died. That way no one was going to buy it and dig up the garden. And I think Mary made the tape as some sort of testament, to tell the story, but not in so much detail that it would incriminate her. It's her justification for what went on.'

Hart was leaning back in his chair, his hands behind his head. 'I think it's curious that Bella stayed there. I do find that odd. You would have thought that North Walk held unhappy memories for her.' He paused. 'So where do you go from here?'

'I was hoping you would have some ideas.'

'Well, one good thing is that we don't have to wonder if the answer is in the Selton Park archive. People don't take notes of their dirty secrets and leave them for generations of historians to come across. I don't think there's going to be a note by the Duke recording the illicit garden burial of his syphilitic son-in-law.'

'But is there enough? Do you think you could write it up as it is?'

'Why don't you?'

She was stunned. 'Because you're a professional journalist and I'm a full-time mother?'

Hart gave her a shake of his head. 'It's your project, Sally. *Yours.* I only got involved because I happened to go to the archive years ago. You're the one who's inspired us, kept going, pressed on through all the obstacles and false starts. And now you're going to Shanghai it's a heaven-sent opportunity. What else are you going to do? Sit by the pool filing your nails? I don't think you're the type.'

'I wouldn't know where to begin.'

'No one does. Just start. And if it doesn't work start again. Do another draft. The story's waited long enough, it can wait for you to get it right.'

'Do you really think I can do it?'

'I know you can do it.'

'But … But there's no ending!' she said woefully. 'Hart, I *know* it's true. Don't ask me how, I just know it. But to the outside world it's a theory. I can't prove it without a body. And I don't think Edward's going to agree to me digging up the garden.'

'Have you asked him?'

'Actually, I did. He said if I was still determined to when we came back we could do it then and take the opportunity to landscape the garden at the same time.'

'It would have been pretty hard work digging.'

'I think John did that part.'

'You see. You've got it all in your head already. You just need to put it down on paper.' Hart stood up. 'I don't think that there has to be an ending, does there? Sometimes the journalist doesn't get the story.' He gave her a wry smile. 'But you've got something else here. At least one genuine love story and an enduring mystery.'

'You mean Mary and John?' she said. 'But they never got married or even lived together.'

'But they loved each other for twenty-five years.'

Hart looked at his watch. 'I have to go, Sally. I've got a meeting with Channel 4.' He looked her in the eye. 'Sally, I think you're an inspiration. I think you're kind and clever and tenacious. If you hadn't been married I would probably have …' He stopped himself. 'And I think you must go to Shanghai and write this story. And maybe one day it will be published and maybe it won't. That's not the point. I think you should do it for you – because you can.'

Silence fell between them.

Sally felt she could not leave without acknowledging Anna. She hoped her voice was light. 'Anna's a very lucky woman.' It was the best she could come up with. Because she had fallen in love with

Hart, if only for a brief time, and now she felt an emotion that settled somewhere between love and friendship.

He looked away. 'We're certainly two of a kind.'

And then he caught her gaze and they moved together and it was natural to hold each other, in the shadow of the churchyard and the mysteries of the past. They stood not speaking until they loosened their embrace.

Hart spoke first. 'Shall we walk up to the village?'

'No. I think I'll stay a while.'

She watched him walk away. A warm breeze presaged the heat of the afternoon as it blew through the tall trees, the same chestnut trees that Mary and Bella would have known. She walked back in the direction of Henry's grave but stopped just short, at the headstone for Bella Latham. The design was Victorian ornate, the stone edged with a pattern of evergreen ivy interwoven with lilies. The stone lettering was worn away. She knelt down and ran her finger over the name.

Bella Latham
1878 – 1953

And then it was time to go home.

Preface to *A Very Victorian Murder*
By Sally Kirwan-Hughes

The story of Bella Latham and Mary Kelly has all the elements of a classic Victorian melodrama: the scandalous marriage of a rich heiress and a penniless man; his mysterious disappearance and the relationship between a mistress and her servant, which endured for over fifty years.

And finally there is the last, essential ingredient: a murder. In this case, the murder was that of the penniless man, Robert Latham, whose body was discovered one hundred years after it was buried in the garden of 12 North Walk, Wimbledon.

It is no surprise that the story has captured the imagination of a public already familiar with *Letters of a Victorian Lady*. Delve a little deeper, as this book hopes to do, and it will be found that there is much in the story that is not melodramatic. Bella Latham and Mary Kelly were women of their time, defined and restricted by a society that limited the role of women, and yet each in their own way found the means to snatch freedom and a measure of happiness from their unpromising circumstances.

I am often asked why I chose to investigate the history of North Walk. The answer is that once I started I had no choice but to continue. The story took hold of me, leading me away from suburban Wimbledon to the country house of Selton Park, onto the hushed archives of an Oxford College and north to the Liverpool docks, overseas to the streets of Cincinnati and in between entangling me in all manner of false starts and dead-ends.

I found that I could not journey alone. Hart Rutherford was an invaluable source of information and advice. His articles for the *Independent* newspaper, covering the forensic investigation into Robert Latham's murder, form the basis for the later chapters of this book. Hope Kirwan-Hughes and Jo Stanley were skilled and enthusiastic researchers. And Anna Miller, a neighbour who became a friend, provided the crucial break in the story when she uncovered the North Walk tapes.

The discovery of Robert Latham's body reopened a story that I believed I had concluded two years previously. Instinct had told me that Robert Latham had been murdered but prior to the discovery of his body I could not prove it. I had gone as far as it was possible to go. As if to signify this, I had left North Walk to join my husband who was working in Shanghai. Once there, I wrote an account of what I knew, secured the manuscript with a rubber band and stored it in my desk drawer where I thought it would remain for ever.

It would have done so had nature not intervened.

After I had been in Shanghai for two years, I received a worried telephone call from my neighbour, Anna Miller. Temperatures had remained scorching all summer. Large cracks had appeared in the lawn of North Walk and, more alarming still, a half-inch crack had opened up in the rear wall of the house. A structural survey revealed that a neighbour's plane tree was the culprit. It would be necessary to dig a tree root barrier across the garden to prevent further root damage and to carry out underpinning in the basement flat to prevent any further subsidence of the house.

Anna Miller's account of the garden excavation is detailed in Chapter 9. Some three feet down the body of a man was discovered.

In Chapter 10 I go into greater detail about the forensic techniques that established Robert Latham's identity and the cause of death, multiple fractures to the head. His throat had been cut. At the time of his death he was suffering from the third and final stage of syphilis and was very probably delusional. The murder weapons, an Italianate marble statue and a bone-handled kitchen knife, were buried with him.

In Chapter 11, I argue that Bella and Mary acted in concert to murder Robert Latham, Mary concluding what had begun as a crime of passion by Bella, most probably occasioned by an unwanted sexual advance by Robert Latham towards his frightened and grieving wife. It was a classic joint enterprise. Mary finished what Bella had begun and so it was that these two women became secret sisters, irrevocably bound together by ties of love and guilt.

Finally, in Chapter 12, I follow the lives of Mary and Bella after the murder. This part of the book, in particular, would not have been possible without the assistance of my husband who has come to share my passion for the North Walk story and who devoted his annual company leave to flying back to the UK to do much of this later research while I remained in Shanghai expecting my second child.

As for Joseph Kelly, he had a successful career, was a founder of the Sisters of Mercy Children's Hospital and an owner of the local baseball team. His papers revealed a photograph of Mary taken outside the Cincinnati Marys Brewery in 1955. Joseph Kelly died in 1970.

For Bella's later life story and her late blossoming love affair I am indebted to the family of Major Stephen Archer who allowed me access to their family's private papers and to invaluable correspondence.

I am grateful to Anne Bayliss at the BBC who has commissioned the story to be made into a six-part television series and to the BBC audio department who will be releasing a full version of Mary Kelly's original 1962 taped interview to coincide with the series. Listeners will draw their own conclusions, but for my part I think that the tapes are Mary's secular confession. Mary left behind a subtle and deliberate record of everything that happened at North Walk.

Finally, my greatest thanks are for my husband who has lived with me, Bella and Mary for several years now.

This book is therefore dedicated to Edward.

Sally Kirwan-Hughes